AGENT OF ROME
TARCHON

NICK BROWN

Copyright © Nick Brown 2023
All rights reserved.

The right of Nick Brown to be identified as the Author of the Word has been asserted by him in accordance with the Copyright, Designs and Patents Act 1988.

All rights reserved. No part of this publication may be reproduced, stored in a retrieval system, or transmitted, in any form or by any means without the prior written permission of the author, not be otherwise circulated in any form of binding or cover other than that in which it is published and without similar condition being imposed on the subsequent purchaser.

All characters in this publication are fictitious and any resemblance to real persons, living or dead, is purely coincidental.

Paperback ISBN: 9798372402898

TIME

The Romans divided day and night into twelve hours each, so the length of an hour varied according to the time of year.

The seventh hour always began at midday.

MONEY

Four sesterces (a coin made of brass) were worth one denarius.

Twenty-five denarii (a coin made partially of silver) were worth one aureus (partially gold).

I

Byzantium, 248 AD

When he saw the cart coming, Atrius Tarchon felt the nerves in his stomach. His fingers were already slick with sweat as he lifted the hood over his head. Even the little grass snake seemed to sense his anxiety; twisting and curling in the bag hanging from his belt. He lifted the heavy length of timber, balanced it on his right shoulder and moved up to the end of the alley. The street was as quiet as he had hoped; it was only the first hour of the day.

The cart was now close enough for him to hear the squeaking wheels. Not long now. The doubts came thick and fast but Tarchon pushed them aside. He had struggled for too long, spent too many days hungry and too many nights without a roof over his head. If he was going to make something of himself, he had to take a risk.

The horses' hooves clattered on the flagstones.

Closer. Closer. Close enough.

Tarchon reached into the bag, grabbed the little snake then strode out from the alley. Affecting the manner of a weary labourer shifting a bit of wood, he crossed the street. Glancing to his right, he was relieved to see only the expected driver and two legionaries on the cart.

They were headed to the harbour, their cargo two chests of silver denarii: pay for some far-off legion. Tarchon had been tipped off by a cook who worked at the fortress; a man who wanted a quarter of the money in return for the information.

When he'd first heard about it, Tarchon couldn't believe the low level of security but – as the cook said – nobody robs the Roman army.

So, it was without question a risk. But what a reward.

Passing just ahead of the two horses yoked to the cart, Tarchon subtly dropped the snake on to the street.

At first the horses didn't react but when one pulled up, the other did the same, eyes bulging when it saw the slithering reptile. Soon both animals were rearing, the driver cursing at them and reaching for his whip.

Once on the pavement, Tarchon calmly turned right, walking past the unsettled horses to the cart. The legionaries were sitting on either side of the vehicle, the chests between them. The closest man had turned to see what was going on. Thanks to the eight-foot timber, his helmeted head was in easy reach. Tarchon dropped the wood off his shoulder, adjusted his grip and swung hard. With a hefty clang, the timber hit the top of the soldier's helmet, sending him sprawling into the back of the cart.

'Hey!' The second legionary stood and drew his sword. But with the horses still moving, the cart was unsteady and Tarchon made the most of it. Darting as close to the vehicle as he could get, he stretched out the timber and prodded the soldier in the chest. It wasn't a hard blow but when the back of his knees struck the side of the cart, the man dropped his sword, overbalanced and fell.

Tarchon could hardly believe how well this was going; the driver had even managed to calm one of the horses. Dropping the timber, he ran to the back of the cart and pulled the first man out by his boots. The soldier was too dazed to resist and landed on the street just like his mate. Tarchon hoped they weren't too badly hurt; part of the reason he had used the timber was to avoid killing someone.

Enjoying yet more good fortune, he climbed up into the cart and grabbed the dropped sword. Leaping over the two chests, he planted himself on the bench beside the driver.

'Get us out of here!' he yelled, aiming the blade at the man's neck.

Though he was still struggling with one horse, the driver forced a nod.

It was then that Tarchon felt something very sharp touch his right flank.

'Drop the blade, son, or I'll stick you.'

He turned to see a man of at least seventy standing beside the cart. Despite his spindly frame, his unblinking eyes were set as hard as his grip on the army-style dagger.

'What's it to you, grandad?'

Gritting his teeth, the old man pushed the tip of his dagger through the tunic and far enough in to Tarchon's flesh to persuade him. He threw the sword to the ground.

'I suggest you call me by my proper name, you little turd,' added the old interloper. 'Centurion Servius Terentius. Retired. Once a legionary, always a legionary.'

Tarchon knew Byzantium prison quite well, having found himself there for six weeks while awaiting trial at the age of sixteen. On that occasion, he'd been fortunate to encounter a lenient magistrate, who'd sentenced him to three months' manual labour. His crime – theft – could have earned him a severe lashing or even the loss of a hand.

Tarchon wasn't exactly sure of the sentence for the attempted robbery of a pay cart and multiple assaults on imperial troops, but he didn't expect to be lucky a second time. In fact, it seemed that luck had entirely deserted him. Hands tied behind his back, he was dragged out of a covered wagon by two legionaries, one of whom was the man he'd knocked out of the cart. His name was Magius and he had hit Tarchon quite a few times while they waited for reinforcements to arrive. His compatriot had been taken to the fortress hospital: apparently, he was still dazed.

'Come on then, you dirty little criminal.' Along with a second legionary, Magius grabbed Tarchon under his arm and marched him up to the prison entrance. It was an imposing brick building only a stone's throw from both the fortress and the basilica. Once inside, they were met by an officer who listened patiently to Magius' description of events then fetched a young clerk to write it all down. Tarchon was asked only his name and address, which he gave. He didn't expect to be asked about what had occurred but – to be fair to Magius – he didn't exaggerate or embellish. Then again, he didn't really need to.

'See you in court,' said Magius coolly as Tarchon was led away by two guards, each armed with a cudgel. 'And I hope you get Aegeus.'

This man was known to be the harshest magistrate in Byzantium. But even if Aegeus didn't preside, Tarchon had no doubt that he'd face a serious punishment; likely flogging or mutilation. If there were games planned, he might even find himself in the arena.

For now, he had a more immediate problem: surviving prison. The building's interior didn't seem to have changed since his last visit. It contained only a few smaller cells for wealthier criminals and those who needed protection from others. The rest were invariably chucked into the big holding cell. During his previous stint, Tarchon had benefited from his age; the older criminals being impressed by his youthful ingenuity in robbing a well-protected merchant. But in the intervening years, he'd made a few enemies in the city; he hoped none of them were present.

A third guard unlocked the holding cell and Tarchon was pushed inside. It was as sweaty, dirty and smelly as he remembered. In one corner was the filthy latrine, above it a tiny window. Along one wall was a bench, along the other a smattering of mouldy straw and sack cloth. As the door clanged shut behind him, Tarchon perused the selection of characters he would be sharing the cell with. Of the two dozen there, he immediately discounted half who were too old, young or weak-looking to cause him any problems. Of the remainder, there were a couple of familiar faces. Picking a space near the iron bars at the front of cell, he leaned against the wall.

His left side ached, as did his right cheek and the back of his head: all a result of the blows inflicted by the vengeful Magius. Tarchon made sure he showed no sign of the pain. He simply gazed blankly ahead, feeling the full weight of what had happened settle upon him. Thanks to that interfering old bastard, he had failed. And now he would pay the price. There were indeed many good reasons not to rob the Roman army.

Just after sundown, food came: a pail of watery soup and some mouldy bread. Tarchon had no appetite. As the hours of the day passed, the ache in his stomach had grown and grown, and this pain was not due to any physical blow. His scheme now seemed idiotic, regardless of how close he'd come to pulling it off. It wasn't as if all his other plans had worked so why should this one be any different? Everyone told him he was too impetuous; too confident in his own ability. And he hadn't even prayed to Minerva. His mother had always told him that she watched over their family. It was one of the few things he could remember them doing together; praying to the goddess.

As the prisoners slopped down their mugs of soup and chewed on the bread, a middle-aged man walked over. He was skinny, his face obscured behind a bushy beard flecked with white and grey. His tunic was worn and stained, and he didn't appear to have any shoes. He was one of the familiar faces.

'Do I know you, young fellow?'

It was the voice that did it. He had a strong Cappadocian accent and a deep, distinctive tone.

'You're Hasta. I'm Tarchon. We both crewed on Cyril's boat a couple of seasons back.'

'That's it.' Hasta's weathered face broke into a smile. 'Mullet and sardines. Tight bastard wouldn't cough up our wages. You changed his mind though. Here.' Hasta tore off half of his bread and offered it.

'No thanks. Not hungry. What are you in for?'

'Forgery scheme. I ran the papers around the city for some rich sod. I didn't know what he was up to but did they listen? They haven't decided what to do with me yet. You?'

'I tried to rob an army pay cart this morning.'

Hasta's eyes widened as he chewed the bread. 'Blood of the gods. Not on your own?'

Tarchon nodded. He'd considered roping in some others but, of the people he trusted, none had the balls for it. He supposed that made them brighter than him.

'It was stupid. I almost hope they hang me. Better than walking around without a hand. I've got no chance of finding work then.'

'You don't mean that,' said Hasta. 'You're still young. All depends on the magistrate. As long as you don't get A-'

'Aegeus. Yes, I know. Any idea how long it will be?'

'I've given up trying to predict. Some people are called in after a day or two. I've been here three weeks. Simpler cases tend to be dealt with swiftly. Especially if...'

Hasta hesitated and avoided eye contact.

'Go on.'

'Especially if the army are involved. You know how they like to set an example.'

Tarchon shook his head and glanced at the window. All he could see now was a square of darkness.

Hasta continued: 'If the magistrate gives you a chance to speak, praise the Emperor and the Empire. Then offer yourself to the legions.'

'The army? No chance. Nothing but a bunch of bullies, killers and cheats. Don't suppose you know a lawyer?'

'Er...only one. I told you about him – the man who forged the papers I was carrying.' Hasta grimaced. 'They beheaded him five days ago.'

As night fell, the prisoners slumped against the walls and slept. The only light came from an oil lamp outside the cell that barely illuminated the guard who sat there, dozing. Tarchon sat with his knees up and his arms resting on them, head bowed.

He had only a few memories of his mother but he treasured them: walking along the shore as sailing ships eased by; watching her weave, singing as she worked; feeling her lie close behind him, her warm hand on his.

Fourteen years she'd been gone; taken by plague. Once she became very ill, she'd had to leave the city, live on an island with the other afflicted. Father had taken Tarchon out in a little boat to say goodbye. Though they were close to the shore, Mother could only croak a few words. She didn't look like herself then; her face ravaged by the disease, body hunched and wracked by pain. Tarchon tried not to think of it. He wished he'd never gone, wished Father had never taken him. It was impossible to shake that memory and for years it had replaced the good ones.

After that, Father's drinking got worse and worse. He had never been one to put much water in his wine and then he stopped entirely. Tarchon only saw him now and again, when he was sober long enough to remember he had a son. The last occasion had been more than a year ago. He'd heard a rumour he was shacked up in the countryside with some farmer's widow.

His mother was buried in a cemetery on the western edge of the city. Like most of the dead poor, her body had been placed in a large amphora, twisted and crushed in a way that made her son wince and weep. The plot was marked only by a stone which Father had engraved himself – badly. He couldn't even do that right.

Whenever Tarchon visited the cemetery, he pledged that he would find enough money for a proper tombstone, engraved with Mother's name. But he'd never got close to having enough coins. Perhaps now he never would. If he died, would anyone even bother to bury him?

Just before dawn, the wind came up from the east, momentarily blowing the familiar salty tang of the Bosphorus in through the window. Tarchon loved the sea; to him, it had always suggested the possibilities of life: travel and wealth and adventure. Now he wondered if he would ever see it again.

The next day passed with an awful slowness, though Hasta did his best to keep Tarchon's spirits up and persuaded him to eat something. From the guards, they learnt that the criminal court was to sit later that week and rush through cases on the order of the governor. No one was sure whether this was to impress an important visitor or create more fodder for upcoming games; possibly both. The guards also told Tarchon that his failed robbery was the talk of the fortress. Apparently, the admiration for his bold attempt among the garrison had not deterred officers from demanding the harshest of punishments. Hasta contended that the guards were purposefully winding him up – their method of passing the time – but Tarchon wasn't so sure.

That night, he finally turned to Minerva. Among the goddess's many associations were weaving and wisdom. This had been enough to convince Mother to devote herself to the goddess from an early age. Mother was a realist; she knew that no god granted every wish, yet she maintained that Minerva did hear her. In the last weeks of her life, she made Tarchon pledge that he would remain loyal to the goddess. For though Minerva might not be able to save Mother's life, she would surely repay her sacrifice by helping her only child. He had dutifully prayed and given offerings – scant though they were – for many years after Mother had died. But he'd not been to the temple in years, nor even thought of the goddess.

Tarchon summoned a simple invocation, asking only for salvation. Sitting alone in the crushing darkness, he whispered it again and again. He wanted to repeat it one thousand times but he kept losing count. So, he kept counting until he was *sure* he had passed that number. Minerva *must* have had heard him.

On the second day, four prisoners were taken to the court. That afternoon, several punishments were carried out, as usual, in the nearby yard. Two men lost their hands.

One, somehow, made little noise. The pleading – and then the shrieking – of the second unsettled even the most hardened criminals in the holding cell. By the time it was over, the mutilated man sounded like a little boy.

Both were thieves. According to the guards, two others had been sentenced to execution: to be carried out at the next games. One man was a rapist and murderer, the other a former slave who had defrauded his master – a wealthy man who sat on the city council. The guards took great pleasure in announcing that the magistrate who had decided these sentences was none other than Aegeus, who was also to sit the following day.

Shortly after dawn on the third day, the guards approached the cell, one holding a waxed tablet. He read out the names of those scheduled to appear in court that morning. Tarchon was the third name. Hasta wished him well and told him he was sure they would meet again. As Tarchon followed the others out of the cell, one of the guards grinned at him.

'Hope you've been praying.'

II

Tarchon was fourth in the line of six. They had all been bound at the wrists and now walked through the prison, two guards in front, two behind. As they rounded a corner, another guard emerged from a doorway and ordered them to halt. He was an older man and now whispered instructions to the leading guards. They listened attentively then continued on their way. As Tarchon passed him, the older man clamped a hand on his wrist and moved him aside as the others continued past.

'Not you. For you we have something special.'

A second man stepped out of the doorway. He didn't appear to be a guard or a soldier but he was an imposing character: broad-shouldered, bald, with faded tattoos on his forearms and a silvered dagger-sheath on his belt. He pointed at a nearby set of stairs that led downward.

Hand still on Tarchon's arm, the guard led him to the stairs. There was only a dim light at the bottom and the passage was so narrow that they could only proceed single file. Tarchon stopped at the top.

'You can walk down or I can throw you down,' said the guard.

Despite the chill from the stone, Tarchon was sweating as he descended the nine steps. There were only two lanterns in the dank corridor in which he found himself, casting a thin yellow light on the stones of floor and wall.

'Can we hurry this along, gentlemen? I have an appointment at the third.'

Tarchon had also not expected to hear such a gentle, refined tone in such a place. It had come from an open doorway to his right. The bald man dismissed the guard with a flick of a finger, then gestured to the doorway.

As the guard headed up the stairs, Tarchon walked along the corridor and into the room. It was rather better illuminated, thanks to a large lantern hanging from a hook. Sitting at the table below it was a slender, middle-aged man with wavy, grey hair. He sat sideways, legs crossed, arms folded, and he ran his eye over Tarchon with calculated curiosity. His clothes somehow matched his voice: a pale orange tunic with a flashy belt buckle and expensive shoes. He was not armed.

'Have a seat, Tarchon.'

Though the stranger was in a high-backed chair, the seat opposite him was a low stool. As Tarchon approached and lowered himself onto it, the bald man leaned against the wall, watching him.

'Can you read and write?' asked the older man, running a finger across his bottom lip.

It took Tarchon a while to reply. He was utterly confused by his situation.

'Er ...I can read a little. I can't write a thing.'

'How old are you?'

'Twenty. Sir, who are you?'

'If this meeting progresses well, I'll *consider* telling you. Where do you live?'

'Just north of Second Hill.'

'You have a house? An apartment?'

'I live in a shed outside my aunt's place.'

'Any closer family? Parents? Siblings?'

'No.'

The man cast a brief glance at his compatriot. 'Your occupation?'

'I've been a fisherman, a labourer, a water-carrier, a runner, a-'

'-Armed robber.'

'Only this week.'

The man smiled. 'What gave you the idea?'

Tarchon sensed that this was not a time to lie.

'I got a tip off about the carts from a cook at the fortress. The legionary pay comes from the mint four times a year and the soldiers deliver it to ships for the eastern provinces. I watched what happened in March, realised there was an opportunity.'

'Apparently you got close to succeeding.'

'I would have if not for some old soldier. Do-gooder prick ruined my plan.'

Hearing an odd sound, Tarchon turned to see the bald fellow grinding his teeth.

'He's a veteran.'

'No offence,' Tarchon said to the ex-soldier.

The older man examined his nails for a moment. 'Regardless of its ultimate failure, your scheme showed considerable verve, not to mention tenacity.'

Tarchon wasn't entirely sure what either of those words meant but it sounded like a compliment. He was beginning to think this meeting might not be a bad thing. It was certainly better than being taken to the magistrate – or out to the yard.

'We keep an eye out for such people. Especially young people, who we can employ.'

'Doing what?'

The man cleared his throat then leaned forward, arms on the table. Tarchon noted the excellent colour and quality of his cotton tunic. 'Our organisation carries out certain tasks on behalf of the Empire and the Emperor. We ...solve problems.'

'What kind of problems?'

'It varies.'

'Are you part of the army?'

'Technically yes, practically no, though we do deal with them from time to time. Everyone sees what the army does and the army likes it that way. If we do our job well, no one ever sees us at all. Or even knows we were there.'

'Spies.'

'In a manner of speaking, though we do far more than spying. I have a proposition for you, Tarchon. If I can extricate you from this...difficulty, you will complete a trial for us: a series of tasks that will allow us to assess your abilities, decide if you're worth our time and energy. If you do well, we can offer you a solid wage. I won't lie to you – the work is difficult and dangerous. But I believe you might succeed.'

'Do I have a choice?'

'Absolutely. You are free to take your chances with Magistrate Aureus.'

'You'd pay me?'

'Only if you do well. As I said, it's a trial.'

Tarchon let out a long breath.

'I expect you're wondering about your case. You mentioned an informer. If you give me his name, we can ensure that everyone believes *he* is the true culprit. We can claim that he blackmailed you or concoct some such story. As long as *someone* is blamed and punished, the army will go along with it.'

'What will happen to him?'

'It's difficult to be sure. The real question is: would you rather it happen to him, or to you?'

Tarchon believed that his prayers had been answered. This turn of events seemed so sudden and unlikely that surely Minerva had somehow presented him with this opportunity. He was not about to turn it down.

'I'd like to accept your offer.'

'Very good. In that case, some introductions. I am Gargonius, he is Korax.'

Gargonius left shortly after. Korax unsheathed his dagger, lifted Tarchon to his feet and cut the rope securing his wrists.

'You are fortunate. Very fortunate.'

His voice was deep and harsh, as if he'd swallowed a mouthful of grit.

Even after he'd sheathed his dagger, Korax remained close; rather too close for Tarchon's liking. He didn't like people getting in his face, trying to intimidate him. He wasn't all that tall or particularly strong but he'd been in endless scraps on the streets. In normal circumstances, he might have pushed the man away. But not this man; and not today.

'I suppose so.'

'I'll make the arrangements regarding your partner in crime but that will take a while. In the meantime, we don't want you out and about. You'll stay here until I say you can go. If anyone asks, you follow the agreed line: the army and the court decided to show mercy as you had been blackmailed.'

'You can do that? Convince the army and the court?'

'Gargonius is influential. Our organisation's authority is bestowed by the Emperor himself. We tend to get what we want, which is probably why many in the army dislike us.'

'But *you* were in the army.'

Korax glared. 'We're not here to talk about me.'

'Right. Sorry.'

Korax walked to the door. 'I'm not going to lock this. When you leave here later, you are a free man. You might be tempted to escape the city.'

'I'm not going to do that. We made an agreement. I'll stick to my side.'

Korax seemed to like that but he still aimed a finger at him. 'Be in no doubt, young man. Master Gargonius has given you your life back. He can just as easily take it away.'

Tarchon spent the entire day in that little room and – despite his abrupt change of fortune – it was not a pleasant day. He couldn't avoid the feeling that something would go wrong and, every time one of the guards passed the narrow stairway, he feared they would drag him off to the yard. Even so, he issued a sincere prayer of thanks to Minerva, and pledged to visit her temple before he did anything else.

The lamps and the lantern ran out of oil in mid-afternoon. Dusk came, casting the room into total darkness. Tarchon sat there alone, growing cold, not daring to leave. He felt sure that if he saw a guard, they would instantly take him back into the holding cell – or worse.

'Tarchon, you down there?' It sounded like Korax.

He hurried to the stairwell and up into the well-lit corridor.

'What are you doing lurking down there in the dark?'

Tarchon shrugged. 'Waiting.'

Korax ran a hand across his bald head. 'Your associate has been arrested. Master Gargonius has spoken to the magistrate. If all goes well-'

'Do I have to hear the details?' The cook was not a close friend of Tarchon's but he had drunk with him on a couple of occasions. He was like Tarchon: a man with an eye for an opportunity. He didn't deserve this.

'You're going to have to toughen up,' said Korax. 'In our line of work, we get the result we need – whatever it takes. Anyway, you're to meet me at the statue of Hadrian, midday tomorrow. Until then, lay low. Come, you should walk out of here with me to avoid any difficulties.'

'Sorry, but do you have any money? I haven't a single coin.'

Korax tutted. 'How sad.'

Once they were out of the prison, Korax silently went on his way. Tarchon stood there for a moment, hands at rest on his belt, drinking in the quiet and the bliss of freedom. The familiar salty tang was in the air, the scent of woodsmoke too. Within the towering basilica, a few windows emitted a faint glow where clerks and officials still toiled. Somewhere, a watchman was calling out to his compatriots that all was well.

Tarchon headed north, crossing two broad plazas before passing the largest structure in Byzantium, the enormous hippodrome. Here the smell of the stable was thick in the air and he overtook a pair of men leading a lame horse, debating how to treat it. Spying two watchmen with lanterns up ahead, he crossed to the other side of the street. Some would leave you alone, others would insist on an explanation of why you were out after dark. It wasn't illegal to move around the city at night but it was unusual enough to attract attention. There had been a spate of robberies and rapes and the magistrates were clamping down.

Narrowly avoiding a pan of slops that splattered into the gutter, Tarchon wove his way through the apartment buildings west of the centre. Here he was approached by a prostitute. Though he couldn't see her face in the darkness, he knew the voice of Old Cecilia, and politely declined her offer. Tarchon always felt sorry for women and children who had to make their way on the streets. It wasn't easy for anyone but at least he could defend himself.

Passing under the city's main aqueduct, he stayed in the middle of the road to avoid the bands of homeless, diseased and poor who gathered there. Every new magistrate pledged to sweep away these unwanted people – and many did – but, somehow, they always returned. As usual, Tarchon heard numerous voices and accents and languages. He saw only the glitter of eyes in the inky darkness; no one here could afford the luxury of light.

Though his aunt owned many lamps – and one lantern – she used them sparingly, and he was not surprised to find her house in darkness. Her husband was a wheelwright and the pair had allowed Tarchon to sleep in a storage shed at the back of their yard for seven months. There had been many arguments and – as Aunt Cassia often stated – he was only still there out of her loyalty to her long-dead sister. As he had essentially been missing for three days, Tarchon knew he would be in for a lecture. Cassia's husband, Hostus, had refused to take him on as an apprentice but the couple insisted that he do certain chores, even though his 'accommodation' amounted to a patch of floor. As for food, he was only ever given something on festival days.

Yet, as he hurried along an alley to access the yard from the rear, Tarchon did not feel downhearted. His risky undertaking had – through a bizarre twist – presented him with an opportunity. If he could impress Korax and Gargonius, there might be a chance to really progress and free himself from dependence on his aunt.

Despite the darkness, he found his usual holds on the wall and swiftly clambered over it. He did, however, stumble over some timbers as he crossed the yard. Hoping the sound hadn't travelled as far as the house, he reached the shed and eased the latch open. Leaving the door ajar to admit what little light there was, he knelt down and crawled over to his corner.

His flask had a little water in it and, though it was stale, he downed every drop. He had no food left but eating was currently the least of his worries. With a weary sigh, he removed his boots. The soles were so worn that they would inevitably fall apart before long. Tarchon then pulled his tunic off over his head and climbed into bed, clad only in his loin-cloth. His mattress was a sewn-up sheet full of straw that rested on a pallet but it was comfortable enough for him. He pulled his blanket up to his chin and, despite the remarkable events of the day, was close to sleep when he heard footsteps outside.

'Oh shit,' he murmured as the door opened. Aunt Cassia was holding the lamp, Hostus beside her.

'Look what the cat dragged in,' he said.

'He's certainly got the morals of a rodent,' added Cassia, brushing an errant strand of greying hair away from her eyes.

This was unusually harsh, even for her; and caused Tarchon to worry that they might know something about where he'd been.

'Sorry I've not been around. I'll catch up with my chores-'

'Don't bother, boy,' said Cassia. 'Vindex's brother saw you on your way to prison. What in Hades did you do this time?'

Tarchon was now sitting up but still feeling rather dazed.

'Er...it wasn't my idea. Honestly.'

'Tell the truth, boy,' implored Cassia. 'Just this once. For your mother's sake.'

Though she didn't do it often, Tarchon hated Cassia for mentioning his mother's name. His aunt always acted as if she'd looked after him for years. In fact, she'd barely bothered with him for most of that time, claiming that two was enough children to support. Both her daughters had been married off now but Tarchon suspected she'd only taken him in because his father had disappeared.

It might have been his exhausted state but he couldn't summon the energy to create a convincing lie. They already knew he'd committed a crime.

'I tried to rob an army pay cart. But like I said, it wasn't my idea, and in fact it turns out that-'

'He admits it,' said Cassia, turning to Hostus. 'Just like that. No shame. No guilt.' She looked back at Tarchon and wiped her eyes. 'Honestly, what *would* your mother say?'

There really was no answer to that.

'We have a business,' added Cassia. 'You *live* here. Your actions impugn our name.'

Again, Tarchon could think of nothing to say; certainly nothing that might change their minds.

'You're leaving, boy. Not tomorrow. *Now*. I don't want to see your face around here again. I'll not have a criminal in my house.' She sniffed and wiped her face. 'May the ...'

Aunt Cassia sometimes faked her tears but there was nothing fake about this pause; this emotion. 'May the great gods watch over you.'

Taking the lamp with her, she walked back across the yard to the house.

'Lad, you must learn to *think*, said Hostus. 'It is as simple as that.' Over the years, he had generally followed his wife's line, though he could be generous at times.

'I didn't just *decide* to do it,' replied Tarchon quietly. 'I planned it properly. I almost did it.'

'Sometimes I think you're beyond help, young man. I hope not. But you must go now.'

Hostus slipped his hand into his pocket and handed Tarchon what felt like a denarius. Tarchon might normally have refused it on account of his pride but he was in desperate need.

'Be careful,' added Hostus as he left.

Alone in the dark, Tarchon gathered his belongings.

*

A painful blister had formed on his right heel by the time he reached the Temple of Minerva. As expected, the priests didn't want to admit him at this late hour but – also as expected – they were amenable to a dedicated worshipper desperate to offer a votive. Once the senior priest agreed, a younger man escorted Tarchon inside; between the high columns and through the great wooden doors embossed with studs of bronze.

Leaving the sack containing his belongings close to the entrance, he followed the priest across the marble floor, to the altar dominated by a seven-foot statue. Illuminated by candlelight, the great stone figure stared defiantly across the temple. On one shoulder sat an owl, in one hand was a spear. The legend above the goddess read, *WISDOM AND COURAGE*. Tarchon had stood in this place many times, the first of them with his mother.

The priest withdrew, leaving him alone with Minerva. Tarchon wished he had previously visited at such a late hour. Without others here, the temple seemed a different place. A strange calm settled over his confused mind. Though the building was cold, he felt a warmth radiating from the statue.

Great Minerva, I thank you for your help today and pledge now to honour you with a life of worship. I give this to you.

Reaching over the bronze bar that protected the statue, he placed the denarius at the base, alongside many other coins of varying value.

Tarchon heard no answer. But he felt something. The warmth was still there and, for the first time, a feeling of connection. A connection not only to the goddess but, through her, to his mother.

Kindness. Love.

Mother had also been wise and brave, taking on the many challenges of life as best she could. After her death, Tarchon had tried to reach out to her with his mind yet she had never answered. Perhaps this was the answer he'd been waiting for.

Soon he was back on the streets, his sack over his shoulder. He made his way towards the eastern shore, knowing he could find shelter for the night beneath an upturned boat.

Perhaps it was Minerva's will that he be cast out like this, left alone with only her to turn to, knowing that she had already given him a chance. It was a chance he did not intend to waste. Perhaps it was true what people said; perhaps the gods did work in mysterious ways. He had no doubt that it would be hard but it seemed Minerva had found a new path for him.

Wisdom and courage.

He would need them both.

III

'Get out of it, freeloader!'

Tarchon knew many of those who kept their boats on the eastern shore. But not this man.

'All right, I'm going,' he said as the impatient sod and his mate flipped the boat over, exposing Tarchon to blinding sunlight. Still groggy as he dragged himself up, he let out a mighty yawn. He would normally have woken and got moving before dawn; evidently the boat's owner was starting late too. Grabbing his blanket and sack, Tarchon trudged away and sat on another upturned hull.

The majority of the fishing boats were already out and they'd left marks in the sand where they'd been dragged into the water. Covering his eyes, Tarchon looked out at the sparkling surface. It was so bright that he could see only a few boats close to the shore, nothing of the Straits or the city of Chalcedon. Though it was just a mile away, Tarchon had only been there a couple of times. In fact, other than the odd trip to the rural areas west of Byzantium, he'd never left his home city.

He put on his boots, then rolled up his blanket and placed it in the sack. Twenty yards away, two brawny wrestlers were practising moves on the sand. Tarchon watched them for a while then gazed dolefully at the sack. His worldly possessions didn't amount to much. In terms of clothes, he had two more tunics, two more loin cloths, a *very* old cloak and a spare pair of socks. Other than that, he owned a small leather bag, a blanket, a spoon, a mug and a plate (all wood), a fire-starting kit, half a candle, plus a needle and thread. He'd had to sell his dagger earlier in the year and now realised that he'd left his fighting stave at his aunt's place. This he would need; he'd adjusted the grip and the strap and had always liked the lightness and balance of the weapon. It was the only one he had.

Within the pocket of his tunic was his most prized possession: his mother's brooch, which was framed with silver and contained an image of Minerva carved in faded carnelian. Tarchon hadn't had it valued but reckoned it would be worth at least an aureus, possibly more. He often told people that he would starve rather than sell it; a pledge he'd fulfilled on many occasions.

When a seagull chose that moment to deposit something very unpleasant only inches from his sack, Tarchon decided it was time to move. Judging by the sun, he guessed it was around the second hour. He had some time to kill before the meeting with Korax and his first priority was to find some food.

Later in the day he might encounter returning fishermen and those he knew might give him something. He also knew many of those who ran the stores and little taverns close to the shore. But he was too late for delivery time and too early for leftovers. And the truth was that he'd called in too many such favours of late. But there was always Mehruz.

The pair had known each other for many years, after first crossing paths as pickpockets. But while he lacked Tarchon's nerve, Mehruz was a keen cook and, two years previously, had opened an eatery with his wife. Like him, she was Persian. Their parents had settled in Byzantium after initially arriving as prisoners captured during one of the many wars with Rome. Mehruz and Anahita cooked traditional Persian food and their unusual, spicy stews were popular with the working folk of the city.

The eatery was only a quarter-hour away. Passing some rich folk, he almost considered a quick bout of pick-pocketing. But he had long wished to leave such desperate thievery behind; and this was clearly not the path Minerva wished him to take.

*

He was surprised and bemused to find the eatery closed, with shutters bolted and door locked. He hadn't eaten in more than a day and let out a groan.

'Mehruz!' He backed out onto the street and looked up at the first floor, where the family lived. The shutters were open and washing was hanging from a line on the narrow balcony.

'Ruz, you in?'

The Persian appeared, bushy hair framing his dark, narrow face. His movements were unusually slow and, instead of replying, he wearily raised a hand.

'Morning, Tarch.'

Even his oldest friend didn't use his given name, which was the way Tarchon liked it; only his parents called him Atrius.

'You all right?'

Mehruz shook his head. 'Some bloody fever. Anahita and the little ones got it yesterday, me this morning. Can hardly move. How you doing?'

The Persian clearly hadn't noticed that Tarchon was carrying all his possessions.

'Er...not bad. Can I fetch you anything?'

'No, no. Seems like a two or three-day thing. Nobody's getting worse, at least.'

'That's good.' Tarchon wasn't all that happy about admitting his poverty to the entire street but he had little choice. 'I don't suppose you've got any spare food?'

'Sorry, mate. None of us have eaten a thing and no delivery today. And I don't want to give you this fever.'

'No worries. Hope you all feel better.'

Mehruz turned back inside, then back to Tarchon. 'Anahita says good day.'

'Same from me. I'll see you soon.'

'All right, Tarch. Stay out of trouble.'

*

If Minerva had intervened previously, she seemed to be ignoring him on this day. Tarchon reckoned that was fair – a goddess could hardly watch everyone all the time – but his search for food seemed a cursed undertaking. At one of the markets, he trailed a fruit cart but was beaten to a fallen apple by a sprightly urchin. Elsewhere, every single vendor seemed to be on alert and – with numerous watchmen on duty – he wasn't about to take a risk. Presumably, any brush with the law would ruin his chances with Gargonius and his mysterious organisation.

In the hour before midday, while slowly wending his way to the statue of Hadrian, he considered what Gargonius had said about working for the Empire and the Emperor. There had been eight rulers during Tarchon's lifetime and his uncle Hostus, like many, often complained about how useless they all were. The current emperor – Phillipus – had at least bucked the trend by lasting four years. All Tarchon knew of him was that he was Syrian and had made peace with the Persians. In the spring, Phillipus had ordered celebrations to mark a thousand years of the Roman Empire. That didn't mean a lot to Tarchon but he and his friends had enjoyed all the free wine.

He rarely mentioned the ongoing conflict with Persia to Mehruz. Despite the Emperor's peace agreement, everyone assumed it was temporary because they had rarely held before. Tarchon knew it was a difficult subject for his friend. On several occasions, local men had insulted Mehruz because of his origins and once had even attacked the eatery. The fact that he had been born in Byzantium and that there were also city-folk from dozens of different provinces seemed to make no difference. Another fellow had made the mistake of cursing at Mehruz while the pair were out drinking, both aged sixteen. Tarchon, who had no older and better friend, had headbutted the man.

He supposed it was another part of the same flaw. The same impetuous nature that had led him to attempt the robbery often caused him to lose his temper. He thought of his anger like a dammed river. When the dam burst, the flow was hard to stop and impossible to reverse.

Reaching the statue, he saw no sign of Korax, so sat down on the steps. To distract himself from thoughts of food, he considered what type of task Gargonius and Korax might have for him. If their organisation solved problems for the Empire, what might those problems be? One of them was certainly wars. Rome seemed to start some conflicts but on other occasions the Empire was attacked. Rome had conquered most of the world and Tarchon guessed that maintaining that was pretty bloody difficult. Then again, they did have the best army and he couldn't imagine what someone like Gargonius could accomplish that the legions couldn't.

As for the Emperor, it seemed that his main problem was staying in power; not being poisoned or stabbed or otherwise betrayed. But most of that went on in Rome and Byzantium was a very long way from the capital. Tarchon looked over his shoulder at the great bronze statue of Hadrian. He had ruled a hundred years earlier. But the Empire had begun a thousand years ago. Tarchon found it difficult to even grasp such a length of time but he did arrive at one conclusion; shouldn't they have *solved* all these problems by now?

When Korax arrived, the first thing he did was point at Tarchon's sack.

'What's that?' he growled in that deep, gravelly voice.

'My gear.'

'What gear?'

'My belongings.'

'Don't tell me you're homeless?'

'Only temporarily.'

The ex-legionary rolled his eyes. 'Now we're hiring vagrants.'

'My aunt found out I'd been taken to prison. She kicked me out.'

'You told her the story we agreed?'

'I did but…she didn't care. It's not the first time we've had a fight.'

Korax eyed him sternly. 'I really have my doubts about you.'

'Just give me a chance. I'll show you I can do the job.'

Korax kicked away a rotting apple core with his boot. 'First step – listen carefully to your instructions.'

'We're doing it here? What about somewhere quiet? A tavern, maybe?'

Though he knew the meeting was far more important than filling his stomach, Tarchon was now painfully hungry. He thought if they went somewhere, he could order lunch and Korax would pay.

'It won't take long. We're not about to give you anything too complicated.'

With that, Korax sat down on the steps, soon turning his sharp gaze on Tarchon's battered boots. Tarchon, meanwhile, noted the bulky calves common to soldiers and the many scars on Korax's legs, visible despite the thick, black hair.

The ex-soldier rubbed a finger along his stubble-covered jaw. 'Some time tomorrow, a coaster is due in at North Harbour. The *Lampra*. She's carrying cargo but also a few passengers. One of those is a man named Evaristos. He's around thirty years old and should be in the city for a few days. Your task is to follow him.'

'Do you know what he looks like?'

'No. We just have the name. Which is?'

'Evaristos. Due in on the *Lampra*, North Harbour, tomorrow.'

'I'll meet you here again at sunset and I'll expect a full report. Where he went, when, who he met, how else he spent his time. Accuracy and detail. A pity you can't write but we'll have to depend on your memory.'

'I have a good memory.'

'I'll be the judge of that. Any questions?'

'Who is he? What's he done?'

Korax sighed. 'That's not how this works. If we decide you need to know something, we'll tell you. Anything else?'

'Well, it'll be hard to do all that without any food in my belly. I promise I'll pay you back. A couple of sesterces would be fine.'

'You can't even feed yourself and you really think you're going to be working with us?' The ex-legionary stood and pointed at the steps. 'Here. Sunset tomorrow.'

'Korax, can *you* read?' Tarchon hadn't intended to be rude but, as far as he was aware, most soldiers could not.

'Yes. I taught myself.' He now leaned over Tarchon, dark eyes narrowed. 'Tell me, are we friends?'

'Er…'

'I'll save you any further thought. We're *not*. So you don't call me Korax. You call me *sir*.'

Fearing that his fighting stave might be turned into firewood, Tarchon traipsed across the city to his former home. Fortunately, neither Hostus nor his assistant was in the yard so he was able to recover it swiftly and hop back over the wall. He thought it important to have some kind of weapon, even though the stave was impossible to hide.

He knew his best chance of avoiding starvation was Galla. He wasn't entirely sure when the two of them had first met but he reckoned it was soon after he'd arrived in the area. Her father was a successful cobbler, his premises only a minute from Aunt Cassia's place.

When Tarchon arrived, Master Vesonius was with a customer, so he lurked outside until the man had gone. He hadn't actually seen Galla but she was invariably working; either dealing with clients or doing something out the back.

'Good day, Master Vesonius,' said Tarchon, wishing there was some way of hiding both his sack and his stave.

He was never entirely sure what Galla's father thought of him. Early on, he had done the man a favour by hauling a nasty customer out of the shop. But that was a long while ago now and he felt sure that Vesonius knew of his criminal history.

'Tarchon. You going somewhere?'

'Er...'

Fortunately, Galla's arrival helped him avoid the question.

'Hello, Tarch,' she said with a welcoming smile. 'I haven't seen you since the Festival of Luna.'

Tarchon flushed, suddenly feeling both guilty and embarrassed at having to stoop to this.

'Hello, Galla. Have you got a minute?'

He really hoped they hadn't noticed the colour of his face.

'Can I speak to Tarchon, Father?'

He gave a solemn nod, and returned his attention to the elegant pair of shoes sitting on his counter. They were not far from the shoe-making district here, and Vesonius specialised in men's shoes. Though he mostly carried out repairs, he did have some on sale, arranged neatly on shelves. The room to the rear was his workshop, which contained numerous tables, woven baskets and tools. It was a comparatively large property; Galla lived with her father, mother and younger brother on the first floor.

She continued through the workshop to the shady courtyard at the rear. Tarchon had always liked the smell of leather and oil that permeated the house. He reckoned they were the tidiest family he'd ever come across. There was never a single thing out of place and every corner was spotless. Galla sat on a bench that faced a little herb garden. Tarchon put down his sack and leaned his stave against the wall before joining her. He could hear her mother and brother talking on the floor above them.

'You all right?' asked Galla, arranging her long tunic as she crossed her legs.

When assisting her father with practical work, she put her hair up and wore a dark apron, but today she wore a simple diadem over her black hair and silver hoop earrings. Galla was friendly, kind, intelligent and pretty. She also had a remarkable singing voice. If not for the withered arm that she usually kept covered by white cloth, Tarchon reckoned she would have been just about perfect. Though he'd never discussed the matter with her, he knew that she was twenty-four but had never received an offer of marriage. Tarchon had glimpsed her arm a couple of times while helping her in the workshop. It was not only strange in shape but colour and texture. He had always been intrigued that – despite this cruel twist of fate – Galla and her entire family were devoted to the Roman gods.

'Not exactly,' he replied. 'Aunt Cassia kicked me out.'

'Permanently?'

'I think so.'

'What did you do?'

Tarchon didn't think it wise to offer the whole truth now but he also hated lying to Galla.

'I made a mistake. Can we leave it at that?'

'I suppose.'

'Galla...sorry, I don't like to ask. But is there anything to eat?'

She gave him a familiar look; part sympathetic, part annoyed. 'I'll see what there is. Wait here. And then you and I can talk.'

Tarchon knew what that meant. Galla had repeatedly tried to put him on the straight and narrow: with limited success. He wished she wouldn't bother but he was also glad that she kept trying. He knew many, many people in Byzantium but it was only Galla and Mehruz that he considered *true* friends. In any case, a lecture was a small price to pay for a feed.

While he was waiting for Galla to return, her mother came down to say hello. Unless busy, she was generally very pleasant to Tarchon. On one occasion, when they were briefly alone, she had commented on his body, which she said was good enough for a sculptor's model. She also seemed to approve of his friendship with Galla. Tarchon guessed this was because Galla didn't have all that many friends, even female friends. She didn't like to leave the house, on account of her arm.

Thankfully, Mistress Vesonius didn't question him about his current situation but affectionately ruffled his hair and departed when her daughter arrived with the food. Galla had put together a plate of bread, pepper sausage and dates. Tarchon tried to control himself but the food tasted *so* good and he wanted to enjoy every mouthful. While he ate, Galla pulled a few little weeds from the herb garden. As he finished, she washed her hands in an amphora of water.

'Can I save these for later?' he asked, pointing at the remaining three dates.

'Of course.'

As he threw them into his sack, Tarchon noted Master Vesonius lurking in the shadowy workshop. The cobbler watched Tarchon for a moment before selecting some tool and returning to the store. When Galla returned, Tarchon moved to his right so there was space to his left; she liked to keep her withered arm away from people.

They sat there for a moment in silence, though there was noise around them: the familiar hammering from the nearby stone-cutter's yard, some vendor announcing that he had a new delivery of fresh prawns, a bickering couple on the other side of the rear wall.

Tarchon looked at Galla. To him, she had a very Greek face: full lips, strong nose, big, dark eyes, masses of curly, black hair.

'You look nice,' he said.

She pointed at his hand, specifically his dirty fingernails.

'When did you last wash?'

'I'll take a dip in the sea when I get time.' Tarchon hoped he didn't smell. One time, Galla had dabbed her perfume on him, much to her little brother's amusement.

'Do you have any work at the moment?'

The truth was that he had recently put most of his time – and hope – into planning the robbery. Prior to that, he'd been able only to secure a few days' labour here and there. Part of the difficulty was his involvement in a mass brawl after the most recent chariot race at the hippodrome. He'd been caught in the fight by accident but when a supporter of the Green chariot team had kicked him for absolutely no reason, Tarchon had chinned him and laid him out flat. Though he couldn't often afford to attend, he supported the Whites and the incident had been witnessed by many. Apparently, this Green was a well-known thug and his fellow Whites had been so impressed that he'd been hoisted on their shoulders and bought several mugs of wine. It was the latest in a long line of unfortunate incidents that had solidified his reputation on the streets of Byzantium as a violent thief. Such a reputation made it hard to find work – until recently.

'Actually, yes. I do have something. Starting tomorrow.'

'Oh,' replied Galla, her face brightening. 'What's that?'

'Working for a city official.'

'Really? You?'

'He thinks I have "potential".'

Tarchon couldn't really blame Galla for the cynical expression that greeted this comment.

'What kind of work?'

'Delivering messages and doing other little tasks around the city.' It wasn't the truth, but then it wasn't exactly a lie.

'Ah. Well, nobody knows Byzantium better than you. How did you get the job?'

'Er...just in the right place at the right time, I suppose.'

Galla put her hand on his arm. 'I'm pleased for you. You need something regular. Did you tell your aunt? She might change her mind.'

'I think it's for the best,' he said honestly. 'I need to do my own thing, try to get my own place.'

'That will be expensive.'

'I know. Actually, the thing is...I don't get my first pay for a couple of weeks. I was wondering...could you ask your father if I could stay – maybe in the cellar or somewhere? Just a roof over my head until I get my coins.' Tarchon hated to ask – especially just after being fed – but he couldn't think of any alternative, and he needed a safe place to leave his things.

'Mehruz and his family are ill,' he added. 'Sorry, Galla. You've already been so kind.'

'It's all right. You know I'll always help you when you need it.' She lowered her voice. 'But it's not up to me. I'll go and ask.'

The wait was not pleasant. Galla first went through to see Master Vesonius, then upstairs to fetch her mother. During this time, her little brother, Marcus, came out to see Tarchon. The lad was eleven and very interested in the fighting stave. He wanted to see some attacking moves but Tarchon was wary of looking like he was trying to ingratiate himself. Marcus told him about some soldier who lived down the street who'd had his leg chopped off by a Goth warrior in a famous battle, though he couldn't remember its name.

When the other three members of the family came out, Tarchon stood up, already blushing.

Master Vesonius spoke: 'Young man, you should know that Galla has advocated for you; and that we trust her view that you are trying to better yourself. I can't have you staying in the house – that would be improper. However, there's a spare pallet in the cellar and if we put it under the rear balcony you'll be protected from the rain. We have a good mattress and pillow for you. On the day you receive your first pay, this arrangement ends. You're not to go up to the first floor or bring anyone else here. And if you hang about in the day, be assured that I'll put you to work.'

Galla and her mother smiled.

'You can teach me how to stick-fight!' exclaimed Marcus.

Tarchon kept his eyes on the stern face of Galla's father. 'Thank you, Master Vesonius. Thank you, all.'

IV

Tarchon left too early to get any breakfast but he still had the dates and a bread roll he'd saved from his evening meal. Master Vesonius had invited him to join them for dinner and, as usual, he enjoyed the relaxed warmth of a family occasion. Afterwards, he helped young Marcus make a repair to a wooden chariot and spoke to Galla before everyone turned in. Tarchon actually preferred sleeping outside (providing he wasn't getting wet) and he was woken by some warring dogs, which at least got him up before first light. He had also managed to borrow a pair of old sandals from his host, which meant his blister didn't bother him as he hurried down to North Harbour.

There were in fact two walled harbours there, situated where the Bosphorus became the busy waterway known as the Golden Horn. The eastern harbour was the Prosphorion, its neighbour to the west the New Harbour. They were separated only by a narrow promontory and were jointly referred to by locals as the North Harbour. This meant that Tarchon had double the wharf space to watch but some enquiries to the dockers told him which vessels had already come in. As the day was young, this amounted to only two ships: a pair of Cappadocian freighters, neither of which was called *Lampra*.

Most of the promontory was occupied by a low-walled yard belonging to a firm specialising in storage. Outside the warehouse, sat row after row of closely-packed amphoras. As he hurried through the short grass beside the yard, Tarchon saw an area of broken containers; the clay fragments were sure to end up on one of the city's many dumps.

'What you up to?' grunted a middle-aged man who had just emerged from the warehouse.

Tarchon pointed towards the end of the promontory. 'Just keeping a look out.'

'Stay out the yard.'

'Piss off.' He had never liked being taken for a criminal, even though by strict definition he was one.

'What did you say?'

Ignoring the fellow, Tarchon pressed on to a muddy patch where watchers such as himself often positioned themselves. He dropped his small leather bag and sat down at the promontory's edge, reflecting that he'd been lucky with the weather. It was a fairly bright day but a thin layer of cloud prevented too much glare.

Tarchon looked out at the concrete moles that defined the two harbours. The defensive chains that protected them hadn't been needed for years and were currently wrapped around spindles. There were only a few large fishing vessels in North Harbour – mainly due to the mooring fees – but a couple were already on the move. Out on the Horn were at least a dozen ships, great sails swollen by a strong northerly. Countless vessels plied their trade up and down the waterway, which continued deep into Thracia before narrowing.

Tarchon shifted his gaze to the east, where he could see vessels travelling in every direction. Here, the Horn met what most called the Straits: the narrow channel that ran north for fifteen miles before reaching the Black Sea. To the south lay the Propontis: gateway to the Great Sea. Tarchon didn't think he had all that much to be grateful for but he'd always been glad to have been born in Byzantium. To many who lived there, *it* was the centre of the world, not Rome. Here was where east met west, and here could be found people of almost every religion and race. As Mehruz was fond of saying, a man bored of Byzantium was bored of life.

With his eye on a ship that was lowering its sails, Tarchon decided it was time for breakfast. As he chewed on a date, he ran his hand across the worn surface of his leather bag. He'd had it for years, having found it in the middle of a street, full of women's clothes. It was a very good bag; sturdy but light and with a matching strap. People had tried to steal it several times but he'd always fought hard to keep it. Tarchon smiled; it really was a very good bag.

Korax had described the *Lampra* as a coaster, which wasn't hugely helpful. This basically meant a two or three masted sailing vessel capable of travelling from port to port. It would be larger than a fishing boat but smaller than a big ship of the type that sailed out of sight of land and across seas. Within the first hour or so, only one such vessel came in. Tarchon could not make out the whole name but could see it was made up of three words, so it wasn't the *Lampra*.

'Typical. Bloody typical.'

His annoyance was a result of two ships turning in at the same time. One already had its sails down and the other had only a foresail still up. Both were three-masted but the first of them was longer, with a prominent prow and a high sternpost. Tarchon stood and shaded his eyes. The first vessel was now approaching the narrow entrance of New Harbour, oars propelling it southward. The second coaster then lowered the foresail and soon her oars could be seen too. Picking up speed, it altered course, confirming that it too was headed for New Harbour.

'At least they're going to the same place.'

Tarchon grabbed his bag and hung it in the usual fashion: from his right shoulder, under his left arm. This kept it out of the way and he'd adjusted the strap so it didn't move much when he ran. And while he often needed to run, a swift walk would get him down to the harbour in time.

The *Ceres* and the *Fortuna Redux*. Once he'd learned that neither were the *Lampra*, Tarchon walked back along the mole, hands tucked into his belt, checking names on vessels he'd already checked. Though he'd never been schooled, he knew his letters and could generally read names; anything more complicated and he got confused. When sober, his father had taught him basic mathematics but he'd never seen the point in really studying.

On one of the vessels, a loud crew chief was reminding his underlings that the captain needed to depart within three hours. Catching sight of Tarchon, he asked him if he was in need of work: at the rate of one sesterce per hour. Tarchon had to refuse and, as he walked away, cursed his luck. How many times had he asked for work down on the docks? And how many times had he got any? One in ten? More like one in twenty!

He told himself to focus on the job in hand. If he could find this Evaristos and stay on his tail for the day, Korax might be impressed enough to keep him on. Tarchon knew it wouldn't be easy but if he could make the right impression on the old soldier and Gargonius, he might have a chance at a real job. A job that paid well, a job that meant he wouldn't have to worry about where his next meal was coming from. If he could achieve that, then he would never again have to beg for work, or food, or a place to sleep.

Once at the landward end of the mole, he turned left, along the wharf at the heart of New Harbour. Mornings were always busy and dockers, passengers, sailors and port officials fought for space. Where the approach road reached the wharf, the harbour-master's assistants directed newly-arrived carts, horsemen and pedestrians to impose some kind of order. These men wore a blue stripe on the sleeve of their tunics and were generally well-informed, if not overly friendly. Waiting for one of them to bellow at a youth and his unruly mule, Tarchon addressed one politely.

'Good day, sir. Any news on the *Lampra*?'

'Never heard of it.'

Tarchon repeated the name but the official just shook his head and turned away. Tarchon was used to such reactions. Young men like him with old, grimy tunics weren't worth the time of a man with a paying job; or at least that's how they saw it. Tarchon knew where he could find men of his station and they could also be very useful.

These were the dockers and though some got sick of being asked if that ship had come in or that ship had gone, they were generally a friendly breed. And while many worked for chiefs who pushed them hard, others were happy to pass on information or have a moment's respite from their labours.

Tarchon dodged his way across the road and continued along the wharf, where more than a dozen vessels were docked. Reaching the first of several dockers, he began his questions. He learned nothing about the *Lampra* until the fifth man: a grey-haired-fellow counting kegs beside a tall, wooden crane. Tarchon was careful to let him finish his count before speaking.

'Due in, is she?' The man picked something out of his teeth, then examined it.

'Today, I was told.'

'Mmm. That's one of Cassander's.'

'Who's he?'

'Owns a shipping firm. Been to Prosphorion today?'

'No. Why?'

'Because if there's space at the wharf, the *Lampra* will put in there. That's where Cassander's offices are.'

'Much obliged.'

Within a quarter-hour, Tarchon had identified the offices of Cassander Shipping, one of the brick buildings set back from the main wharf in Prosphorion. There was indeed still space for at least two ships, so he sat on a stone bollard and waited. Unless the *Lampra* arrived very late, he knew he would not be bored. There was simply so much to watch:

First, he saw a captain and his crew prepare their ship for departure. While they took on some last bits of cargo and an apologetic passenger, the Prosphorion herald announced that this vessel, the *Artemis*, was bound for Neapolis, calling at Perinthus and Lampsacus. As the sailors detached fenders and lines, two of them cursed at a crow circling the mast. Tarchon knew that if a dark bird landed in the rigging, the superstitious sailors would fear the worst for their voyage.

Later, he observed an argument between a sailor and a passenger who seemed incensed that a departure had been put back to the following day. He unleashed all manner of curses, only desisting when the sailor began to clench his tattooed fists.

Around midday, Tarchon spoke to a friendly fellow carrying a box of trade items on his back. Tired from shifting this load down to the harbour, he opened it up and showed Tarchon the contents: a selection of nautical signalling mirrors, mainly polished metal discs. After catching his breath, he set off to try and sell his wares.

Tarchon kept an eye on Cassander all the while and eventually a man who looked like a shipping agent stepped out. A few minutes later, two carts drove up. Tarchon left his bollard and casually moved closer but he couldn't hear the conversation between the agent and the cart-drivers. He didn't want to draw attention to himself by asking them outright but reckoned their arrival was a good sign.

Sure enough, less than an hour later, the *Lampra* came through the harbour entrance. She was a three-masted vessel, quite broad, with a sharp prow and a goose-head at the stern. The shipping agent recruited a couple of dockers to take the *Lampra*'s lines and the coaster tied up directly opposite Cassander Shipping. Tarchon had already identified the captain: a tall, loud man who wore a pale blue tunic of some quality. He had also identified the only passengers: a family of four who were ready with their bags and a single wooden chest. The father might have been in his thirties but surely this Evaristos was not a family man?

Once the gangplank was down, the four said their goodbyes to the captain. One of the crew grabbed the chest and two more escorted them across the narrow plank and onto the wharf. Tarchon was close enough to see grey in the passenger's beard. He was at least forty.

His gaze moved across the ship again but he could see only sailors; most of them now bringing up cargo from the hold.

However, just behind a sailor lugging a hefty amphora, were two more men, and both looked like passengers. One was very well-built, carrying a pack over his shoulder and wearing boots befitting a soldier. He carried himself confidently and Tarchon reckoned him to be an ex-legionary. The second man was slight, darker in complexion and with curly, black hair. He wore a dark brown cape over his tunic and also carried his belongings in a pack.

Ensuring that he didn't keep his eyes on them for too long, Tarchon observed them exchange farewells with the captain and – once on shore – pay the shipping agent. Now Tarchon walked past, hoping to catch a name, but the talk was of weather and flying fish. He stopped by another vessel, pretending to be interested in other goings-on. After a few minutes, the two departed: in opposite directions. While the soldierly type headed for the buildings that lined the wharf, the slender fellow headed for the road.

Tarchon cursed. He felt sure that the muscular fellow was the more likely target. But if he was wrong, he would lose the other man, who – once out of Prosphorion – would soon be lost in Byzantium's enormous crowds.

'Master Philo!' A youthful sailor ran nimbly across the gangplank and along the wharf. He was carrying a pair of socks, which he duly handed over to the muscular passenger.

Grinning to himself at this good fortune, Tarchon turned around and walked after the slender man. He had to be Evaristos.

Following anyone for a distance in the city was difficult. Many of Byzantium's streets were narrow and most were busy. Then there was the usual issue of keeping the right distance: not so close that you were noticed, not so far that you lost contact. And with Evaristos' lack of height and nondescript clothing, he blended easily into even a small crowd. Tarchon imagined a seagull depositing a nice white dropping on the man's back to make the job easier.

While pursuing his target, he wondered what Evaristos might have done to draw the interest of Korax and Gargonius. Though he'd learned a little about their organisation, he still found the whole affair difficult to grasp. He was sure of one thing: the man was no stranger to Byzantium.

Approaching First Hill, Evaristos turned off into an alley and trotted up a steep set of steps. Not wanting to draw attention to himself in the confined space, Tarchon paused behind a corner wall before following. It was fortunate he didn't wait any longer because, when he did look again, he glimpsed the fast-moving Evaristos turn right at the top. Tarchon hurried after him, stepping as lightly as he could. He emerged onto a street that ran most of the way around the lower slopes of First Hill. He looked left and right but Evaristos had disappeared.

A pair of squealing piglets was dragged past by a cursing youth as Tarchon stood there, beginning to sweat, eyes scanning the nearby buildings. The most likely destination was an inn: the Three Sisters. It was a middling place but quite popular due to the proprietor's wide selection of affordable wines.

When he opened the door and stepped inside, he saw there were about a dozen patrons. He tried not to register his relief when he spied Evaristos at the counter, talking to the proprietor. They were already discussing his choice of wine.

Before the man had a chance to turn and look at him, Tarchon crossed the room and sat at a shadowy table beside the hearth. The proprietor cast a disapproving glance at him before fetching Evaristos his wine. Tarchon was again relieved when the man didn't speak to him; hopefully he'd come to the table. Keeping his head down by pretending to look at something in his bag, he noted Evaristos take his mug of wine and move to a stool beside one of the tavern's two windows. Nearby, a quartet of what looked like sailing officers were deep in conversation.

The proprietor lifted the counter hatch and approached. 'You do know our prices?'

Tarchon knew he wouldn't get away with pretending to be a man of means. 'I do. My uncle's meeting me here. He promised me a mug of Naxos' best in return for a favour.'

This was greeted by a cynical expression. 'So, you're not ordering yet?'

'Not just yet, thank you. Unfortunately, he's usually late.'

Another raised eyebrow but the man left. Tarchon had kept his voice quiet and thankfully the proprietor had done the same. He hoped Evaristos hadn't noticed him at all.

Tarchon had just begun to relax when the door opened and two men entered. They were clearly regulars because the proprietor greeted them by name and immediately poured them some wine. Unfortunately for Tarchon, one of those names was familiar and Myron noticed him almost immediately.

Of all the people in Byzantium who Tarchon owed money – or who *thought* he owed them – Myron had long been the biggest problem. The previous year, the smuggler had organised an illicit shipment of Persian perfumes to Byzantium. Tarchon had been no more than hired help; shifting the precious contraband from ship to rowing boat to cart. Three of them had rowed ashore with Myron but due to an unforeseen incident – the arrival of a squad of city guards – they'd been forced to abandon the boat close to shore. They all fled but Tarchon had done so with a box tucked under his arm, which he lost in the waves. Unfortunately, Myron had only seen him *take* the box, not lose it, and insisted on recompense. Many months had passed but Tarchon had escaped him on at least three occasions.

'Well, well,' said Myron as he planted both hands on the table and leaned forward. 'It's been a while. The last time I saw you, Tarchon, you were running away. *Again.*'

Myron was as tall as Tarchon but with the bulk of an older man: wide neck, barrel chest, big hands. One of his eyes always seemed to be facing the wrong way and he possessed an unsightly double chin.

Not wishing to draw any attention, Tarchon gestured to the chair to his right, so there was less chance of Evaristos seeing or hearing them.

'Good day, Myron. Have a seat.'

'I'll have one. And then I'll smash it over your head.'

Some of the patrons heard this; faces turned their way.

'Have a seat. I've just finished a good deal. Maybe I can settle our debt.'

Face set in a glare, Myron rounded the table and took the chair beside Tarchon. He sat so close that the smell of sweat, wine and some noxious food was hard to avoid.

'As I remember it, your debt is twenty denarii.'

'Twenty? Let's be realistic. I'll get you ten.'

'The number is *twenty*. You should consider yourself lucky, mate.'

Myron moved closer, his chair scraping on the stone floor. He put his left arm around Tarchon's shoulder and when he spoke, Tarchon grimaced at the foulness of his breath.

'You've made me look a fool time and again. Embarrassed me. You're going to pay up. Now.'

Stay calm. Deep breaths. Don't let this idiot ruin everything.

'Listen, Myron, I don't have it on me but let's make an arrangement for later. I can-'

Myron's fingers encircled his shoulder and squeezed hard.

'I said *now*.'

Tarchon hated a lot of people. He hated the rich because they treated everyone else badly and they had what he wanted: wealth, comfort and freedom. He hated soldiers and city guards and watchmen because they loved power and thought they were above the law, even though they were supposed to enforce it. But the people he hated most were those who thought they could intimidate him. Because for all his disadvantages, he was no slave: he was a freeborn man and he wasn't going to roll over for some overconfident bully.

Knowing he was about to snap, he told himself once more: *Stay calm. Stay calm. It's not worth it.*

But the smell of the man and the touch on his shoulder had ignited an anger that he just couldn't quell.

'Myron,' he said, voice low. 'Take your hand off me right now or you're going to regret it.'

Instead, Myron gripped harder. 'Do you seriously think I'm scared of you, you little street-rat?'

Tarchon looked away and relaxed his body so Myron wouldn't feel him about to move. His arm was currently at rest on the table between them: until he drove his elbow up and back with power and precision. The crunch of bones and the outraged cry of pain from Myron confirmed that he had done plenty of damage. Tarchon was planning to head for the door but hadn't got far when Myron's left hand gripped his belt.

But with blood pouring from his nose, the man could not maintain his grip; especially when Tarchon chopped a hand onto his wrist. Without a glance at Evaristos, Tarchon made for the door, only for his path to be blocked by Myron's companion.

'I knew you'd cause trouble!' spat the proprietor, already throwing open the hatch to come and join in. Tarchon snatched a glance over his left shoulder. Despite his injury, Myron was also moving, holding his nose with his left hand and grabbing a stool with his right. Tarchon reckoned he had no more than ten seconds to get out of the tavern.

Myron's friend was not as well built as the smuggler but clearly unafraid of a scrap. Tarchon thought he'd dodged neatly around him but the man flailed at his sleeve and grabbed hold. The material ripped but it slowed him down and the bastard followed up with a low, swinging punch that caught Tarchon in the gut. The impact of the blow was not unlike being hit between the legs and for a moment the pain stalled him. But he knew he had to get out before he faced three men instead of one. His punch slid across his enemy's cheek but was sufficient to knock him off balance.

Despite the sickening pain in his stomach, Tarchon dived for the door, wrenched it open, and threw it shut behind him. Knowing that the nearby Sanctuary of Apollo represented his best chance of escape, he ran to the right, almost knocking over a young lad towing a hand-cart. He could hear footsteps behind him and he glanced back to see the man he'd just struck burst out of the inn.

Pumping his legs to get some distance, Tarchon ran through the pain, though he couldn't stop himself throwing up. Vomit sprayed from his mouth as he cut left, then left again: into the alley that ran along the rear of the sanctuary. Looking back to ensure his pursuer wasn't close enough to see him, he launched himself up, gripping the rounded top of the wall. Once he had his elbows set, he levered the rest of his body over and dropped blind into the middle of what turned out to be a spiky bush.

Though it scratched his legs, he was at least well-hidden from the other occupants of the sanctuary, as the bush was behind a sprawling tree. He then heard fast-moving footsteps: two men, at least. They halted – perhaps at the end of the alley – and then moved on, the noise soon fading.

Tarchon stepped out of the bush. Wincing at the nasty scratches, a dozen of which were bleeding, he then remembered the pain in his stomach and promptly vomited again. Leaning back against the wall, he eventually began to feel better. Only then did he think about how badly he had screwed this up; and what in Hades he was going to say to Korax.

V

Returning to the Three Sisters – or going anywhere near it – was out of the question. Myron's rage would not pass quickly and he was well connected in the area around First Hill. If he got hold of Tarchon, any chance of passing Gargonius' test was gone. As if finding Evaristos again wasn't enough of a challenge, Tarchon would now also have to look out for himself.

Waiting a half-hour, he casually exited the sanctuary, noting the couples walking hand in hand amid the fountains and flowers and wishing his life was so easy. Pausing at the gates, he checked in both directions before braving the street. Keeping to alleys and quiet areas where he could, he descended the northern flank of First Hill, headed back to Prosphorion Harbour. There was simply nowhere else he might hope to learn more about Evaristos. While he began with only a vague plan, by the time he reached Cassander Shipping, he knew exactly what to do.

Tarchon straightened his tunic, knocked on the door and entered. The office was quite large, with a broad table facing the door. Most of one wall was taken up by shelving full of scrolls and waxed tablets. There was no sign of the shipping agent he'd seen earlier but a younger man sat at the desk, making notes on a tatty piece of papyrus with a stick of charcoal. He was no more than twenty and dressed in a dull, plain tunic. Tarchon guessed he was a clerk.

'Good day,' he said. It was even harder to make a good impression when your tunic was torn and your legs were covered in scratches. Fortunately, the man didn't notice.

'Good day, sir,' said the clerk politely, though his expression and manner changed when he saw who had entered the office.

'I'm here on behalf of Titus, proprietor of the Three Sisters tavern.' Tarchon stepped forward and showed the clerk the Minerva brooch already in his hand. 'A customer dropped this and we wanted to return it. We only know his name and that he came in today on the *Lampra* – thought you might know of an address or way to find him? Evaristos.'

Tarchon had used this trick many times before; another reason why he would never get rid of his prized possession.

The clerk peered at the brooch for a moment then leaned back into his chair and sighed, as if this was another great burden among many.

'Master Gennadius deals with clients. He's out for the afternoon.'

Though the agent might have known more, Tarchon reckoned he stood a better chance with this fellow.

'Perhaps he's used your firm before,' Tarchon suggested. 'There might be a record.'

'The name doesn't ring a bell.'

'We *must* try to get it back to him though. Might be a reward. If so, I'm happy to share.'

With a little nod, the clerk stood and walked to the shelves. Reaching into a wooden box, he retrieved a pile of small papers, which Tarchon guessed might be receipts. After a minute of searching, he held one up.

'Here's the name and record of payment. No address though.'

Tarchon winced but also remembered that Evaristos had clearly struck up a friendship with the other lone passenger – the bald man.

'He did mention that he'd spoken to a gentleman named Philo while on the ship. He might know where we can find him.'

'Possible, I suppose.'

'And do you have an address for him?'

'Probably – Philo is a regular client – but you won't need it. He's a buyer for the fleet. Spends all his time in one harbour or another. I saw him only an hour ago – talking to an agent outside Axius.'

'Axius?'

'Another shipping agent. Eight doors down.'

'Ah. Thank you.' Tarchon wasn't overly keen on the idea of trying this ruse with a navy man but at least he had some information.

As he headed for the door, the clerked cleared his throat. 'And if you do receive any reward...?'

'Of course.'

Philo was not to be found at Axius shipping but, after asking for him there and at the harbour-master's office, Tarchon tracked him down to a warehouse situated behind the wharf. The buyer seemed to be inspecting a shipment of grain and was discussing numbers with a merchant. Standing outside the warehouse, Tarchon waited for a lull in their conversation before introducing himself. At such times, he tried to moderate his accent, which he'd often been told was rather "rough".

Philo seemed annoyed at the interruption but at least listened. 'Yes, I spoke to him. I believe he lives near Third Hill – can't tell you more than that. You should ask the shipping agent, lad.'

'I have. They don't have an address.'

Philo shrugged and wiped some sweat from his hairless head. He turned back to the merchant but suddenly raised a finger and addressed Tarchon once more.

'We did talk about food. Eateries. Pelagia's. He's a regular. You could try there.'

Tarchon was not in the mood – nor the physical state – for another long walk but that was what he faced. To get to Third Hill, he had to head west. Traffic was slow at the gate of the

Severan Walls but, once through, he hadn't far to go to reach the eatery. Pelagia's was known throughout the city for its excellent shellfish and wealthier customers from Chalcedon often crossed The Straits just to dine there. Mehruz often spoke of the establishment in envious terms: this was what he was aiming for. Tarchon couldn't see the city-folk being as enthusiastic about a Persian eatery but he never told his friend that.

He had no chance of getting in the front door so instead loitered at the back. Here staff came and went: taking deliveries, fetching firewood or simply coming out for fresh air. Tarchon was snapped at by a well-dressed fat man but most of the others listened to his brooch story. He had to question five of them before he got solid information.

'Master Evaristos, yes, I know him,' said a middle-aged maid. She had come outside for a snack and spoke to him while sitting on a barrel, nibbling at a plate of sardines and green beans.

'Any idea where he lives?'

Using her fork, the maid pointed north. 'Bottom of the hill, not far from the Great Avenue. Merchant's street. Nice places down there.'

'Much obliged. Is it numbered?'

'I think so. Don't know which one is his.'

Tarchon doubted that his haphazard pursuit of Evaristos was what either Gargonius or Korax had in mind. By the time he spoke to some locals on Merchant's Street, he'd probably mentioned the man to over a dozen people, but at least he'd made progress. The street consisted mainly of large townhouses, so he was clearly a man of some standing.

Two of those Tarchon spoke to agreed that Evaristos dwelt at number eleven. The building was only a single storey but the frontage was thirty feet across and Tarchon reckoned it would go back twice as far. The walls were bright with fresh white paint, the sloping roof topped by red tiles. There was only one door facing the street and that was sturdily made of iron and wood. There were four windows: all small, grilled and high.

Tarchon's intention was to observe the place for a bit but it was difficult to dwell in the street without attracting attention, especially as some of the townhouses were staffed by doormen. He had only been watching number eleven for a minute or so when he realised that Evaristos had his own enforcer. This fellow came out, chewed his fingernails, then wandered down the street to talk to a compatriot.

Tarchon looked to the west. The sun was low and already more orange than yellow. There was no time to tarry any longer. He had an appointment to keep.

He had aimed to arrive looking calm and professional but it was quite a way to the statue of Hadrian and he found his path blocked by not one but two throngs of cultists. When he finally got there, Korax was sitting on the steps, sipping from a metal flask. As Tarchon sat down beside him, breathing hard, the ex-legionary peered at his legs. Tarchon had hoped that the gloom of dusk might hide the scratches but Korax apparently missed nothing.

'You're late.'

In truth, the sun had only just dropped the horizon but Tarchon chose not to argue the point. 'Apologies. How are you?'

He regretted this inane comment as soon as he said it.

Korax ignored it entirely. 'Report.'

'The *Lampra* came in about midday and I saw Evaristos get off.'

'How did you know it was him?'

Korax' voice was so deep and harsh that Tarchon wondered if his throat had been injured somehow. He sounded like he'd swallowed a mouthful of grit.

Tarchon had decided not to disclose any more than he needed to about his difficult day. 'I heard someone use his name.'

'Go on.'

'I followed him to a tavern called the Three Sisters. It's on First Hill.'

'I know it. Go on.'

Tarchon had hoped Korax didn't know it; that he'd never heard of it, in fact.

'Evaristos drank wine and left after an hour or so.'

'Did he meet anyone?'

'No.'

'You were inside?'

'Yes.'

'But you don't have money for wine.'

'I got credit.'

Korax raised an eyebrow. 'You're *sure* he didn't meet anyone?'

'I'm sure.' Tarchon really wished he didn't have to lie so he quickly moved on. 'From there I followed him to his home. Eleven, Merchant's Street.'

'How do you know that's his home?'

'I asked around – only a couple of people.'

'What time did he arrive there?'

'About the ninth hour.'

'Tell me about the house.'

'It's big, even for that street. Nice white paint.'

'Nice paint? Gods, next you'll be telling me which flowers he has in his garden. Who gives a shit? What about residents? Layout? Security? Access?'

'Er, not sure on residents other than him. He has a doorman. Door looked strong – only way in at the front. I couldn't get round to the back.'

'You didn't check the rear of the property?'

'There is a reason,' replied Tarchon, desperately trying to think of one. 'Workers. Labourers repairing a wall. I couldn't get close without looking suspicious.'

Korax sighed. 'Did Evaristos remain there until you left?'

'Yes.'

'Did anyone else go in or out?'

'No.'

'Tell me about him. Appearance.'

'You said thirty. I'd say more like thirty-five. Short – around five feet four. Black, curly hair. Light brown tunic, dark brown cape. Large pack. Fine shoes.'

'Better,' said Korax.

For the first time that day, Tarchon felt a moment of optimism.

'All right then,' growled the veteran. 'Your next assignment. We have just learned that Evaristos returned in possession of a fine vase of lapis lazuli. Your task is to secure it and bring it here at dusk in two days' time.

'What?'

'You heard me.' Korax stood.

Tarchon just slumped back against the steps. 'How?'

'Young man, if you can't work anything out for yourself, you're of no use to us.'

Though he didn't feel like it, Tarchon forced himself to his feet. 'Yes, sir. I'll do my best.'

He reckoned it sounded like something a soldier might say but Korax didn't seem all that impressed. Still, he had to try his luck:

'Er. I don't suppose-'

'-If you ask me for money again, I might just lose my temper. You'll get it when you've earned it.'

'Right.'

'Two days then. And *don't* be late.'

By the time he reached Galla's, the street was fairly quiet. The store, however, was unexpectedly busy. Master Vesonius had two lanterns alight and was helping a customer, along with Galla. The cobbler greeted Tarchon with only a nod while Galla swiftly conducted him to the rear of the store.

'It's late,' she said.

'Busy day.'

'I'll get you some food in a bit but I must stay with Father for now.' She leaned in close. 'Master Bernardus has been here for *two* hours.'

While Galla returned to the front of the store, Tarchon leant against the wall, safely in the shadows. Master Bernardus looked to be at least sixty-five and was now walking back and forth, eyes fixed on his new-looking shoes. Vesonius watched, hands clamped to the straps of his apron, trying – but failing – to hide his displeasure.

'The right is better, certainly.'

'Ah,' said Vesonius, exchanging an optimistic glance with Galla.

'But the left,' said the old man. 'Something's wrong. I'm off balance.'

Vesonius rolled his eyes.

'The heel again, Master Bernardus?' said Galla.

Tarchon had seen her deal with customers before. She often smoothed the way between her father and some of their more demanding clients. Proper shoes were so very expensive; Tarchon guessed that was why so many insisted that they be just right.

'It's the toe. The left side.' For a man of his age, Bernardus had a very loud voice. He sat down on a bench. 'Just have another look, would you, Vesonius?'

'Of course.'

The cobbler helped the old man remove his shoe and took it into the workshop. Galla went to help him.

Bernardus slowly stood up. 'Who's that there?'

'Tarchon.'

'Come forward so I can see you.'

Tarchon wasn't all that keen on following this old fool's orders but he had to be respectful to his host's clients.

'And who is young master Tarchon?'

'A friend of Galla's. Master Vesonius has been kind enough to let me stay here for a while.'

'Ah. The gods have smiled upon you.'

Bernardus was solidly-built for an old man, with quite a stomach hanging over his belt. He had a strong nose, pale eyes and a beard more white than grey. There were only a few strands of hair remaining on his head.

'Have you a trade, Tarchon?'

'Not exactly. I've done many jobs.'

'How old are you?'

'Twenty.'

Bernardus looked him over. 'You look strong. Healthy. Have you considered the legions?'

'Not really. Were *you* a soldier?'

'I was. Twenty-five years.'

'Which legion?'

Bernardus pushed up his left sleeve. The ink was faint on his leathery arm but Tarchon had seen the lightning bolt symbol many times. The Twelfth Legion had been raised originally in the West but based in Galatia and Cappadocia for centuries. The lightning bolt was the legion standard.

'Ah,' said Tarchon. 'So, you probably killed a few Persians?' There were plenty of veterans in Byzantium and few were slow to boast of their service.

'A few,' admitted Bernardus. 'Goths too, zealots, brigands…'

'And anyone who wouldn't pay up, right?' said Tarchon with a grin.

'What?' said Bernardus with a frown. 'What does that mean?'

Tarchon wished he'd kept his jape to himself. Some veterans were realistic about the army's reputation for fleecing civilians but apparently Bernardus wasn't one of them.

'Well, speak up, lad!' barked the old soldier.

'Just a joke, sir,' replied Tarchon quickly. 'Twenty-five years, eh? You must have been in a few scrapes. You must have some excellent stories.'

This seemed to placate the old man a little but he was still giving Tarchon a sharp look when Galla and her father returned.

Tarchon offered a bow and withdrew to the shadows once more.

'A pleasure to meet you, sir.'

He wasn't sure Bernardus even heard him. The old man was more interested in his shoes.

It was only afterward that Tarchon realised he could have asked the veteran about the organisation Korax and Gargonius worked for. Though it seemed obvious that they were spies of some kind, he was keen to know more. Hopefully, he'd have a chance to learn directly from them.

Already considering how he might infiltrate Evaristos' house, Tarchon took himself out to the rear courtyard. There was no sign of Galla's mother or brother, which was a relief. It had been a tiring, unpleasant day, though at least his stomach didn't hurt as much now. Touching it, however, he found that the skin was tender. If he ever saw that friend of Myron's again, he would get his revenge – and it would be more than a punch to the gut. Tarchon grinned at the thought of Myron's ruined nose; at least he'd done some damage to that cocky bastard.

He ran his hands across his lower legs. None of the scratches were too bad but there were dozens of them. The darkness at least prevented Galla from seeing the injuries when she brought him out some dinner.

'Has the old bugger gone?'

'Tarchon!'

'I bet your father calls him worse than that.'

Galla sat with him on the bench and handed him the plate. Tarchon tucked in immediately: a bread roll and a cold sausage.

'At least he's happy with his shoes now,' said Galla, leaning back against the bench.

'Difficult job – cobbler,' said Tarchon after a couple of mouthfuls of bread.

'Most jobs have their difficulties.'

'I won't argue with you there.'

VI

It wasn't as if it was the first time. He wasn't proud of it, but Tarchon had robbed several homes. On most occasions, he'd simply been after food; and he'd only done so out of utter desperation. These had been during his younger years, the other robberies being a case of taking what was owed to him from cheats and double-crossers.

But this was different: this was the house of a wealthy man, and therefore a difficult house to break into. He first needed to learn more about the layout of the place and identify weak spots where he could gain entry.

Leaving Galla's place with half a roll and a small flask of watered wine saved from the previous night, he set off just before dawn. Master Vesonius was an early riser but Tarchon had already tidied his pallet, blanket and pillow away before the cobbler came downstairs. His scratched legs had at least scabbed up a bit overnight and his bruised stomach didn't trouble him much as he strode north, passing traders moving their wares and storekeepers opening up. Despite all he faced, Tarchon was surprised to find quite a spring in his step. He even offered a brief prayer to Minerva, though he suspected she'd given him all the help she was going to for a while.

When he arrived at Merchant's Street, his first task was to get a good look at the rear of number eleven. Running along the back of the property was a broad, muddy track, not paved like the street at the front. It was perhaps ten feet across; wide enough to admit carriages and carts to courtyards. Tarchon strolled along it, passing the rear of several similar properties on both sides. One well-dressed gentleman on a fine horse trotted imperiously out of his courtyard. Though he seemed oblivious to Tarchon's presence, his underling gave a suspicious glare before securing the gate. This townhouse was to the right; number eleven was to the left.

Slowing as he reached it, Tarchon was glad to see a barred metal gate that he was able to look through. It was as high as the rear wall – about eight feet – and with enough decorative touches to make it easy to climb. Better still, he got a good look at the rear courtyard. Two doors faced onto it, one of which was open. Inside, a woman was vigorously chopping something on a board. Nestled between the rear of the house and the wall was a small stable where a lad was mucking out. Passing the gate, Tarchon switched his gaze to the windows. The shutters were open but he saw no movement inside. The tiled roof was identical to the section at the front, the gentle slope running up to a ridge parallel to the street. He felt sure that the front and rear sections of the house would be connected by two more, forming a large atrium in the centre – a common arrangement.

As he walked on, Tarchon concluded that the rear was undoubtedly the best method of getting onto the property, though accessing the interior presented a problem. Then there was the even greater problem of locating the vase and getting away undetected.

Now he passed the rear of number ten, which was similar to eleven in both design and size. Though the houses shared a wall, getting onto the roof of number ten would be no easier. There was a narrow alley between ten and nine which he now turned into. The wall was not only very high but topped by vicious-looking shards of broken glass. Tarchon cursed under his breath. This was not looking good.

Once at the end of the alley, he turned left onto Merchant's Street. As he passed number eleven, the wall loomed over him defiantly, the big door apparently impenetrable. Number twelve had a weaker door (without iron reinforcement) and a row of accessible windows. But it didn't really matter; the front was just too exposed, especially with all the doormen around.

At the other end of Merchant's Street, he turned left again and paused at the end of the track. He wanted to take a closer look at the rear of numbers twelve and thirteen but couldn't risk arousing suspicion. Peering around the corner, he saw two men on horseback coming his way, so retreated and leant casually against the wall. They rode out and away, laughing uproariously at some jape.

Hoping no one would notice him retrace his steps, Tarchon approached thirteen slowly. The wall was high – again eight feet or more – and the gate topped by spikes. It would be very difficult to scale without either making noise or risking injury. This was doubly annoying because, on the right side of courtyard, within a ring of soil surrounded by bricks, was a fine oak tree. It was least forty feet tall and several boughs hung over the house. The tree looked very climbable and – crucially – gave access to the roof, which was connected to the roof of number twelve…and number eleven.

Tarchon knew from bitter experience that negotiating sloping tiled roofs could be treacherous but he'd resolved to consider one problem at a time. Number twelve had no tree but the gate was similar to eleven's – easy to climb over. Whistling amiably as he passed a woman carrying a basket of vegetables, Tarchon glanced back at the wall separating twelve and thirteen. It was no more than six feet tall and of a design containing numerous gaps or – as he thought of them – footholds.

With a grin, Tarchon accelerated into a striding walk. He had to speak to Mehruz.

The cockerel stood with its red beak open, as if ready to attack. The black tail feathers were high and proud, giving the creature an air of elegance. It was, Tarchon concluded, a very good painting. And the other paintings on the stone counter of Mehruz's eatery – a pig, a loaf of bread, and a plate of figs – were equally good.

'Don't get me wrong,' he said, 'Anahita is an excellent artist. But why not draw a piece of *fried* chicken? If I'm a customer, I don't come here to buy a *live* chicken: feathers, claws and all. If I see a piece of fried chicken, then I'm hungry and I'll buy.'

Busy with a steaming stew, Mehruz shrugged. 'I don't know. More artistic or something.'

'How is she anyway?'

Mehruz exhaled despairingly. 'She got out of bed today, at least. Don't think I'll see her down here though.'

'At least *you're* better.'

'I was.' The Persian wiped his brow. 'At this rate, I'm going to have a relapse. Maybe you can help out? You know I'll pay you.'

'Sorry, busy day.'

'This new job?' Mehruz looked up as a middle-aged man approached the counter. 'Good day, Iulius. The usual?'

'Good day,' said the customer with a yawn. He was carrying a sack over his shoulder from which he produced a large cloth. Once he'd laid this out on the counter, Mehruz put out a bread roll, a cut of hard cheese and a handful of walnuts.

Iulius paid with a sesterce, wrapped up his food and departed with a weary wave.

'So?' said Mehruz, adding a handful of spices to the stew.

'It's a big opportunity. Can't say much about it. Not yet anyway.'

'I don't much like the sound of that, Tarch. Listen, you've got a roof over your head-'

'-Sort of.'

'So why not just work a solid job for a bit, get some coin together.'

Tarchon felt oddly guilty that Mehruz and Galla knew nothing of the failed robbery and his brief imprisonment. It made the resulting events seem even more bizarre and unreal.

'If this job happens, I'll have more coin than you've ever seen, mate. Listen, I need to ask you something. That Persian you used to hang around with, what did they call him – The Fox?'

'What about him?'

'Any idea where I might find him?'

'No. But I heard he's with Diamandis' gang. You know where to find them.'

'Aye'. Approaching Diamandis and his cohorts was never pleasant but at least he didn't have far to walk.

'Why would you want to talk to The Fox?' asked Mehruz suspiciously.

'Don't worry about it.'

As he had the rest of the day to find The Fox and prepare for his night's work, Tarchon decided he could help his friend.

'I'll stay for the breakfast rush. How's that?'

'Good,' replied Mehruz with a grin. 'Like I said, I'll pay you.'

'You can pay me all right – in bread, cheese and walnuts.'

Once the breakfast rush was over, Mehruz declared – not for the first time – that while Tarchon was quick, his manner with the customers left something to be desired. After he had grunted at a couple of them, the Persian kept him away from the counter. Though Tarchon had little interest in cooking, he had helped out before and didn't make too many mistakes.

Even though the eatery was still busy when he departed, Mehruz grabbed his arm and fixed him with his most serious stare. Tarchon would have shrugged off virtually anyone else in the world, but not his oldest friend.

'Tarch, don't do anything stupid. And be careful around Diamandis.'

Tarchon simply smiled and left. It actually suited him to leave Mehruz' place just before midday because, by the time he arrived, the quail fights were already under way. It was traditional for the betting and action to start around the seventh hour and there were already at least fifty men there. The location was a patch of dusty, rubble-strewn ground between a building site and one of Byzantium's meat markets. Tarchon had always assumed that the fights were held here because the quail could be easily purchased.

Though he'd had a couple of run-ins with Diamandis and his associates, Tarchon generally got on with them well. This was mainly because they also supported The Whites and Diamandis liked nothing better than to lead a group into battle against the Greens or the Blues. In fact, it was commonly said that he had only the vaguest interest in the actual racing. Not a large man, he was nonetheless an utter brute; his face a mass of scars, his preferred weapon a home-made club studded with nails. He was one of the few in Byzantium that Tarchon was truly afraid of.

As he approached a small crowd watching a quail fight, he was glad to see Noctua. The pair had known each other for many years, and he was one of the more friendly members of Diamandis' crew. Even so, he was focused on the fight, and offered only a wave when he noticed Tarchon.

Cheers and boos sounded simultaneously as one of the two chubby quails flapped forward and raked the other with a claw, drawing blood from its neck. While the fight continued, Tarchon looked around but saw no one else he could ask about The Fox. Fortunately, the aggressive quail struck twice again, sending the other bird fleeing to its owner. As such contests went, quail fights were less bloody than most and the referee declared the bout over.

Noctua turned away and spat in disgust. 'Fortuna! Prayed to her for a bloody hour this morning! What's the point?'

'Tough luck, mate,' said Tarchon. 'I don't suppose you know where I'd find The Fox?'

Noctua kicked a pebble away before replying. 'Don't see all that much of him these days. Diamandis reckons he's keeping his head down. Someone robbed the Palmyran envoy's place last week. The Fox claims it's nothing to do with him but Diamandis don't believe him.'

Tarchon grimaced.

'Why'd you want to see him?' asked Noctua. 'Got a tip off or something?'

'Actually, I need a bit of advice.'

'About what?'

'About getting across tiled roofs without making noise – or falling off.'

'What's the job? Need another pair of hands?'

'No, no. More of a test run.'

'I might know someone who can help you.' Noctua held out a hand with an expectant look.

Tarchon held out both of his. 'I've not got a coin, Noctua. The great gods are my witness. But if this mate of yours helps me out and I get the job, I'll give you a finder's fee. A denarius.'

'Make it two and I'll show you to his door.'

An hour later, Tarchon was five denarii in debt. Of course, that debt was really only theoretical but Noctua and his associate had been very helpful, so – if he ever got the money – Tarchon would try to pay it. The associate, an ageing thief named Diogenes, had offered three key pieces of advice regarding the efficient crossing of tiled roofs and Tarchon planned to make use of them all. Now feeling slightly more confident about his perilous assignment, he set off for a familiar destination.

There were several dumps within Byzantium and many more outside the walls. None were anywhere near the centre but the largest was situated in a natural depression just south of Second Hill. There were some apartment blocks in this area but most of it was occupied by workshops of various kinds. They were the ones who'd created the dump in the first place but it was now used by everyone, despite the best efforts of the authorities. Tarchon had been there many times to find certain objects he could use or adapt and, on this particular occasion, he was in need of a rope. He knew from experience that he wouldn't need to search the dump himself.

Most people called them divers, and they were the poorest of the poor. Tarchon had occasionally seen adults engaged in this work but most were children between the ages of six and twelve, usually boys. While some were on the streets, others had homes and families: they were simply sent there to claim what they could. There were numerous tales of great treasures being unearthed (almost entirely untrue, Tarchon was sure) but for the most part if was a case of locating valuable materials that could be reused: timber, metal, glass. It was filthy, dangerous work and Tarchon counted himself lucky that he'd never had to stoop so low.

Passing a row of carts where young labourers were offloading rotten fruit, he approached a pair of lads who were no more than eight or nine. They were burrowing into one section at the edge of the dump, flinging useless rubble and rubbish aside. From his position, Tarchon could see at least forty others doing the same. The dump was about a hundred yards across and gave off the same harsh, fetid smell as the others.

'Lads.'

The two of them turned and hurried over to him, sensing an opportunity. Neither had any shoes and their tunics were in an awful state. One had a nasty sore on his cheek and the other had a harelip.

'I'm Tarch. Who are you?'

'Eagle,' said the one with the sore. He aimed a thumb at his compatriot. 'That's Hawk. He don't speak.'

'Ah. Like the names.'

Tarchon was joking but the lads took him literally, exchanging proud grins.

'Listen, I've got no coin but I do have this.' He reached into his sack and showed them the cheese, bread and walnuts he had earned that morning. 'The one who brings me a rope can have his choice.'

The cheese was three inches across, the roll as big as a hand and there were two dozen walnuts. The boys knew a good feed when they saw one.

'This rope – how long?' asked Eagle.

'I need fifteen feet.'

'Does it have to be one length?'

'No. I don't mind tying a couple of bits. Long as it holds my weight.'

The two of them set off around the edge of the dump, as if they had a particular area in mind.

Tarchon retreated to one of the few trees in the area and squatted in the shade. He watched the various divers at work and listened to the banter of the lads unloading the rotten fruit. They were discussing the maids at some inn and couldn't agree which of them had the biggest breasts.

After a quarter of an hour or so, the silent Hawk came running, a coil of rope in his hand. He handed it to Tarchon, who examined it thoroughly. There was at least twenty feet of it. He'd seen a lot better but then he'd also seen plenty worse.

'Now that's a good find. Let's test it out.' He tied it off around the tree and pulled hard with both hands. The rope held.

'Nice work, Hawk.' Tarchon coiled the rope and put it over his shoulder.

Just as he unwrapped the cloth and laid out the food, Eagle came running up. He had a short length of rope in his hand but it was clearly frayed in several places.

'That's no good to me. Looks like Hawk's the one with the best eyes.'

To his credit, Eagle didn't seem all that upset. The reason for this soon became clear.

When invited to choose his prize, Hawk pointed to the cheese. Tarchon had expected as much; cheese was filling and a rarer treat than bread. Without a word, the pair sat side by side in the shade. Hawk used his teeth to make a dent, then broke the cheese in two. Soon they were both eating, smiling at the taste. They took their time, savouring each mouthful.

'So, you're a solid team, eh?' said Tarchon. 'Good for you – there's nothing worth more than a friend. Slow down a little, eh? A quality cheese needs a quality bread.'

He handed the roll to Eagle. 'Save some for tomorrow, maybe.'

The lad stared at the bread in near disbelief then looked up at Tarchon. 'May the gods smile upon you, sir.'

'And you.'

VII

Use bare feet.
Spread your weight at all times.
Take a rat with you.

Tarchon easily understood the first two pieces of advice from Diogenes, and the veteran thief had gone into quite a bit of useful detail on both. The third surprised him, but the explanation made sense. Having returned to Galla's in late afternoon, he asked for some meat – any meat – and headed for the alley behind Hostus' yard. When he arrived there, he took a quick look over the wall. He saw no sign of Hostus or his aunt. A glance at the shed where he'd spent so many nights sparked a brief pang of sentimentality but he dropped down off the wall and got to work.

There was one particular spot close to a broken sewer grate where he had often seen rats. After placing the meat (chicken's feet) near the grate, he sat against the nearby wall, a wooden box at the ready. As he knew from experience, the key was to remain utterly still, so still that not even your eyes were moving when the rat appeared. Before long, one rodent poked its nose out but swiftly retreated. Then another managed to pilfer one of the chicken's feet without getting caught. But twenty minutes later, Tarchon dropped the box and captured a small, young-looking rat that would do the job nicely. Having transferred it to a sack, he'd hurried back to Galla's to ready himself. He wasn't sure if she believed he was helping out a friend with some night-fishing but he had to come up with something.

*

He reached Merchant's Street around the third hour of night and wasn't surprised to find it better illuminated than the poorer parts of the city. These people had the money to afford candles, lanterns and lamps.

Even so, the track to the rear was dark, which helped him reach number twelve undetected. He peered through the gate. There were lights in the kitchen and from there came the faint sound of voices. He raised his hood and adjusted his shoulder strap so his bag was tight against his back. The rat had moved around while he'd been walking but had now gone still. He hoped it was still alive, though it might also serve its purpose if dead.

Hands on the gate, he felt for a good hold, then put his left foot on one of the horizontal bars and lifted himself up. With his right up on the next bar, he was soon over the top and down the other side. He immediately heard a low growl and the unmistakable sound of four legs pounding across the courtyard.

Knowing he had only seconds, Tarchon ran for the wall that separated number twelve from number thirteen. He recalled the useful handholds but knew he'd have no need of them now. Even in the gloom, the top of the dividing wall was clear and this is what he leapt for. His left hand did no more than smack painfully into sheer brick but his right found the edge. Fortunately, his left boot had also found a grip because the barking dog – quite a large one by the sounds of it – had just skidded to a halt.

'Shut it, Marius!' shouted a deep-voiced woman from the kitchen.

Feeling the dog's snout strike his heel, Tarchon hauled himself up, swiftly levering his legs onto the wall. Hearing the kitchen door fly open, he winced as he dropped over the other side. But there was no spiky bush this time and he landed on level ground.

Marius, however, was not to be deterred. He continued to bark, snarl and paw at the wall.

Then he suddenly quietened.

'Here, boy,' said the woman. 'Look what I've got for you. Master and Mistress left all these roasted snails. Here you go. Good lad.'

Tarchon listened as she and the dog returned to the house, only relaxing fully when he heard the kitchen door close.

Thank Jupiter that Master and Mistress didn't finish their snails.

He surveyed the rear of number thirteen. There was only the dimmest of lights visible behind a single window. The tree was between him and the house, its twisted bulk rising up into the darkness, the higher branches clear against the moonlit sky. Tarchon wished there were a few more clouds; he would be vulnerable while on the roofs.

Approaching the tree, he felt the soil that surrounded it under his boots and began to feel for holds. There were no branches within reach but, after a minute or so, he found a combination of hollows that would get him off the ground. Once at this first hold, he wedged his arm into a space where the trunk divided and scrambled his way upward. In the process, he scratched his ear and the back of his hand but kept the volume of cursing to a minimum. Looking up once more, he saw that the crucial branches were about ten feet above. There were no easy holds but this section of the trunk was not vertical; it sloped up towards the house. It was also a good size for him to hold with his hands while the surface was rough enough for his boots to grip. Ignoring the rat – which had begun to shift around – he started climbing.

Tarchon was halfway up when a door opened. He froze. Hearing a man whistling, he looked down and saw him pass by, lamp in hand. He saw nothing more but heard the gate rattle as if being checked. A few seconds later, the man returned to the house, his whistling fading as he closed and locked the door.

Tarchon hauled himself up the trunk to the first big branch. Gripping the trunk with his thighs, he reached out and decided this branch wasn't thick enough. Climbing another ten feet, he found a better one. Looking down, he was pleased to see he was directly above the edge of the tiled roof.

Manoeuvring himself around the trunk and onto the bulky branch was not easy but he was glad to find it supported his weight without moving. Sitting astride it, he grabbed his bag and retrieved the rope. The rat was writhing around once more and now squeaking.

Keep quiet or I'll throw you to that dog.

Returning the bag to his back and placing the rope over his shoulder, he braced his hands between his legs and levered himself forward, a few inches at a time. After five feet, the branch began to bend but Tarchon wasn't concerned. He had loved climbing trees as a child and always dared to climb higher and farther than anyone else. He was sure he would know if – and when – there was a danger of the branch breaking. Around ten feet from the trunk, he found himself a similar distance above the roof. Ahead, the tip of the branch actually hung close to the tiles but he couldn't risk going further.

He now tied the rope around the branch using one of the many solid knots he'd learned while fishing. Earlier, he had added several rounded knots to the rope to aid his descent. Once it was secure, he carried out the awkward job of removing his boots and placing them in the bag. Thankfully, the rat had calmed down again.

Now around twenty feet off the ground, he was struck by doubt. Maybe he'd slip from the rope; slide down the unstable tiles and dash his head against the flagstones, spilling his brains out in the courtyard. Tarchon had once seen a dead child that had fallen from an apartment block, body and limbs smashed into a bloody pulp.

He took a deep breath.

Great gods, please watch over me. Especially, you, Minerva.

Rather than swinging down, he lowered himself: one hand on the branch, one hand on the rope. Then, gripping with his thighs, he descended, using every knot. Already sure that he was far enough over the roof, he didn't look down until he was close.

Halting – both hands on knots – he freed his feet but then realised he wasn't quite there. He lowered himself another few inches and the toes of his left foot touched the rough surface of a clay tile. Waiting until his right foot was down on another tile, he at last let go of the rope, wincing as his entire weight was transferred to the roof.

The edge was three yards to his left. To his right, he could make out the lines of the tiles rising up to the roof's ridge; even the semi-circular *tegula* tiles that divided each line of flat *imbrex* tiles to ensure solidity and keep out water.

He knew from past experience that a fast or unplanned move across such roofs would easily dislodge tiles and create damage and noise. But, as Diogenes had told him, by flattening his feet across each tegula and moving slowly, he could avoid cracking or moving the tiles. Tarchon now did exactly that: staying low, feeling his way with his hands, always trying to spread his weight. Close to the top, his back scraped low-hanging foliage but his confidence had grown and he was soon at the ridge. Halting to catch his breath, he now moved up onto the row of tegula tiles that topped the roof.

Bare feet were again useful here because he could grip with his toes. Now he stayed upright, arms outstretched to help him balance. Tarchon halted when he reached the edge of number thirteen's roof, which adjoined a small, perpendicular section of number twelve. Though it was merely one long step, the impact was heavy and he heard the tile crack. He brought his other foot across and knelt, listening for a while before continuing upwards. He paused again when he reached the ridge of this section but heard nothing that concerned him.

Left across this part of number twelve, right across the section that faced Merchant's Street, right again until he found himself clambering onto number eleven. Tarchon paused once there, realising that this period of intense concentration had made him lose track of time. But now he took even more care, scaling one side of the roof then turning around and descending step by step, stretching out his arms again to distribute his weight. Eventually, he reached the roof's edge which, as expected, overlooked a spacious atrium.

The moonlight upon the rectangular pond at its centre offered some illumination; enough for him to see that all four sides were porticoed: supported by a series of narrow columns. He could also see that the roof-edge was no more than nine feet from the ground. Evaristos' townhouse seemed quiet.

Now Tarchon employed an old trick. Squatting low, he removed two of the imbrex tiles that ran along the roof-edge. Placing them carefully behind him, he was relieved to feel the timber frame underneath. This would provide the handholds that would enable him to drop to the ground. But, before that, he needed to put his boots back on: not an easy process. The young rat was now so quiet that Tarchon thought it might be dead. But when he reached down further, he found it alive, breathing and oddly placid.

Once he had his boots on, he shifted the bag to his back. That was when his elbow struck one of the imbrex tiles. It slid away from him and his despairing grasping dive did no more than knock it off the roof.

NO!

The tile landed with a loud crack, the noise seeming to reverberate out into the quiet night. In moments, Tarchon heard movement from the front of the house.

Now I'm in trouble.

Grabbing the other tile, he replaced it and moved himself gently up the roof, bag still in his hand. Hearing footsteps, he laid out flat on his back. Looking downward, he couldn't see much: only a light approaching from his left. There also seemed to be someone coming from the rear of the house.

Take a rat with you.

Tarchon reached inside the bag. When he gripped the rat's body it began to struggle. He grabbed its tail, plucked it from the bag and threw it off the roof.

'What in Hades is that?' said a gruff voice. The light was close now and Tarchon imagined the big doorman, a lantern in one hand, cudgel in the other.

'Bloody rat!'

'Rat?' The female voice came from the right. From the accent and tone, Tarchon guessed it was a housekeeper.

'There it goes!' said the doorman.

The woman emitted a fearful groan.

'Can't see it now,' added the man.

'Good.'

'Oh, look here. Bloody thing knocked a tile off. That's what the noise was. Master won't be-'

'Vala, what's going on out there?'

This was a rich man's voice – presumably Evaristos – and he did not sound happy. It sounded as if he was inside the building, directly below Tarchon.

'Nothing, sir, just a fallen tile. I'll deal with it.'

To Tarchon's relief, Evaristos said nothing more.

'Do rats go on roofs?' asked the woman.

'They go everywhere. I'll fix it in the morning.' Vala the doorman lowered his voice. 'Anything good left over from dinner?'

'No,' she replied sharply before walking away.

Tarchon thought he heard Vala curse quietly before he also left, leaving the atrium in darkness once more. He felt as if he had held his breath the entire time and, when his body relaxed, he realised his hands were shaking.

All this and I haven't even seen this stupid bloody vase yet!

He waited. Some loud lads passed down Merchant's Street but then all fell quiet once more. Removing the tile – and putting it well out of the way – he turned around, both feet on the timbers. He then knelt down, gripped the wood with both hands and lowered himself towards the ground.

Tarchon paused, hanging in the air. If anyone saw him or raised the alarm, he could pull himself back up. Hearing nothing to worry him, he dropped, letting his legs relax so that he landed smoothly. Straightening, he found himself facing a darkened doorway, presumably leading to where Evaristos and his family slept. Tarchon reckoned he could now at least be confident of one thing: they didn't own a dog.

If some, or all, of the bedrooms were on this side, the dining room would likely be on the other: this was where many rich men displayed their valuables. However, if the vase really was a form of payment, it might also be in the owner's office or study. Aware that the doorman might see him if he crossed the atrium openly, Tarchon hurried to the front section of the townhouse. Reaching an open door, he peered around it and saw the enforcer sitting on a stool by the main entrance. Vala was whittling something out of wood, sitting under a lantern hanging from a hook.

As he seemed focused on his work, Tarchon stepped across the doorway and continued around to the other side of the atrium. The first room he came to was protected by a heavy curtain. Tarchon listened carefully, then pulled it back and looked inside. The two windows admitted enough light for him to see three couches: definitely the dining room. With a glance over his shoulder, he entered. The only ornament on the central table was a bowl containing fruit. From there, he moved to the far wall, where there were two wooden cabinets. On top of one, he found a small candelabra and a glass bowl – but no vase. He opened the cabinets and felt around but there was only crockery. After a brief check that there were no small tables he'd missed, Tarchon slipped back outside.

He continued along the side of the atrium and easily identified the latrine by smell. Next was an open doorway that led only to a small space containing firewood and garden tools.

Though the house was still quiet, Tarchon's throat felt tight and sweat was running down his flanks. He was taking a huge risk breaking in here. Would there be any reward? He doubted that Korax would appreciate the effort if he didn't deliver a vase of lapis lazuli.

The next room was the second to last on that side of the atrium. He tried the door but it was locked. Reaching lower, he found the lock itself and an L-shaped hole. He moved along to the single window, where the shutters were ajar. He eased one open, hoping to reach inside. But, unlike the rest of the windows, this was covered by a solid metal grate. It had to be the man's office.

Bloody paranoid bastard. A locked door and a sealed window on the inside of your house? Bastard Tightwad Prick!

Tarchon had tried picking locks a couple of times but had no real skill or the necessary equipment. He guessed it was possible that the vase might be in a bedroom but he could hardly search those. This *was* the most likely location. So, he needed a key. Assuming it was with the other keys, he also knew where he might find it.

Vala the doorman was still whittling. He was a good twelve feet from Tarchon and between them was a corridor and two doorways. These rooms would face onto the road and included those high, barred windows: almost certainly staff quarters. Tarchon reckoned he might need to get inside one of them. First, he had to locate the keys.

Advancing three steps along the darkened corridor, grateful for the sound of Vala's whittling, he saw them. They were hanging from a ring on another hook close to the door. There were four and all except one were short and simply made. This one had the distinctive L-shape and the intricate shape of an expensive key.

Vala stopped his whittling and held the carving closer to the lantern, then set to it again. With slow, careful steps, Tarchon slipped through the shadows into the room to the right. Passing a bed and hoping there was nothing on the floor he might inadvertently kick, he approached the nearest window. He unlatched the shutters and opened one side, wincing at a faint squeak.

This allowed a little moonlight in and he spied a mug sitting on a chest. Grabbing it, he stuck his hand through the bars and threw the mug onto the street. Seconds later, he heard Vala get up and unbolt the door. Tarchon padded immediately to the corridor.

Unfortunately, the doorman was simply standing there, gazing out at the street. The keys were no more than six feet away but the danger was too great.

Then one of his mates on the other side of the road hailed him. Vala answered and stepped onto the street. 'You hear anything?'

'Something. Didn't see anything though. What's that you're carving? Another chariot for the nephew?'

As they continued speaking, Vala pulled the door to behind him. Tarchon moved as quickly as he dared, easing the ring off the hook, holding the keys together so they didn't jangle. He kept his eyes on the door as he retreated and was soon back in the safety of the shadows. Hurrying around the pool, he found the right key with his fingers and tried it in the lock.

It didn't fit.

Until he shifted it around and was rewarded with a satisfying click. He turned the key and heard a second, even more satisfying click. Once the door was open, he hurried inside. There wasn't much light but he spied a table, a desk and – on the wall beside the window – shelves. Here were several objects and only one felt like a vase. Moving close to the window, he held it up and could just about make out the blue of lapiz lazuli.

The sweating had receded but now he felt his heart beat faster. Grabbing his bag, he wrapped the vase in the cloth he had brought for the purpose and left the office, locking the door behind him. Now there was a decision to make. Returning the keys to the hook was very risky but it would buy him time. Another alternative was to-

'Marta, the keys! Do you have the keys?' Vala sounded panicky.

'The keys? No, why?'

She came speeding out of the kitchen and took the right side around the pond. Though he was deep in shadow beside the door, Tarchon remained utterly still as she ran past him, sandals slapping. He decided to leave the keys in the lock. Once she was inside the front section of the townhouse, he headed in the opposite direction. Raising his hood, he sprinted through the kitchen and unbolted the back door.

From there, he ran across the yard to the gate. A horse in the stable puffed and shuffled around but made no great noise. Determined not to do anything stupid at this late stage, he climbed carefully over the gate. Next door, Marius the dog barked suddenly, causing Tarchon to misjudge his landing and fall on his backside into the mud.

Inside number eleven, Vala shouted, the housekeeper shouted and then Evaristos shouted. Once out of the mud, Tarchon sprinted away, a triumphant grin upon his face.

VIII

Tarchon awoke to find the angry face of Master Vesonius glaring down at him. It caused such surprise that he almost rolled off the pallet but he swiftly sat up, rubbing his tired eyes. He knew instantly from the light in the courtyard that it was late; more than an hour after dawn.

'Well, lad?'

'Master Vesonius?'

'Only the gods know what the hour was when you got in. Climbing over the wall? I thought it was some robber. If Galla hadn't assured me it was you, I might have cracked you over the head with a hammer.'

'Very sorry, sir. Really. It won't happen again.'

Tarchon now saw two pairs of eyes looking on from the kitchen window to his right: Galla and her mother. He pushed his blanket aside and stood, patting down errant strands of hair.

'What exactly were you doing out at that time?'

'This new job, sir.'

Vesonius' eyes narrowed. 'Galla says you're working for some official – running messages.'

'That's right. I did know it would involve some odd hours but…sorry. I was just trying not to disturb you all.'

'What's his name, this official?'

'He did ask me to keep that a secret. I would tell you if I could.'

'What's in there?' asked Vesonius, nodding at the bag beside his bed.

'Nothing that shouldn't be.'

'You won't mind me looking then.'

As Vesonius went to grab the bag, Galla came flying out of the house.

'Father, you can't accuse Tarchon like that!'

'I shall do as I please, girl. And you best remember your place.' She seemed to consider another protest but her father's glare kept her silent. Vesonius picked up Tarchon's bag, peered inside, fished around for a bit, then dropped it.

'I heard a rumour from a customer yesterday that you'd been in trouble with the court. He heard it from someone who heard it from your aunt.'

'Not true, sir,' replied Tarchon, thinking quickly. 'She just wanted everyone to think she had a good reason for kicking me out. She doesn't want me under her roof anymore.'

'If I hear different, you and I will talk again. Working all hours of the night? You must have been paid by now.'

'Hopefully today, sir. Then I'll be able to rent somewhere.'

Vesonius aimed a final glare at him before heading inside.

Galla turned to Tarchon. She looked close to tears. He felt no guilt at the lie, which had been necessary, but he never liked to see her upset, especially not if he was the cause.

'You *were* very late.'

'It won't happen again.' He hoped that delivery of the vase would at last earn him some money, meaning he might not have to stay with the family any longer. Though he'd arrived back exhausted, he'd at least had the presence of mind to secrete his prize in a broken amphora at the rear of Uncle Hostus' yard.

'Are you hungry?' asked Galla.

Tarchon smiled. 'Starving.'

His meeting with Korax wasn't until sundown and he wasn't sure how to spend the rest of the day. While he and Galla were tidying up breakfast, he considered walking out to the west of the city, to visit his mother's grave. Though these visits always caused him pain, they also gave him energy. He would not – could not – rest until he had enough money for a proper tombstone. He also toyed with the idea of selling the vase, which he felt certain was worth more than a few gold coins. But that would be sacrificing long-term advantage for short-term gain. He also had enough enemies in the city without adding Korax and Gargonius to the list.

As Galla took the breakfast tray inside, young Marcus arrived, demanding that Tarchon help him with his wrestling practice. Tarchon resisted until Galla's mother came out and persuaded him. As the courtyard was covered by flagstones, Mistress Vesonius brought out a mat for them. Tarchon had never studied wrestling properly but he was able to teach the lad some basic holds and throws. To Marcus' credit, he didn't mind being chucked around and kept coming back for more. When they took a break, Tarchon complimented him on his attitude.

'Come out hard and just keep going. That will win you a lot of fights.'

'My instructor says that it's good to fight bigger and stronger people. Have you heard of my namesake – Marcus the Macedonian?'

'Who hasn't?'

Tarchon had never had much money to spare on watching entertainment or sport. He quite enjoyed the chariot racing but preferred beast hunts to gladiatorial contests. The fighting intrigued him but he felt such pity for the gladiators. It was one thing to be imprisoned or mutilated or killed. But to have to fight for your life for the entertainment of others? An apt fate for the very worst criminals but some, he knew, were just prisoners of war. Others chose to fight and achieved wealth and fame, like Marcus the Macedonian.

'Do you think he could beat a bear?' asked young Marcus, wiping his brow. 'I do. They say he has the strength of four men.'

Tarchon snorted. 'I can think of at least two problems about fighting a bear. One – claws. Two – teeth.'

'A boy bit me once,' said Marcus. 'The teacher beat him for it.'

'Quite right,' replied Tarchon. 'But in the real world, sometimes you have to do what you have to do.'

'You mean fight dirty-'

'I'm sure that's *not* what Tarchon means.' Master Vesonius came out into the courtyard holding a broom.

'Only if there's no other choice, I mean,' said Tarchon. 'He's got some real guts, this lad.'

Vesonius ignored this comment but offered him the broom. 'The shop and the front, right?'

'Of course.'

Tarchon didn't mind doing it at all. He generally preferred working to idling and while Vesonius was hard with him, you couldn't call the man unfair. A customer came in and so he found himself outside in the sun, sweeping up dust and dirt. His task was made somewhat harder by the people coming and going along the pavement. He had just finished filling the dust pan when the old soldier turned up. Bernardus was carrying a net bag in which Tarchon could see a circular loaf and a big fish wrapped in leaves.

'Imagine if you were with the legions,' said the old fellow, pointing at his brush. 'That could be a sword.'

Tarchon was impressed by the veteran's memory. 'Or a spade. Don't legionaries spend most of their time digging ditches?'

'Some. Not most.'

'Master Bernardus, can I ask you something?'

'Lad, now that I have my bread and fish, I have nothing else to do. Ask away!'

'I heard about this organisation that's part of the army. Sort of spies. Apparently, they work directly for the Emperor.'

'Sounds like the grain men.'

'The what?'

Bernardus stepped into shade and took his time, apparently enjoying the explanation. 'Many centuries ago, they were the administrators tasked with finding grain for the legions. Dull enough, you might think. But they built up so many contacts that they knew more about what was going on in the provinces and over the borders than anyone else. Over the centuries they became a sort of specialised force, like the scouts or the engineers. The organisation has changed over the years, as has the name. These days it's known as The Imperial Security Service.'

Tarchon thought this a very grand title. 'And do you know anyone in the city who's in it?'

'No idea. I retired many years ago. Why do you ask?'

'Just curious.'

'They're a nasty bunch,' added Bernardus. 'Not much liked by your common soldier. Tricky, sneaky, double-crossing sorts. Always got some scheme or plan going on. I remember one occasion in Egypt. We were supposed to be building a bridge but this officer collared the lot of us as an escort. We went across a border to a secret meeting at an oasis. He disappeared into a tent with some tribal leader and then back we went. The word was that it was some sort of payoff – to keep this leader on the side of Rome.'

'So, they do work for the Empire? Just in a different way.'

'They *say* they do. Another time, two grain men turned up and nabbed three soldiers on accusations of spying for the Persians. There was nothing to it – I knew every man – but we never saw the poor buggers again. Never liked the Service. No legionary does.'

Tarchon wasn't sure what to make of what he'd heard. Despite his dim view of soldiering, it was at least clear what a legionary did. He was still far from clear on what this Imperial Security Service did. Then again, he supposed it suited spies to stay in the shadows.

'All finished out here?' It was Master Vesonius, and he only just managed to force a smile when he saw the old soldier.

'Ah, Master Bernardus. Good day to you.'

'Good day, Vesonius. You'll be pleased to hear I've had no further problems with my shoes.'

'Very pleased indeed.'

*

Once his sweeping was done, Tarchon was sent – with Marcus – to fetch some firewood. Vesonius had a hand-cart for this purpose but it still took them more than two hours. By the end of it, Tarchon was sick of the lad, who insisted on asking him which animal he thought would come out on top in a contest: Bull versus bear. Bear versus lion. Crocodile versus tiger.

As they unloaded the firewood from the courtyard and into the cellar, Galla and her mother sat on a bench in the garden. While Tarchon and Marcus worked, they sewed: both were repairing various garments.

Once the firewood was unloaded, Galla prepared a bowl of warm water for Tarchon and Marcus to clean themselves up. By then, the afternoon was getting on. After eating two bowls of a tasty stew, Tarchon grabbed his bag and left, his first stop being a certain amphora in his uncle's yard.

He didn't have time to visit his mother's grave but it was still too early for his meeting with Korax, so he called in at a house not far from Mehruz's place. Here lived a woman named Rhea. Tarchon had worked for her husband on and off, mostly delivering messages and laying wagers. He had died the previous year but had been one of those fellows with the knack of making money. Most of his profits had been invested in an apartment building only three streets over from Mehruz and Anahita's. It was a cramped, old building but there was a considerable advantage in knowing the owners.

Tarchon spoke with Rhea's son in the doorway for a while before she arrived, wiping greasy hands on a greasy apron.

'Not seen you for a while.'

'New job. Should be getting my first lot of pay soon. I was wondering if you have any apartments spare?'

'One room?'

'One room is fine.'

'There's one on the third floor. Bit of fire damage. I can give it to you for ten denarii a month. Actually, make it eight. My husband always liked you.'

'That's very kind. You'll hold it for me?'

'I will,' said Rhea. 'Just don't leave it too long.'

He was close to the statue when he saw two centuries marching along the Avenue of Marcus Aurelius. Few weeks passed without Tarchon observing such a sight but it was always impressive. On this occasion, it wasn't just the legionaries in their gleaming armour but a great bolt-thrower mounted on the biggest wagon Tarchon had ever seen. The engine was being towed by a team of eight horses and behind it came a cart bearing the ammunition: huge arrows as tall as a man.

'Should we be worried?' called out an onlooker.

'Just Goths,' remarked a tall centurion with a ready grin. 'Some sea raid. We'll sort them out.'

'May the gods watch over you.'

From the others watching came a range of approving remarks.

'The best there is.'

'Greatest army in the world.'

'Greatest there has *ever* been!'

Even amongst the other soldiers, the centurion cut quite a figure. As well as his crested helmet, the officer wore old fashioned segmented armour. Tarchon knew that the four discs upon his chest – one bronze, two silver, one gold – were awards for service. He wondered what such a man might have seen – remote parts of the world, great battles, triumphs and tragedies. It was difficult to imagine old Bernardus as one of these fellows but at such moments it was easy to see the appeal of the legions. True, many of them were rogues and thieves, but presumably there were plenty of noble heroes too.

Korax clearly didn't want anyone to see the vase. He kept it within Tarchon's bag while examining it, then surreptitiously moved it into his own.

'Good work, young man,' he growled.

Tarchon resented the happy feeling that this rare moment of praise gave him.

'Wasn't easy. Had to cross three roofs, escape a dog, a housekeeper and a doorman. What's so important about that thing anyway?'

Korax stood up and shouldered his pack. 'I have another appointment. Walk with me.'

They set off across the square. A few hawkers were still plying their trade and two rich fellows passed by in a luxurious carriage. Other than that, there weren't many people around.

'I'm not going to go into the wider issues but we know that identical vases have been used as a form of payment. For services rendered to a…foreign power. Now that we have some evidence to use against Evaristos, this is an ideal time for an interrogation. He'll be on his guard after the theft but I'm sure you'll think of something.'

Tarchon stopped walking. 'Think of something? How do you mean?'

'We need you to bring him in. Don't worry, I'll handle the interrogation.'

'How?'

'Again, that's up to you. What I can tell you is that this is the last stage of your trial. Well, *initial* trial. You get this right, and we'll take you on. And you'll get your first pay packet. Twenty denarii.'

This was an even greater shock than the revelation of his latest assignment.

'Twenty?'

'Per month. But we can discuss all that with Gargonius. First, get us Evaristos.'

Korax kept walking – and he did not walk slowly – so Tarchon had to jog a few steps to catch up.

'When?'

'Tomorrow. You know Linus, the sardine seller?'

'Yes.'

'Six doors down is a small stock house. I'll leave a knotted rope on the door so you can't miss it. Get him there between midday and sundown: tomorrow or the next day.'

Tarchon could still hardly believe what he was hearing.

Reaching the edge of the square, they passed into a street where a queue had formed outside a theatre. Illuminated by several braziers were wealthy Byzantines in immaculate togas and colourful dresses. An actor wearing a comical mask was parading up and down, promoting the play to draw in more custom. Korax didn't give the scene a second look but soon came to a halt outside an inn. The circular sign above its door featured a striking image of a black bird in flight. The Crow was well known on account of its long history and many rooms.

'I'll be here for the next couple of days. If you need anything from me or to notify me of your plan, let me know. Ask for Kallikres.'

Tarchon had a hundred questions but it was clear that Korax again wanted him to find his own answers.

'All right?'

'Right.' Tarchon watched Korax enter the inn. Ignoring the loud imprecations of the actor, he walked away down the street. Once again, he had a lot to think about.

It didn't seem like a one-man job. There was no question of recruiting Mehruz or any of his friends. He couldn't get them mixed up in all this spying business (nor did he want to risk someone outshining him). There were associates, like Noctua, but how would he convince them to help him abduct a rich, powerful, well-protected man with no payment up front? No doubt he could find a couple of desperate fellows down on the waterfront but that might cause as many problems as it solved.

And yet, how else to get someone like Evaristos to some shady shithole miles from his house?

Tarchon still hadn't found an answer when he arrived back at Galla's. He was glad to see some light behind the windows; the family hadn't yet turned in so he wouldn't disturb them. No one came after his first knock. He was about to try again when the door was opened by young Marcus. The boy said nothing, instead simply standing aside so that Tarchon could enter.

'You all right, lad?'

Marcus remained quiet as he bolted the door and led the way through the store and into the house. As they passed a lamp, Marcus reached up and seemed to wipe away a tear. Another lamp was alight in the courtyard and here were gathered the other three members of the family. Master Vesonius stood by the far wall, with arms crossed and jaw set. He gave Tarchon only the briefest glance.

Galla and her mother were sitting together on the bench, both clutching handkerchiefs. Galla looked up at him with a weak smile. Tarchon was curious but didn't want to say the wrong thing.

'Sorry, Tarchon,' said Galla.

'Stop apologising!' snapped her father. 'You have done nothing wrong. You *never* have!'

Tarchon and Marcus took evasive action as Master Vesonius stomped towards the house. He stopped abruptly by his daughter and cradled her face in his hand. Shaking his head, he continued on his way and went inside, closely followed by his wife.

Marcus instantly sat by his sister's side and took her hand.

If there *were* any right words to be found, Tarchon was yet to locate them. He simply sat down on the other side of Galla. The glow of the lamp barely reached them and he was quite glad of the darkness.

'There was a band of musicians playing down at the square,' she said after a while. 'Cappadocian.'

'Your favourite,' replied Tarchon.

'Marcus came with me.'

Tarchon knew this would have been difficult for Galla. She didn't often leave her home and much preferred familiar surroundings.

'After the music there was a juggler. Marcus wanted to see him.'

'So did you!' added her brother.

'I did, you're right,' Galla conceded. 'At the end of his act, he juggled three daggers.'

'He wasn't very good,' added Marcus. 'Anyone could see that.'

'He had an accident,' said Galla. 'One of the blades struck his foot, cut off two of his toes.'

'Ah,' said Tarchon.

'That girl Helena was there,' continued Galla. 'She'd seen me earlier and when the accident happened, she started shouting at me, blaming me again. She said that the gods had cursed me because of my arm and that bad fortune followed me around. She was with those friends of hers. Soon they were all saying it.'

Tarchon remembered that Helena had previously blamed Galla for an outbreak of pox at a nearby market. He had seriously considered giving the spiteful bitch a good slapping but Galla had persuaded him not to.

'We had to run home,' she said. 'Father was angry and went down to the square. It got nasty.'

'If not for Butcher Gaius it would have got a lot nastier,' said Marcus.

Gaius was a former city official and a well-known character around the area. Tarchon knew it wasn't the first time he had calmed a situation.

'Sorry I wasn't here,' he said.

'Marcus, would you get me some wine?' asked Galla.

After his sister had ruffled his hair, the lad hurried into the house.

'That silly whore,' said Tarchon.

'Language!' admonished Galla.

'Sorry but that's what she is.'

'It doesn't matter.'

'Of course, it does, Galla. It's wrong.'

'There will always be people like her. There were when I was a child and there are now. It will never be any different with…with this.'

Galla struck her withered arm with her good one. For Tarchon, it was a terrible thing to see. Brave, cheerful Galla so seldom felt sorry for herself and he always wondered how. He wasn't sure he could have lived with such an affliction. Life was hard enough with a strong, healthy, complete body. And if life was a race, some cruel god had placed Galla well behind the start line.

Tarchon put his arm around her shoulder. He wanted to kiss her. It wasn't the first time this desire had struck him; sometimes he just wanted to make her feel better, sometimes he was excited about what it would be like. But this wasn't the moment, especially not with her family so close.

'They really hate me. I could see it in their eyes.'

'Idiots like that always hate something. They're not worth worrying about.'

'Helena has had three offers of marriage. *Three*.'

'Another three idiots.'

'And how many offers have I had?'

She'd never been so direct about the subject of marriage before and Tarchon couldn't help feeling that the remark was at least partly directed at him.

'What man would marry me?' she added.

He almost said it. He almost said *I would*. But that was dangerously close to *I will*.

He still had his arm over her shoulder and he squeezed it but neither of them said anything more. In fact, Tarchon was relieved when Marcus returned with the wine. He moved away, certain he hadn't helped Galla feel any better. In fact, he suspected he'd only made things worse.

IX

Jucundius looked up at him, reed pen poised over the small sheet of paper. 'Say it again.'

'If you want your vase, meet me at the store-house six doors down from Linus the sardine seller.'

Jucundius had very bushy eyebrows and now raised both of them. 'Sounds nefarious, young Tarch. Definitely sounds nefarious.'

'No idea what that means but don't worry about it. Surely it's worth a denarius.'

'With the cost of paper and ink these days – barely. But, fortunately for you, I always was a soft-hearted fellow. Say it again.'

Tarchon did so and then watched as the bookmaker crafted the words in his neat, even hand. He'd been surprised the first time he'd seen Jucundius write; for a fat, clumsy fellow, he was unerring and delicate with pen in hand. As always, Tarchon felt a pang of jealousy that Jucundius – that anyone – had access to the secret world of writing and reading. He wouldn't even know how to *hold* a reed pen. Having finished, Jucundius placed his on a blotter. Tarchon went to grab the page but found his hand blocked.

'Let it dry, you fool.'

The bookmaker pushed his chair back and stood, releasing his considerable bulk. Tightening his belt, he slipped on a pair of sandals and walked to the window. As usual, he was sweating heavily, underarms ringed by damp. He picked up a fan and handed it to Tarchon.

'If you please.'

'I don't work for you anymore.'

'But you are in my debt. Again.'

With a shake of his head, Tarchon took the fan – a dried palm mounted on a stick – and obliged his old employer.

For more than two years he had run messages in and out of Jucundius' office, mostly wagers from his many clients. The days before a chariot race had been a blur of activity, with Jucundius growing ever hotter and hot-tempered. His assistant (and girlfriend), Katya, had been the only one capable of calming him down and ensuring that debts were collected and pay-outs delivered. She'd been very kind to Tarchon, often bringing in leftovers to supplement his meagre diet. But she'd run off with some sailor a while back and things had gone downhill for Jucundius ever since. It seemed that Katya had in fact guided many of his business decisions and, since her departure, he had been overtaken by competitors. His sister had a quarter share in the business and, when times became hard, she offered her sons as free labour, meaning Tarchon was out of a job.

However, he and Jucundius had remained on good terms and Tarchon even provided the bookmaker with security now and again. But it was never easy work. Even if you were tough, you needed a decent sword to convince people that you were professional. Tarchon also wasn't really old enough. Or big enough.

Jucundius yawned and took a date from a dish. After inspecting it for a while, he frowned and put it back.

'So, what is it now then – robbery?'

'It's complicated,' replied Tarchon between wafts.

The bookmaker wiped sweat from his double chin. 'You did steal some poor bastard's vase though?'

'You steal from poor bastards every day.'

Jucundius grinned. 'But I do it *legally*. Hope that aunt of yours doesn't find out.'

'Not living there anymore. She kicked me out.'

A rare expression of concern flashed across Jucundius' round, shiny face. 'Do you have somewhere?'

'Hoping to get my own place soon.'

'I've heard that before.'

'Don't you live with your sister now?'

At that, they both grinned. As Tarchon had grown older, and more confident with his employer, such banter had become common between them. Not for the first time, Tarchon felt regret that things had worked out as they had. Jucundius' sister had always disliked him.

'A temporary arrangement.' Jucundius aimed a finger at him, then used the same hand to wipe sweat from his forehead. 'Move that elbow – you're barely creating a breeze!'

Tarchon had no idea if his scheme would work but, after much consideration, it seemed to him the least risky method of luring Evaristos to the store-house. It was possible that he would alert the city sergeants, even have them accompany him. Tarchon didn't imagine Korax would be particularly impressed by that. But, overall, he thought it unlikely. If Evaristos really was a spy for some foreign power – and the vase was indeed a payment – he was unlikely to alert anyone. Tarchon had some alternatives if the merchant didn't show up but was currently more concerned that the next stage of his scheme went well.

The young lad he had earlier recruited came around the corner with a beaming smile. 'All done, chief. Now hand over the grub.'

'Did anyone see you?'

'No. Pushed it under the door and scarpered like you said.'

'Very good.' Tarchon reached into his bag and retrieved the piece of fried fish he'd saved from breakfast at Galla's.

'Thanks, chief,' said the lad. He grabbed the fish and ran off towards the square where Tarchon had found him, scouring the streets for dropped coins with a gang of other youngsters.

Tarchon peered around the corner, along Merchant's Street, towards number eleven. He could only hope that Evaristos would receive the note quickly and consider it worth his while to proceed. Tarchon would not wait there to find out. If

Evaristos did take the bait, following him all the way would be very difficult. More importantly, Tarchon needed to intercept him at the store-house if he was to successfully deliver him to Korax. His first job that morning had been to secrete his fighting stave in the burned-out shell of a building close to the meeting point. Korax had selected the area well. It was set back from the shore and relatively quiet. With luck, Tarchon would be able to rough Evaristos up a bit and get him to Korax swiftly and without incident.

As he set off, Tarchon considered a prayer to Minerva. But he had already asked her for enough. She had answered by presenting him with an opportunity. It was up to him to take it.

It was a still, warm day in Byzantium, with hardly a breath of wind coming in off the water. And in the two hours since he'd taken up his position, Tarchon had grown warmer and warmer. In fact, his tunic was beginning to itch and he was having to regularly wipe sweat from his top lip and brow. His location did not help; he was cramped into a narrow space between two store-houses, one of which stank of fish guts. He was at least pleased to find the street quiet. Linus the sardine-seller closed up at midday and only a few people had passed by.

Hearing the familiar squawk of gulls, Tarchon looked up to see a pair launch themselves off an old watch tower on a neighbouring street. Stone-built and round, the abandoned structure was popular with the homeless of Byzantium. As a lad, Tarchon had once climbed forty feet to the top but the stones were notoriously loose and few tackled the exterior these days.

One of the few others who had made it was a boy named Lysander. He was one of the most daring, skilful climbers Tarchon had ever met but he had not reached his fifteenth birthday. Tarchon winced as he remembered what had been left of Lysander after he'd fallen from the high walls of the arena. He had foolishly accepted the challenge of some drunken rich folk; they had each put in a denarius if he could climb to the top and back down. The only thing worse than the sight of Lysander's broken body had been the noise of the impact.

The store-house was twenty feet to Tarchon's left and the street ran another sixty beyond that before joining another. Forty feet to the right it turned ninety degrees. Close to that corner, a crew of three had been loading amphora onto a cart but they had just left. So now the street was empty again and Tarchon remained in the shadows, fighting stave beside him, waiting for something to happen.

'Blood of the gods,' he hissed.

He hated waiting. Always had. Simply didn't have time for it.

Hearing an approach from the left, he stepped warily forward and peered around the brick. But it was just an old man shuffling along, humming to himself. He shuffled and hummed his way slowly down the street, taking so long that Tarchon imagined jumping out and clobbering him on the head just for something to do.

Then he thought about Galla. Her mother had given him his breakfast that morning. He asked about Galla but Mistress Vesonius had simply shaken her head. Even young Marcus seemed preoccupied; he had sat alone in the courtyard, painting one of his toy chariots. Though he wished he could help, Tarchon was now even more keen to leave. It was nice to be close to Galla – and sometimes nice to be with her family – but now he felt *too* close.

Voices. A conversation. He was trying to make out what they were saying when he peered to the right and saw Evaristos round the corner. He was not alone.

It was Vala. In daylight, Tarchon got a much clearer idea of the doorman's size. He was a full foot taller than his employer, heavy with a bit of fat and a lot of muscle. Hanging from his belt was a cudgel.

'Shit.' Tarchon withdrew. Holding his breath, he watched the pair walk past, noting the hairy bulk of Vala's forearms.

'This is it,' said Evaristos, stopping at the store-house.

The doorman slipped the cudgel from his belt.

Tarchon's scheme suddenly seemed ridiculous. Why in Hades *wouldn't* Evaristos have brought his doorman with him to confront the thief? It was an entirely predictable turn of events. And yet, Tarchon was close to achieving everything asked of him. He had come too far to back off now. And he still had the element of surprise.

Vala knocked on the door with his cudgel. Tarchon knew he had to strike now, with the pair preoccupied. Stave in hand, he tiptoed out of the space, keeping his weapon well off the ground. Praying that no one else entered the street, he had soon cut the distance in half.

'Perhaps they meant outside?' suggested Vala.

'Or perhaps this whole bloody thing is a trap?' On the last word, Evaristos spun around. Seeing Tarchon – and presumably the fighting stave – he yelped and backed towards the building. With no intention of attacking the merchant first, Tarchon dropped his grip to the bottom of the stave and swung at the big doorman's head, hoping to knock him out with one blow. But Vala was already turning and had enough time to throw up his arm. The stave whacked into his shoulder, knocking him off balance but doing no serious damage.

Evaristos used the opportunity to try and flee. Though Tarchon couldn't shift the stave in time to hit him, he did get a leg out and trip him. Evaristos went down hard on his face.

Tarchon returned his attention to Vala, aiming a couple of jabs at his foe's head. Vala was clearly no amateur; he swatted away each intended blow with his cudgel. He was also very quick for a man of his size: he snatched the stave out of the air one-handed and pulled it clean out of Tarchon's grip. Knowing he was in trouble, Tarchon risked a glance at Evaristos. The merchant was on his knees, staring at his scratched hands, blood dripping from his nose.

Now holding stave and cudgel, Vala smirked. 'You really think you're a match for me, you thieving little shit?'

Tarchon stepped back – suggesting he was giving up – then ran straight for the enforcer. He swung his right boot, aiming for the big doorman's balls. A dirty move but – as Vala himself had pointed out – it was not an even match. Once again showing considerable agility, the doorman brought his cudgel down into a neat block. Tarchon's boot connected with it, hard enough to knock the weapon from his grasp.

But Vala still had the stave and he swung it with power and accuracy. Tarchon only avoided it by dropping so sharply that he lost his balance and staggered backwards. A hand that could only have belonged to Evaristos pulled on his ankle and over he went, landing on his backside next to his victim. Evaristos looked to his employee, who was not slow to take advantage. In seconds, Tarchon's own weapon was at his neck, pressing hard, causing him to cough and choke.

'Do it,' ordered Evaristos, wiping blood from his nose. 'Squeeze the life out of him.'

I've had it. I'm dead.

What was I thinking? Another mistake. Another failure.

I'm dead.

'Drop it!'

Vala and his employer turned around. Through the doormen's legs, Tarchon watched as two men approached. Both wore dark grey tunics and held short swords. Both were short-haired and carried themselves with the easy confidence of soldiers. One halted behind Vala, while the other walked around the three combatants.

'We're not in the habit of repeating ourselves,' said the swordsman behind Vala. He looked around twenty-five; compact and muscular with a thick, black beard. 'Drop it and get on your knees with your friend.'

At a nod from Evaristos, Vala complied.

Spluttering once the stave was off his neck, Tarchon scrambled away and got to his feet.

'Lucky boy,' said the bearded man.

'Who are you?'

'It's more a case of who *we work for*.' The interloper used his spare hand to point up at the old tower. A figure had appeared at the top, leaning casually against an uneven wall, sun gleaming on his bald head.

Korax.

Tarchon watched as the two men took charge. His neck felt very tender but he knew it could have been a lot worse. The bearded fellow was clearly the leader of the pair. He continued to give the orders while the second man – whose grim expression hardly changed – kept his eyes on their prisoners. While Evaristos dabbed at his nose and cursed at his three enemies, Vala maintained his composure, repeatedly asking the two swordsmen who exactly they did work for. The bearded man had just told him to shut up when a covered wagon turned into the street.

Korax was beside the driver and jumped down when the vehicle stopped. He said nothing but pointed at the wagon. As the swordsmen guided their two charges into the vehicle, Vala shot Tarchon a last venomous glare. The swordsmen jumped in behind them, blades still at the ready. After another gesture from Korax, the driver set the horses away.

'Sorry about that,' said Tarchon.

Korax exhaled loudly. 'You did all right, up to a point.'

'Thanks for helping me out. Sorry you had to. I suppose I've messed everything up?'

'That's not my decision to make. But I expect you'll know by the end of lunch.'

'Lunch?'

X

A plate full of top-quality shellfish served with half a dozen vegetables and a lemon sauce. Though unused to the pleasant surroundings of a plush restaurant and uncomfortable in the intimidating company of Korax and Gargonius, Tarchon nonetheless enjoyed the meal, which was one of the best – and certainly the most expensive – he'd ever eaten. Gargonius insisted that they discuss nothing relating to him until they had finished eating. He and his employee spoke only of an upcoming election in the city of Cyzicus and a rumoured revolt in far off Arabia.

While Tarchon and Korax filled their stomachs, the slender Gargonius picked at his food and seemed more interested in the wine. As their plates were collected, two well-dressed ladies approached and greeted him. Gargonius complemented them both and went as far as to finger the material of one of their dresses. Tarchon thought this all rather odd but Korax looked on impassively. As the ladies departed, Gargonius made an adjustment to his wavy hair and moved his chair back so that he could cross his legs. Blinking up at the sunlight, he gestured to Korax.

'Would you?'

The veteran stood and adjusted the parasol over the table so that his superior was shaded. They were sitting on a terrace at the rear of the restaurant. It included only four tables, situated so far apart that conversation could not be overheard.

Gargonius turned to Tarchon. 'Well then, young man, did you enjoy that?'

Actually, he had eaten so much that he was beginning to feel sick – but in a good way. 'I did, sir. Very much.'

'You have done quite a bit for us. It seemed the least we could do.'

Tarchon now suspected that the lunch might be all he would be receiving.

'I do appreciate the opportunity. I know I-'

Gargonius silenced him with a raised hand. 'Tell me, where did you go wrong today?'

'I needed more men. I should have known he'd have the doorman with him.'

Gargonius glanced speculatively at Korax, who shrugged before speaking.

'As Evaristos didn't take him on the trip, it wasn't a given.'

Gargonius sipped his wine. 'Korax tells me that you used a note to draw him down to the stock-house. Good thinking, especially for an illiterate.'

'I could have told him to come alone.'

'You could, though there's no guarantee he would. In any case, you faced two men, and you still had a go. Quite the risk – attacking a big fellow like that and still hoping to hold on to Evaristos.'

'I didn't want to fail.'

'Evidently.' Gargonius rested both hands on his thigh and interlocked his fingers. 'The truth is that, in our trade, the line between failure and success can be very thin. There are always risks, variables, unknowns. You're inexperienced, rather rash, but overall, I think you've done quite well. Korax?'

The veteran crossed his arms and leaned back. 'Master Gargonius asked what you should have done today. Why attack alone? You made no attempt to contact me. We could have helped you. You achieved half the task, then took an unnecessary risk. I've fought alongside many a man who thought himself brave but was in fact no better than reckless. Not many of them lasted long enough to retire.'

'I understand. I just thought it would look better if I-'

Korax continued: 'But getting that vase out without being detected...really not bad.'

Only now did Tarchon begin to think that the pair might not cast him aside after all.

'Praise indeed,' said Gargonius. 'Tarchon, you've shown a bit of brains and a lot of guts. You work for us, you'll need both. There might be...something coming up. Something outside the city. If you can make a success of that, then the wage Korax is about to give you will be the first of many.'

'Thank you, sir.'

Gargonius stood, walked over to him, and placed a hand on his shoulder. He spoke quietly.

'Just remember – you do not talk about your work to anyone. Not family. Not friends. Not lovers. *No one*. If we ever learn that you've been...indiscreet, you'll find yourself on a slave ship bound for the salt mines of Cappadocia. Am I exaggerating for effect, Korax?'

'Never, sir.'

With a light slap on Tarchon's shoulder, Gargonius walked away, offering a flamboyant wave to his female friends, who returned the gesture.

Once outside, Korax belched and walked over to a low wall between two hawkers selling cheap jewellery laid out upon cloth. On the shore below, three fishermen were sorting through their catch.

Korax nodded to the east. 'You've been to the other side?'

'A couple of times.'

'Beyond Chalcedon?'

Tarchon shook his head.

Korax sighed. 'If he uses you for the job he's talking about, you'll be travelling some distance. I presume you can't ride?'

'Actually, I can. It's been a while, but-'

'Then I suggest lessons. This should buy a few.' Korax slipped a little leather bag from his pack and handed it to Tarchon.

'Don't start throwing it about,' added the agent. 'You're also going to need a sword. If you're happy to leave it to me, I'll find you something basic but effective. Maybe a dagger too?'

'Yes, thank you.'

'What about training?' asked Korax. 'With a blade?'

'You'd help me?'

'No. But I can probably arrange some tuition – it will cost, mind.'

With his existing debts, Tarchon was beginning to think that his first wage might not go far. Even so, the weighty bag in his hand felt so, so good.

'Actually, I might know someone.'

'Up to you. It's your neck on the line. Judging by what I saw this morning, you could use some help.'

'I suppose that's why Gargonius uses soldiers. They already know weapons and how to fight.'

'True, but there's no shortage of tough bastards. Sneaky bastards are a rarer breed.' Korax placed one boot on the wall and re-tied an errant lace. Tarchon noted an odd, diamond-shaped scar on his calf, one of several.

'I'm serious about the riding. If he does give you this job, you'll be covering a lot of miles.'

Despite all he'd been through that day, Tarchon felt a fearful chill in his stomach when he heard that. In this city he was on familiar ground, where he could use local knowledge and contacts to his advantage. He was always keen to hear of life beyond Byzantium – in other cities, other provinces, in the capital itself – but he had virtually no experience of it. Everything would be new.

'I understand. I'll be prepared when you call on me.'

'I hope so. Still staying with the cobbler?'

Tarchon hadn't told Korax that but he supposed it wouldn't have taken much to find out.

'No. I've found somewhere else.'

'Good. You wouldn't want to put them at risk.'

This raised numerous questions in Tarchon's mind but he didn't get anything out before Korax spoke again.

'Statue. Tomorrow. Usual time. I'll get you the weapons. Bring your coins.'

'Right. Sir, what will happen to Evaristos? And the doorman?'

'Time will tell. It all rather depends on whether he cooperates.'

'What's it all about? This foreign power?'

'You don't need to know – so you don't. I know twice as much as you, half as much as Gargonius. That's how it goes.' Korax pointed at the bag in Tarchon's hand. 'Don't get robbed.'

At the first convenient location – which turned out to be a shadowy sanctuary occupied only by an elderly gardener – Tarchon got off the streets. Standing beside a wall, shielded by trees on three sides, he tipped the coins from the bag into his hand. Small though they were, the silver denarii felt *so* heavy compared to sesterces and the minor denominations. He counted them. Twenty.

Twenty denarii!

Tarchon smiled, then shook his head, then chuckled, and it was about all he could do not to cry with joy. While working for Jucundius, Katya had sometimes let him hold big handfuls of coins just for the thrill. But this was better. Ten times better.

Twenty denarii!!

Though he knew he would have to visit the temple later to give real thanks, Tarchon closed his eyes and uttered a prayer.

Great and honoured Minerva. Thank you for the opportunity you have given me and the wealth I now hold in my hands. I know it was you that came to my aid in a difficult time. In return for your favour, I offer my eternal loyalty and faith.

He made two stops before returning to Galla's. The first was to Jucundius. The bookmaker welcomed the swift repayment of his debt but again warned his former employee about 'nefarious activities'. As it was close to midday, Tarchon then headed to the quail fights but Noctua was not there. He left a message with a mutual acquaintance that he was looking for him and would return the following day. Once he'd paid off Noctua and his robber friend, he would be down to fourteen denarii – but that amount of silver could still go a very long way.

With Korax's words in mind, Tarchon now found himself wary of every shady-looking character on the streets and, even in daylight, there were quite a few. Despite his knowledge of the city and its inhabitants, Tarchon had been the victim of thieves more than a dozen times. On most occasions, he'd either escaped his assailants or convinced them that he possessed nothing. On two occasions, he'd had to fight. As a fourteen-year-old he'd suffered a nasty beating from three youths, leaving him with a broken finger and a gashed head. By seventeen, he'd been in enough scraps to take the initiative; the two men who tried it on soon wished they hadn't bothered.

Despite the fear of losing what he'd worked so hard to gain, two words continued to pulse through his head.

Twenty denarii!!!

Back at the cobblers, Tarchon first saw Master Vesonius, who was talking to a customer at the front of the store. Tarchon loitered on the street and waited for the customer to leave.

'Good day.'

'Good day, Tarchon. You were up early again this morning.'

'Not an easy job. But I received my first pay packet today. I'd like to give you something. Is two denarii fair?'

'I'd say so. But don't give it to me, give it to my wife. She can use it to replace all that food you've been eating.'

The cobbler was a dour character by nature and so Tarchon took the remark at face value, reddening with embarrassment.

'A joke, young man,' said Vesonius, knocking a fist against his shoulder. 'I know I don't make many of them.'

'Ah, right. Good one. Sir, can I ask you where Master Bernardus lives?'

'He has an apartment. Timaeus' block on Goat Lane. Why?'

'I like his war stories. I'd like to hear more about the army.'

'Rather you than me.' Vesonius' usual serious expression now returned. 'Listen, young man, Galla won't be happy that you're leaving. She knows it couldn't go on but she likes looking after you, I think. Just promise me you'll come when you can, perhaps even take her out if she'll have it.'

'Of course.' Tarchon was quite surprised by this; perhaps the cobbler didn't have such a dim view of him after all.

Master Vesonius apparently wasn't finished. 'I'll be frank; I've never been sure about you. But for all I've heard about what you've been involved in, you've always been decent with me and my family, and kind to Galla. Try to keep yourself on the straight and narrow. Remember that's what your mother would have wanted. Ever hear anything about your father?'

'Not for a long time.'

'Well, I'm sure that's what he wants too.'

Tarchon said nothing more. This was starting to sound like advice and he didn't much like advice. The people who doled it out tended not to actually know him that well, and certainly not know how many nights he'd spent on the streets, how many days he'd spent hungry. He didn't care much for Master Vesonius' opinion, nor his father's. As for his mother, he always remembered some of her last words:

The worst in all this is that I can't look after you anymore. You have to look after yourself. No one else will. Do whatever you have to.

Galla was in the kitchen with her mother, kneading dough. When her father told her that Tarchon had returned, she came out into the courtyard where he was waiting. As usual, her withered arm was wrapped in cotton and Tarchon sensed that her mood had not lifted. She first wafted insects away from some young plants in the herb garden before sitting on the bench.

'I've barely stopped today,' she said. 'They're trying to keep me busy, keep my mind off things.'

Tarchon couldn't think of anything particularly helpful to say so settled on, 'feeling any better?'

'Mother keeps asking me that. Today I said yes, even though I don't. She makes us thank the great gods for our blessings but these days I just mouth the words.' Galla leaned back and gazed at the sky. 'I'd rather shout – ask them why they did this to me.'

'I don't blame you.'

When she finally looked away from the sky, Galla turned to him. 'I'm sorry, Tarch. Your life's not been easy. I expect you've done the same.'

'Now and again. But I prayed to Minerva a while back and I think she may have heard me. I got my first pay packet today.' He couldn't resist showing her the coins and gave her two.

'For your mother.'

'Are you sure?'

'Of course.'

'I'm happy for you, Tarch. Really.' She reached across and gripped his arm. 'I do hope you're going to buy a new tunic.'

'Definitely. And lunch for you, if you'd like to come.'

He hadn't planned it but felt he had to do something to lighten her mood.

'Would make quite a change,' he added, '*me* providing *you* with food.'

She laughed, for what seemed like the first time in a while. 'I'd like to. I really would. Just not right now. You'll ask me again, won't you?'

'Of course.'

She looked at the coins as he replaced them in the bag. 'You're leaving us then, I suppose?'

'Looks like I've found an apartment.'

'Tarch, your own place! You must be excited.'

'I am.'

'And you'll come and give me the address if it all works out.'

'Of course.'

He wasn't actually sure he would. Bearing in mind Korax's earlier warning, he wondered if it was sensible to tell anyone. He would sleep a lot better in that place if he felt safe there. Other than a couple of old enemies, Myron would still be looking for revenge, not to mention Evaristos, Vala and whoever else he crossed on Gargonius' orders.

'The new job will keep you busy,' said Galla.

'Yes. Lots of messages to deliver. I'm supposed to use some of this to pay for riding lessons.'

'They'll give you a horse?'

'Not sure. Probably a pony knowing my luck, or a mule. They said I might be going over to Chalcedon – even further.'

'I'll worry about you.'

'And I about you.'

Galla turned and kissed him on the cheek. It felt like a sisterly kiss. At times, her kisses hadn't felt like that but, to Tarchon, that was the best way for them to be.

'Cursed things!' Galla stood and hurried over to the plants, deterring more insects. She stayed there, facing away from him, for longer than seemed natural.

Tarchon joined her there and saw that she was crying. He'd rarely seen her so upset for so long.

'Sorry,' she said. 'I really am happy for you. But I'm jealous too. Because you can change things, make things better for yourself and move forward. I'm stuck, Tarch. Just stuck.'

Despite her words, Galla soon recovered herself and helped Tarchon pack, which did not take long. Marcus was with his tutor but Tarchon said farewell to Mistress Vesonius, who thanked him for the two denarii and gave him a warm embrace. Galla kept up her smile even as he departed and Tarchon felt tears form in his eyes.

He had always tried to harden his heart against such softness. As a child, during the worst times – such as his father's drunken fits of rage – his mother had used a practical way of achieving this. She had let him cry until the age of four but after that it was, 'time to grow up'. When one of their many turns of ill fortune caused him to shed tears, she would pinch his nose, hard, near the top where there's not much skin. After she died, Tarchon began to do it to himself. Though he'd not needed it for a while, he did so now as he set off towards Bernardus' place.

The apartment building where the veteran lived was a good deal better than the one Tarchon was about to move into. The block had been built around a central yard where children played and women hung washing. The interior walls were well painted, the corridors quite clean, and someone had even added potted plants, though most had wilted in the early summer heat. Like most apartment buildings in Byzantium, there were no numbers. At the first place he knocked at, a nervous-looking woman took one look at his stave and shut the door in his face. Behind the second door was a man who directed him one floor up. Fortunately, the old soldier was at home.

'Well, well,' said Bernardus when he saw his visitor. 'Young Tarchus.'

'*Tarchon.*'

'Ah, yes.'

Just then, it seemed foolish to think that this forgetful old fellow could really help him. But Tarchon had come this far; he might as well ask.

'You must come in,' said Bernardus, standing aside. 'I don't get many visitors.' Tarchon didn't feel overly encouraged by that either; the old fellow did have a tendency to go on a bit and he didn't have a lot of time to waste.

'Some cold milk? Fresh today.'

'Thank you.'

As Tarchon had expected, this was a two-room apartment, with one bedroom and a living area. While the veteran gestured to a round table and two stools, Tarchon placed his bag and stave in a corner. As befitted an old soldier, Bernardus' place was orderly and neat. He owned several expensive-looking chests and on one wall was a bronze plaque with writing inscribed upon it. Tarchon inspected it while Bernardus poured the milk.

'My diploma.'

'You get it when you leave the army.'

'That's right. For many of my compatriots, it meant they became a Roman citizen.'

'Not you?'

'My father was a man of means. He never could understand why I joined up.'

As he placed a mug of milk on the table, Bernardus kept his eyes on the diploma. 'Receiving that was more a relief than a pleasure. Twenty-five years in the legions. By the gods.'

Only once they'd both sat down on the stools, did Bernardus realise he'd left his own drink on the counter. Tarchon fetched it for him.

'Ah. Thank you.' Bernardus scratched his prominent nose and drank his milk. 'So, what can I do for you? I suppose if my daughter were here, she'd tell me not to let a young man I don't know into my home. But my instincts have always served me well enough.'

'You've nothing to fear from me, Master Bernardus, I promise you that. Remember I asked you about the grain men? It looks like I might be working for them. Sort of a trial. It seems I'll need a sword. I'm all right with my fists and a dagger is simple enough but well, sword work – there's an art to it. I wondered if you might be able to teach me a few things.'

'I see. Well, it's been a while. Do you have a blade?'

'I should have one by tomorrow.'

'I can show you some drills. It's all about repetition and practice – so it comes naturally when you need it.'

'My thanks. That would be very helpful.'

Bernardus pulled at the hairs on his chin, where his white and grey beard was thickest. 'I daresay I'm a bit out of touch but men have been sticking other men with pointy things for many a century. I doubt much has changed.'

'True enough,' replied Tarchon, finishing his drink. 'Lovely milk. Thank you.'

'Did I tell you about the Battle of Cremna, young man? Now that was a terrible day. It all began with–'

'-Master Bernardus, I'm very sorry but I have an appointment I can't miss. Would you mind telling me the story the next time I see you?'

The veteran sighed. 'As you wish. Come when you have the blade.'

'Excellent. Thank you again.'

Bernardus remained on his stool, watching as Tarchon fetched his stave and his bag. 'Can't be using a stick to fight all your life.'

'Definitely not.'

Grunting as he stood, Bernardus followed Tarchon to the door. 'Then again, use a stick, you've got less chance of doing permanent damage, or having it done to you. Not true with a dagger, certainly not true with a sword. I remember one fellow who didn't seem to grasp that – I believe he was Galatian.'

Tarchon was by the door, and ready to leave.

'Did you just roll your eyes?' demanded Bernardus.

'No sir,' Tarchon replied, though he had.

Bernardus aimed a broad, scarred finger at him. 'You roll your eyes again, lad, and you'll be getting no favours from me. If I help it's to help a young fellow trying to make the best of himself and – from what I hear at the cobblers – hasn't had the easiest of starts.'

'I am sorry. I won't do it again.'

Bernardus took a step closer. 'You want to learn about fighting? About war? My old centurion said you need strong feet for marching, strong hands for fighting, and a strong stomach for all the nasty sights you'll see. But you'll need a strong head most of all.'

'Good advice.'

'No one knew better than him, believe me. He went on to join the Praetorian Guard. Now where was I ...'

'You mentioned a man. A Galatian.'

'Yes, yes. Like all of us, he had to learn on the job. He hadn't been with us long when we were sent after a tough bunch of Lycian rebels. We hunted them for days. And all the time he was telling us older hands how he was going to cut them up, do this, do that. We eventually cornered the Lycians in a gully and they had no choice but to fight for their lives. It was a messy affair and when the shield wall broke up it was every man for himself. This Galatian waded straight in and a moment later I saw him staggering out of the scrap holding onto his guts. He'd been sliced right across: blood, tubes and all kind of bits coming out of him. Nasty way to die.'

Tarchon was surprised by the effect Bernardus' tale had on him. He felt rather ill.

'The point is, the Galatian spent so much time thinking about what he was going to do to the enemy, it had never occurred to him that they'd be trying to do the same to him.'

Bernardus formed two of his fingers into a point and poked Tarchon in the side.

'Only takes one moment and it's all over. You want a long life, lad? An easy life? A pleasant life? Don't pick up a blade.'

XI

By sunset, Tarchon was in his new home. Rhea had just left, having apologised for the state of the place, particularly the blackened wall in one corner where some idiot had started a fire. The apartment was ten feet by twelve, the only furniture a half-wrecked pallet for sleeping and a wooden chest that Rhea had moved in from another of her properties. There was also black mould on one wall and one window provided a view of nothing but bricks. On the third floor, he had a long way to carry his water up and his slops down but Tarchon could not have cared less.

He looked at the big iron key in his hand and smiled. It was the first home he had ever paid for himself. He had given Rhea eight denarii, securing the apartment for a month. Having already cleaned out the chest and placed his possessions inside, he now left, locking the door behind him. Because the heavy door was not flush to the frame, this took three attempts but it at least looked secure. That would help him sleep better.

'If it isn't the neighbourhood's newest resident!'

Tarchon looked to his right to see the familiar figure of Mehruz striding along the grimy corridor.

'What are you doing here?'

'Just saw Rhea at the market.' Reaching his friend, Mehruz playfully knocked a fist against his shoulder. 'Going to show me the palace then?'

Tarchon still had the key in his hand and now replaced it in the lock. 'It's not much – but it's home.'

*

Though he initially protested, Mehruz eventually agreed to a celebratory drink. The Persian suggested Diana's, a quiet place without music where they could catch up. They were about halfway there when Tarchon spotted Myron. Fortunately, the streets were dark and the bastard was facing away from him – one of two men sitting in a barber's getting a shave. Tarchon said nothing to Mehruz but was glad when they turned off the street. With his new job in mind, he wondered if he might be better off paying the man something just to keep him off his back. But he really didn't want to give that bullying prick any of his hard-earned coin.

'Riding lessons?' spluttered Mehruz when they got to talking.

'I know,' said Tarchon, shaking his head as he drank.

'And we're on the good stuff too,' added Mehruz, holding up his wooden mug. Tarchon had bought them a two-sesterce flask and the wine was considerably smoother and tastier than their usual fare.

'So, when do you buy your eighteen-hand black stallion?'

'Might be a bit early for that.'

Tarchon nodded towards the door of Diana's. A middle-aged man had just walked in with his two daughters; both were pretty.

Mehruz took a look and smiled. 'Nice.' He then let out a long sigh and leant his head back against the wall. 'I'd forgotten how much I enjoy this – doing nothing.'

'Life as a family man – and a hard-working man.' Tarchon reached out and grabbed a tuft of his friend's curly, voluminous hair. 'Uh-oh. I think I see grey.'

'Honestly, it wouldn't surprise me. So, what are you going to spend your money on, apart from furniture?'

'I'm getting a sword tomorrow. Won't be cheap but I should get a decent price.' Tarchon couldn't resist telling Mehruz about the blade but he knew it would only make his friend more suspicious.

'This "opportunity" – going to tell me anymore? We don't often have secrets between us.'

'No great secret. It's delivering messages for a man. An important man. Which is why I need the sword.'

'So, who is this important man?'

'I'm not supposed to tell anyone. I would if I could, Ruz, it's just I can't risk losing this.'

'Fair enough. How'd they hear about you?'

'I...came to their attention. They need someone who knows the city well, how to stay out of trouble.' This he said with a provocative grin.

'Just be careful, Tarch. Sounds to me like you could be in over your head.'

'Say a prayer to Ahura Mazda for me.'

'I always do. So does Anahita. Now that we're all well again, you must come over for dinner sometime.'

'Definitely.' Tarchon filled their mugs. 'Drink up – we've got a whole flask to get through.'

As it turned out, Tarchon drank two-thirds of the flask and so, when he met Korax the following day, it was with a slightly sore head. He also had a sore back due to the old pallet but he planned to fix up the bed when he could. Despite the soreness, he had happily laid there for some time, watching the early sun gradually illuminate his new home. Dozing, he had also heard the sounds of his neighbours waking and others passing by. Like many in the city, this street had no name but that didn't bother Tarchon at all. It would make him harder to find.

Arriving at the statue just before midday, he waited around but saw no sign of Korax. He was beginning to wonder if he'd got something wrong when a lad of about ten approached him.

'Tarchon?'

'Yes,' he replied, getting up off the steps below the statue.

'Master Korax sent me. He said you're to follow me.'

'Lead on.'

Tarchon assumed the lad might work for an armourer but he wouldn't say a word about his employer. He was therefore surprised when his guide eventually led him into the back of a bakery. Here, two women stood at a counter, making rolls. In one corner was a large oven, where more rolls were cooking, giving off a delightful smell.

The lad walked through the back room and stopped before entering the front, where Tarchon spied a queue of customers. He pointed up a set of steps, then hurried into the store, where he was cuffed around the ear by a large woman demanding to know where he'd been.

At the top of the stairs were two doorways. To the left was a room full of amphoras containing fine flour and rough bran. To the right was a second room furnished with a table and a few stools. Sitting there was Korax, chewing enthusiastically on a large roll. There were three more on a nearby plate. He said nothing, simply watching Tarchon as he entered and sat opposite him.

'Mmm. Best in the city.' He showed Tarchon the half-eaten roll. 'They put olives and nuts in.'

'Actually, I haven't had any breakfast,' said Tarchon, reaching for one.

'Hands off,' growled Korax. 'Those are mine. Grab a couple downstairs on the way out. The owner's an old friend.'

Though determined not to show it, Tarchon was excited about the prospect of a free breakfast. He really was moving up in the world.

'I must admit,' continued Korax, 'I'm slightly disturbed that the first thing you noticed in this room was the food.'

Leaning against the wall behind the veteran were a sword and a dagger, both in plain leather sheathes. Unable to suppress a grin, Tarchon walked over and first picked up the dagger. He drew the blade and saw that it was similar in design to those used by the army, if rather shorter and narrower. The wooden hilt was rounded, the flat blade made of iron. He placed the dagger on the table, then picked up the sword. Once out of the sheath, it was surprisingly light, again a basic version of a legionary weapon, though this blade was steel. There were no adornments on handle or pommel but the sheath was equipped with a shoulder strap.

'Nothing special but they'll do the job,' said Korax, finishing his roll. 'Nine for both. You can pay a third now, the rest when you have it.'

'Very kind.'

Sheathing the sword and placing it next to the dagger, he retrieved his money and counted out the coins.

'Thank you,' he said as he sat down.

'No one will look twice at the dagger but I'd advise against carrying the sword around unless you're on a job. You might get the odd watchman or soldier who'll start asking questions.'

'There's no law against carrying a sword.'

Korax cleared his throat. 'Perhaps you'd prefer me to not offer advice.'

'Sorry.'

'Good. Because we're going to be spending a bit of time together. This job on the other side of the Straits has become more urgent. Gargonius wants the issue dealt with as soon as possible. I'll get you to the right place but from there you're on your own.'

'What is the job?'

'All in good time. We leave tomorrow, at dawn. I'll meet you at East Harbour. We'll hire mounts on the other side.'

'I haven't had time for the riding lesson.'

'You'll have to learn as you go. Don't worry.'

Tarchon eyed the weapons. 'I've barely any time to practise with those either.'

'Don't worry.'

'What *should* I worry about?'

'Same thing I worry about. Same thing the chief worries about. Getting the job done.'

Though part of him wanted to discuss all this with Mehruz or Galla, he knew he couldn't. And though he needed to purchase a few items for the trip, he was still left with several unoccupied hours. He didn't want time to grow even more nervous about the impending mission and there was one obvious alternative.

When he arrived at the apartment on Goat Lane, Bernardus was about to fetch some water, so he instead despatched Tarchon. When Tarchon returned with a third bucketful from a nearby fountain, he found the veteran examining his unsheathed sword.

'What do you think?'

'A fair blade. Rather light but it's not as if you're joining the legions.' Bernardus removed some tiny pieces of leather from the shiny steel. 'A good place to start, I would say. Move the table aside.'

'I thought we would practise outside?'

'We shall. When you bring wooden swords, we will need more space. But for now, you should simply practise some basic moves.'

'Very well.'

While Tarchon shifted the table to the wall, Bernardus sat on a stool, loosening his belt around his stomach. 'Ugh. I must eat less and exercise more. Hard to believe I was a soldier for twenty-five years. Now then, what do you think of the sword's handle, young man?'

'Er, not bad.'

'Grip is crucial. You realise that the first time you lose your blade in a battle. Some men add rope or other bindings. Find what works for you and maintain it – the rest of the weapon too, of course. By the time I've finished with you, you'll have blisters all over your fingers but your hands will toughen up in time.'

Having spent much of his life labouring, Tarchon reckoned his hands were tough enough but he said nothing. This old man had valuable knowledge and he intended to obtain as much of it as he could – starting today.

'Forget what you might have seen of a gentleman duelling.'

Don't know many gentlemen, thought Tarchon as Bernardus continued.

'What you hold in your hands is an infantry weapon, designed primarily for short-range stabbing, with the odd slash thrown in. It's not the best for attacking, nor the best for defending but if you've only one weapon, you could do a lot worse. We shall start with defence.'

Tarchon hadn't noticed the long-handled brush leaning against a cupboard that Bernardus now picked up. 'Chances are that if you've gone for your sword, you're facing someone else with a sword, or maybe a spear. And we know you won't have armour or shield so your priority is to not get hit. It's the blade that can hurt you so the blade you must watch. Now, this is where it's important to have what we call a soft hand. Blades can come at you from all directions, all angles. Getting your blade into the right position to parry or block is essential. We'll start there. Now, I know you're strong and keen but don't try and knock the handle out of my hand. You just need to keep the end away from you. Understood?'

'Yes.'

The old soldier unscrewed the head of the brush and put it on the floor.

'All right then. Let's make a start.'

When the old man approached him, Tarchon didn't anticipate a lot of difficulty. And, in fact, it wasn't initially hard to bat away the jabs aimed at his face and body.

'Steady on,' said Bernardus after a minute or so, 'or you'll be buying me a new brush.'

It took about five minutes – and by then the veteran was sweating – but he seemed to get into his stride, increasing the speed and variety of attacks.

'Move those feet!' he ordered in that surprisingly loud voice, thrusting the handle straight at Tarchon's groin, then coming in wide towards his face, then angling up at his armpit. Tarchon kept his eyes on the handle, shifting as the tip came towards him, always knocking it away.

It was a low, straight thrust that caught him out. He was still recovering from the previous parry and as he rotated his wrist to the right, he reached the limit of that rotation. The handle slid inside the blade now pointed at the floor and tapped Tarchon lightly against the stomach.

'Balls.'

'Bit higher actually,' said Bernardus.

They both chuckled at that, and the veteran lowered the handle.

'Get the point?'

'Luckily for me, the handle doesn't have one.'

Grinning, Bernardus put the brush down and went to fetch a mug. 'Some refreshment before round two.'

Tarchon swapped the blade to his left hand and shook his right, grimacing at the ache.

'Gets heavy quickly, doesn't it?'

'It does.'

'Nothing compared to a shield. Or full armour, for that matter.' Bernardus sipped his water. 'You know, lad, sometimes when I look back, I honestly can't believe I was a legionary.'

'Did you lose many friends?'

'I did. I suppose I should be grateful – at least I have the chance to look back.'

By the time they were done, Tarchon was sweating more than the old veteran. Bernardus insisted that they stick with defensive techniques and gave him some exercises to practise alone. He was surprised when he heard his new student was leaving the city. Tarchon played down the importance of the trip but Bernardus instructed him to be very careful around "the grain men". Thankfully, he also agreed to keep the matter between the two of them.

Of his first pay packet, Tarchon had six denarii left and four of that was gone by the time he returned home. He purchased everything from the second-hand stores at Third Hill: a blanket, a tunic, a pack, a narrow leather belt and a pair of boots. The boots were army cast-offs but looked in good condition. He could hardly believe that almost all his pay was gone but the pride created by his new acquisitions more than compensated.

Despite his circumstances and lowly beginnings, Tarchon had always felt that he was meant for great things; that he would do something in the world, be a man of influence. Only a few weeks ago, he had made a desperate gamble to improve his lot. What seemed initially like a disastrous failure had somehow turned into a promising success. He shook his head in disbelief at how things had turned out. He had his *own* place. He wasn't dependent on the generosity or pity of others. At last, he was *someone*.

A hundred thanks, Minerva. A thousand!

XII

The six oarsmen were as good as he'd seen. Strong currents ran through the Straits and the twenty-foot ferryboat was carrying eight passengers, two heavy chests and various other bits of luggage. As they neared the middle of the mile-wide channel, facing a worsening headwind, the chief oarsman began to call stroke. A lad aged no more than six sat in the bow, alerting the chief to anything coming their way. So far this had included two other ferryboats and a hundred-foot freighter named *Dacius*.

Tarchon – who was feeling dozy, despite an early march across the city to meet Korax – dipped his hand into the cold water and splashed it across his face. As the two merchants behind him began muttering about the price of vinegar, Tarchon glanced across at Korax. The bald agent was gazing calmly across the Straits, hands clasped between his thighs. He was armed only with a dagger and between his boots sat a well-packed saddlebag. Tarchon wondered what he'd done for Gargonius and the Service in his time. He wondered if the man was as tough and ruthless as he seemed.

Typically, Korax had said little before they departed and though Tarchon had a dozen questions, he knew it would be inadvisable to ask. He also knew that he would not help himself by constantly worrying about what was to come. He would take this trip day by day, hour by hour if necessary.

As they approached Chalcedon, Tarchon looked along the coastline, which was less developed than the western side, with patches of beach and rock between the harbours and rows of warehouses. Here the lad was needed again as the ferryboat avoided a trio of coasters bearing Cretan flags. When they at last neared a rectangular concrete quay, the rowers were breathing hard. The chief put down his oar and, along with the lad, neatly tied up to a pair of iron rings. The passengers then faced a steep set of slippery, weed-strewn steps. Korax was first off, which meant Tarchon had to be second, earning him a sharp look from a woman he had overtaken.

Once at the top of the steps, Korax put his saddlebag over his shoulder and set off along the quay towards shore. A couple of other ferryboats had recently arrived and a queue had formed at the far end. Stationed there were three legionaries, intercepting new arrivals.

Korax tutted.

'Is that a problem?' asked Tarchon.

The agent did not reply. Pack over his shoulder, Tarchon followed him to the queue, where they awaited their turn. As they approached the three soldiers, Tarchon listened in and realised the legionaries were questioning the travellers about the reason for their trip, their destination, starting point and so on. According to the two merchants, this was due to the Goths, who were apparently moving south again. He recalled the column of soldiers he'd seen in the city and wondered if the two were connected.

When they reached the soldiers, Korax pulled out a worn piece of paper and showed it to them. With a nod, the senior man swiftly waved the pair through.

'We're headed for Nicomedia,' explained Korax.

Tarchon knew he was now in the province of Bithnyia and that Nicomedia was the capital.

'My papers are good enough for them – they're from the Fifteenth Legion, not local. But outside Chalcedon we might run into local soldiers, guards and officials. For that, we'll need a cover story.'

'Right,' said Tarchon as they turned onto a busy street that ran along the waterfront.

'Something simple and hard to disprove.'

'Right. And you'd like me to…'

'Yes. By the time we have the horses. So, take that stupid look off your face and start thinking.'

These thoughts occupied Tarchon while they marched through the streets of Chalcedon, dodging heavily-loaded carts headed for the port and the usual variety of people going about their day. There were fewer of them here, however, and far fewer of the great structures visible in Byzantium. Heading inland, they passed a group of twenty or so priests clad in colourful, flowing robes. They were clearly men but had grown their hair long and arranged it in feminine fashion.

Korax gave them a distasteful look. 'Cultists – followers of Cybele.'

'Ah. I've heard some stories about them.'

'They're causing quite a bit of trouble here.'

'Is that anything to do with our mission?'

'Don't use that word again,' said the agent as he turned into a narrow street that ran up one side of a hillock. 'We're on a *job*.'

At the top of the slope was a stable and paddock, where a man was trotting a horse around in circles.

'That's where we're picking up the mounts. What's our story?'

'Right. You are a former soldier with a nice pension, looking for investments in Nicomedia. I'm your nephew and you've taken me along for experience.'

Korax grimaced.

'No good?'

'Not terrible but why suggest a family connection? If we're supposed to know each other well, we can easily be caught out.'

'You're taking me on as apprentice? It's often said that the best lies are close to the truth.'

Korax rolled his eyes, then rubbed them. 'All right, the old soldier thing is not bad but why look in a different province? Why not closer to home?'

'Er…you don't want to be limited to Byzantium. Looking for a broad range of opportunities for the long term.'

'Who are we going to see in Nicomedia? No appointments made?'

'First trip. You'll be visiting all the main commercial areas and making enquiries.'

Korax bobbed his head from side to side. 'It's not terrible.'

'Good.'

'I didn't say it was good. What do you know about trade and business – if asked?'

'I used to work for a bookmaker. Lots of clients with money. You pick things up. And one way or another, I've been involved in half the trades in the city. Glassmaking, carpentry, oil-pressing, fishing–'

'All right. We'll go with it. While we're riding, we'll fill in the details.'

As they neared the stable, the hillock provided a view out over the south of Chalcedon. Tarchon saw three great pits carved out of the earth, huge piles of spoil beside them. Two of the pits were presently unoccupied but one was busy with workers. A long line of men entered a broad tunnel with empty baskets on their backs. The baskets of those coming the other way were almost overflowing with chunks of pale grey rock.

'The quarries,' he said. 'I've never seen them before.'

'Main reason there's a city here,' said Korax. 'There's barely a building in Byzantium without stone from Chalcedon.'

Though Tarchon's occasional attempts at riding had been successful, few of them had involved a saddle. Korax hired all the tack with the mounts, insisting that Tarchon would have to use the proper gear if he was to ride long distances. He informed the stable-owner that Tarchon was inexperienced, so he was given an eight-year-old grey named Ambler. Korax chose a taller, more expensive horse named Swiftfoot. As Nicomedia was only forty miles from Chalcedon, Tarchon was surprised that Korax secured both mounts for two weeks.

He didn't question that but he did learn a good deal about the man as the day unfolded. As Tarchon had said himself, it made sense for their stories to reflect reality where possible and Korax disclosed a surprising amount. Tarchon learned that he had been born to a farming family in the Rhodope mountains of western Thracia, some two hundred miles from Byzantium. Hearing tales of adventure from his legionary uncle, Korax had joined at seventeen. Enrolling in the Eleventh Legion based in the neighbouring province of Moesia, he had seen action in half a dozen provinces and fought as many battles, four of them against the Goths.

He had eventually reached the rank of optio, spending a decade as second in command of a century before retiring after the usual twenty-five years. Korax was guarded about how exactly he had ended up with Gargonius but remarked that he had worked with Imperial Security while still a member of the Eleventh. Like many of the soldiers Tarchon had met, he insisted on proudly listing the historic battles at which the Eleventh had fought, which included Dyracchium, Philippi and Actium. The Eleventh had been originally raised by Caesar himself, three centuries earlier: another point of pride for Korax.

The quickest route to Nicomedia was to follow the coast road, which led south from Chalcedon, then east. Much of the road ran close to the shore and Tarchon looked out over a smattering of small islands. He had only a loose idea of geography beyond his home city. Korax informed him that – if they kept heading south-east past Nicomedia – they would pass through the provinces of Galatia, Cappadocia and Cilicia before finally reaching Syria and the eastern borders of the Empire.

Persia, as Mehruz had told him many times, was over a thousand miles away. Tarchon could barely conceive of such a distance. It occurred to him that they were very much in a central area of the Empire and it seemed odd that the Service would find something to concern them. But Nicomedia was a capital and he supposed all manner of intrigues might unfold there.

Tarchon was relieved to find riding quite a bit easier with a saddle, or perhaps it was because Ambler was so calm and obedient. Around midday they stopped and bought bread, cheese and wine from a stall beside the road. As they stood there eating, a cart halted. Lying in the back was a boy being tended to by his mother and sister. According to the father, the hapless lad had been gored by a bull. The family were bound for Chalcedon and a cousin who cleaned the house of an army surgeon. While the father swiftly watered the horses, the boy wailed. His sister and mother sobbed incessantly, their tunics already wet with tears. Tarchon was keen to get moving and the awful sounds of suffering put him right off his food. Korax sat on a rock, impassively enjoying his lunch.

In the afternoon, the veteran asked Tarchon about his earlier life. Tarchon was honest – even about his mother's death – though he didn't mention all his encounters with the law. When he told Korax of the many times he'd not been able to make ends meet, he sensed a rare – and surprising – sympathy from the ex-legionary.

As the afternoon wore on, clouds appeared and released a burst of heavy rain. Korax pulled a hooded cloak from his pack and covered himself. Tarchon had only his nice new blanket and he had no intention of getting that wet.

After half an hour of plodding onward, the veteran turned to him. 'Got nothing to cover yourself?'

Tarchon shrugged. 'It's only water.'

Though Ambler was a steady horse, Tarchon felt very sore when they at last dismounted at an inn situated only a stone's throw from the shore. The rain ceased just before sunset so he was also very wet. According to the most recent milestone, they had twenty-two miles to go before reaching Nicomedia. Once they had left the mounts with the innkeeper's son, the owner himself showed them to one of his four small rooms. It was at least equipped with proper wooden-framed beds, which Tarchon had only enjoyed on a handful of occasions. Korax dumped his saddlebag and headed down to the parlour without a word. Tarchon changed into his spare tunic and took the other downstairs with him. Fortunately, the innkeeper's wife took it instantly, offering to dry it at the kitchen's hearth, along with Korax's cloak.

The former soldier was sitting in the parlour with a mug of wine. When Tarchon sat opposite him, the innkeeper brought him one too.

'Thank you.'

'My pleasure, young sir.'

Tarchon could count on one hand the number of times he'd ever been called "sir": young or otherwise. He supposed that was what happened when you wore nice new clothes, travelled by horse and stayed at inns.

'Pleased to have a couple of guests with us,' said the innkeeper, a stocky fellow with livid red veins upon his cheeks. He took a damp cloth from his belt and began wiping down the table. 'Been a quiet week. Quiet *year* for that matter. No one's got money to spend.'

'What do you put that down to?' asked Korax.

'Probably best I don't say.'

'You needn't worry about us. In fact, we're interested to hear about what's going on here. My apprentice and I are looking for business opportunities in Nicomedia.'

'I hope the gods smile on your endeavours, sir, but I'm afraid there's a good deal of uncertainty in the capital. And no one likes uncertainty when it comes to business.'

Korax said, 'I hear there's been some unhappiness in certain circles.'

The innkeeper finished his cleaning and threw the cloth onto the counter. 'If I may, sir, that's something of an understatement. I've seldom known a more unpopular governor, and I've known a few. We've had three consecutive years of tax rises, all the strange trial decisions and then these bloody cultists.'

Korax glanced at Tarchon, clearly expecting him to say something.

'The followers of Cybele? We saw some in Byzantium.'

'We see them on the road all the time, young man. They used to keep to themselves, but they're always out looking to convert these days. I ask you, what mother or father wants their son to end up half a man? First sight of the bastards, I get the wife and the boy in and lock the door. I've no issue with folk following whatever god they please but what they get up to…Gods, it turns the stomach.'

Tarchon needed no prompting to press him further on this. 'What exactly *do* they get up to?'

The innkeeper was clearly more interested in talking than working. While the sounds of energetic chopping emanated from the kitchen, he went to the counter, grabbed a flask and poured himself some wine. He also took a dish of walnuts and placed it on the table.

'You don't mind if I join you for a moment?'

Korax gestured for him to sit.

'It's best that I speak of this *before* dinner. I hope you both have strong stomachs. You've heard of the Day of Blood?'

Both men nodded. Tarchon knew that the priests of Cybele sometimes flogged themselves until they bled.

'The followers are zealots but it is the eunuch priests that are truly out of their minds.'

'The Galli,' said Korax. 'They believe that the goddess Cybele fell in love with the god Attis. When Attis married a mortal woman, Cybele avenged herself by forcing him to castrate himself.'

The innkeeper swigged down some wine. 'I remember when the Day of Blood meant blood only from their *backs*. Not now. I couldn't bear to watch it myself but I'm told that they drive themselves into a frenzy, then take up some rusty old sword and chop off their parts. Can you imagine? From that day, they grow their hair long and walk around dressed as women.'

'They are not alone in that,' said Korax. 'The emperor Elagabalus, for one. And there was a tribune from the Fifteenth Legion who was found by another officer clad in the clothes and jewellery of his wife.' The ex-legionary gave a rare chuckle. 'He'd even made up his face with paint and powder!'

The innkeeper didn't crack a smile. 'It wouldn't be so bad if they kept it all behind closed doors but their temple is one of the most popular in the city. I sometimes wonder if people just enjoy the show. Worse, the governor does nothing about them.'

'There may some…extremists,' said Korax, 'but Cybele originated close to here. There are followers all the way from Antioch to Rome. Ordinary people.' Korax took a walnut from the bowl and ate it. 'You mentioned something about court decisions.'

The innkeeper looked towards the kitchen and lowered his voice, clearly not wanting his wife to hear. 'Well, the worst was this army officer who raped a ten-year-old girl. Apparently, he was a favourite of the governor's and therefore spared punishment. When he first took over, Lucretius was admired and well-liked. He had done very well as procurator. But these last few years, the man has lost his way.'

'Any idea why?'

'Some say he's too old – infirm perhaps. Others say it's his staff – divided by in-fighting. Who knows? We're so far from Rome that the Emperor seems not to care who represents him here. I daresay he's got his own problems. Well, speaking of problems, I best go see how the wife's getting on.'

The innkeeper departed, taking his mug with him.

Once he was in the kitchen, Korax leaned across the table.

'Only one man's opinion but you can learn a remarkable amount from innkeepers.'

'You knew all that already, I suppose.'

'Most.'

'And you know why the governor has lost his way?'

'I do.' Korax popped another nut into his mouth. 'As a matter of fact, that's why we're here.'

XIII

They reached Nicomedia around the tenth hour. There was another cloudburst in the morning but by mid-afternoon the sun had dried the broad slabs that paved the road. Nearing the capital, they had a clear view south across the narrow inlet that divided the north of Bithnyia from the rest of the province. Nicomedia was situated close to the eastern, landward end of the inlet. A warm breeze was blowing; ships and smaller boats eased gently across the sheltered, placid waters. As the road passed over a promontory, Tarchon spied an area of large warehouses and high cranes, and two partially-built vessels up on scaffolds. Nicomedia was famed for its shipyards and he knew a couple of men who'd worked there.

Though not on the scale of Byzantium, the Bithnyian capital was still impressive. Just outside the city, the road turned inland from the coast and passed under a high aqueduct. Here, a team of at least thirty engineers were hard at work, some of them hanging from slings and nets at dizzying heights.

'Don't much fancy that job,' said Tarchon.

'Took them bloody decades to finish that thing,' remarked Korax, slumped back in his saddle. 'There was a governor who finally got it done. Built a couple of canals too. Became some famous writer. His uncle was one too. Er…Plinius. Heard of him?'

'Can't say I have. Don't know many writers. Not much point when you can't read. Do you read, sir? Books, I mean?'

'No chance,' said Korax as they passed beyond the shadows of the aqueduct. 'Too pricey. The chief has a few but he's an educated man.'

Tarchon considered asking how long his companion had known Gargonius but he doubted Korax was in the mood for revealing more personal details.

Reaching the arch that marked the capital's west gate, they dismounted and were questioned by a local official seated at a table. A squad of legionaries were also on duty but they paid the new arrivals no attention. The official was interested only in whether they were carrying trade goods and sent them through.

As sunset was near, the streets of Nicomedia were not busy. Korax clearly knew the place well and they led their mounts past an open square where a few knots of people had gathered. Ambler was as relaxed as usual but Swiftfoot clearly preferred the open road, taking some time to settle down. There were notably more soldiers than Byzantium: patrols often mixed with city sergeants carrying clubs. Passing a street vendor grilling a couple of big pike, Tarchon felt his stomach grumble. Then he grinned as he thought of another nice dinner courtesy of the Imperial Security Service.

'What's wrong with you?' said Korax, frowning as they stopped outside an inn with a sign bearing an odd-looking creature.

'Nothing.'

'Stupid smile on your face again. You ought to be careful – people will take you for an imbecile.'

There was no pike for dinner but Tarchon greatly enjoyed the mushroom soup and blood sausage laid on by the two sisters who ran the inn. He had discovered that the poorly-rendered creature on the sign outside was in fact a camel, and that he was now staying at The Camel Inn. He and Korax ate in a central courtyard with other guests. Korax resisted the attempts of one man to engage him in conversation between the soup and the sausage. As the larger of the two sisters waddled over to collect their plates, she flashed a smile and put a hand on Korax's shoulder. The ex-soldier greeted this with his habitual grim expression and Tarchon had to look away to ensure his superior didn't see another "stupid smile".

He'd been told before dinner that they had an appointment at the second hour of night. Korax ordered him to leave his sword in their room but both men left armed with their daggers. As the less friendly of the sisters closed the door behind them (asking them not to return too late), Korax spoke:

'Street of the Carpenters.'

He had consistently tested Tarchon's navigational skills and had earlier pointed out certain streets and landmarks.

'Er…left.'

'And then?'

'Not sure but I'll get us there.'

'How?'

'My nose.'

'Your nose? Blood of Mars, you're not a hound. What if you were in the army? You'd need to describe a route to your men.'

Tarchon shrugged. 'My friend Mehruz says I've got a good nose.'

'We'll see about that.' In the dim light of the lantern outside the inn, Korax gestured to the left.

Tarchon led the way along the centre of the street, where the moonlight wasn't blocked by the buildings. Nicomedia was just like Byzantium at night: a sea of darkness had settled on the city, with only a few islands of light with which to navigate. Over the years, the darkness had been Tarchon's friend more than it had been his enemy.

He took two rights and a left, leading them to what he believed was the Avenue of Antioch. A moment of doubt struck him after a couple of minutes – everywhere looked different in the dark – but his nose then led him off the avenue and he felt fairly confident that he was heading for the west gate. Korax said nothing, staying a pace behind him and occasionally sighing. They passed two patrols bearing lanterns but the locals paid them no attention.

'The Street of the Carpenters,' he announced as they halted beside a high plinth not currently adorned by a statue. Predictably, there were no congratulations; Korax simply marched on along the street. He approached two men standing on the pavement talking loudly and asked them about a leather store owned by a man named Galanis. They directed him to the right side of the street. Several of the ground floor stores had lanterns out front; the leather store was not one of them.

Before knocking on the door, Korax whispered to Tarchon. 'Keep your wits about you. Unlikely to cause us a problem but I've not met him before.'

The knock was answered swiftly, the door opening to reveal a man of about thirty, holding a smoky oil lamp. His expression was nervous and his fine tunic and belt were certainly not those of a leather-worker.

'Master Orfius?'

'Yes,' answered Korax. 'Panagos?'

'Yes. Who's that with you?'

'My associate. You're alone?'

'I am,' said Panagos with what sounded like regret. He held the lamp higher and eyed Tarchon.

'Are you going to let us in?' asked Korax. 'I'd prefer not to attract any attention.'

Panagos opened the door, watching them suspiciously as they stepped in. Tarchon was not surprised by the familiar harsh, earthy smell of the store. Panagos' lamp gave out enough light for him to see a range of goods arranged on shelves along two walls, mainly belts and bags of various designs. They looked to be of good quality, many adorned with expensive buckles and clasps.

Bearing in mind Korax's instructions, Tarchon glanced towards the gloomy rear of the store. There was a desk to the left and a pitch-black doorway to the right. In the middle of the space was a circular table across which the three men now faced each other.

'I was told four aurei,' said Panagos, scratching his neck.

Korax reached inside his tunic and retrieved four golden coins, which he placed on the table close to the lantern. Panagos was already reaching for them when Korax held up a finger.

'Not yet. First you tell me what I need to know.'

Korax placed his hands on his belt, the right only inches from the hilt of his dagger.

Panagos straightened up and gulped nervously. 'Very well. He has been in the city for several months, travelling between the basilica and his home. Recently, he's taken to using a carriage and added a bodyguard to his detail. He's not been seen publicly for some time.'

'So, *two* bodyguards now?'

'Yes.'

'You've seen this for yourself – the carriage and the guards?'

'Of course.'

'He meets the governor at the basilica?'

'Yes. It's not possible to ascertain anything of what goes on in these meetings.'

'And the house?'

'A villa on the coast. It used to belong to a city council member who fell out of favour and was exiled. Now Lucretius has given it to his favourite. It's a couple of miles south of the city, one of several with their own beach. It's called Green Cove – on account of the water.'

'Security?'

'I've not been. I didn't want to risk it.'

Korax reached forward and reclaimed one of the coins.

Panagos frowned theatrically. 'I've spent days on this, neglected my-'

'I was assured you could tell me *all* there is to tell.'

'I…I have a position here. I can't risk being seen *spying* on the governor's favourite.'

'What's the view of him amongst Lucretius' staff?'

'They hate him. They can't believe that the governor would listen to his ramblings above the advice of old friends and wiser heads. Publicly, they have to toe the line.'

'Is he known to visit anywhere else?'

'Previously. Not now, though some visitors do go out to the house. The head priest of the Temple of Cybele, for example. There are some jokes going around – about which of them is the more depraved. I'm led to believe that the procurator and the magistrate have already tried to resign but Lucretius gave them pay rises to ensure they remain in post.'

'So, he at least still values them?'

'It appears so.'

Something made Tarchon turn to the left, towards the darkened doorway. He had heard and seen nothing to suggest there was someone there and yet his instincts had offered a warning. Had Panagos brought someone along to back him up? Observe the meeting? Something more dangerous?

'What is it?' asked Korax.

'Hopefully nothing, sir,' said Tarchon, taking one of the candles sitting on the worktable and lighting it from the lamp. All things considered, he didn't much like the idea of entering the darkened passageway but he wanted to show Korax he was fearless.

'Thought I might check the back – make sure we *are* alone.'

Korax glanced at Panagos.

'Go ahead, I've nothing to hide.'

Korax pointed towards the rear. Tarchon walked that way, the candle offering a weak glow. Beyond the doorway was a narrow corridor. Swapping the candle to his left hand, he drew his dagger and stepped forward. Opposite was another doorway which led to a small storeroom. Tarchon peered inside and saw only piles of stock.

Heading left, he followed the corridor to a right turn. Six feet beyond that was the rear door of the store. It was fitted with a hefty lock but the door was slightly ajar. The floor was covered with reed matting which offered no evidence of movement. Still able to hear the low tones of Korax and Panagos, Tarchon went outside and found himself in an alley no more than five feet wide. On the far side was a high wall. If there *had* been anyone in the store, they could have only escaped along the alley.

Lowering the candle to give his eyes a chance, Tarchon looked to the left. He saw no movement. Turning right, he glimpsed a dark shape nip swiftly around the corner, about fifty feet away. It might easily have been someone who'd used the alley as a short cut or emerged from one of the other buildings; it was impossible to be sure.

He returned inside to find Panagos pocketing his three coins.

'All right?' asked Korax.

Tarchon nodded as he put the candle out, then sheathed his dagger.

'If you ever need any more information,' said Panagos, 'feel free to contact me through our mutual acquaintance.'

'Oh, you won't hear from us again,' said Korax. 'Not ever. Unless you tell anyone about us and this meeting of course. Then we may have cause to return, Panagos.' Korax tapped the hilt of his dagger with his right thumb. 'Or…to be accurate, Statius Egnatius Vitalis, son of Nonus and Marte.'

Despite the dim light, "Panagos" visibly blanched. 'There is no need for threats.'

'Experience tells me otherwise. But it seems we understand each other. We'll leave you to it. That way, if you don't mind.'

Tarchon followed Korax out of the store, though the dark corridor and out into the alley.

'I may have seen something. Someone turning at that end of the alley.'

'Not sure they could have got from here to there without you hearing them.'

'Probably right.'

'Better safe than sorry. Good that you stayed a distance from me too. Keep that up – if someone pulls a weapon, the other has time to react. Now, find us a different route back to the Camel. And tell me why.'

'Changing routes makes it harder to be followed – and tracked over time.'

'Good.'

Tarchon almost made a comment about the rarity of praise from his superior but kept his mouth shut. Half way along the alley, he spoke up:

'Do you always finish such meetings like that – with a threat?'

'If he were to become a regular source, I'd likely be more pleasant. But in this case, we have to get in, do what we have to, then get out.'

'And what exactly *are* we doing, sir?'

'Patience. I'll tell you everything you need to know tomorrow.'

They left The Camel just after dawn, fighting their way through the morning crowds before eventually striking the coast and heading south. The road itself was busy with carts and riders heading into Nicomedia, so Korax elected to follow a narrow path that ran through dry grass not far from the main route. Their own mounts were back at the inn's stable; Korax had explained that they would be more trouble than they were worth on this particular job. It was clear to Tarchon that they were going to see this villa Panagos had described. He still knew very little about the man who lived there, other than the fact that he seemed to be a bad influence upon Governor Lucretius. He was further confused when Korax stopped beside a patch of mud, put some on his finger and rubbed it into his belt buckle.

'So the shine doesn't give us away,' he explained after telling Tarchon to do the same.

A mile south of the city, the main road curved away inland so – after consulting a goatherd – they turned onto a wide, dusty track. This route followed the contours of a promontory about a hundred feet above the water, though it never got close to the attractive beaches below: these had long been claimed by the wealthy. In fact, there were only a few ordinary people around, mostly heading for Nicomedia with something to sell. Twice, however, the pair had to make way for grand covered carriages.

'Might have been our man,' said Tarchon as the second vehicle trundled past.

'Possibly,' replied Korax. 'If anyone asks, we're taking the sea air.'

'Got it.'

Shortly afterward, they stopped to eat the breakfast packed for them at The Camel. The larger sister had handed the food over and Tarchon noted that Korax had been given not only a bigger roll but also an apple.

'You're definitely her favourite, sir,' he said with a grin.

Korax just chewed his roll.

'Maybe we'll get a discount on our bill.'

Korax glared at him so he shut up.

By mid-morning, they had passed four large estates, each surrounded by walls. Only one was visible; the others were situated lower down, closer to the sea. The fifth, however, was unmistakably Green Cove, the enticing waters visible before the house. Realising that they were approaching their destination, Korax cut off the track and across the scrubby terrain to a patch of dense bushes. He carefully selected a location between two bushes, took off his pack and sat down, eyes fixed on the area below.

The cove was perhaps a quarter-mile across: a narrow beach enclosed by two rocky headlands. On the near side of the southern headland was the dark mouth of a partially submerged cave. The beach was of pale sand and ran up to the front of the villa, which had been built into the slope. The building was not actually that large but the colonnaded front (which faced inland) and gleaming white paint gave the place an air of grandeur. The broad front door faced a well-maintained garden where a man tended a flower bed. A path bisected the garden and ran up to the main gate, which was flanked by a five-foot wall. A paved section led up to the track the observers had just walked along.

As they gazed down at the property, a squat, powerfully-built man approached the gardener. Though he was at least three hundred feet away, his sword was obvious against his pale tunic. Korax reached into his pack and retrieved his flask and a straw sun hat. After drinking, he placed the hat on his head and sat with his hands in his lap, still scanning the scene below.

'I take it we're here for a while then?' said Tarchon, drinking from his own flask.

'You should have a hat.'

'I'm all right. I have hair.'

Korax again turned his stony glare on Tarchon, which caused the younger man to look away. He knew his comments weren't furthering his cause but the former legionary was a grim companion and he sometimes couldn't help himself.

'I was going to take first watch,' said Korax. 'But you can do it. I expect you to not only watch the house and the road but memorise every inch of what you can see. Understood?'

'Yes, sir.'

Korax moved to a partly-shaded area beside a bush, laid out using his pack for a pillow, then placed the hat over his face. 'And wake me if anyone comes near.'

Tarchon reckoned Korax had chosen their observation point well but he adjusted his position so that he was better hidden from both the road and the villa. His view was slightly obscured by one of the bushes but he did as he'd been told and first directed his gaze from left to right across the cove and the property. He repeated this five times, then simply watched.

Other than the gardener going about his work and the guard ambling slowly around the property, he saw only two other people. The first was a woman wearing an apron who came out to polish the bronze studs on the front door. The second was a lad who spent half an hour mucking out the small stable situated to the right of the house. Other than that, the most exciting moment was when Tarchon spotted two lizards scampering across the slope just below their position.

Korax did not move or make a sound until he suddenly sat up about an hour after settling down.

'Well?'

'Not a lot going on. Also saw a woman and a stable lad. Other than that, everything-'

At the sounds of the carriage, they both ducked. Then, looking to their right, they watched the heavy vehicle rumble down the track before reaching the paved section close to the villa. The driver was hunched forward, arms tense as he slowed the horses. Beside him was a second guard, this man steadying himself with one hand. The carriage was not one of those they had seen earlier; it was painted a distinctive dark blue. The window was open with the curtain drawn back and Tarchon thought he glimpsed a face.

'Move over.'

Tarchon did so, allowing Korax the best position. As the carriage stopped in the courtyard that divided the villa from the stable, the driver climbed down and steadied the horses. The lad trotted forward holding a step, which he placed below the carriage door. The guard opened it and stepped back as a fat, white-haired man slowly descended. There were rolls of flab below and above his belt and he possessed larger breasts than many women. He was dressed in a pale blue tunic and sandals which audibly slapped as he made for the villa at surprising speed.

'Good,' said Korax. 'Plenty of daylight left. We might get a chance to observe more of this fat bastard's habits.' He turned to Tarchon. 'That will be helpful for you.'

'For me?'

'I did say I am only here to guide you this far. What happens next is up to you. That man is named Demetrius. He is a seer, specialising in the reading of animal entrails and the weather. Over the last few years, he has somehow convinced Governor Lucretius that he can see the future and, as you now know, his interference has caused no end of problems. Master Gargonius has been ordered to remove him. You should be pleased that he believes you're capable of the task.'

'Remove him? What exactly does that mean?'

'What do you *think* it means?'

For seven more hours they sat and watched the villa. Korax gave him an opportunity to rest but Tarchon didn't take it. He tried to put aside the issue of Demetrius' fate and absorb the details that Korax pointed out. They saw more of the guards' routines and watched Demetrius amble down to the beach for a swim around the ninth hour.

Only when the sun began to set, did Korax decide they should leave. There was a little light to see their way and before long they were back on the main road, walking at a brisk speed. Tarchon found himself so preoccupied that he could eventually remain silent no longer.

'Kill him. You want me to kill him.'

'We need to stop him influencing Lucretius. We could cut out his tongue but killing him is probably the best choice, yes.'

Tarchon didn't know what to say; he had expected the sternest of tests but this was something else.

'I don't blame you for having doubts,' said Korax. 'You weren't in the army like me but it's really no different. The Emperor pays us to get rid of his enemies.'

'It's not the same as fighting on a battlefield. Nobody gets a medal for killing a fat, old man.'

'Don't bet on it. In any case, that fat, old man is endangering this entire province. One way or another, he's going to Hades.'

'How...how would I do it? How would *you* do it?'

'That's up to you, lad. I'm leaving in the morning.'

'What?' Tarchon stopped in the middle of the road.

Korax kept walking.

I don't believe this. I've barely known this bastard two weeks and he wants me to kill a man?

But as he stood there, Korax's footsteps growing increasingly faint, Tarchon admitted to himself that he shouldn't really have been surprised. In fact, hadn't part of him expected this?

He ran and caught up with Korax, who eventually spoke again.

'If it helps, you should know that there's not much honour on the battlefield either. Killing's killing. If fortune goes your way and some poor sod drops his sword, you stick him. If he trips at the wrong moment, you stick him. And you thank the gods for their favour.'

'But in cold blood, sir. You know what I'm saying.'

At last, Korax stopped. 'I do, lad. I do. And if you can't manage it then this will be your last job. Like I said, Demetrius' time is up. The question is, are you going to pass the final test? You get this done for Gargonius, and you'll be set fair.'

'Is this what the job is? Killing?'

'Sometimes. Not often. But if you can't do it, you're no use to us. No use at all.'

Tarchon just shook his head. Thanks to an unlikely turn of fate, or the hand of Minerva – or both – he had somehow escaped mutilation or worse at the hands of the law. There was always going to be a price to pay.

'I saw the look on your face when I gave you those coins,' said Korax. 'It was a bloody long time ago but I remember getting my first pay packet from the legion. Second best day of my life. You know now where I came from – a family of shepherds. We never ate *one* of those sheep. Sold every last bloody one. I barely knew what meat tasted like. In the worst winters, my mother and father would go short so we could get something in our stomachs. My first leave I walked back there loaded down with more silver coins than my father had ever seen. That was the *best* day of my life. You want *your* handful of coins next month? Every month? For five years? Ten? Then you do as you're ordered. No questions asked.'

XIV

It was unusual for Tarchon not to fall asleep quickly, but that night he lay awake, eyes open, mind racing. Only feet away, sleeping silently once more, was the man who had brought him to this place and told him of his task. Tarchon could not forget the image of the fat seer, Demetrius. How would it be done? Sword? Dagger? With his hands? The more important question was, *could* he even do it? Twice in his life, he had set out to take revenge on enemies; attack in cold blood. And he had done damage both times; once to a crook who'd cheated him, once to a man who'd insulted his aunt.

This was completely different. Could he even deal with the fear of it? And how would he feel when it was done? As the hours wore on, into the depths of the night, he realised he could never know.

Close to dawn, he did fall asleep, only to soon be woken by Korax.

'Breakfast is on its way. We're eating in here.'

The agent was already dressed and now opened the shutters of the room's single window. The morning sun and the noises of the street burst inside. Korax dragged over the tiny table and two accompanying stools, then stood gazing at the street below. Throwing off his blanket and sitting up, Tarchon saw his companion's full pack leaning against his neatly-made bed.

Predictably, it was Korax's admirer who delivered their breakfast. Today, it was hot fare: thick wheat pancakes with dates and honey. As Korax took the two plates, the woman remarked that she was sorry to hear he was leaving. After she left and Tarchon joined him at the table, Korax shook his head.

'Gods, imagine bedding that one – you'd be lucky to come out alive.'

Tarchon was not in the mood for humour but a jape from Korax was a rarity and he grinned as he tucked into the pancakes. Oddly, given the circumstances, the earlier tension between them seemed to have lessened. He supposed it was because they were about to go their separate ways.

'Can you give me any help?'

'Don't think you need it,' said Korax, finishing his last mouthful of pancake. 'You've handled everything else we've thrown at you.'

'It's not just finding a way to do it.'

'I know. You wonder if you can live with it.'

'Yes.'

Korax turned towards him and ran a hand across his shiny scalp. 'Unlike our fat friend, I can't claim to know the future. What I do know is that *you* didn't make this decision. *You* didn't decide his fate.'

Korax moved his stool so that his back was resting against the wall. He gazed at the floor for a time before speaking. 'Second campaign against the Goths. We were south of the Dacian mountains, trying to push them back north, as usual. For months we fought them, with no reinforcements and not a day of rest. Our legate had orders that we were not to take a single backwards step.

'I was a guard officer then – third in command. But my centurion was long dead and my optio recovering from a nasty head wound. So I was in charge. But not of eighty men: we were down to fifty by then and, if memory serves, I had only thirty or so with me on that day.

'Winter was near. We were out looking for food, raiding hamlets in the foothills, though the locals had already been robbed repeatedly by both sides. They had never resisted before but that day they fought back. Ambushed us. Forty, maybe fifty men, but they didn't have our weapons and they fought like a rabble. Brave bastards though. Didn't stop until we'd cut them all down. Must have killed half, wounded the rest. Lost six legionaries.

'I couldn't go back to the camp empty-handed; the senior centurion was depending on me. We cut off the head of the leader and walked into the village. I stuck the head on a stake and told them to give us everything they had. What I didn't know was that the man had lost his daughter only days earlier. Some idiot from another century had his way with her, slit her throat and chucked her down a well.

'I only found that out afterward. But as soon as we walked into the village, they came for us. Women and children, throwing stones, sticks, anything they could lay their hands on. Gods, they hated us. One woman came at me with a pitchfork. I ran her through.'

Korax showed no trace of unease or guilt as he said these words. Tarchon imagined that he'd thought or spoken of the incident many times. It was as if he had made his peace with it.

'That stopped it, at least. Stopped *them*. Stopped *my* men too. Afterwards, it didn't seem right to take anything. We left without a morsel. All for nothing. The whole day. All those lives.'

Korax turned and glanced out of the window, eyes narrowed against the sun. 'It wasn't my decision. I was ordered to do it by the legate, who was ordered to do so by the Emperor.'

'Do you regret it?'

'For many years, I thought of it every day. The noise of the blade going in, the sigh as she fell. The screams that came after. I wish it could all have been different but it was not. I did the right thing for my century, for my army, my Emperor.'

'You don't think of it now?'

'Sometimes. I'm telling you, lad, because there is no sense getting hung up on the rights and wrongs. The likes of us do not give orders, we carry them out.'

'What if the gods punish us? For doing wrong?'

'I'll tell you what a tribune told me. Rome has ruled most of the world for a thousand years. If the gods are not for us, who *are* they for?'

After Korax left, Tarchon laid back down on the bed. He somehow felt both a great pressure and a great freedom. He had money in his pocket, new clothes, weapons, and a horse in the stable. If he so wished, he could forget Korax and Gargonius and the mission: go south or east, anywhere he wanted. But if he was to continue the mission and return to Green Cove, he needed to leave immediately. Korax had instructed him to carry out his task and return to Byzantium as swiftly as possible.

Sick of the stuffy room, Tarchon went downstairs and into the stable. The young lad was there and told him that Ambler was happy enough. Tarchon went to the stall and even raised a smile when the horse shuffled about and raised its head to greet him. He patted the animal on the muzzle.

You don't have all this to worry about do you? Lucky sod. Wish my life was so simple.

Tarchon wandered out of the stable, feeling a little better on the streets, anonymous once more in the busy city. With no thought other than to find his way forward, he kept on the move, striding swiftly but turning corners with little thought to his direction. Despite the movement and noise around him, he thought only of Green Cove, of the villa and the beach, and the man he had been sent to kill.

Despite all the tests they had thrown at him in Byzantium and his discussions with Korax, he could still not quite believe that they expected him to do it.

'She is with you!' said a female voice brimming with conviction.

The woman who'd said it was already past him. He turned to see that there were actually three of them: all clad in long robes, one carrying a painted figurine. Tarchon had no idea which god or goddess the trio followed but the moment gave him a sudden clarity:

He would find out if there was a Temple of Minerva in Nicomedia. He would go there and see if the goddess could help him once more. So far, the signs suggested that she had offered him this opportunity and expected him to take it. But if he did what he'd been ordered to, nothing would be the same again. He needed to be sure.

Heading back to the inn to ask the sisters about the temple, he turned left at the next junction into a quieter street. He hadn't gone far when he passed a small building squeezed between two walled townhouses. Four columns flanked a wooden door scarred by numerous holes and discolorations. A pigeon was pecking something in one corner of the courtyard and in another lay a shattered amphora. The place had seen better days but the altar at the courtyard's centre left him in no doubt that this was a temple.

Tarchon was about to ask a passer-by about the place when he spied the small, crude sculpture carved below the apex of the roof. It was no more than two feet high, the features and detail heavily weathered. But the shapes on the goddess' shoulder and in her hand were clear. The owl and the sword.

Minerva.

He did not need to pray, nor enter the temple.

She had spoken.

Within an hour, he was already on the outskirts of the city, headed for Green Cove. He bought some bread and cheese on his way, placing it in his pack with a water-filled flask borrowed from the sisters.

Now without Korax's guidance, he approached the villa even more warily, staying on the coast road for longer and waiting until there was no one in sight before cutting down to the observation post. He completed the last quarter-mile on his belly and moved three times before settling on a position within the clump of bushes. Wiping sweat from his brow and face, he sat down and surveyed the villa. The first thing he noticed was the carriage in the courtyard. This was a promising sign; he needed to see at least one more whole day of activity.

That day was a warm one and it passed slowly, the only scare coming when two hares bounded across the slope, momentarily convincing Tarchon that he was being attacked from behind. He ate the cheese early on because it was beginning to sweat and smell and nibbled the bread until it was gone. He only moved to stretch his limbs and relieve himself, having drunk most of the water by mid-afternoon. But by the time the sun began to sink over his left shoulder, he had learned much more about the staff's routines and seen the target himself three times.

It was essential that he leave before sundown because he wanted to get a sight of the terrain beyond the southern headland at the far end of Green Cove. Once there, he discovered that it was far from ideal but acceptable for his purposes. Still refining his plan, he completed a final task then made his way back up to the road. He waited for two horsemen to pass, then headed back to Nicomedia at a run.

Fearing that he wouldn't be able to sleep, Tarchon asked for some strong wine and took a mug up to his room after dinner. He then set about readying his gear to the accompanying sound of drums and flutes drifting in through the window from somewhere. On the way back to the Camel, he had purchased thirty feet of good quality rope and a water bladder. He looped up the rope and retied it so it would take up less space. The bladder was of the type used for transporting liquids, the dried skin topped by a wooden cap. This and the rope he placed in his pack along with his dagger and another flask of water. He gave no thought to food.

His sword, blanket and other gear would stay in the room until he left the following evening (assuming all went to plan). As far as the sisters were concerned, he had stayed on to conclude some business for Korax. With his brief work done, he stood at the window and looked out at the night, the mug in his hand. The music had stopped now and, other than footsteps and muted conversation, all was quiet outside. He drank the wine quickly.

Reaching the south gate just after dawn, he was ignored by the officials and guards there and was soon back on the coast road. He was determined not to get distracted and didn't allow himself to think beyond what he could see and hear and smell. This was something he'd often done when he faced a difficult task that required effort and concentration. And so, he inspected the flowers growing by the side of the road, inhaled the salty tang of the sea, listened to the cries of the seagulls above.

Coming around a bend, only a mile or so from Green Cove, he encountered what looked like a full century of the Roman army. They had occupied a large field enclosed by a stone wall and seemed to be carrying out battle drills, supervised by two officers with crested helmets. Three lads in threadbare tunics were sitting on the wall munching apples, only yards from the coast road.

By the time he reached them, Tarchon had muttered a series of bitter oaths.

'What's all this about then?'

'Fifth cohort,' said one the lads, as if he was an expert in military matters. 'Getting some practice in.'

'Why here?' asked Tarchon.

'They often use this field. There's not much space in the city.'

Tarchon tried to tell himself that this needn't affect his mission but the presence of eighty soldiers so close to Green Cove wasn't a particularly good start to the day. After a final glance at the century – who were now rearranging themselves into a box formation – he hurried away.

Having turned off the coast road onto the track, he'd gone only a few yards when he spied a cart coming up from the villa. Diving to his left and lying on the ground behind a low bush, he avoided detection. As the cart trundled past, he smelt fish and assumed that the driver supplied Demetrius' household. Cursing himself for even setting foot on the road, Tarchon took to the dusty, scrubby ground above it, staying low until he reached the observation post. Once there, he swigged down some much-needed water and watched the villa.

To his right, in the courtyard, the lad was by a stall, petting one of the horses. Only a few yards away, two men were doing something to one of the carriage wheels. Within the sparkling villa itself, the shutters were already open but Tarchon spied only glimpses of movement. The gardener was currently visible at the front of the house, meticulously picking flowers from the beds and placing them in a basket. To the left was the path that led down to the beach. An easterly breeze had created a little chop on the water which Tarchon reckoned would work to his benefit. If the wind strengthened too much, however, his chances of success would diminish.

Around the third hour, Demetrius came outside with what looked like the housekeeper. Sitting in a large chair brought out by the gardener, the seer had his hair cut. One of the bodyguards appeared and stationed himself nearby. Demetrius sat with his hands clasped upon his heavy stomach. He seemed fussy; regularly issuing orders to the housekeeper and demanding to see the back of his head in a mirror.

After a while, Tarchon found that he couldn't look at the man, knowing what he was supposed to – no, *knowing* what *he was going* to do. Then he cursed himself for such weakness and forced himself to look.

It is Minerva's will. It is not my decision. It is for the Empire. It is not my decision.

It was for the money too, of course, but he preferred not to dwell on that.

Around the fifth hour, Demetrius reappeared in the garden and for a time stood utterly still, gazing up at the sky. It was then that Tarchon remembered that the seer apparently used the weather to aid his prophecies. Demetrius shouted an order and a younger man joined him, holding a tablet and stylus. The clerk followed his master, making notes as Demetrius paced back and forth across the garden, dictating.

By the sixth hour, the men in the courtyard had finished with the carriage wheel and had also cleaned the entire vehicle. Tarchon feared that Demetrius was headed to the city but the horses remained in their stalls and he knew that such men preferred to conduct their business before noon.

With the sun directly above, Tarchon knew it was time to move. He carefully extricated himself from the bushes and retraced his steps up the slope. He never actually reached the road but continued south across the dusty ground, avoiding some of the spikier bushes and areas of treacherous shale that could send him tumbling.

Soon he was on a steeper slope, ascending the headland that enclosed the far end of Green Cove. At the top, he kept low and looked back along the coast. The villa and the beach looked small from this elevated position. Tarchon pressed on, aware that he would only have limited time to strike.

The far side of the headland adjoined one end of a very different cove: there was no beach there, just a wall of rock. Having descended this way once before, he moved from slippery, sandy earth on to solid rock before finally reaching the water. Here, the sea slapped and sloshed against the rocks, a sharp contrast to the placid beach on the other side of the headland.

First checking that there was no one above who might observe, Tarchon removed his pack and took off his tunic and sandals. Now clad in only his loincloth, he sat on a ledge beside the rock he had placed there the previous day. It was about the size of a melon and he reckoned it weighed at least twenty pounds, which would be enough. Taking the bladder from the pack, he unscrewed the cap and blew into it until it was almost fully inflated. He lost a bit of air when he put the cap back on but knew that wouldn't matter. He then took out the rope and tied it around the rock, circling it five times and checking carefully to ensure it was secure.

Moving closer to the water, he lowered his feet in and then dropped the bladder between them. He placed the rock on the bladder and was relieved to find that it easily supported the weight. He knew from his fishing experience how tough and buoyant they were. He grabbed the end of the rope and tied it into a slipknot of the kind hunters used in snares.

From there, he took a final look around, satisfied himself that he was alone, and slipped down into the water, which wasn't too cold at all. Wary of unseen obstacles below the surface, he gently pushed off and headed around the rocky headland.

It was not easy going. The incoming waves pushed him towards the shore, which heightened the risk of injury or losing the rock. Nearing the promontory's rounded tip, he glimpsed a pair of small fishing boats offshore, glad they were too far away to see him. Hands on the bladder, he used only his legs, pushing himself through the water at a steady speed.

Suddenly, a larger wave came out of nowhere, lifting him up and casting him towards the rocks. Fortunately, he was opposite a niche in the formation and he escaped harm. But when he kicked out to get clear, his right foot grazed solid rock. Feeling warm blood flow, he could only hope that the injury wasn't too bad. Freeing one hand to pull away from danger, he then ingested a mouthful of water and swam into a patch of weed.

By all the gods! What next?

With a wary eye on the incoming waves, he steadied himself and pushed on. Rounding the headland, he was surprised by how far away the villa seemed. And when he saw the beach unoccupied, he wondered if Demetrius was not taking his early afternoon swim on this day.

Though confident that he couldn't be seen at such distance against the dark grey rock, Tarchon accelerated, now benefiting from the waves running into the cove. He soon reached the gloomy cave, and here the current also pushed him in. The water and the air were colder inside, the roof and walls unusually smooth. Eventually finding a hold, he secured himself on the landward side of the cave, his free hand on the bladder, his gaze fixed on the beach.

He saw no one. The seconds passed, then the minutes. Now still, he felt cold leeching in through his fingers and toes. After what he guessed to be about a quarter of an hour, he left the bladder and swam around the cave just to warm up. It didn't seem to make any difference. He had just returned to the bladder when he saw movement on the path that led to the beach.

Demetrius, wrapped in the flowing robe he normally wore before his swim.

Minerva, I thank you.

Behind the seer came the shorter of the two bodyguards. As they reached the sand, Demetrius took off his robe and handed it to the bodyguard.

Yes. Stick to your routine. Same as before.

The seer stood there for a while, evidently unconcerned by his nakedness upon the private beach. He gazed out at the water, then began to move his arms in circles to warm up. The bodyguard walked over to the stone bench Tarchon had earlier observed close to the path. He carefully laid out his master's robe then sat beside it.

Demetrius yawned, then ambled into the water. When it reached his waist, he began flicking handfuls onto his flabby chest. Smoothing down his hair, he took a few steps, then dived in with surprising grace. Emerging some distance away, he turned onto his back and languidly propelled himself away from the shore.

Stick to your routine. Same as before.

As if listening, Demetrius turned onto his front and began his usual breast stroke, heading towards the villa end of the cove. Tarchon moved up to the edge of the cave. He waited and watched, the cold now forgotten.

Demetrius halted only a few feet from the rocks of the opposite headland, turned and began his gentle, steady strokes once more. Tarchon found his eyes drifting up into the blue sky and his thoughts drifting to the question he'd tried so hard to avoid.

Why? Why kill him? Why?
The decision has been made. It is Minerva's will.
You want this new life? This is the price you have to pay.

The bodyguard was slouched on the bench, arms crossed. Demetrius passed him, the features of his face now visible. Tarchon estimated that his target was a hundred and fifty feet away. Time to move.

He swam out of the cave and along the side of the headland, towards shore. He held the bladder to his left, obscuring his face. At that distance, with that slight chop on the water, he thought it unlikely that Demetrius would see him. In any case, he had only to reach a sharp outcrop, close to where the old man usually turned. That was where he would strike from.

By the time he got there, he could hear him. The seer had switched to backstroke and it was far from smooth. Tarchon watched him from the landward side of the outcrop, which was covered in little shells that fell off at the slightest touch. Demetrius glided a little way on his back then returned to breast stroke. He was no more than twenty feet away now: close enough to see his pink cheeks, his bushy eyebrows, the white hair plastered to his brow.

He slowed again, drew in some deep breaths, then turned around, revealing a broad back marked by dark moles. Twelve feet away, no more. Tarchon looked past him: the guard was still on the bench, sunning himself.

Gripping the rope just above the knot, he pushed himself away from the outcrop, then dived gently down. Once his feet were submerged, he kicked hard, also using his spare hand for power. Only when he was a good ten feet under did he head up towards Demetrius, already aiming for the large white legs. Though the incoming waves moved Tarchon around, they did not slow him. He kicked hard again as he closed in. He hadn't the breath to let the doubts in.

Now or never.

Once within reach, he gripped the old man's left ankle and yanked him downward. He heard a splutter and hoped the noise hadn't reached the shore. Head now submerged, Demetrius initially seemed too surprised to struggle. Tarchon slipped the snare over his foot, then pulled it tight. He turned, yanked the rope and saw the splash as the rock came off the bladder. It sank swiftly towards the sand far below.

He still had hold of Demetrius and now the old man was kicking. Gripping hard, Tarchon pushed water with his spare hand, holding himself – and Demetrius – below the surface. Then the rope went tight, pulling the leg down. Already struggling, Demetrius was hauled lower. Tarchon glimpsed flailing arms, a terrified face and an open mouth, trailing bubbles.

But by then he was running out of breath himself. Spinning around, he swam for the outcrop, only allowing himself up when he could touch it. Though his head broke the surface slowly, he sucked in breath, lights flashing in his eyes.

When those lights cleared, he turned around.

Of Demetrius there was not a trace.

On the beach, the guard had not moved and there was no one else in sight. Tarchon looked around for the bladder but saw that it had been washed towards the rocks at the corner of the cove. He wasn't going to waste time recovering it. If they found the old man, they would know he'd been murdered anyway.

Using the outcrop for cover, he swam directly towards the headland, inhaling deeply to ready himself for the next dive. Then he went under again, breathing evenly but swimming strongly, now fighting the currents. When he came up and glanced back at the shore, the bodyguard still hadn't moved. Under again, ten more strokes, and up he came.

He was tiring quickly but making good progress. He glanced back at the shore. On the beach, the guard had just jumped up from the bench. He looked out across the cove, hand shielding his eyes. Then he shouted up at the house, threw off his sword-belt and sprinted across the sand. Tarchon waited until he flung himself into the water before diving again. Two more spurts took him to the headland.

When he took his last look back, he realised that the bodyguard wasn't much of a swimmer. He was still fifty feet from the outcrop, yelling, his voice laced with fear and panic.

'Master? Master!'

XV

They seemed like the wrong feelings. As he dragged himself back onto the rock ledge and flicked a string of weed off his hand, Tarchon felt only relief and satisfaction. He knew it should have been guilt and shame but perhaps those would come later. Still breathing hard from the swim, he was pleased to see that the damage to his foot was only minor: some skin torn off his toes. It was no longer bleeding, just stinging.

He wiped water off his shoulders and chest, then smoothed his hair back to keep it out of his face. He put on his tunic and his sandals. As he swung the pack over his shoulder, he imagined the scene on the other side of the headland. The guards might already suspect foul play and it wouldn't take much to work out where the threat could have come from. Picturing them marching towards him, Tarchon began clambering up the rocks. And then – having avoided making any obvious mistakes – he made a terrible one.

Only yards from the sandy section of the slope, he jumped across a little gully no more than four feet wide. As he landed, his left foot slipped and he came down hard, his left arm smashing into a nasty little point of solid rock. He knew instantly it was bad. Still on his knees, he turned the arm to inspect the wound and watched the blood begin to flow. The neat gash in his skin was an inch across and alarmingly deep.

Oh gods no. Not here. Not now.

Tarchon had cut himself many times before but not like this. The blood wasn't dripping, it was streaming out, splashing the rock below. Vision blurring, he lurched backwards, somehow retaining his balance. He knew that if he didn't act quickly, he was going to faint.

Get off the rocks. Sit down. Tie it.

Forcing himself to take steady, slow steps – arm held up – he negotiated the remainder of the rock, then slumped down onto a patch of sand. Shrugging the pack off his right shoulder, he pulled out his dagger and unsheathed it. Holding the pack steady with his feet, he cut off the leather strap, which was about three feet long. Forcing himself to not look at the wound – or listen to the thick gouts of blood dropping onto the sand – he wrapped the strap around his arm. The pain turned his stomach but he kept at it and tucked the end in. By now, most of his left arm was covered by blood. He held it up with his right hand.

Gradually, the blood began to slow, until there was only a single stream running down his skin. Only now did he allow himself to look up the slope of the headland. Thankfully, there was no one there.

Yet.

Tarchon just sat there with his aching arm in the air, bleeding, cursing himself for this almost laughable mistake. He cringed as he imagined explaining to Korax that he had carried out his mission successfully, only to slip over and cut himself up like some old codger.

The bleeding had slowed to a drip. Holding his pack in his right hand, he hauled himself to his feet and started up the headland, every step now doubly trying. All that mattered was getting as far away from Green Cove as possible. He doubted he could reach Nicomedia but if he could just find somewhere to hide out until nightfall, he would have a chance. Plodding upward, blood dripping onto the sandy ground, he wondered if he was dreaming.

Concentrating on not fainting and putting one foot in front of the other, he didn't realise he had scaled the headland until the ground levelled out. Passing through a small patch of ground blackened by fire, Tarchon walked between two ruined trees and found himself facing an old wall. He staggered over to one of the more solid sections and slumped against it, holding his left arm clear. It hurt more than anything he had ever experienced; a sharp, pulsing ache that made him want to throw up.

Thankfully, there was a damaged section of the wall nearby and he was soon through it. And there – no more than fifty feet ahead – was the ditch that edged the seaward side of the coast road. Part of him just wanted to get on it, walk to Nicomedia and not stop until he reached the safety of his room. But he knew he'd need to find another way.

His first step towards the road was an unsteady one but he told himself to keep going, just keep moving. Dimly aware of a rhythmic tapping sound, he forced himself to take step after step until he reached the ditch. Though it was no more than a couple of feet deep, getting across was quite a struggle.

Straightening up, he found himself gazing down at the broad, smooth stone slabs. The tapping was louder now. He put his finger in his ear but the noise remained. He saw blood colouring the stones, only belatedly realizing it was his. He lurched back a step, almost fell.

Keep moving. You can't stay on the road. Keep moving.

He glimpsed movement to his left. Men. Many of them, marching towards him. His memory flashed to that morning – watching them drilling in the field. Soldiers. Legionaries.

Keep moving. Get off the road.

He started across it, saw a flash of sky then felt his chest thump into stone. The thunder of the century's boots was still pounding in his ears when all became dark.

A spot of dim, yellow light.

The smell of food. Meat. Spices.

Beneath his right hand, smooth strands – grass or straw.

'Chloe? The one with the big arse?'

'No, that's Anastasia. Chloe wears the yellow tunic – she brought the vinegar out.'

'Mmm. Can't picture her.'

'I can.'

'I bet you do – every night. Oh look, he's awake.'

Propping himself up on his right elbow, Tarchon saw the light come towards him. It was a lamp, in the hand of a man with spiky, fair hair wearing a red tunic and wide belt.

'How you doing, mate?'

Tarchon tried to speak but his throat was horribly dry. The soldier put the lamp down and sat on a stool. He then reached for a flask and offered it to him. Tarchon only remembered the left arm when he tried to move it.

'I wouldn't. That's worse than some sword wounds I've seen.'

The legionary held the flask so that Tarchon could drink.

Now he remembered; falling on the rock, reaching the road, fainting.

So, they had him now. He was a prisoner. He had failed.

'Slipped on the rocks, did you?' asked the soldier. 'We reckoned you'd been swimming. Good idea to strap it with the belt but you lost a lot of blood. Good pint or two, that's what Egnatius reckons.'

Tarchon couldn't believe it. They didn't know.

The second soldier spoke up. He was leaning against the wall, arms crossed. 'He's our medic. Better than most of the surgeons I've met. He cleaned you up, stitched your arm. You are one lucky bastard.'

Tarchon couldn't argue with that. He winced as he turned his arm over. The stitches were black, the flesh swollen and coloured yellow and pink.

'Still hurts, I expect,' said the first man.

'Not too bad,' croaked Tarchon.

'That'll be the strong wine Egnatius gave you. It'll wear off.'

'Is he here?'

'Nah. Getting his dinner. And nobody interrupts Egnatius' dinner.'

'Where are we?'

'Way-station outside Astakos. About eight miles south of Nicomedia. We should have been going back to the capital but some tribune wants us to help with a section of road outside Liada.'

'Our centurion would have walked right by you,' said the second man. 'But Egnatius thought we should do you a good turn. He said the gods might remember it next time we face battle.'

'You carried me?'

'We're legionaries, mate. Took turns. Not a problem.'

'I'm very grateful,' said Tarchon. 'Thank you. But I really should be going. My...father will be very worried.'

'No, no,' said the legionary, placing a hand on his shoulder. You're staying here until dawn. Egnatius' instructions.'

Lacking the energy to argue, Tarchon carefully turned onto his back and laid down, slowly lowering his arm onto the mattress. It was very comfortable, too comfortable in fact, because he almost drifted back into sleep.

Stay awake! You have to stay awake.

But his eyes were closed, and it soon became clear that the soldiers thought he was sleeping.

'Seems all right.'

'He's fine. Just needs rest. Let's go and get our grub.'

Minerva stares with spear in hand, gazing into the distance, marble face impassive.

Her eyes snap open.

Her eyes?

No. Mine.

Tarchon was alone in the little room. After a couple of deep breaths, he shook off the dream and sat up. The effects of the wine must have begun to wear off because he now just felt *very* tired. But he knew that this was a chance – possibly his only chance – to escape the soldiers. They had inadvertently saved him but if news of Demetrius' demise reached the way-station, he was in serious trouble.

Using his right hand, he removed the two blankets covering him. He was still wearing his tunic, which had only a few bloodstains on the left side. Turning onto his front, he then got to his knees. Dragging the stool close, he used it to steady himself and slowly stood. The aches across the rest of his body subsided as his left arm began to throb. The flesh there – inside and out – had been torn up, knocked about, then stitched. No wonder it hurt.

Where's my gear?

The only pieces of furniture were a table and a chest. Tarchon searched them but saw no trace of his pack. He wondered if the soldiers might have looked inside, perhaps even stolen his money and dagger. Suddenly feeling faint again, he leant back against the table and took five deep breaths. Then he saw his pack and his sandals; he had inadvertently covered them with the blankets. Thankfully, the money, dagger and flask were intact. He put his sandals on and picked up the pack.

The door had not been closed. Peering out through the narrow gap, Tarchon spied a shadowy corridor leading to what looked like the parlour. He eased the door open and slipped through it. Male and female voices laughed at something and he used the noise to advance a few paces. He passed another open door and a room with two bunk beds. There was only one occupant: a snoring man lying on a top bunk, leg hanging over the edge.

Through the parlour door, Tarchon could see a dozen legionaries gathered by a counter where a woman was stacking plates. But there was only a weak lamp in the corridor and he was sure they couldn't see him. Staying away from the lamp, he took a few more paces and reached the adjoining corridor outside the parlour. To the left it led to more rooms. But only ten feet to his right was a larger door with a muddy mat in front of it and a wicker basket containing a couple of walking sticks.

Hoping that the legionaries stayed where they were, he tiptoed to the door. Careful with the latch and handle, he opened it and stepped outside. The chill wind cooled his warm face and he felt a surge of relief as he closed the door behind him. Hearing some horses stirring nearby, he briefly wondered if he should take one. As it stood, he doubted the soldiers would pursue him; but the outcome could be very different if he stole a horse. He also had to consider the likely possibility that – in his present condition – he would fall out of the saddle.

Judging by the activity in the way-station parlour, he adjudged it was late evening. That meant he had many hours of darkness to get away from this place, so he immediately walked onto the road and headed north. He needed to cover a lot of ground but had no intention of passing anywhere close to Green Cove. Then he had to reach Nicomedia, fetch his gear, then get out of Bithnyia. But for now, he had a single concern.

Don't faint. Just don't faint.

The wind was a blessing. Chill and sharp, it blew in off the sea and kept him cold and alert. There was scant cover and this section of the road seldom strayed far from the coast. Other than the gusts whistling through rocks to his left or rustling the trees to his right, the only sound was his sandals on the paving stones. The noise helped him keep a good rhythm and pace.

Once he started at what sounded like someone approaching from behind but after an hour or so it truly seemed as if he was the only person alive, stalking along the exposed road through the night. The pain from his arm did not lessen and he walked with his right hand circling his left wrist to take some of the weight off.

He imagined the scene the soldiers had come upon that afternoon: a bleeding youth lying in the middle of the road. How fortunate he'd been that Egnatius and the others had taken pity on him. Legionaries were not known for their acts of charity.

You absolute idiot. You bloody fool.

But at least he was out of the strange trap he'd found himself in; and with his arm stitched up and now able to escape.

Two hours? Three?

He halted and drank the remaining water in his flask, wishing he had a bucket full. Replacing it in the pack, he gazed out at the dim outline of a long, curved bay. He had no idea how far he was from Green Cove but was sure of one thing; he didn't want to get any closer.

Tracks ran inland from the coast road at regular intervals and he took the next one, hoping this would give him room for manoeuvre in the morning. After a couple of hundred paces, it took him up a slope, then veered north down one flank of a broad, low valley. It was only when the path became muddy and wet that he realised the valley was bisected by a river. This at least confirmed that he was still some way south of Green Cove because he and Korax had not passed over or near any river.

Even though the water glittered under the moonlight, it was hard to estimate its width. Now dotted with puddles, the path veered to the right, running parallel to the river. Tarchon halted and looked in both directions but he could see no sign of a bridge. He was about ready to drop and so decided to do exactly that. Retracing his steps to a drier patch of ground, he located some low bushes that would at least provide a little cover.

Having slowed down since turning off the coast road, he was already cold when he sat on the ground. He undid his sandals and removed them and used his pack for a pillow. He lay on his good side and tucked the fingers of his left hand into his belt so his injured arm wouldn't fall. Cold had seeped into the tender flesh, magnifying the pain. Close to the ground, the piney scent of the bushes mingled with the brackish water to unpleasant effect. Tarchon closed his eyes, glad at least to be still.

There was so much he could have thought of then: the fact that he had killed a man; the fact that he was in all likelihood being hunted, the fact that he'd suffered the worst injury of his life. But only one fact – one oversight – seemed to matter.

Why, why, why did I not pack my blanket?

XVI

Whiskers trembling, the vole's beady eyes examined the big, strange shape in front of it. A loud yawn from the newly-awake Tarchon sent the rodent scampering back into the bushes.

'Shit and shit again.' Sitting up, he looked down at a tunic stained with mud, blood and rabbit droppings. Wincing, he turned his arm over. The stitches were a livid red, the swelling visibly worse. Thirsty once more, he opened the flask and drank the last few drops. Getting to his knees was unpleasant, getting to his feet even worse. He again felt faint and knew he was in desperate need of food and water if he was to reach Nicomedia.

By the looks of it, the sun had been up for about an hour and he could now see the lay of the land. The river was about fifty feet across; a slow-moving waterway thick with weed. The far side looked similar to the near, though there were more banks of reed. Beyond them, the land rose up and – north of where the river met the sea – was a headland very much like those at Green Cove. Clear now in the morning light was the dark arch of a bridge that crossed the river close to the sea.

The next sight caused Tarchon to smile. About a quarter-mile to his right, two deer were halfway across the river: the water was barely up to their haunches.

Wading across turned out to be the easy part. The riverbed was much softer on the far side and it took an age for him to drag himself through a series of mudflats and reedbeds. Some of those reeds were as tall as a man, which was why he failed to notice the two cutters until he was almost on top of them.

Coming around a bend, he found the men tying great handfuls of the plants, ready for a pile of those already baled.

'Gods!' exclaimed the older of the pair, putting a hand to his heart. 'Where'd you come from?'

'Across the river.'

The younger man peered at him from below a low fringe and made an odd sound.

'Don't mind him,' said the older man, chucking a newly-tied bale onto the pile. 'He don't talk. Where you headed?'

Tarchon was careful to keep his left arm down so that they didn't see the wound.

'The city.'

'Should have crossed the bridge.'

'Saw a couple of deer crossing – seemed like a good short cut.'

'Mmm.' The local nodded at the path that led out of the reeds and up to the higher ground. 'Follow that, turn left and you'll meet the coast road. Four miles to the city.'

'Thank you. Is there anywhere closer – where I might get some food?'

'If you can spare the time, turn right towards Bithynion. The road passes Delai.'

'Is that a village?'

'Small one. Dozen houses. No stores but someone will make you something or give you something if you have coin.'

Tarchon had at least packed that: he still had three denarii.

'Much obliged.' He walked on, now moving his arm across his body to obscure the wound.

'Gods' favour,' said the man.

'And to you.'

The Bithynion road was busy, mostly with carts full of produce headed for the capital's markets. As well as hides, wicker and fine ware, there were baskets and amphora overflowing with greens, artichokes, beans, plums, apricots and cherries. Though he walked alongside the road to draw less attention to himself, Tarchon couldn't help eyeing the fruit and by the time he reached Delai, he was famished.

A stone's throw from the road, the hamlet consisted of a few mud-brick houses built on either side of a track that ran north. Unsurprisingly, the triangular roofs were covered with dried reeds. At the first house, a man and a woman were piling bunches of dried flowers on the back of a pony.

'Good day,' said Tarchon, holding up a denarius. 'Do you know of anyone who will cook me a meal?'

The woman answered: 'Eulalia – third house on the right. She's a decent cook.'

'Decent?' said the man. 'Compared to you, she's brilliant.'

The woman shot him a glare. 'You can finish loading up yourself.'

The man rolled his eyes as Tarchon continued. Reaching the third house, he could see someone moving around inside through the open door.

'Hello? Eulalia?'

A plump, barefoot woman wearing a brown tunic and a woollen shawl appeared in the doorway.

'Yes?'

'Your neighbours said that I might buy some food from you.'

'I'm not baking this week – no good wheat.'

'Ah.'

'But I can make you a hot plate of food,' she added. 'Yesterday's pork stew with greens? I've a few almond cakes left over too.'

'Sounds good to me. Do you have any wine?'

'Yes.' Eulalia stepped out into the sunlight, revealing a lined, pleasant face and greying hair tied in a ponytail. 'Food won't be long.' She gestured to a short, narrow bench under a window. 'Move it into the sun if you like.'

Tarchon did just that and, when he sat down, almost toppled off the bench. He didn't dare look at his left arm but rested it on his lap. Eulalia came out with a large wooden mug of watered wine. He thanked her, then downed half in one go. Though it was thin and bitter, he was so thirsty that every drop was a delight. He heard Eulalia putting more wood on a fire, presumably to heat his stew and greens.

He looked over to his left and watched the warring couple set off on the cart. On the road beyond, he counted no less than eight vehicles headed for Nicomedia.

'A few days' old but the taste is still there.' Eulalia brought out a plate with three small cakes.

'Thank you,' said Tarchon. 'Tell me, if I continue along this track, is there another way to the capital?'

'There is. Not easy to follow but this early there'll be enough people around to ask the way. You'll come in at the east gate. Six miles or so. The Roman road is quicker.'

As Eulalia returned inside, Tarchon sipped his wine and he thought about Green Cove. Not about what he'd done – he could not face that yet – but what might have happened in the hours since. Was the death considered murder? Did the governor know of his friend's demise? How would he react? Send out the army? Tarchon wondered if he even dared return to the inn. Should he avoid the city completely?

Though gripped by these questions and the fear they provoked, Tarchon's appetite remained unaffected. When Eulalia brought out the stew, he took a spoon and immediately tucked in. The stew had smelled good while cooking and lived up to expectations: the meat was tender, the vegetables not too soft and the sauce spicy. Even the greens tasted better than usual.

'You're a good cook,' he said between mouthfuls.

'Thank you,' said Eulalia, now hanging washing on a rack that she'd also placed in the sunshine.

'I don't suppose you'd have a long-sleeved tunic or shirt I could buy?'

She frowned. 'You do know that there are hundreds of sellers in the city?'

'I do.'

Eulalia walked over to him. 'You're about the same size as my husband. I might have something but it won't be anything nice.'

'That's all right. I just need something to cover my arms. Got sunburned yesterday.'

He wasn't sure she believed this but she went into the house nonetheless. He polished off the remaining stew and greens in the meantime and barely resisted the temptation to lick the plate.

'Only this,' said Eulalia when she returned, holding up a very thin and very tatty tunic. There was large brown stain on the shoulder and several holes.

'That'll do fine,' said Tarchon, who had worn plenty worse in his time.

'Really?'

'A denarius for the food and the shirt?'

Eulalia frowned as she took the plate from him. 'You must be richer than you look.'

Having thanked her sincerely, he set off along the track and – once well away from the village – replaced his tunic with the "new" one. It would also function as an effective disguise, especially with his muddy sandals and pack. Relieved to finally have the wound covered up and with his spirits raised by the meal, Tarchon found himself walking quickly in the warm morning sun.

As Eulalia had promised, there were indeed enough locals to guide his way. He did, however, fear he was going to get wet again when he encountered another waterway. This river was not wide but deep and fast-moving and there was no sign of a bridge. Before long, however, a skiff came along and the owner was happy to take him across for the sum of one sesterce. Tarchon thanked the gods that he still had a few coins and marvelled at how much he'd been able to do with his first wage: the world was truly different when you had money.

Having eaten two of the three almond cakes for lunch and filled his flask at a village well, he reached the city in early afternoon. The east gate was similar in appearance to the others: a high, decorated arch set within a bulky building. Though not every part of Nicomedia was walled, here the slabs of stone towered twenty feet above the ground.

Trailing back along the road was a long line of carts, packhorses and pedestrians. The reason for the delay was quite obvious: at least a dozen legionaries were present at the gate, under the command of an officer wearing a red cloak. His men seemed to be questioning every new arrival. Before reaching the line, Tarchon turned left onto the road that encircled Nicomedia. This, he knew, would lead him eventually to the south gate. He expected a similar scene there but hoped to find another way into the city.

Within a few minutes, he reached the first unwalled section. A team of engineers was present, marking out distances with pegs and string but this part of the city was secured by nothing more than a wooden fence. However, there was also a squad of city sergeants and Tarchon could see no way of getting past them.

He encountered two more such sections between old chunks of wall as he followed the road around Nicomedia's uneven perimeter. Again, both areas were manned by city sergeants; it was quite clear that the authorities didn't want anyone to pass in or out undetected. If anything, there were even more legionaries at the south gate. They were checking those leaving the city but seemed far more interested in those entering. Without breaking stride, Tarchon glanced along the road that he had started on the previous morning – the road that led to Green Cove. He did not plan to pass that way again.

He watched two tall legionaries grip the arms of a man who cried out in protest. Were they looking for an assassin? Were they looking for *him*? Could information from the helpful soldiers have reached the city already? If they'd searched the headland and discovered the blood, his wounded arm might give him away.

Beyond the road was the inlet that ran into the city's centre, the walls abruptly ending where the ground became marshy and soft. It would have been easy to sneak in via this route, if not for the two-man patrols of legionaries criss-crossing the area. Desperate to find another way in, Tarchon followed a broad, well-used track that led directly to the water. Part of him thought it advisable to leave the city entirely but the sisters at the Camel would surely be suspicious if he didn't claim his gear, nor did he want to embark on the return journey without a horse.

On this side of the inlet were mudflats where dozens of long-beaked white birds plucked out worms. Three slender timber piers ran out into the water. At the end of each, a few small craft were tied up. Passing a trio of men hauling baskets of shellfish, Tarchon walked to the end of the nearest pier.

Once there, he gained a good view along the inlet to his right. Half a mile away were the great workshops and half-built vessels of Nicomedia's shipyards. Beyond that, was a dense thicket of masts that marked the docks. It occurred to Tarchon that both areas would be much more difficult to secure than a solid perimeter.

'Good day,' said a boy of about twelve. He was sitting in a rowing boat, mopping up water with a sponge in each hand.

'Good day,' said Tarchon. 'Got a leak?'

'Looks that way.'

'Shame. I need a boat to get to the docks.'

'Say no more, sir,' said a gruff voice. Tarchon turned to see a middle-aged fellow climb out of a punt. 'I can take you. One sesterce.'

'Now?'

'Of course.'

Tarchon felt sorry for the lad but the youngster didn't seem to care; he was already back at his sponging. The boatman untied his punt and stepped nimbly down into it. He then took up his pole and stationed himself at the stern, feet well spread. Steadying the narrow vessel with the pole, he invited his new customer to take a seat on the single, central bench. Tarchon stepped aboard and sat down, his pack between his feet.

The boatman pushed off, drifted away from the pier, then stuck his pole in and propelled the punt towards the city.

Tarchon reminded himself that this stretch of water was actually part of the Marmara Sea, but the narrow inlet was so calm that they might have been upon a lake.

Gazing down at the water, he was about to put his hand in when something stopped him. That something was the thought of Green Cove. That something was Demetrius being dragged to his death.

No.

No.

Think only of what's in front of you. No more weakness. No more mistakes.

You're getting out of this. You're getting back to Byzantium to tell them the job is done.

'What's your trade?' asked the boatman.

Tarchon would have preferred not to talk but stuck to the story agreed with Korax.

'Looking for new business for my master.'

Given his muddy, tatty appearance, this probably sounded fairly ridiculous but the local seemed to accept it.

'Business, eh? Sounds promising.'

Tarchon thought of falling, slicing his arm up, fainting in the middle of a road and being rescued by the legionaries.

'Er…I hope so. Lot of troops around today. Any idea what's going on?'

'In the city?'

'Yes – guarding the gates.'

'I stick to the water,' replied the boatman. 'I don't like all the people, all the noise.'

The man clearly knew his work; expertly pushing the punt along at an impressive speed as they passed the many workshops and boatsheds. The thumps and clangs seemed to be amplified by the water and Tarchon saw scores of men at work: carrying spars, fitting ropes, repairing timbers; painting, tarring, cleaning, polishing.

'That one there is for a Cilician prince,' said the boatman as they passed a great ship inside one of the sheds. The huge prow dominated the waterfront and there was barely enough room for men to squeeze between it and the water.

The local chuckled. 'It was originally named after his wife but she had an affair – now it's to be named after the daughter.'

They were almost past the shipyard now and approaching the docks. Tarchon realised he hadn't seen a single soldier or city sergeant on the busy waterfront.

'I just spotted an old friend!' he said. 'Can you drop me there? Between those two ships?'

'I'm not really supposed to, sir, the foremen don't-'

Seeing the two sesterces in Tarchon's hand, the boatman quietened, slowed the punt and turned it towards the shore. They did get a couple of sharp looks from workers nearby but, having handed over the coins, Tarchon slipped off his sandals and stepped out of the punt. From there, he hurried up the sloped ramp that fronted the boatsheds.

Keeping his head down, he put the sandals back on and made his way along the waterfront, noting the slicks of paint and oil running out of the sheds into the water. His path was momentarily blocked by a crew shifting a long spar but he ducked under it. From there, he waded through a mass of shavings produced by three men working a spar with heavy planes and passed the last of the boatsheds.

Here he turned inland on to a wide street. He was concerned that there might be some gate or guard-post controlling access to the shipyard but he passed only a cart coming the other way and soon found himself in a quiet part of the city. After getting some directions from a man selling crabs, Tarchon headed north, hoping his trusted nose would get him back to the Camel Inn.

Slow yet relentless, the fear grew.

With every step of the journey through Nicomedia, he saw more city sergeants and legionaries. They were mostly in pairs or threes and had clearly been deployed to cover a lot of ground.

Tarchon avoided the centre but there were still so many: some on the move, some stationed at corners, junctions and squares.

He reckoned he wasn't far from the Street of The Carpenters – and therefore the inn – when he passed two soldiers with identical circular shields upon their backs. One glanced at him and, once past, he soon heard four hob-nailed boots tapping away. He covered twenty paces, then forty.

Great Minerva, keep them away from me. Please protect me.

But the tapping continued; the soldiers weren't going anywhere. He reached the Street of the Carpenters and turned off it, now only a minute or so from the Camel. The legionaries were behind him but had still done nothing. Surely it was a coincidence? They just happened to be going the same way. If they wanted to question him, they would have stopped him by now.

As he approached a small square, he saw a squad of city sergeants move off, one man thumping his club into an open palm. Tarchon would have been glad to see them go, except that their departure revealed another threat: two legionaries, leaning against the surround of a fountain in the middle of the square. They were equipped with the same shields as the other pair: red, with a metal boss and a white wreath design around the edge. Both looked thoroughly bored.

But when a whistle sounded from behind Tarchon, they looked up. Certain that the first two had given a further signal, he watched the legionaries stride towards him, the harsh sound of their boots fusing with the others. He tried to appear calm, even while fighting the urge to run.

The soldiers were clearly aware of this possibility. They spread out and, when he stopped, he found himself completely surrounded. There were several stores facing onto the square and some of the vendors and customers were now watching the unfolding incident.

'Could be him, right?' said one of the men behind him.

'Right age,' said the oldest of the two from the square, a brawny bastard who – unlike the others – wore a mail shirt over his red tunic.

'Name?'

'Linus, sir.'

'You local?'

'No, from Byzantium, sir.' Tarchon knew – as everyone knew – that the first rule of dealing with soldiers was to be respectful.

'Here on my master's business.'

The legionary looked him up and down. 'What business is that?'

'Investment opportunities. We arrived together last week. He departed two days ago. I remained behind to keep looking for him. I'm staying at the Camel Inn.'

'How long have you been in Nicomedia?'

'Four days, sir.'

'Mmm.' The legionary glanced at his compatriot. 'Doesn't seem the type, does he?'

The other man Tarchon could see grimaced and scratched his chin. 'They're crafty bastards though.'

'True. Well, there's one way to find out for sure.'

The legionaries closed in, so close that he could smell them.

'You're going to have to show us something, mate,' said the older man.

They know. They know about the blood. The wound will give me away.

'Lift up your tunic. So we can be sure you're not one of them.'

'One of *them*?' said Tarchon.

'The Cybele freaks. One of them desecrated the Temple of Mars last night and the chief centurion is out for blood. They're easy to identify – if you know where to look. Come on now, we've got you covered.'

Tarchon almost laughed. He lifted up his tunic and pulled down his loin cloth.

'Sausage and beans,' said the legionary. 'Fair enough. On your way, mate.'

Tarchon could not have thought of any other circumstance in which displaying his privates in a public square would cause him relief but he felt only that as he walked away.

'Gods, what a way to spend the day,' complained one of the soldiers.

'You're just jealous, Hector,' said the old legionary, drawing a laugh from the others. 'His equipment is twice the size of yours.'

Tarchon was desperate to leave Nicomedia but he wasn't about to blunder into the Camel without watching the place first. He found a nice spot in an alley nearby and observed the inn for an hour. He saw no sign of any soldiers or anything else suspicious so entered via the parlour, where he found the smaller of the two sisters sweeping the floor.

'Well, well – you're back.'

'One of my master's associates is very generous with his wine. I had a few too many so he let me stay the night.'

She frowned at his tatty tunic. 'What are you wearing?'

'The other one is dirty – you know how it is.' Tarchon mimed vomiting.

She did not find this amusing. 'Will you want the room for tonight?'

'No thank you. My master settled up, correct?'

'He did. You'll want the lad to ready your horse?'

'Yes. Thank you.'

All Tarchon could think about now was the city gates and facing another interrogation by more legionaries. He hurried up to the room, fetched his gear – including his sword – then said farewell to the proprietors. Out in the courtyard, the lad already had Ambler saddled. Tarchon gave him a tip and asked him about the quickest route to the west gate.

He reached it surprisingly quickly. Perhaps due to the patrols, people seemed to be staying off the streets. He was again questioned at the gate but repeated the cover story. The soldiers did ask about his sword but he claimed that his master had insisted he take it as he was travelling alone. As they waved him through, he overheard other legionaries discussing the fact that two suspected cultists had now been apprehended.

As he guided Ambler out onto the coast road, Tarchon felt another wave of relief. In front of him were two old men on ponies. As he passed them, he listened in. They were talking about the governor's favourite seer, Demetrius. Rumour had it he was dead.

XVII

Three days later, Tarchon found himself at the most famous bathhouse in the East: the Baths of Zeuxippus. This was a luxury he had seldom enjoyed, and normally he might have taken the opportunity for a swim. But his wounded arm ached and he had applied new bandages that morning. Once in the changing rooms, he rented a towel, undressed, wrapped the towel around himself, and asked one of the attendants to show him to private pool four.

The baths were so named because they had been built upon an ancient Temple dedicated to Zeus, constructed during the reign of Septimius Severus. Bypassing the exercise area and the spacious hot and cold pools, Tarchon saw the numerous statues mounted within the niches. He knew that these had been brought to Byzantium from across the Empire; the baths and its unique decorations were a point of pride amongst many locals.

The attendant led him to a low, arched entrance partly obscured by steam. Standing there armed with a sword was the black-bearded fellow who had rescued Tarchon and apprehended Evaristos. He was sweating profusely and ignored Tarchon's 'good day', instead nodding toward the arch.

Inside, Gargonius sat on one side of a square pool, sinewy arms propped up on the edge, watching the new arrival. In a corner was a wooden screen and racks for clothes. The warm air was suffused with a powerful, floral scent.

'Ah, young man,' said the agent in his soft, cultured tone. 'Welcome.'

'Good day, sir.'

Korax had instructed Tarchon to go to the baker's and leave a message when he returned to Byzantium. There he was told by another of Gargonius' employees to meet the senior agent at the baths.

'Please.' Gargonius gestured to the narrow steps that led down into the steaming water.

'I can't, sir.' Tarchon showed him his bandaged left arm. He wasn't sure if it was healing or not. The ache was no better and the flesh around the stiches remained a livid red.

'I shall have my surgeon take a look at that for you. We can't risk it turning bad. Sword, was it?'

Tarchon looked at the water as he answered. 'No, sir. I fell. Stupid of me.'

'These things happen. I must congratulate you on your success.'

Tarchon did not reply. With time to dwell on what he'd done at Green Cove, another chilling image – Demetrius' white, terrified face as he was pulled into the depths – appeared whenever he closed his eyes.

'At least sit down, put your feet in.'

Tarchon sat on the edge of the pool opposite Gargonius. The private bathing room was illuminated by a skylight directly above, casting the sun's rays on to the agent. Though the water was very warm, he was not sweating and, even when wet, his grey hair appeared well-cropped and neat. Tarchon saw that his body was as slender as he'd expected, though he was surprised by how pale he was. Meeting the agent's blue eyes, he realised that he too was being appraised.

'Tell me, how did you manage to make it look like an accident?'

'Sir?'

'The report from the governor's office in Nicomedia stated that Demetrius was lost while swimming. No body has been recovered. Apparently, they're putting it down to his age and excessive weight.'

Though he would rather have spoken of any other subject, Tarchon described how he'd used the rock, the rope and the bladder.

Gargonius listened keenly throughout. 'You passed the statue of Homeros on your way in?'

'Not sure, sir. There are so many.'

'You know the story of the Trojan Horse, though?'

'I do.'

'A neat trick, no? Ingenious, resourceful. You have shown such qualities, young Tarchon. I must say it all went rather better than I was expecting. Korax will be impressed.'

'He's not in the city, sir?'

'Expected back today.'

Gargonius dipped his hand into a nearby bowl and scattered petals into the water. 'I do love this place. There is nowhere in all the Empire quite like it. You've been before?'

'Only the public area, sir. Couple of times.'

'Of course. Expensive.'

Tarchon had forgotten how pleasant warm water was but he still preferred the jolting cold of the sea.

'How did you find it?' asked Gargonius. 'Working alone?'

'Not easy. I need to improve my riding and fighting. And planning.'

'The last of those is the most important in our profession. I am glad to see that you are willing to learn. You have the raw materials, particularly the looks.'

Tarchon wasn't sure what to make of that.

'Relax, young man, I'm not trying to seduce you – I do not mix business with pleasure. Looks are more important than you might think. You're taller than most, but not unusually so. You're strong, well-built but, again, not unusually so. You have nice, thick, hair but your features are slightly asymmetrical. Overall, you're fine-looking and, again, better than average. But nothing special. Perfect for our line of work.'

Gargonius took his arms from the sides and allowed himself to sink under. Re-emerging, he put a hand through his hair.

'Alas, the same cannot be said of me. I would be disastrous in the field, for any number of reasons.'

Tarchon had heard enough to know that Gargonius rated him. Perhaps that meant he could afford to show a little weakness by asking for some advice.

'Sir...it is difficult to forget...' Even though the guard was too far away to hear, Tarchon lowered his voice. 'To...to take a life.'

Gargonius nodded knowingly, his chin touching the water. 'What's done is done. For better or worse, you're one of us now.'

Despite the warmth of the bathhouse, Tarchon felt a chill run through him. What Gargonius said next, however, made him feel a little better.

'And you're in good company. There are men like us in Britain, in Spain, in Egypt and in Syria. We don't particularly *want* to do these things but we do them for the greater good. And we are well rewarded for it.'

'You see the bag there, Tarchon?' Gargonius pointed to the clothing racks. In one of them sat a previously unnoticed bag of money. 'For you. Your next month's salary – silver. And a bonus for a successful outcome – gold. My advice is to save that; not every assignment will go so well.'

Tarchon almost smiled when he heard about the gold. He had held golden coins but they had never been his.

Gargonius continued: 'I've always found that a good, heavy bag of coins does wonders for a guilty conscience.'

That bag was surprisingly, pleasingly, wonderfully heavy. Tarchon had to carry it back through the baths to the changing rooms and he felt as if everyone was watching him when he placed it in his pack. That was not all he'd been given. The guard, who was named Solon, had also passed on directions for this surgeon friend of Gargonius. The agent had also told him to rest for a few days but to not leave the city. Apparently, events to the north were in flux and there was talk of the Goth king, Cniva, ordering more attacks on Roman targets.

Knowing it was important to have the wound checked immediately, Tarchon hurried to a large townhouse north of Second Hill. Upon giving a password supplied by Solon, he was told to return at sunset: the surgeon was busy with an important client.

As he walked back to his apartment, Tarchon worried about where to keep the money. He hadn't actually opened the bag yet and he smothered a smile at the thought of touching and counting all those silver and gold coins.

After the events of the last few days, he was desperate to do something normal, something familiar, and he soon found himself changing direction and heading for Galla's. He made two purchases on the way. The first was a new dark green tunic; long-sleeved to ensure Galla didn't see the wound. The second was a gift.

'Tarchon, it's so pretty!'

Having never had enough money to buy any, he knew virtually nothing about jewellery. But he could see that Galla's reaction was genuine and he reckoned the silver bracelet studded with tiny emeralds was indeed a pretty piece. It had set him back eight denarii but he could think of only one other thing he'd rather spend money on; and that was also in hand. There was always the risk that Galla might get the wrong idea but it seemed to him that, if anyone deserved a gift, it was her.

The bracelet attracted an approving look from the maid who had just placed a flask of wine on their table. Tarchon had taken Galla to a local restaurant that specialised in shellfish, and they'd already ordered oysters and mussels in wine sauce.

'Shall I help you?' he asked.

As usual, Galla's left arm was wrapped up. He remembered her complaining that no one ever bought her rings or bracelets because they thought it insensitive and that she'd have difficulty putting them on.

'Please.'

She beamed as Tarchon stood and affixed the bracelet using a simple clasp. The jeweller had polished it and the silver now caught the golden light coming in through the restaurant window.

'Oh, it's lovely. Just lovely.' She watched him as he sat down. 'And you look so smart. What a nice shade of green.' She gazed down at the bracelet. 'Thank you.'

Tarchon thought Galla looked pretty good too. When her curly black hair was tied up, he always noted her big brown eyes and full, tempting lips. But he told himself to stop thinking of her in this way. They were just friends.

'You were very kind to me,' he said. 'Before my fortunes changed. It's the least I can do.'

'You've been away a while. The new job?'

'I've been travelling quite a bit. The second pay packet was better than the first.'

'Mother ran into Anahita at the spice market. She said you have an apartment?'

'That's right. Third floor. Bit of a mess but it'll do.'

'A place of your own, Tarch.'

'I know. My riding is improving too.'

'Don't tell me you've bought a horse?'

'The pay packet wasn't that good. They hired one for me.'

'And the work is still delivering messages?'

'Mostly, yes. But not your day-to-day stuff – *important* things.'

Galla admired the bracelet once more, then drank some wine. 'I'm proud of you. Do you know that?'

He shrugged. 'I do now.'

What Galla said should have meant a lot. No one had ever said they were proud of him. But the truth got in the way. The truth of what he was involved in, what he had done. He said nothing for a while, sipping his wine, fighting off the thoughts, raising a shield against the truth. He hadn't actually lied to her, after all, and hadn't he done a good thing today?

Before he could say anything more, the mussels arrived.

'These look delicious,' said Galla, already digging in.

And they were, the wine sauce fortified with herbs and honey. They both ate several mussels before Tarchon spoke again.

'Galla, I just wanted to say that…things can get better. Sometimes it happens when you least expect it.'

'What a philosopher.'

He reddened slightly, then they both laughed.

They stayed for two hours, and each put away several mugs of wine. By the end, they were laughing about some of the odder customers that Galla had encountered at the cobblers. Eventually deciding that she needed an afternoon nap, she asked Tarchon to escort her home. Claiming that he had an appointment with Mehruz at the tenth hour, Tarchon didn't go inside for fear of encountering her parents. It had been the most pleasant occasion he could recall; the wine and the cheerful atmosphere eventually allowing him to forget all he'd endured. How fine it was to take a friend to dinner, to eat the best of food, to spend the afternoon doing nothing but talking and laughing.

On his way out of the city, as his drunken head began to clear, he passed a crew of filthy labourers unblocking a stinking sewer pipe. He'd worked on such a crew more than once.

Not again. *Never* again.

The cemetery was just north of Fifth Hill, in the area of Petrion, close to the walls that enclosed the city's western flank. It was a sprawl of dusty tracks and pale stone, resting place for thousands. Tarchon's father had insisted on his mother being placed here, where his family were buried, even though most of hers were in a smaller cemetery closer to the centre.

Buying some purple and red dried flowers from a vendor, Tarchon shamed himself by not being able to immediately find the grave. It had been a while since his last visit but that was no excuse. Like all the other family members here, his mother had been placed in a large amphora and buried beneath the sandy soil. The haphazard collection of circular marking stones on the surface was faded and dusty. His mother's was closest to the path. Tarchon knelt by it, brushed away the worst of the dust, then used spit to clean up the cheap green stone.

TO THE SPIRITS OF THE DEPARTED,
PHOEBE, WIFE OF MARCUS TARCHON.

Though it was traditional, Tarchon had always hated that she was listed as his useless father's wife – as if nothing else about her mattered. No one who ever read it would know that she'd been a far better person than him; stronger, kinder, more loving.

He placed the flowers on the stone, then stood up. This was an area of graves for the poor; there were only a few humble tombstones. But he had passed through a section for the rich, where there was coloured marble and many arches, columns and elaborate designs.

Tarchon wondered if his mother was watching him. Could she see his fine new tunic? The coins he had earned? She had been right about Minerva, that much was certain. Gazing down at the stone, he tried to remember what her voice was like, how she looked, what it felt like to embrace her. All this became more difficult as time passed. What would he give to see her again? Every coin he had and every coin he would ever have.

And his useless drunk of a father? Why had the gods allowed him to live and taken her? Why hadn't Minerva protected her? It made no sense.

After a time, a man passed by with a brush over his shoulder.

'You work here?' asked Tarchon.

'Aye.'

'Those nice tombstones – the marble ones as tall as a man. They have the stone boxes underneath, I suppose?'

'Sarcophagi.'

'That's it. How much? For one of those and a big stone with an inscription?'

'More than you can afford, mate.'

'Just tell me how much.'

'You need gold for that, mate. Handfuls of the stuff. Ten for the box. Twenty for the stone.'

Tarchon was surprised by how much they were but now, incredibly, this huge sum was actually in reach.

'Better get saving, mate,' added the man with a sneer.

'Already started.'

He reckoned he'd already walked ten miles that day, so his feet and legs were a little sore by the time he returned to the surgeon at Second Hill. The physician was very direct and assured Tarchon that anything he told him was in confidence: apparently the same applied to anyone Gargonius sent his way. Even so, Tarchon didn't tell him that he'd been stitched up by an army medic. The surgeon pronounced that the work had been well done. He also applied a salve and told Tarchon to return in two days' time for the stitches to be removed. He would then decide if the wound would need another set or could be left to heal.

The salve stung unpleasantly, though it was not nearly as unpleasant as what happened on his way back to the apartment. Just two streets away, he rounded a corner only to almost walk into his aunt.

'Well, well,' said Cassia, in her usual dismissive tone. Hostus was with her, and at least offered a friendly half-smile. Tarchon's aunt looked him up and down, instantly appraising the fine green tunic.

'Where did you steal that from?'

Tarchon just shook his head. He was about to walk on when his aunt fired another question at him. 'And why are you still walking the streets after trying to rob that cart?'

This he felt he needed to answer; if only to stop others asking the same question.

'The court gave me a second chance, aunt. I'm working for the army as a messenger. Got my second pay packet today.'

'Good for-'

Hostus was instantly cut off by his wife. 'I don't believe it. The court showed mercy? To *you*? A known criminal?'

'I've just been out to the cemetery. I'm saving up – for a proper stone and a sarco…sarcophi...'

'Sarcophagus,' said Hostus.

'Yes.'

'I'll believe that when I see it.' Aunt Cassia looked up at him, eyes narrow. 'You're mixed up in something. I can always tell when you're lying.'

That was far from the case, though she was certainly better than most.

'Believe what you want,' he said. 'I don't want to argue with you.'

'Fine by me,' she replied. 'Our house is a lot happier without you in it.'

'I was never really *in* it, though, was I?'

'That nasty mouth of yours,' she added. 'You never did respect me.'

That was not true. Cassia's face and some of her mannerisms reminded Tarchon of his mother and he'd always been grateful for that. He wished they could have been close but it had never happened.

'I have an apartment now,' he replied, enjoying the expression this provoked. He looked to Hostus. 'How's business?'

'Not bad. Good for you, Tarch.'

Aunt Cassia sighed and shook her head. Tarchon wondered if – now he was out of her hair – there would come a time when they might reconcile. For all their disagreements, he hated the thought of not seeing her and his uncle again.

'Perhaps I can come by some time?'

'Fine,' she said. 'But make sure I'm not home. You're up to no good, just like that father of yours. You can't pull the wool over my eyes, boy. I'll not have you bring shame on me again.'

With that, she walked on, leaving Hostus to mutter an oath. 'She might come round eventually.'

'I won't hold my breath,' said Tarchon.

His uncle clapped a hand on his shoulder before following his wife. 'I'm going to assume that she's wrong and that you're not mixed up in anything. Either way, be careful, eh?'

XVIII

Four days later, Tarchon woke to a brisk knocking. Once up, he looked through the door (there was a half-inch space between two planks). At first, he saw no one there but, when he looked lower, he saw the head of a boy. After he'd unlocked and opened the door, the lad – who was no more than six or seven – looked up at him, squinting and wrinkling his nose.

'From Korax,' he announced. 'The Wheel. Fourth hour. From Korax. The Wheel. Fourth hour.'

'Got it.'

The lad put out an upturned palm. Tarchon knew Korax would have paid him but he walked to his chest and found a bit amidst the higher value coins.

'Much obliged, sir,' said the boy politely, before sprinting away along the corridor.

Tarchon could smell cooking from the apartment opposite, which he'd learned was occupied by two middle-aged sisters. He could also hear some vendor bellowing about his cakes and workmen hammering away at something.

He had acquired two more pieces of furniture: a stool and a table, and he now sat there, drinking the last of the fresh milk he'd bought the previous day. He looked at the apples and rolls he'd also purchased; at the chest that contained his clothes and his sword; at his pack (complete with new strap); at his new boots; at his new blanket and soft pillow; and at the pallet, which Mehruz had helped him repair.

Mine. All mine.

He had also fitted in a riding lesson and a useful sword session with Master Bernardus. Tarchon was surprised at the detail of the veteran's instructions; it must have been fifty years since he himself was taught how to use a blade. As for the riding, the trainer had seemed appalled by Tarchon's technique and had immediately insisted that he change virtually everything he was doing. This was not a surprise; without Korax around he had made a couple of mistakes with Ambler on the return journey and knew that most mounts were much less obedient. It would not be a swift process.

Neither sword play nor riding was made easier by his injured arm but the stitches were out and the surgeon said it was healing well. Tarchon kept the bandage on when outside, mainly to avoid awkward questions.

Another of his recent purchases was a brush, which he now used to clean the apartment floor. The dust was deposited into his slop pail, which came with a well-fitting lid. Having dumped this down the sewer grate in the building's small yard, he returned upstairs and changed into his new green tunic. He eyed the sword for a moment but decided that his dagger was sufficient protection.

Having put a denarius aside as a votive, he paid a visit to the Temple of Minerva before walking to the Wheel, which was situated south of Prospherion Harbour. Outside, a work crew was mending one of the inn's two front windows: replacing parts of the wooden frame. Tarchon was only a couple of steps from the entrance when someone grabbed him from behind and spun him around.

'Myron sends his regards.'

Two of them. The one that had hold of him was six and a half feet tall, wide with it, and his left arm was already swinging. Tarchon couldn't break free from his assailant's grip but he at least bowed his head, which meant the fist hit his skull instead of his face.

Even so, the impact flashed light and pain into him and sent him flying back into the column beside the door. The unforgiving wood knocked the wind out of him and he collapsed to his knees.

'Look out!' cried one of the workers, who had stopped to watch.

Tarchon looked up in time to see a boot coming at him. It belonged to a shorter man with the stoutest set of legs imaginable. Throwing himself to the right, Tarchon felt the boot nick his shoulder. Knowing the man would be unbalanced, he grabbed a handful of calf and pushed. With a grunt of outrage, the second thug tottered away.

Stout did not fall, but he impeded the advance of his compatriot. Tarchon used the brief opportunity to spring to his feet. Still dazed, he put his arms out to steady himself. By now, several passers-by had also stopped to watch with the workers. Tarchon was dismayed to see that there were no city guards or soldiers among them. He had no choice. He drew his dagger.

Tall approached the workers, who backed away. He picked up a long saw and passed Stout a hammer. The shorter man was curly-haired and blunt-nosed, sweat glistening upon his face.

'We *were* just going to beat you up,' said Tall, who possessed very dark eyes, one of which was notably higher than the other. 'But if you want to get nasty...we have absolutely no problem with that.'

Tarchon didn't know what to do. A fistfight was one thing but if one of them was seriously injured, the authorities might hear of it. He did not need that kind of attention.

'Let's be reasonable,' he said. 'I can pay-'

The length of wood seemed to come out of nowhere, cracking Stout across the back. The thug's head snapped up and – face contorted by pain – he fell forward. Having apparently appeared from nowhere, Korax turned his attention to Tall. The agent had his own dagger on his belt but evidently wanted to avoid a lethal battle. He kept his eyes locked on his foe, every movement measured and calm.

Tall craftily dropped the saw and made a successful grab for the other end of the six-foot-timber. As the pair fought for control of it, Tarchon ran towards them. He had mistakenly assumed that Stout was out of the fight but the man flailed with a hand, sending him stumbling past the other pair. He was caught and shoved back into the fray by two enthusiastic onlookers who laughed as they did so.

Stout pawed sweat out of his eyes, then came at him with a right cross. Tarchon got his left arm up in a block but the meaty fist thumped into his bicep with shuddering force. Side-stepping and wincing at the pain, he looked over at the other two.

Korax pulled the timber towards him, let go, then darted forward and launched a well-aimed boot between Tall's legs. Teeth bared, eyes bulging, the big man staggered away, scattering boys at the front of the crowd.

The agent went for Stout, who did not punch this time but caught a handful of Korax's tunic and pulled him near. This was a mistake. Korax chopped a hand into his ear, drawing a squeal of agony and loosening Stout's grip. He then grabbed one of his assailant's fingers and bent it back on itself, somehow without breaking it. In seconds, Stout was on the ground, begging for mercy.

'You going to be a good boy?' asked Korax.

Stout nodded readily.

'And you?'

Tall was bent over, gripping his groin, apparently unable to respond.

'Good,' said Korax before turning to Tarchon. 'You know these two?'

'Sent by a man who doesn't like me.'

'That sounds like an understatement.'

The crowd of onlookers broke up to let a squad of four legionaries through.

'What's going on here?' asked one.

Korax beckoned him close and whispered in his ear. He then reached into a bag tied to his belt and showed the soldier something. After briefly inspecting it, the legionary nodded and ordered his men to apprehend Tall and Stout. Nabbing a length of rope from the carpenter's pail, Korax threw it to the soldier.

'Use that. Have them held at the prison. I'll be along later.'

As the legionaries complied, the crowd began to break up.

Korax walked into the Wheel, closely followed by a bemused Tarchon.

'Come on,' said the agent. 'Fighting always makes me thirsty.'

Having ordered some wine, Korax then led Tarchon to a table in a corner, which gave him a good view of the door. He held up his wrist in order to remove a splinter, then cleared his throat.

Tarchon sensed he was about to get a telling off, so jumped in first. 'I should have told you. I know that.'

'So why didn't you?' asked Korax, brushing something off his hairless head, then swigging back the well-watered wine delivered by the innkeeper. Tarchon guessed he had chosen The Wheel because it was murky and quiet, especially this early in the day.

While he considered his answer, Korax interjected. 'Because you didn't want to endanger your nice new job.'

'Yes.'

'You're lucky that Nicomedia went well. I'll have to tell Gargonius.'

Tarchon winced as he reached for his wine, not only because of what Korax had said. Though his head had cleared, he had no doubt that the thumping punch from Stout to his arm would result in a nasty bruise.

'Lucky for you I came along,' added the agent.

Tarchon had already thanked him once but did so again.

'Who sent them?'

'A smuggler named Myron. I was part of a crew unloading Persian perfume for him. There was a raid by the city guards. I took a box when we scattered and lost it in the sea. He thinks I stole it and that I owe him. He tried to collect a while back. I broke his nose.'

'You don't lose all your fights then?'

It didn't seem like the moment to mention that he'd actually won far more than he'd lost; or that, on this occasion, it had initially been two against one.

Korax sighed. 'If this problem affects your work for us, we need to solve it.'

'You're not going to-'

'I'll do whatever I think needs doing. Now, the chief gave me the basics on Nicomedia. Tell me the rest.'

Tarchon had little desire to do so but he could hardly refuse. In typical fashion, Korax listened intently and regularly pressed him for details. Tarchon admitted how he'd sustained the injury to his arm but repeated the lie he'd told Gargonius; that it was Eulalia the villager who had stitched him up.

When he finished, Korax drained his mug and belched. 'The chief seems more impressed than I am but you got it done. That's what counts.'

'What you did outside – can you teach me to fight like that?'

'Perhaps,' said Korax. 'When there's time.'

'You're busy?'

'Yes, and so are you. There's another job.'

According to Korax, it was to be his last night in Byzantium for a while. With this in mind, Tarchon invited himself along to Mehruz's place. As he walked there – sword over his shoulder in case anyone else attacked him – he wondered what exactly this new job might be. Korax had simply told him to report to the New Harbour at the second hour, where both he and Gargonius would brief him. It seemed obvious that he would be travelling by ship. But where? And why?

'Tarch!' Though clearly surprised to see him, Mehruz embraced him and invited him in. He bolted the door behind them, then led Tarchon through the darkened eatery. Mehruz and Anahita habitually closed at sunset, so Tarchon had waited an hour or so before calling in.

'How are you?' asked Mehruz. 'It's been weeks.'

'Not bad, thanks. Away with the job.'

'Ah yes. Got another pay packet yet?'

'As a matter of fact, yes.'

'Is that a sword?'

'It is.'

'By Ahura Mazda, riding lessons and now a sword! You'll show me later?'

'Of course. Hey, Ruz, can I leave these with you?' Tarchon reached into his tunic pocket. 'My mother's brooch and a couple of golds.'

'Golds? You really are moving up in the world!' said Mehruz as he took them. 'I'll stick them in the strongbox.'

The pair ascended the stairs at the back of the eatery and emerged into a corridor that led past a curtain and the family's bedroom. Tarchon was relieved to learn that the two children – Farhad and Delara – were asleep. He would always feel affection towards them because they were his friends' children but he never quite knew what to say or how to play along with them. Mehruz had taken to fatherhood easily and it was Anahita who more often complained about the burdens of being a parent. Tarchon could hardly imagine anything worse than having to care for two whining, helpless creatures that could do nothing for themselves.

'They've only just gone off,' said Anahita, after raising a finger to her mouth. 'Lucky you didn't wake them banging on the door like that.'

'I thought it was quiet.'

'It was,' said Mehruz. Though the apartment was lit only by a couple of candles, Tarchon noticed the reproachful look aimed at his wife.

He offered the cake he had bought with him. 'Date and honey.'

'Thank you,' said Anahita. 'The children will love that.'

'You hungry?' asked Mehruz as they walked out to the narrow balcony at the front of their apartment.

'Got some leftovers for me?'

'Lamb stew all right? It's cold.'

'Sounds good.'

'Come and sit,' offered Anahita.

'Yes, you two go and sit,' moaned Mehruz, 'because I haven't served enough food today.'

Ignoring him, Anahita and Tarchon walked to the stools on the balcony and sat down. Mehruz's wife was on the larger side, possessor of wide green eyes and a warm smile that she rarely used: and certainly not with customers. She wasn't actually a particularly good cook but she was excellent with money, always budgeting well and securing good deals on produce.

Anahita seemed not to approve of Tarchon when they'd first met but she'd warmed up over the years. Once, after a lot of wine, she'd told Tarchon that Mehruz was fortunate to have such a loyal friend. That had meant to lot to him.

She watched as he took off the sword and propped it against the balcony wall.

'Why does a messenger need a blade?'

'Important messages.'

'Ruz says this new job pays well.'

'Not bad.'

'And an apartment too? The gods have favoured you of late.'

'About bloody time.'

Candlelight illuminated a half-smile from Anahita, which to Tarchon was a small victory.

'The sun shines on all of us sometimes. I am glad for you.'

'Thank you. Are the children well?'

'*Too* well. Noisy. Disobedient. My father says we're too soft on them.'

'He's probably right,' said Mehruz as he handed Tarchon the bowl of stew. 'So where did this trip take you?'

The version he told them was considerably different to the one he'd given his superiors. Lying to these two did not come easily so he told the story quickly.

'So, it's for the army?' said Mehruz.

'A branch of the army. Officers.'

'Did you have to take the oath? Legionaries have to take the oath.'

'No. Looks like I have a new job starting tomorrow. I think I could be on a ship.'

'Going where?'

'Don't know yet.'

'Sounds very secretive,' observed Anahita.

'Not really,' countered Tarchon, suddenly anxious to change the subject. 'Anyway, enough about me. What's your news?'

Anahita sighed. 'Father's ill. Some lump in his throat. Mother says he should have it cut out. He's hoping it disappears.'

'I shall offer a prayer for him,' said Tarchon, largely because it was just something you said.

'Thank you,' said Anahita.

'How old is he now?'

'Sixty-one.'

'Getting on,' added Mehruz.

'You know what,' said Tarchon. 'Your *cold* stew is better than most hot stews.'

'Course it is,' said Mehruz. 'That's the last of it so I'll have to make another bloody pan tomorrow. When you're back, we *have* to go and see the chariots. It's been too long.'

Anahita looked out over the balcony. There were only a few dim lights visible on the opposite apartment block.

'What?' demanded Mehruz, apparently noting some reaction that Tarchon has missed. 'You can go and look at dresses we can't afford but I can't go to the odd race?'

'Buy me a new dress, Ruz, then you can go to as many races as you like.'

Husband and wife glared at each other before eventually sticking their tongues out and laughing.

'Your mother still helping out with the children?' asked Tarchon.

'Yes,' replied Anahita. 'Though she's not always free. Could you do a few hours here and there?'

'Well of course I'd love to but er…with the new job-'

Anahita snorted. 'Calm down, you fool. I'm joking.'

'Ah.'

Mehruz picked up the sword, drew it from the sheath and held it close to the candle. 'Light. Well made. Do you know how to use it?'

'It's just for show, really,' said Tarchon.

Mehruz sheathed the sword and looked down at his friend, a troubled look upon his face. 'Hope so.'

XIX

The fisherman swung a hand at the diving gull but missed by a couple of feet. He at least kept it away from its target – hundreds of sardines packed into three amphoras – and the gull returned to a nearby wall, still eyeing its prey while parading back and forth on its yellow feet.

'Bastard thing!' spat the fisherman, before throwing his hands in the air. 'Where is Glabrio with the cart?'

He and his catch were at the top of the ramp that led down to New Harbour. Just below, a quintet of sailors lugged an enormous rope out of the harbour. Six inches wide, it had been looped into sections but looked a heavy, ungainly load. Nearby, a pair of well-dressed gentlemen discussed shipping costs, surrounded by bored-looking attendants. At the base of the ramp, flames spewed from an iron cauldron heating bitter-smelling pitch. Labourers wielding heavy brushes slathered the thick, black liquid onto timbers mounted on frames.

Once past them, Tarchon saw Korax step out from behind a covered carriage. The bearded Solon stood with the two horses, one hand on the reins. Without a word, Korax opened the door to the carriage and indicated for Tarchon to enter. Tarchon stepped up into the cramped confines and sat on a comfortable bench, facing Gargonius. The senior agent sat with one leg crossed, dressed in an orange tunic, a white cape over his shoulders. He looked like he was going to a party, but the expression on his narrow face was grave. There wasn't enough space on the floor for Tarchon's pack so he set it on his lap.

As Korax sat down beside him and closed the door, Gargonius waved a hand at him. 'This other issue.'

'Myron. You needn't worry about him or those two cretins from yesterday.'

'Right,' replied Tarchon.

'Relax,' said Korax. 'We didn't chop their hands off. Once he realised who he was dealing with, Myron could not have been more cooperative.'

Gargonius said, 'So, you are now entirely free to focus your efforts on this: a task at least as important as your last.'

'Yes, sir.'

'What do you know of the Goths?'

'I know they have attacked some provinces. Dacia, for one.'

'Any others?'

'Er…'

Though he hadn't seen it, Tarchon felt sure that Korax had just rolled his eyes.

'Do you know anything *else* about them?' asked Gargonius, wetting a finger before smoothing down an errant hair on his right eyebrow.

'Strong warriors. Good at riding horses. Good at training birds, falcons especially. But they're barbarians: no great cities, no great empire.'

'If current events are anything to go by, they actually appear intent on acquiring our empire,' said Gargonius. 'Several years ago, they captured the Scythian capital and they continue their march west. Much of the northern coast of the Black Sea is within their grasp. King Cniva grows ever bolder with every passing year. They threaten Dacia, it's true, and Moesia. If they conquer those provinces, they are at the borders of Thracia, and then us here in Byzantium. I don't need to tell you of the strategic importance of our fair city.'

Tarchon wasn't entirely sure what "strategic" meant but he knew why Byzantium was important. 'We control The Straits, sir. Ships moving north and south; armies moving east or west.'

'Quite so. The Emperor has his hands full with the Carpi, not to mention rumblings of discontent in Pannonia. It will likely fall to the eastern legions, and ourselves of course, to guard Thracia and our city against the Goths. Would you see

Byzantium fall to the Goths, Tarchon? See our great buildings torn down, our beacon of civilisation ruined and burned?'

Gargonius spoke with an odd gleam in his eye, which reminded Tarchon of an actor giving a performance. If it was a game, Tarchon was happy to play along. Truth be told, he'd never given a great deal of thought to the wider Empire but he did love his city and, well, *some* of the people in it. From what he'd heard, the barbarians of the north deserved their fearsome reputation. If he could help defeat them, he'd feel proud.

'No, sir. I would not.'

'Cniva's forces are now – for the first time – threatening our cities on the Black Sea. We have agents placed in some of them, and they must be recalled. It appears that our usual method of communication has been compromised. We need you to go and fetch one of those agents and bring them home.'

'Understood. Where is he?'

Gargonius gestured to Korax.

'A city named Odessos. About a hundred and forty miles north. You're booked on a freighter leaving this morning but the wind is currently not favourable so it might not be a swift trip. You will make contact with the agent by going to a tavern named Thalia's.'

'How will I know him?'

'Oh, easily,' said Gargonius with a mischievous smile. 'He is a *her*. Her name is Kallisto and she's one of our finest agents. She is currently going by the name Cassandra. Amongst her many talents is music and she performs on...when is it?'

'Festival days plus every Tuesday and Friday.'

'Ah, yes. Korax, I do believe our young friend looks shocked. Believe me, I wish the majority of my male agents were half as effective as Kallisto.'

'We've never met,' said Tarchon. 'How can I convince her you sent me?'

Korax handed him a piece of cold metal. Looking down, he saw a very well-made miniature spearhead, no longer than three inches.

'Keep that hidden,' said Gargonius. 'Show it only to her. The Goths know we have agents and that they carry those. The wrong person finds that – they'll kill you for it.'

As the carriage trundled away up the ramp, Korax led the way along the busy main quay of New Harbour. Tarchon wasn't sure how to feel about this new mission. Fetching another agent didn't seem all that hard but, until recently, the barbarian Goths had been no more than an unseen foreign horde. He had no particular desire to meet them face to face. And then there was this female agent; it hadn't occurred to him that there would even *be* female agents.

'This Kallisto – how did she end up with…'

'The Service. Just call us that. Not sure.'

'What's she like?'

'How do you mean?'

'Er…to work with?'

'Knows her own mind. Let's leave it at that.' Korax aimed a finger at Tarchon. 'But you need to be very clear with her. Whatever's going on up there, she's to return with you immediately.'

'Understood.'

'Morning!' This greeting came from a young man walking towards them along the quay. He looked to be a few years older than Tarchon; tall and sturdy with a long mane of black hair. Just above his right eye was a narrow, dark red scar that ran diagonally up to the left side of his brow. As he grinned, his right eyelid flickered open and shut.

Korax nodded to him. 'This is Tarchon. Sardenos, captain of the *Erythrai*.'

Sardenos seemed young for a captain but was at least friendly. 'So, you're the brave one heading up to Odessos?' he said, before winking at Korax with that oddly flickering eye. 'I suppose that's what underlings are for, right?'

Before leaving the carriage, Tarchon had been briefed on the cover story. He was again to be a merchant's assistant, this time going to recover his superior's niece.

'Fear not, Tarchon,' added Sardenos. 'We'll look after you. We've nine passengers as a matter of fact, though they're not all going as far as Odessos. I was hoping for a full load but there's not much going north now and I doubt there'll be much coming south – other than people.'

Tarchon's passage on the ship had already been paid for. He had been given an additional six aurei, though this was solely for expenses. Korax had made it clear that he was expected to account for every last sesterce.

'I doubt we'll see you back here before ten days,' said the agent. 'We'll be waiting.' He locked eyes with Tarchon as they shook forearms, which actually did give him a little encouragement. 'Careful on the ship.'

'Bit of a landlubber?' asked Sardenos.

Tarchon had been swimming and sailing for as long as he could remember.

'Don't worry about me.'

As Korax departed, he followed Sardenos back along the quay, pack over his shoulder. 'You've done well – captain at your age.'

'Wish I could take credit for it. The *Erythrai* is my father's boat. He died last year.'

'At sea?'

Sardenos gave a strange bark of laughter. 'In a way. He was at a beach, swimming on his back, went straight into a mass of jellyfish. I think he would have survived a couple of stings but there was more than we could count.'

Tarchon wasn't sure what to say to that.

'Makes for a good story at least,' added Sardenos.

They continued past two broad, deep-hulled freighters before reaching *The Erythrai*, which was more of a coaster; narrow and elegant.

'Seventy feet?' asked Tarchon.

'Just sixty-five. Not a lot of hull space but she's quick and good on the wind.'

'Useful if we're fighting a northerly.'

'Gave Neptune a goat this morning,' replied Sardenos. 'I'm hoping he'll at least turn it into a north-westerly for us.'

Sardenos' crew were loading heavy amphora. Each required two men and the gangplank shuddered under the weight.

'What's in them?'

'These are dried fish. We're also carrying raisins, vinegar and olive oil. Most of it is coming off at Apollonia Pontica.'

'Korax said you have plenty of water and wine.'

'Yes, all included, so just ask. We'll freshen the tanks at Odessos.'

Sardenos pointed to three men sitting on the far side of the gangplank, watching the loading. 'They're off at Apollonia too. Hopefully, the other passengers will be here before long. I better get to it.'

The young captain certainly wasn't afraid of getting stuck in and his crew worked with great efficiency. Another load turned up on a cart shortly after Tarchon arrived. This contained heavy iron fittings which Sardenos welcomed aboard as 'useful extra ballast.'

Realising that loading was going to take a while yet, Tarchon sat on the edge of the quay beside his three fellow passengers. Though he was ready to greet them, they cast not even a look in his direction and continued to talk quietly amongst themselves. They were dressed very modestly and carried only a small bag each. One aimed a suspicious glance at Tarchon's sword.

He turned his attention to the *Erythrai*, knowing his fortunes might depend on the quality and strength of the vessel. Like the prow, the stern angled in sharply. Above was a traditional sternpost, though it was impossible to see if the worn, damaged carving was the usual goose-head. Hanging over the stern was a flag bearing the name of the vessel's guardian deity: *JUPITER, THE SAVIOUR*. Forward of the sternpost and tiller was a low, solidly-built shelter. Just beyond the mast was the single hatch, which led down into the hold. The yard was laid out along the centre of the hull, the sail currently stowed at the bow, along with the oars. Between the mast and the shelter, the deck dropped down three feet; here were the benches for the oarsman, six on each side.

As a pair of boys walked past – giggling at the crab one of them was holding – Tarchon glanced at his pack, which was very full. As well as his new clothes, it contained his dagger and some food for the journey he'd purchased on his way to the harbour. He was glad to have his new boots for this new assignment.

As the loading neared completion, the remaining passengers arrived. First, there was a family of four, with a teenaged son and daughter. Then came a fellow about Tarchon's age, wearing a sleeveless tunic. He possessed an athlete's build and there was not a sign of fat on his lithe frame. His brown hair was cropped short and his eyes darted around as he moved. He greeted Sardenos merrily and introduced himself to his fellow passengers. The quiet trio offered nothing more than silent nods.

'Morning. Name's Pelopidas. You?'

'Tarchon.'

'Good to meet you. You headed to Odessos?'

'I am.'

'You going to the games?'

'The games?'

'Never heard of The Odessos Games? Very famous. Held every five years.'

'Actually, now that you say it, maybe I have. What's your discipline?'

'Boxing.'

That didn't surprise Tarchon at all.

Pelopidas gazed out at the sea. 'I hope we get fair winds. I'll need a few days on land for my stomach to recover. My trainer was supposed to be with me but the old fool broke his ankle last week.' The boxer nibbled his lower lip. 'Won't be the same without him.'

'There's an arena in Odessos?'

'Large one. They get athletes and visitors from all over. My trainer says there won't be as many this year due to this trouble with the Goths but the organiser has some wealthy patrons. The winner gets a medal and twenty aurei. Even a semi-finalist gets six.'

'Not bad. I've done a bit myself. Maybe we can spar on the deck?'

Pelopidas sighed. 'I'll be lucky if I'm not throwing my guts up. Don't like boats. Don't like water much either.' He then pointed at Tarchon's bandaged arm. 'What did you do to yourself?'

'Burn – from a fire.'

'Honoured guests!' announced Sardenos, standing on the gangplank. 'We will shortly be departing. Please feel free to come aboard.'

Despite the captain's warm welcome, the passengers were swiftly ushered forward to the bow and out of the sailors' way. Sardenos did, however, introduce his second-in-command: a brawny fellow of at least fifty with the dark, leathery skin typical of a lifelong mariner. His name was Metrobius, and he possessed an unruly shock of grey hair that looked to have been fixed permanently in place by brine. The man did not shout, but was evidently respected by his subordinates, who obeyed his every growl of instruction without question.

The three wary passengers remained impervious to Pelopidas' attempts to befriend them but he did get the family talking. It turned out that they were only going as far as Apollonia Pontica; they had been in Byzantium visiting an aunt who apparently did not have long to live.

The nine passengers sat up against the wooden rails that ran along the sides of the *Erythrai*, watching as the oarsmen took their places. Sardenos and another man untied the lines from the bollards on the quay, then jumped aboard. Having checked that their way was clear, the young captain ordered that they cast off. Using their oars, the crewmen neatly pushed the coaster away from the concrete quay and they drifted slowly out into the channel. Sardenos and Metrobius remained on the higher rear deck, constantly looking around the busy harbour.

'Oars up,' ordered the captain. 'Hold for now.'

Sardenos had seen the bulky freighter coming in through the harbour entrance and waited for it to pass. Suddenly, Metrobius darted across the deck and leaned over the left side-rail. 'Clear out of it, you lot! Or I'll put an oar through your timbers!'

No answer came but the passengers soon saw the target of his ire: four lads in a tiny fishing boat, two of them holding a net. One muttered something but they too seemed in awe of the wild-looking mariner.

'Give him a trident,' said Pelopidas with a wink, 'and he'd make for a passable Poseidon.'

It seemed that the goat had died in vain. After they had cleared the Straits, the wind remained stubbornly from the north, slowing their progress and constantly pushing the *Erythrai* towards shore. Sardenos did not raise any sail, instead relying on his crew's skill and endurance with the oars. Though he'd done more than a bit himself, Tarchon marvelled at the economy and power of the sailors. They rotated by doing an hour on, followed by a half-hour break. The two officers did their share but Metrobius expended most of his energy on berating the crew when – in his view – they slacked off or disrupted the rhythm. The man was clearly a perfectionist. This crew needed no drum; in the parlance of sailors, they had been expertly "beaten together".

The passengers remained at the bow and Tarchon rather enjoyed the afternoon. He certainly enjoyed it more than poor Pelopidas, who literally turned green after half an hour and was then sick at regular intervals. Tarchon offered him water – and the sailors offered him plenty of advice – but the boxer did no more than sit with his hands over the rail, lost in his misery. Sardenos assured him that he would adjust by the next day and feel fine for the remainder of the journey.

As for the three quiet passengers, they kept themselves to themselves, often speaking in hushed tones. The family seemed used to sea travel, though the young daughter attracted the ire of Metrobius when she began clipping her nails. Tarchon knew of the many superstitions of sailors but the girl and her father were considerably less understanding. A bit of diplomacy from the ever-friendly Sardenos smoothed the waters.

An hour before dusk, the family ate their meal and offered Tarchon some dried beef. He readily offered some apples in return and later enjoyed listening in as mother and daughter sang a song. They were actually very good and Sardenos also allowed the crew to stop work and listen. Tarchon couldn't help thinking of the female agent, Kallisto.

As the sun set, the wind eased off. The young captain was able to reduce his number of oarsmen, though they kept hard at it. The son from the family insisted he would never be able to sleep with the squeaking of the oars so his father suggested that he stick bread in his ears.

When the last of the sun's pink light disappeared, Sardenos reduced his oarsmen further to just six, though they still kept the *Erythrai* moving well across the calm sea. Pelopidas had picked up at last, and now accepted some water and laid out beside Tarchon under his blanket.

Tarchon was not yet sleepy so he remained sitting against the side-rail, gazing at the coast. The *Erythrai* was currently opposite a grass-covered headland that was now no more than a dim shape in the darkness. Tarchon wished he'd not seen it before trying to sleep: it reminded him of Green Cove.

XX

In late afternoon of the following day, the *Erythrai* docked at Apollonia Pontica. Tarchon said goodbye to the friendly family and accompanied Pelopidas onto the quay. The harbour was small compared with those of Byzantium and overlooked by a large temple, which had clearly benefited from a new coat of paint. The entrance was dominated by four, huge gleaming pillars and a red door. At the base of the high, wide steps, four braziers emitted more smoke than flame.

Though he'd managed to sleep, Pelopidas seemed immensely relieved to be on solid ground. His relief would, however, be temporary. Due to the clement conditions, Captain Sardenos was determined to press on through the night once again. As the pair walked along the narrow quay towards the town, they were harried by vendors carrying trays and baskets of offerings. Pelopidas simply groaned at the sight of food but Tarchon bought some dried olives and a bit of dried cod. The pair sat on stone bollards and watched as a wagon pulled up.

'That's the *Erythrai*,' said the driver, pointing at the newly-arrived ship. 'That wild-haired fellow is sailing master.'

He halted the horse and climbed down with a second man. They pulled a cover off the wagon to reveal dozens of new-looking copper pots.

'Afternoon,' said Sardenos, waving as he strode down the quay to meet his clients.

'Good day,' said the man. 'Thought we might not see you until tomorrow.'

'We're moving quick,' replied the captain. 'And I want to get these on board now.'

'You're going back out tonight?'

'We are. Got the agreed order?'

'All sixty. Factory tried to give us five with holes in but we're wise to their tricks.'

'Good idea to keep moving, captain,' advised his mate. 'I'd get in and out of Odessos as quick as you can.'

'Don't tell me – the Goths.'

'News came down yesterday of a raid on Callatis. That's no more than two days' ride from Odessos. My cousin's an auxiliary; he reckons two centuries have been sent our way from Cabyle. Hope they get here sharpish.'

The usually cheerful Sardenos looked rather grim as he summoned his men and helped unload the cart.

'Doesn't sound good,' said Pelopidas. 'I hope the games are still going ahead. If not, I'm out of pocket with no chance of winning any back.'

'There must be other games?'

'It's the biggest around. There are plenty of rich folk there, hopefully they'll still want some entertainment.'

Sardenos approached the two passengers. 'You heard that, I suppose? If you'd like to stop here and look for passage back south, I can refund the difference.'

'Not me,' said Tarchon.

'How far to go?' asked Pelopidas.

'About forty miles. Wind is from the south now, so we'll make five knots. Should be in before midday tomorrow.'

'Have you heard anything more about the games?' asked Pelopidas.

'Afraid not. All I know is what I told you earlier.' Sardenos returned to his men.

'Which was?' asked Tarchon.

'He knows a captain who took four runners from Byzantium up to Odessos. But that was three weeks ago.'

Pelopidas stood up and put a hand to his stomach. 'Still bloody aches. Can't work out if it's the sickness or because I've not eaten anything.' He glanced up at the gleaming temple. 'I should really pay my respects. My father is a great lover of Apollo.'

'Best save your strength,' advised Tarchon.

'Admiring our temple?' said a croaky voice.

The pair turned round to see a stooped old sailor with a mangy-looking cat under one arm.

'Aye,' said Pelopidas.

'As temples go, it's not bad,' added the old man. 'But we used to have a *statue* of Apollo. Eighty feet high. Imagine that. Then some Roman bastard took it back to the capital.'

'Ah yes,' said Pelopidas, 'My father told me of it. Lucullus, a general. He later fought against Spartacus.'

The old man grunted. 'Like I said – bastard.'

The sailors never stopped. Though their rowing duties were temporarily suspended, they now had to care for the sails. Every last man was required to haul up the yard, lower the mainsail, set it for the wind conditions, then monitor it closely. Four or five times an hour, either Sardenos or Metrobius would order some adjustment to the yard, the sail or the lines. Those not involved in this duty were oiling the over-worked oar fittings, stitching up another sail, burnishing the signal mirror. The two youngest lads were tasked with producing food, which looked to be of the basic variety. Sardenos did, however, personally give his crew a mug of honey-spirit at sundown.

Knowing he would reach Odessos the following day, Tarchon again found it difficult to sleep. The advance of the Goths was the reason behind his mission, but what if they had advanced even further south? News was always days or weeks old and they were known for their speed of movement. Tarchon recalled some of the tales he'd heard of Gothic warriors. They were said to be much taller and stronger than the Greek peoples, and many possessed that unusual fair hair that he'd occasionally seen in Byzantium. The thought of being in a city under threat from these warriors of the north – however briefly – was not a pleasant one. And yet, sitting there in silence below the sail, beside the sleeping Pelopidas, Tarchon smiled. Only a few weeks after the failed robbery, here he was on a mission for the Empire, and a well-paid one at that.

At dawn, rain came. The wind also dropped, meaning the sail was lowered and the crew took up their oars once more. Sardenos acknowledged that he'd worked them hard but assuaged them with promises of a bonus based largely on the delivery of the copper pots. By now, Pelopidas had recovered himself, even eating a breakfast of bread, cod and olives with Tarchon. The downpour lasted only an hour or so but the breeze didn't return, so Sardenos kept his men at the oars. The grey clouds became white clouds and began to break up. It didn't take long for the deck to dry.

'With the sail down, we can use the bow to spar,' suggested Tarchon, who was bored and always eager to learn from an expert.

Pelopidas made a face. 'Just as I'm feeling well again?'

'It's your last day.'

Pelopidas looked at the bow. There was sufficient space and the sailors were all occupied on their benches or elsewhere. Sardenos was asleep under a blanket but Metrobius was close by, studying the shore, which was no more than two miles to the east. Tarchon approached him.

'All right if he and I spar a bit up forward?'

The lined, lumpen face appraised him briefly before replying. 'Don't see why not.'

Tarchon pointed towards the small settlement opposite their position. White walls and red tiles marked it out from the thick forest that dominated the surrounding land. 'Where's that?'

'Naulochos.'

'Never heard of it.'

'Not much to recommend it,' remarked Metrobius. 'Only the one tavern. Pricey wine and the ugliest maid you ever saw – they call her Hagfish.'

Surprised by the veteran's levity, Tarchon chuckled and returned to Pelopidas.

The boxer was now close to the bow, already warming up. Tarchon had never been properly instructed, so he simply copied Pelopidas, who had been rotating his arms and was now repeatedly touching his toes.

'You done much?' he asked with a grin.

'Proper boxing, no,' replied Tarchon. 'Street boxing – a bit. Mainly at the races.'

'Ah. I have a couple of friends who're always trying to get me along. My trainer forbids it. He's right of course. Broken hand and I'm out for six months.'

'I like how you dodge and cover up – stop yourselves getting hit.'

Pelopidas had moved on to twisting from side to side. Tarchon emulated him once more as he continued: 'Trouble is, on the streets, while you're covering your head, some bastard will hit you low.'

'Let's do some defence then,' said Pelopidas.

'Covering up?'

'Yes. Put your hands up.'

Tarchon tried to copy the classic boxer's stance, with elbows low and forearms protecting his face. Pelopidas made a few adjustments then stepped back.

'I'll try and hit your head.'

'When you say *hit*…'

'Just a tap. Don't worry.'

'I'm not worried.'

Pelopidas went easy on him to start with. It was – as expected – very different to a street fight. Most of those had been over before Tarchon could think about it; won by the aggressor who'd landed the most hits or one telling blow. When Pelopidas realised Tarchon could dodge or duck his more obvious strikes, he began to deploy his full range: straight jabs, upper cuts, crosses. Even his swinging blows were efficient and controlled. What impressed Tarchon even more was that, despite the speed, he could limit the impact.

'Your guard is fine,' said Pelopidas. 'And you're watching me well. Just need to move your feet quicker. Stay on your toes isn't just a saying, you know!'

Tarchon was now sweating and aching; and thoroughly enjoying himself. Pelopidas still regularly landed blows, but – as time passed – he began to evade more shots. One he evaded so well that he almost tripped and went over the side, earning him a stern look from Metrobius.

'How's the gut?' Tarchon asked when the pair took a break.

'Not bad, thanks.'

'Hope the games *are* on. You'll do well, I'm sure. How many times have you broken your nose?'

'Three.' Pelopidas grinned and aimed a finger at him. 'But not recently!'

'So now I get to try and hit you?'

'Hey – just taps.' The boxer eyed Tarchon's frame carefully. 'I reckon you're at least one weight up from me.'

'I'll go easy.'

The next half-hour was as helpful as the first. Tarchon reckoned it was hard to put a value on instruction from men like Pelopidas or Korax or Bernardus. He planned to use much of his earnings on improving every one of his fighting skills. Working for Gargonius, he was sure to meet some tough characters, and his career would be very short if he couldn't defend himself better than most.

By the time they finished, both men's bodies were slick with sweat. They slumped down and emptied their water flasks.

'Not bad,' said Pelopidas. 'You're quick, you're better with your weaker hand than most, and you see things early.'

'Thanks. And for the lesson.'

The last portion of the journey seemed to go on and on. Though the oarsmen of the *Erythrai* kept up their impressive rhythm and speed, progress north seemed slow to Tarchon. He found himself checking that progress against landmarks on the coast. But this made the trip seem even slower, prompting him to swap sides so he was looking out to sea. He and Pelopidas had talked for quite a time after the sparring, but even the cheerful boxer now seemed preoccupied and impatient to reach their destination.

In mid-afternoon, Metrobius alerted Sardenos to a problem. Listening in, Tarchon gathered that a large fishing net had wrapped itself around the rudder. This was slowing them down and would be even more problematic when they had to manoeuvre. Sardenos ordered his men to ship their oars, which they did with more celebration than complaint. Sardenos and two others stripped down to their loin-cloths and jumped off the stern. The captain could soon be heard complaining that the net was also tangled in the mechanism that connected the rudder to the tiller.

Metrobius told the oarsmen to rest and didn't seem overly concerned. The three other passengers, however, clearly *were*. They had been constantly pestering the captain for estimates of their arrival time and now sat in a huddle, talking in urgent whispers.

'What's up?' asked Pelopidas. 'Got to be in before sundown?'

One of the three nodded by way of reply.

Over the next few minutes, as Sardenos and his crewmen laboured to remove the net, the three passengers became increasingly agitated.

Tarchon and Pelopidas glanced at each other and shrugged. Then a frowning Metrobius marched along the central aisle, past the oarsmen on their benches. Climbing up onto the foredeck, he peered over the passengers' shoulders and was suddenly shouting.

'Put that away! We'll have none of your magic-making on here!'

His outburst prompted some of the crew to join him.

'What are they doing?' asked one.

'I saw a cross!' exclaimed Metrobius with a snarl. 'Bloody cultists.'

'So what?' said one of the crew. 'My sister-in-law's one of them. Don't mean any harm.'

'That's fine on land,' said another, stabbing a finger at his compatriot. 'But here we respect the *true* gods – above all the god of the sea. You three – stop whatever it is you're doing!'

The three passengers reacted by scrambling away to the bow, where one of them clasped his hands together and looked to the skies.

'Stop that!' yelled Metrobius, pursing them across the deck, followed by several other sailors. 'You'll put a curse on us all.'

'Maybe get between them,' Tarchon suggested. 'I'll fetch Sardenos.'

'Good thinking,' said the boxer.

Given Pelopidas' earlier display of fighting skill, Tarchon reckoned it unlikely anyone would take him on, so he focused on alerting the captain. These types of arguments were pretty common and Metrobius was not unusual in being a sailor as combative as he was superstitious. Theirs was an unusually dangerous life and they hated ignorant land-lubbers who provoked the gods and made some nautical disaster more likely.

Tarchon ran back to the stern, where a couple of the younger sailors were alternating their attention between the developing row and the ongoing operation below. Tarchon looked down and saw the three divers surface, each clutching a portion of the net, which was thick with weed and shellfish.

'Captain, we have a problem up here.'

'Yes?' said Sardenos, clearing hair from his face, his afflicted eye already blinking.

'The three quiet passengers – they're Christians. Metrobius saw a cross. He and some of the others aren't very happy.'

The captain slapped the water with his hand and cursed.

'All right. I'm coming.'

Passing his section of net to one of the others, he swam to the ladder hanging from the stern and hauled himself out of the water.

Tarchon ran back to the bow ahead of him, where he found Pelopidas doing a good job of keeping the warring factions apart. In fact, the sailors were now arguing amongst themselves, one contending that these were paying passengers who should be left alone.

'I'll leave them alone when they chuck that accursed cross over the side,' said Metrobius.

The Christians weren't exactly helping themselves. While two continued to pray, the third was holding the cross up, as if warding off evil.

'Look at them,' remarked one of the crew. 'They're loving this – nice bit of oppression will make their day!'

Fortunately, the arrival of Sardenos swiftly brought the incident to a close. On his order, most of the sailors returned to their posts, with only Metrobius and another remaining.

'Sorry, cap,' said the sailing master, 'but it's a provocation. They know it's not allowed.'

'I'll deal with you later,' said Sardenos. 'For now, you can get wet and clear the bloody rudder.'

The wild-haired Metrobius ran his tongue around his mouth for a bit before walking towards the stern, his compatriot close behind.

'Apologies,' said Sardenos to the passengers, who at least seemed to have calmed down. The eldest of them; a lean, bearded man, stood up and bowed respectfully.

'And our apologies to you, captain. We are sorry for offending your sailors but we simply wished to invoke the Lord's help. We *must* reach Odessos by sundown.'

'Well, I *am* trying to make that happen,' said Sardenos, still dripping water onto the deck as he strode away.

'What's so urgent?' asked Pelopidas.

'The festival of Andrew the apostle ends today,' explained the bearded man. 'If we are not there before sundown, our pilgrimage is in vain. You are clearly men of good intent. Apollonia is a great centre of worship. Perhaps you would like to join us and learn more of the Lord and the Kingdom?'

'No thanks,' said Pelopidas. 'Got urgent business of my own.'

The Christian turned his eyes on Tarchon.

'Me too.'

Thankfully the net was swiftly removed and the Christians sensibly made no more overt religious gestures. With sundown three or four hours away, the wind came again, this time from the east. It would have been perfect for the sail but Sardenos clearly thought that raising it would cost more time than it was worth. Those at the oars had at least enjoyed a brief break and they now powered the *Erythrai* across an increasingly choppy sea. The captain clearly knew he had worked them hard; he personally doled out another ration of honey-spirit and informed the sailors that they would receive a small advance on their wages.

Tarchon was glad to see that the captain and sailing master had made their peace while recovering the net. With Odessos now only a few miles away, they each took up an oar to do their bit. Tarchon also offered his services but Sardenos refused, apparently concerned that word might get around of him using passengers on the benches.

As the sun descended over the province of Moesia to the west, the *Erythrai* turned in the same direction. The pink light of dusk created a glittering path upon the water that drew murmurs of approval from both the sailors and the Christians, who now had a slim chance of arriving before nightfall.

'That bodes well for our time here,' said Pelopidas, standing with Tarchon just forward of the mast.

Sardenos was at the tiller now, with Metrobius at the bow, occasionally calling out navigational instructions. The westward turn took them around a high headland and into the estuary of the river Devna. Tarchon had learned from Sardenos that, a few miles inland, the river became a lake. At the western end of that lake was another city: Marcianopolis. The captain had clearly not followed this route many times because he was entirely dependent on Metrobius' guidance.

'Quarter-mile more,' shouted the sailing master. 'When we're due south of the tower, we turn in.'

Sardenos kept his course, his men still dipping their oars and propelling the *Erythrai* into the estuary at speed. As they neared the city, Tarchon could make out the wall that protected Odessos. Someway inland was the tower Metrobius had mentioned and, once the turn was made, Tarchon could also see the harbour.

As they got closer, he noted a long, high mole that would protect the vessels moored at the quay. It turned out to be a surprisingly long quay but there were only five ships present. Four were freighters; all longer and broader than the *Erythrai*. The last was a Roman warship.

'Behind the destroyer?' suggested Metrobius, using a term employed by some sailors.

'Aye,' agreed Sardenos, making an adjustment to his course. 'Lads – one last effort. Let's get our guests in before sundown and dock with a bit of light to guide us. Three-quarter speed – follow Agathon.'

This sailor seemed to be third-in-command. Like many of them, he rowed only in his loin-cloth. He was of average size but apparently without a single morsel of fat on his body. His veins throbbed and his muscles pumped but his expression remained impassive. Though most looked considerably wearier, the others matched Agathon's increased pace, and the *Erythrai* cut across the estuary at speed, the only vessel on the water. Once in the lee of the mole, the sea calmed notably and they swiftly reached the harbour, Sardenos ordering quarter-speed as he brought his ship in behind the stern of the naval craft.

Half of the rowers then put down their oars and lowered the fenders that would protect the ship's wooden hull from the stone quay. Metrobius and two others were ready with the lines, which were taken by two helpful locals. As soon as the ship was secure, the Christians paid their dues and leaped onto the quay, instantly questioning the locals about the location of a church-house. As for the sailors, they all joined Sardenos in a brief prayer of thanks to Poseidon, Jupiter, Mercury and several other gods.

'Look there,' said Pelopidas, pointing to the warship. A crew of a dozen were busily working away at the stern, now under lamplight. Half of the men were on small seats, suspended on lines above, tools in hand.

One of the men who'd taken their lines turned out to be the assistant harbour master. When the gangplank was on, he came aboard and spoke to the captain. Tarchon and Pelopidas moved astern to listen in.

'Did you see any warships?'

'Just that one,' replied Sardenos. 'Why?'

'Hoping for some reinforcements.' The local gestured to the ship. '*Hercules* got knocked about by two Goth ships on her way south. There's talk of another warship being sent across from Trapezus but no sign of her yet.'

To Tarchon, this indicated a serious situation. Trapezus was far to the east, many hundreds of miles away, on the north coast of Bithnyia. The port city was close to the edge of the Empire and had long been considered at risk from Goths. If the navy were taking a ship from there, the fleet was clearly thinly-stretched.

'*Hercules* was the last ship stationed at Callatis,' added the assistant harbour master. 'It was overrun two weeks ago.'

'What about the legions?' asked Sardenos. 'Are there enough men here to defend the city?'

'No idea. There are three centuries, three more in Marcianopolis. Plus the local militia. A small cavalry detachment too and they sighted Goth scouts in the hills to the north only yesterday. They're getting closer every bloody day.'

Tarchon turned to the optimistic Pelopidas. 'That does *not* bode well.'

XXI

Captain Sardenos said they could stay onboard with no extra charge but neither Tarchon nor Pelopidas took up his offer. The boxer was clearly keen to stay on dry land and Tarchon wanted to get to work immediately. From what he'd heard, the situation was even worse than Gargonius and Korax had suggested, so he needed to contact Kallisto urgently. The pair said their farewells to Sardenos, Metrobius and the others on the quay. Tarchon had been impressed with the young captain and he hoped that he might sail on the *Erythrai* again.

Sardenos planned to unload his copper pots in the morning, load some previously agreed cargo and then take as many passengers as he could. Though the hour was late, several enquiries had already been made by people hanging around the quay, looking for passage south. Many were families and most were carrying heavy loads; they were clearly planning to leave Odessos for the foreseeable future.

Just as Tarchon and Pelopidas hoisted their own packs – headed for an inn recommended by the assistant harbour master – a trio of armed men marched on to the quay. Spying the twenty or so people congregated near the *Erythrai*, they raised their lanterns and went to investigate. One was a legionary. He was wielding a spear and already seemed annoyed about something. With him were two irregulars – presumably locals – armed with clubs.

'Who's just got off?' asked the soldier.

'These two,' explained Sardenos, pointing to Tarchon and Pelopidas, 'and three earlier. I have all the names.'

'Three earlier? Every single new arrival is to be accounted for. Magistrate's orders.'

'I wasn't to know that. Who are you?'

The soldier answered with an angry glare. 'Legionary Heirax, second century of the garrison, under the command of Centurion Panares, who is in charge of security for the entirety of Odessos. Good enough?'

Sardenos' eye twitched as he held up his hands. 'Good enough. The first three were Christians – they were headed for a church-house.'

'Christians,' said one of the irregulars. 'Least they won't cause any trouble.'

'If they *are* Christians,' countered the legionary. What about you two?'

'Pelopidas. I'm here for the games. Do you know if they're going ahead?'

The legionary exchanged a look with his compatriots, then gave a cynical smile. 'The last I heard – yes. The governor wants everything to continue as normal and the organiser of the games is his brother. Must keep up appearances.'

'Doubt there'll be anyone in the stadium though,' said one of the irregulars.

'And you?' said the legionary to Tarchon.

'I work for a merchant in Byzantium. I'm here to escort his niece back there. Name's Tarchon.'

'Why does a merchant's lackey carry a sword?'

'We heard it could be dangerous up here.'

This Heirax seemed to Tarchon very much like other soldiers he'd met: arrogant bullies with too much power in their hands.

'I'm no one's lackey,' he added.

'I can vouch for them both,' said Sardenos.

'Where are you staying?' asked Heirax.

'The Octopus for tonight,' said Pelopidas.

'Notify the basilica or someone here at an army post if you move. And when you leave. I suggest staying off the streets after dark. Not every patrol will be as friendly as us.'

'I thought the governor wanted things to continue as normal,' said Tarchon.

Heirax held his lantern unnecessarily close to Tarchon's face. 'My centurion has orders to protect and hold Odessos. That means keeping an eye out for spies and saboteurs. And troublemakers.'

The Octopus inn was two minutes' walk away, close to the mole. Passing the other ships, they saw that these crews were also up on the quay, exchanging news with the locals. Unsurprisingly, most of the talk concerned the Goths. One man loudly contended that he was not worried; such enemy forays happened from time to time and he reckoned them to be no match for the Roman troops and local militia.

'Let's hope he's right,' said Pelopidas.

At the doorway of the Octopus, a flickering lantern illuminated a many-tentacled image etched upon a rusty plaque. Lamps were alight inside and they could see several patrons within the parlour. Pelopidas raised the latch and Tarchon followed him inside. The two groups of men present – sailors judging by their clothing and tanned faces – paid the pair little attention as they entered. The front of the parlour's counter was decorated with octopi, squid and starfish and reminded Tarchon of the (less exotic) illustrations at Mehruz's eatery. Behind the counter were shelves occupied by all manner of jars, bottles and flasks. Above these were a series of pegs, each holding a length of dried sausage or salted fish. The counter at first seemed unmanned but then a young man popped his head up, holding four empty mugs. His brow was wet with sweat and he looked rather anxious.

'Where's that round?' yelled one of the sailors.

'It's coming!' replied the young man, trying – but failing – to sound polite. He then returned his attention to the new arrivals.

'Do you have a room?' asked Pelopidas.

'We do, yes, though I've not had time to clean it. Sorry, Mother's laid up with her bunions and Father's off training spearmen. I'll get you clean sheets, of course. Room Three has two singles.'

'That's fine,' said Tarchon. 'Do you know Thalia's?'

'Everyone knows Thalia's,' said the young man as he began pouring the wine. 'Head back along the quay for a quarter-mile, turn right at The Avenue of Gordian, then left into Dyer's Lane. You won't miss it – most popular tavern in the city.'

'Even now?' asked Tarchon. 'With all that's going on?'

Their host nodded towards the sailors. 'When folk are worried, some turn to drink and merriment.'

'Have you heard anything about the games?' asked Pelopidas. 'Apparently, they're going ahead.'

'Really? I'd assumed they'd been cancelled. We did have a javelin-thrower in last week though. Tall fellow. Kept banging his head on the parlour door. I'll just serve this lot, then I'll take you upstairs.'

Fortunately, the room wasn't notably dirty, and their host – who was named Chremes – swiftly supplied both the sheets and a jug of water. He couldn't offer them any hot food but would bring up a cold meal, which was sufficient for Tarchon and Pelopidas. Tarchon unpacked his belongings, hanging his spare tunic and other clothes from a rafter to air them. The sword he hung from his bedpost.

'You useful with that thing?' asked Pelopidas. He had stripped off and was now cleaning himself with a cloth and his half of the water.

'Wouldn't go that far,' replied Tarchon. 'Like I said, my employer gave it to me as a precaution.'

'So, the woman you've come for – she works at this Thalia's?'

'Apparently. I'll go there tomorrow morning.'

'And I'll go to the stadium.'

'What if there are no crowds?'

'I reckon there will be. Like the man said, people look for distractions at times like this. My trainer reckons that was half the reason the old emperors put on games: to keep the people happy. Same as handing out bread.'

'I'd never really thought about it like that.'

'A crowd is good – it helps get your blood up. But if there aren't many there, at least it will be the same for all of us.' Pelopidas now meticulously washed his right foot. It seemed to Tarchon that he was by nature very precise; it had certainly shown in his sparring.

'As long as there's prize money, it was worth the trip.'

'Assuming you win some, that is.'

Pelopidas grinned as he cleaned his underarms. 'Good point.'

Not long after he'd finished washing, the meal arrived. It was simple fare: rather stale bread, half a sausage, and an apple each. The sausage turned out to be quite good; not much fat and well spiced with what the pair eventually decided was basil and sage.

They'd also been given a flask of wine and two mugs. The wine was rather tart but they filled their mugs and sat by the room's only window. Though the *Erythrai* was out of sight to their right, they could see a couple of the ships and mole stretching out into the broad estuary. The three-quarter moon was strong enough to penetrate a thin covering of cloud and glitter on the rippled water. The fading wind rattled ropes and stays but all else seemed quiet.

'Peaceful,' said Pelopidas.

'Yes,' said Tarchon. 'For now.'

Preferring a proper dip to a wash, he rose just before dawn. No one else was up, but he unbolted the front door and walked barefoot across the street. In the half-light, he could see a couple of sailors pottering around and some others on the quay. The concrete mole was in poor repair, covered with many fissures and holes, so Tarchon didn't venture far. A rough staircase had been cut into the inland side. Here, he took off his tunic and walked down into the cool water, wearing only his loin cloth. He hadn't slept well and felt weary as well as sweaty and grimy but a few moments in the water refreshed him. Running his hands over his body, he felt energy returning. During his many nights on the streets, Tarchon had always done this, whatever the season. He'd never been able to understand those who feared the water. The sea had always given him sustenance and employment and, in Byzantium, it was never far away. To him, it was one of the gods' greatest gifts.

Pelopidas was still snoring when he returned, only waking when Tarchon shut the door.

'You're up early. Not even light yet.'

'Fancied a swim.'

'Fair enough.'

As the boxer dozed off again, Tarchon hung up his wet loincloth and put on a fresh one. He lay out on his blanket, knowing he'd be unable to get back to asleep. It was a Tuesday, which meant Kallisto was supposed to be performing at Thalia's. But that would not be until later in the day and – with the current situation in the city – he could not afford to waste those hours. If he could quickly locate her, there might even be a chance of getting away on the *Erythrai*. With this resolution made, he drifted back to sleep, waking only when Pelopidas gave him a nudge.

'Ready for some breakfast? I should really go for a run but I'm going to head off to the stadium straight away. Need to know what's going on.'

'Same here,' said Tarchon.

He considered taking his sword but reckoned that might arouse the suspicions of the local patrols. So, once he had tunic and belt on, he attached only the dagger. He tied his money bag to the inside of his belt and placed within it the miniature spearhead that Korax had given him. Pelopidas let him out first and locked the door behind them.

As soon as they entered the parlour, Chremes apologised for the lack of fresh loaves. Apparently, the magistrate had ordered that half of all bread be delivered to the local fortress, for distribution to the legionaries, auxiliaries and the reserve militia. It was the militia that Chremes' father was training: a well-established force made up of veterans and new volunteers. Chremes expressed his fear that he might be conscripted, despite his flat feet and poor eyesight. Tarchon and Pelopidas were the only ones in the parlour and their host did compensate them for the stale bread with a double portion of sausage and fresh milk. The Octopus' only other guests – a middle-aged couple – came down just as the pair left.

Every hand was at work on the *Erythrai*, unloading the copper pots and the remaining cargo. Tarchon and Pelopidas exchanged greetings with Metrobius, who told them that the absent Sardenos was with the harbour master. Despite the early hour, the quay was already filling up with yet more locals seeking passage out of Odessos. Tarchon reckoned that the skippers might profit well from the Goth advance.

The stadium was situated on the western side of Odessos, some way inland. At the Avenue of Gordian, the room-mates parted, both wishing each other luck with their endeavours. Tarchon headed north, away from the estuary along the broad avenue. Here, Odessos didn't seem so very different to Byzantium. As the city began to wake, wagons of goods and building materials rolled up and down, and people gathered at the usual popular places: taverns, temples, civic buildings and the residences of their patrons. Yet there were signs that all was not well; the locals seemed to move with unusual haste, their expressions anxious and grave. Tarchon also passed a statue of Tiberius lying beside a plinth and two empty building sites covered with wooden scaffolds and ladders.

Chremes had told he and Pelopidas that the city's baths were quite a landmark and so it proved: a sprawling complex of grand buildings surrounded by flowerbeds and boasting a large exercise yard. Apparently, the building had been commissioned by the emperor Gordian only a few years previously. He was known for taking the purple at an exceptionally young age – just thirteen – and dying six years later. Tarchon remembered hearing news of Gordian's death: he had been out raiding an orchard after yet another argument with his father. While the youngster had ruled, Tarchon and his friends had often discussed what it might be like to command such power.

He also passed a number of patrols. The guiding hand of this Centurion Panares was clear because every unit was the same as that he'd encountered the night before: a legionary supported by two local irregulars. Twice he saw these patrols questioning a fearful-looking suspect.

Turning into Dyer's Lane – a street of middling townhouses and three storey apartment blocks – he encountered two families loading a cart while being berated by a red-faced neighbour for their "cowardice". The second part of the lane was less busy, partly due to a collapsed apartment block and the pile of refuse that had grown up around it. Here, Tarchon received some suspicious looks from a group of children scouring the rubbish. He thought of Eagle and Hawk – the pair who'd located the rope for him back in Byzantium.

Thalia's was easily identified; the name had been painted above the entrance in red. On one side of the door was a well-rendered jewelled goblet, on the other a flute. The two-storey building stood alone, with an overgrown garden to the right, and a walled courtyard to the left, where there were many tables and stools. Tarchon could only see these because of a barred section in the middle of the wall, presumably there to show potential customers what they were missing. He saw no sign of life in the garden or the courtyard and was not surprised to find the door locked. He knocked but there was no answer.

He turned around, tapping his thumbs against his belt in annoyance. Opposite the tavern was a low, brick building. Thick smoke was rising from a chimney and he could hear the clanging of tools from within. He wondered if someone inside might know where he could find Kallisto. But as he neared the open doorway, a soft voice called out to him.

'I wouldn't.'

She seemed to have come from the alley between the left side of the tavern and the adjacent warehouse. She was hard to age due to the hood of the dark blue cape she wore over a light blue dress. Only one side of her face was visible but, as she approached him, Tarchon could see that it was a fair one and that she was smiling. Her appearance was so timely that he wondered if he had somehow already stumbled upon Kallisto.

'You wouldn't what?'

'Go in there – Hektor is not a friendly man and he usually has a hammer in his hand.'

'Ah.'

'Can I help you?'

'Perhaps. My name's Tarchon. Yours?'

By this point, he was almost convinced that this was her. He was prepared to show the spearhead and offer the codeword that Korax had provided.

'Zina.'

'Pleased to meet you.' Deciding that he'd perhaps got carried away with himself, Tarchon pointed towards Thalia's. 'I'm actually looking for a woman who sings there.'

'Cassandra? She's never short of admirers.' Zina failed to hide a note of bitterness in her voice.

'That's not it,' replied Tarchon. 'I have a message for her.'

'She won't be in yet. None of them will. Thalia's doesn't come alive until it gets dark.'

'I see. Any idea where I might find her?'

'Of course. Her house. Would you like me to show you?'

'I'd be grateful. Is it far?'

'Not at all.'

'Come then.' With that, Zina turned around and walked back into the alley she'd emerged from.

Tarchon followed her and soon found himself between the high walls of the warehouse and the tavern's courtyard. Zina said nothing more and he could not walk beside her due to the confined space. Passing the rear of the warehouse, Zina continued over a quiet street and into an even narrower alley where Tarchon had to almost turn sideways.

'Is this the best route?'

'A short cut.'

They passed between two low, ruined houses striped by weeds and ivy. Tarchon was surprised that the dwellings still stood; the roofs retained only a few tiles and the walls were holed and uneven. Zina abruptly stopped and turned.

Tarchon's instincts were already telling him that something was wrong; his fingers reached for his dagger.

'Too late,' said Zina.

Hearing movement behind him, Tarchon looked over his left shoulder, expecting one or more men to have emerged from the shadowy door of the dwelling. In fact, it was another woman. Though shorter, she was dressed identically to Zina, holding the folds of her hood close to her face.

'May I introduce my sister, Mina,' said Zina. 'You'll give us what you have. I've a good eye and I see there's a money bag behind your belt.'

Tarchon turned back to her and drew the dagger, his fingers clammy on the wooden handle. 'Can't say I'd like to stab a woman but I'll do it if I have to.'

'You'll give us what you have,' repeated Zina. 'Or we'll give you what *we* have.'

She dropped her hood. Hers was indeed a fair face but the right side – which she'd obscured – was covered with pale blotches of skin. She had no eyebrow over her right eye, and most of her forehead was covered by ugly growths. Tarchon had observed far worse cases but when he looked back at Mina, he saw the worst he'd ever seen. The growths covered most of her face and were so severe that only her left eye was open. She had also revealed her hands. The fingers were no more than misshapen stumps riddled with scabs and scars.

Leprosy. A word and a disease feared by all. In Byzantium, it was illegal for the afflicted to live within the city limits. All knew that the awful illness could be caught by closeness to sufferers.

The sisters each took a step towards him. Tarchon knew they had chosen the location well. He was utterly trapped.

'You'll give us what you have,' said Mina, her voice also identical to her sister's.

Tarchon could not believe he'd been so stupid. While there was generally more to fear from men, he'd encountered a few crafty, dangerous women on the streets. But never a pair as crafty as these two. They possessed a weapon quite unlike any other. He could see only one way out of this situation.

He held up his dagger. 'I could. Or I could throw this at you and take my chances.'

'You'll still have to get past me,' said Zina. 'And Mina is quicker than she looks. Your other problem is that, the longer this goes on, the longer you're close to us.'

The sisters took another step and one more look at Mina's face was enough to convince Tarchon. He took the money bag from his belt, opened it and began to take out the coins.

'No, no,' said Zina. 'The whole thing.'

'You can have the money but there's one thing I must keep.'

'Could be the most valuable thing in there.'

'Not to you.'

'You'll give us what you have,' said Mina from behind him, taking another step closer.

'By all the gods…'

He threw the bag to Zina, who plucked it out of the air with ease.

'The gods didn't help *us*,' she said. 'They won't help *you*. Have a good day.'

Mina raised her hood and retreated into the shadows. Zina calmly backed away before slipping around a corner.

Tarchon looked down at the dagger in his hand.

'Useless,' he whispered. 'Just like me.'

XXII

It cost one sesterce to get into Thalia's, which was one more than he had. The tavern opened at midday but Tarchon had to stand there and watch others walk inside. For the intervening four hours, he had wandered the area, half hoping to catch sight of the lepers and somehow reclaim his money. As he walked, he considered a number of alternatives: return to the Octopus and sell some of his belongings? (It didn't seem a good idea to ask Chremes for a loan, as he would soon have to pay his bill.) Go to the stadium to find Pelopidas and borrow from him? Use some of his old skills and turn pickpocket?

None of these were particularly appealing but, while hanging around, he did at least hear some useful information: today Thalia's was hosting Cassandra/Kallisto's last appearance for a while. To mark the occasion, she would be performing twice: once at the ninth hour of the day and again at the second hour of night. Tarchon assumed that she would therefore be leaving Odessos and that they could do so together. He had the perfect opportunity to make contact that afternoon. Less perfect was the fact that he couldn't actually get in; and he would have to explain his idiotic failure.

By the eighth hour, at least fifty patrons had entered Thalia's and, considering the wider situation, they seemed a high-spirited bunch. Tarchon had hoped to catch some sight of Kallisto but the only women he'd seen were accompanied by men and none looked like performers. He'd already circled the area twice and decided that one way of gaining entry was to sneak into the courtyard. Climbing the surrounding seven-foot wall was not a problem but, when he looked over it, he saw a number of patrons already there. He couldn't risk them reporting him to the two doormen, one of whom had a blood-stained club hanging from his shoulder. They already knew his face having resisted his earlier attempt to enter without paying.

He decided to try the rear of the tavern. Though anyone looking down from the second storey windows would see him, this area would surely be quieter. However, when he found sufficient holds to help him scramble up the wall, he discovered two obstacles. The first was a line of glass shards and long nails cemented into the top layer of brick. The second was three women sitting at a table, peeling vegetables and singing while they worked.

Dropping back down, Tarchon began a search of the surrounding area for some specific items. Eventually uncovering an old sack, he filled it with grass and weeds. This process revealed a hole in the bottom, which he mended using a piece of old twine retrieved from the nearby pile of refuse. Returning to the wall, he heard no singing but someone was evidently moving around. Only when all was silent did he climb up and place the sack on a less lethal looking part of the barrier.

It was then a case of slowly – and carefully – manoeuvring his body and limbs over the numerous sharp points and edges. Chucking the sack back over the wall, he found himself sitting on the edge and facing one of two open doors. Dropping to the ground, he approached the wall beside the kitchen door, from which the smell of cooking meat emanated. The women were at work inside, talking to a man who sounded like he might be the owner.

Crossing the rear courtyard to the second doorway, Tarchon stopped when he heard approaching footsteps. Fortunately, no one appeared. Peering around the frame, he saw another door on the left side of the corridor swing shut. His nose told him this was the latrine. Deciding he was much less likely to be discovered inside, he at last entered Thalia's.

Beyond the latrine were four closed doors and a stairway leading up, which he walked straight past. From there he came to the tavern's main room, which was one of the largest he'd seen. There was no second storey here, just a high roof decorated with faded frescos. To his left was a long counter running almost to the door. One of the enforcers had just stepped inside, so Tarchon slipped into the shadows beside the bar, pretending to study a price list on a mounted wax tablet. The two men behind the counter were occupied decanting wine from a skin into jugs.

Hoping no one had noticed him, Tarchon continued to examine the place. Forty feet to his right, opposite the counter, was a stage. Along the rear wall were three long benches and, in the middle of the space, circular tables arranged around a stone statue on a wooden plinth. This was Thalia, goddess of music and comedy. Robed and crowned, she held a comic mask in her hand.

Glancing at the patrons, Tarchon realised that many had taken the tables closest to the stage. He also noted that all had mugs of wine in front of them. Unfortunately, there were none in reach at the counter, so he headed for a table where two had been left. Grabbing one as he passed, he was not surprised to find it empty. Having recently learned how much easier life was with a bag of coins, he now found himself cast back into his previous existence, where so much seemed out of reach. Hoping that a large party close to the statue would keep him hidden from the doorman, he sat on one of the benches.

Occasionally pretending to drink, he listened in to the group, which numbered about twenty. They were mostly men and seemed very enthusiastic about hearing Cassandra but regretful that it might be for the last time. There was also plenty of talk about the Goths. Three of the group were auxiliaries and would soon be reporting for duty in Marcianopolis. Two others were grain merchants and both complained about the governor fixing the price to avoid profiteering. Over the next few minutes, more patrons arrived, swiftly filling up the remaining tables and half the benches. Tarchon guessed there were now at least a hundred and fifty within the tavern.

Hearing voices behind him and to the right, he realised he was beside a darkened corridor that presumably led to the artist's dressing rooms. He had seen such a place while doing a day's work moving newly-painted scenery into one of Byzantium's theatres. He could hear a female voice and was considering darting into the corridor when he noticed the doorman moving in his direction. This man was not armed with a club like the other but he walked with a swagger and looked like the type who enjoyed cracking heads. Fortunately, he was intercepted by a patron who stood and engaged him in conversation. Unsure if the doorman had actually noticed him, Tarchon was about to move when someone hurried out of the corridor.

Wearing an ostentatious orange cloak, this bearded man walked up three steps and to the centre of the stage, where there was a single table and chair. Beaming, he halted and clasped his hands. He was clearly well known and respected because the patrons immediately turned towards him and quietened.

'Friends!' he boomed, 'welcome once more to Thalia's. I normally reserve a special welcome for newcomers but I doubt there are many today.'

Feeling some eyes upon him, Tarchon was glad that the host continued.

'This fair city of ours faces trying times. We all know that and I won't darken your mood by talking of it any further. That's not why you come here. And it's not why we host musicians and singers, dancers and acrobats, comics and poets. We do it for the love of the form.'

'I certainly love Cassandra's form!' declared one enthusiastic patron leaning against the counter. Some laughed, some gave him stern looks. The host continued, unperturbed.

'I have to admit we've not had a lot of acts coming through recently and I'm afraid it might remain that way for a time. But one talented lady has stayed here and lightened all our lives with her beauty, her elegance and – above all – her talent. She's favouring us with two shows today. Sadly, her last for a while. But that's all the more reason to respect and enjoy this performance. Please welcome…Cassandra.'

He gestured to the corridor and beamed again. Tarchon saw her sweep past and, as she elegantly climbed the steps, her clinging cream-coloured gown demonstrated that the patron's earlier comment was not misplaced. In one hand was a flute, in the other a small lyre. She was tall, long-limbed and possessor of a remarkable head of curly, red hair that reached halfway down her back. Unusually for a woman in a place dominated by men, she seemed confident and assured. Tarchon reminded himself that this woman was anything but usual: she worked for Gargonius.

She put the lyre on the table and touched hands with the host, who departed swiftly, then stood to watch from the corridor along with a few others. The audience had greeted her with the typical clicking of thumbs and clapping. This continued until she took up the flute. Tarchon was about twenty feet away but noted her large, dark eyes and fine, sculpted features. She seemed to him sultry and mysterious and he wondered how much of that was performance. She took several deep breaths, then lifted the flute and began.

The first tune was a jolly one and when she tapped her foot on the stage, the patrons soon joined in. From there, she moved onto a tune known throughout Thracia and Tarchon reckoned he'd never heard it sound better. Her last piece on the flute was one of long, plaintive notes and, by the end, more than one patron was wiping away a tear.

She sat to play the lyre and the instrument looked like an expensive one, much of it covered with tortoise shell. Tarchon knew nothing about playing music but the immaculate silence of those within Thalia's said it all. As if she wasn't entrancing enough to look at, she played with a great variety, sometimes plucking the strings with softness and delicacy, sometimes striking a thrumming tune that could be danced to. Even the nasty-looking doormen stood there, rapt like the others.

The applause began when she put down the lyre but she wasn't finished. She ended with a song that used many old, obscure words but was – as far as Tarchon could tell – about a woman waiting for her warrior lover to return from war. When the applause ended, she thanked the patrons and the host. Dozens of appreciative replies rang out as she bowed and left the stage.

By the time she reached the bottom of the steps, five different admirers were on their way. Four were holding bunches of flowers and one a small wooden box. As Cassandra strode towards the corridor, the admirers' paths were blocked by the bulky doorman and two other employees. Tarchon stood but as soon as he moved toward her, the bearded host sprang from the shadows and put a hand across his chest.

'Stay back, please.'

'Cassandra, may I speak with you?'

'Sorry,' she said, striding past him and the host without turning her head.

'I have a message from Gargonius.'

She stopped and looked at him, then turned to the host and nodded.

'Not very bloody subtle, are you?' she hissed with an accusing glare. The door had just shut behind them and she stood with her back to a table equipped with an oval mirror and covered with pots and little boxes. Tarchon found himself up against the opposite wall in the tiny dressing room.

'And don't crease my bloody dress!' she snapped. Having been as entranced by her as the rest of the audience, it came as a shock to find that beautiful face contorting into an angry expression. He moved away from the dress hanging behind him.

Sighing, she sat down at the table and removed what Tarchon then discovered was a quite remarkably well-made wig. This she placed upon a wooden head sitting on a small, iron-bound chest. She then undid the twine holding down her own hair, which was black and straight, the odd streak dyed brown by the sun. Once the twine was off and she'd coaxed her hair free, she spun around.

'Codeword?'

'Mogentiana.'

Tarchon was greatly relieved when she gave the matching word. Without the spearhead, he had no other way of proving who he was.

'Arrabona.'

A moment later, the dressing room door opened. The bearded host entered and put down the box and the flowers. Loud applause could still be heard behind him.

'Will you come back on?'

'Not now, Hippon. Perhaps tonight.'

'Very well. You were wonderful, as always.' With a hostile glance at Tarchon, Hippon departed.

Still working on her hair, Kallisto looked Tarchon over, starting with his face and ending with his boots. She didn't seem the type to miss much.

'You new?'

'Yes.'

'Things must be bad. What do I call you?'

'Tarchon.'

'Call me Cassandra – and *only* Cassandra while we're here – understood? Now, what's this message?'

'You're to return to Byzantium immediately. I was told not to take no for an answer.'

She frowned. 'What's wrong with the usual method of communication?'

'I don't know – something happened.'

'At least explains why I've heard nothing for weeks. Well, I'll return when I'm ready.'

'And when will that be?'

'Believe me, I have no wish to remain here longer than necessary.' Brushing some red hair off her pale dress, she aimed a finger towards the door. 'Though that lot out there have convinced themselves they're safe, there's every chance half of them will be Goth slaves by the Festival of Mars. However, I have an opportunity to gain a piece of information that our superior will be very interested in. If he were here, he'd understand. I expect you to help me but if you'd prefer not to, I can handle it on my own.'

'Gargonius told me to bring you back to Byzantium. You said it yourself – this place could fall any day.'

Kallisto crossed her legs, smoothing her gown over her thighs. Tarchon forced himself to keep his gaze on her face.

'So, you've been in this game for…what, weeks?'

'Months. Three months.'

'This is my *seventh* year. I'm telling you I'll leave when I'm ready.'

'By the time you're ready, there might not be a ship left in the harbour.'

Kallisto leaned forward. 'If you want to go – go. But if you stay – help me. You can do that best by keeping quiet and doing what you're told.'

Now Tarchon sighed. It seemed Korax was right; for all her beauty and talent, she was not going to be easy to work with. As it was now clear that he couldn't convince her to leave immediately, he reckoned it as good a time as any for his confession.

'Er, listen, Kall – sorry – Cassandra, I had some…difficulties earlier.'

'Why doesn't that surprise me?'

Tarchon reddened. Though somewhat in awe of this lady, there was only so many insults he would take.

'While I was looking for you, I met a woman who claimed to know you. I should have seen it coming – she obviously pulls this trick regularly.'

Kallisto had opened the gift box and taken out a ring bearing a hexagonal orange gem. 'Mina and Zina? By Jupiter, you are truly an asset to the Service. They robbed you of every coin, I suppose?'

'And my spearhead.'

'Brilliant.'

She reached into the chest, took out a purse and gave him four denarii.

'Thank you.'

'Where are you staying?'

'The Octopus.'

'If I need you, I'll get a message to you. Tell me you can at least fight.'

He shrugged. 'I do all right.'

She did not look particularly impressed. 'What's your name again?'

There was little he could do except return to the inn. Fetching the key from Chremes, he went straight up to the room. Desperate for something to distract him from a burning sense of shame and failure, he sat by the window. While oiling and cleaning his sword as Bernardus had shown him, Tarchon watched the ships. One of the freighters had already departed and the *Erythrai* seemed close to doing so. He had given the ship a wide berth, not wanting to be drawn into a conversation with the crew.

Once he'd finished with the blade, he propped it up against his bed to dry and returned to the window. Sunset wasn't far away and the glow on the water was now more pink than yellow. He reckoned he would normally have felt hungry but the day's events had left his stomach in a knot. It had all gone well until he'd made that fateful, stupid decision to follow that thief bitch Zina. All the confidence gained from his achievements in Byzantium and Nicomedia had drained away.

He could hardly blame Kallisto for being so dismissive. He could also not blame her suitors for pursuing her. As well as her beauty, she seemed to possess intelligence, wit and spirit. He wanted to see her again; and he wanted to prove to her that Gargonius' faith in him was not misplaced.

Pelopidas returned with the last of the light. The usually cheerful boxer sloped in with head bowed. Slumping down on his bed, he managed only a morose nod of greeting.

'Bad day?'

Pelopidas gazed at the ceiling for a moment before speaking.

'Started off well. There were already dozens of competitors at the stadium when I got there. But the place was padlocked.

Eventually this fellow turned up and let us in. For the morning, we just waited around. At the eighth hour, the organiser of games arrived. By then there were fifty of us, at least. He told us that crowds and prize money were limited but the city council was determined that the games go ahead. He promised to return with a schedule but he didn't come back. Then his deputy turned up about an hour ago. With four bodyguards. I knew that wasn't a good sign. Apparently, the provincial governor overruled the council. All civic events are suspended until further notice. I should have known. Why did I waste all that bloody time and money? Who's going to hold a sporting contest when there's an invasion coming? Idiot!' Pelopidas punched the bed.

'Sorry, mate.'

'How about you?'

'Er...not good.' Tarchon wasn't going to tell him about Kallisto and his mission, nor the lepers, but he needed to be honest about his money. As it stood, he wouldn't be able to pay his share of their bill.

'I...got robbed. Only four denarii left.'

'What? You hurt?'

'Just my pride.'

'What a shit day. Did you at least make contact with this woman?'

'I did.'

Neither of them said anything for a while. A couple of drunks passed by the Octopus, enthusiastically singing a sea shanty. It was a very well-known song but they could barely get a word out and – at the third mistake – Tarchon and Pelopidas burst out laughing. Tarchon surprised himself, glad to somehow release the tensions of the day.

Pelopidas dragged himself forward and sat on the edge of the bed. He took off his sandals and his rope belt. 'What a pair, eh? I can cover our bill. I know you're good for it. The *Erythrai* is still here. I daresay Sardenos would let us sail back with him, take payment in Byzantium.'

'I daresay he would – but I have to wait for the woman. She has some job to do and won't leave until it's finished. Thanks for offering to pay the bill – but I'll get some money.'

'All right. How was her singing?'

'Very good. Excellent, actually.'

'Pretty?'

'Oh yes.'

They initially concluded that they couldn't afford dinner but, as their hunger grew, Pelopidas decided that they needed something. Having enjoyed his newfound wealth for some weeks now, Tarchon hated having to depend on his friend but he was starving. He just hoped Kallisto would lend him some more coin.

The parlour was surprisingly busy, with three of the six tables already occupied. Chremes was at the counter and seemed addled as usual, though his mother was working in the kitchen. The smell of spiced chicken wafted into the parlour but it was too pricey, so Tarchon and Pelopidas instead asked for soup. They couldn't afford any wine but Chremes filled their flasks from a barrel of water that didn't taste too bad.

As soon as they sat down, Pelopidas asked Tarchon to describe Kallisto and he tried to do her justice. It was not easy, especially when his efforts were interrupted by a loud man at the back of the parlour. Despite being shouted at by some of the other patrons, the man simply would not shut up. Tarchon turned and saw that he was sitting with another man who looked embarrassed by his friend and was now trying to quieten him. In response, the loud man slapped him.

His compatriot drained his mug, cursed at his companion, then marched out of the Octopus. Watched by Chremes, Tarchon and Pelopidas, the drunk pulled himself to his feet, knocking his mug to the floor.

'What?' he exclaimed in Latin, before switching to a language that neither Tarchon nor Pelopidas understood. A nervous-looking Chremes opened the counter hatch. When he passed their table, Pelopidas asked, 'What's that?'

'The northern tongue. He's talking about the Goths. Says we'll all be dead soon.'

Another patron stood and pointed at the loudmouth. 'You'll shut your trap if you know what's good for you.'

Eyes wild, the man stabbed his finger at every patron in turn. 'Death comes!' he shouted, returning to Latin. 'Fire and ruin! Fire and ruin!'

Despite the volume, the man was of average size and didn't look all that tough.

'Want us to get rid of him?' suggested Pelopidas. 'In return for a plate of chicken, maybe?'

'Sounds fair to me,' replied the innkeeper.

Tarchon also reckoned it was a fair trade. The pair walked past Chremes and the others to the rear of the parlour.

'What you want?' demanded the drunk, eyes glazed, unsteady on his feet.

'You're leaving,' said Tarchon.

'Want a drink. Paying customer.'

'No more for you, mate,' said Tarchon, grabbing him by the arm. The drunk tried to pull away but Tarchon tightened his grip. Though the man was a couple of inches shorter than him – and didn't seem the fighting type – he was glad when Pelopidas grabbed his other arm.

'Easy way or the hard way, mate. Your choice.'

'All right. I'm going. Long as you let go.'

Tarchon did so and gestured to the door. He and Pelopidas followed the weaving drunk to the door, which Chremes had opened.

'Last time in here,' slurred the man, shaking a fist at him. 'Hope they burn this shit hole. Fire and ruin!'

Tarchon grabbed his collar and pushed him out on to the street. It might have been the fresh air but something persuaded the man to turn and have a swing. It was a wild blow and easily avoided by Tarchon. The man stumbled off the pavement but was swiftly back up and swinging again, this time at Pelopidas.

Hearing the commotion, Chremes and the other patrons came to the doorway to watch. As Pelopidas ducked and weaved, he and the drunk moved in and out of the weak circle of light cast by the lantern beside the Octopus' sign. Somehow the man seemed to grow in confidence. Though every lunge and charge was evaded by the nimble Pelopidas, the drunk seemed determined to land a blow.

'Bad idea, mate,' said Tarchon, who was staying out of their way.

Ignoring him, the drunk backed Pelopidas towards the tavern. The boxer stood his ground and waited for the next swing. Slipping it easily, he countered with a short upper cut. Landing with a sharp crack, the blow sent the drunk tottering back into the road. Tarchon had seen it coming and got there in time to catch him on his way down. He'd watched a man die after falling onto stone and didn't want to see it again – even if it was this fool. Pelopidas helped him drag their foe to the pavement.

'Nicely done!' said Chremes.

'He's a professional,' said Tarchon.

Straightening up, he saw that another figure – a very different figure – had stepped into the glow of the lantern. Wearing a dark grey tunic and a black cape, Kallisto lowered her hood and glanced admiringly at Pelopidas before turning to Tarchon.

'So, if he's the professional, what does that make you?'

XXIII

Once they'd handed the drunk over to a pair of watchmen, Tarchon and Pelopidas returned to the Octopus. Pelopidas seemed keen on claiming the chicken and hopeful that Kallisto would join them. They found her standing by the door, arms crossed, a satchel hanging from her shoulder.

'I have a proposition for you two.'

'Really?' said Pelopidas.

'Leave him out of it,' said Tarchon.

'Out of what?' asked Pelopidas, already moving towards her.

'Nothing,' said Tarchon. He didn't know what she meant either but he didn't want to drag him into some dangerous operation. He also didn't want the capable boxer to make him look even worse than he already did.

'A little security work,' said Kallisto.

'Can I speak to you for a moment?' said Tarchon. When he walked towards the mole, she reluctantly followed. They spoke in the darkness, unable to see each other's faces.

'I think you're forgetting who is in charge here,' she stated.

'You forgot Gargonius' instruction soon enough. I suppose I could always knock you out and carry you onto a ship.'

'I'd like to see you try. Do you think I'm some tavern girl or housewife? I've bested tougher men than you.'

Tarchon doubted that was true but he knew he had to try and get on with this woman. 'Listen, I don't want Pelopidas dragged into whatever you're up to. Can't you find a couple of legionaries to help out?'

'I don't have time to involve the army. And I'm not about to compromise a hard-earned cover unless I have to. I have a meeting at the third hour of night and it's quite a way. I'm meeting a man who will give me the name of Cniva's top agent in Heraclea.' Kallisto tapped the satchel. 'In return, I am giving him an emerald, worth around fifty aurei. It may be that this man decides he doesn't want to leave me alive to tell anyone of his betrayal. So, some help would be useful. But if you don't want to give it, I'll go alone.'

'I'll come. Just me. I have a sword.'

'Glad to hear it. But you're unproven. Your friend looks useful with his fists. Don't worry, I'll pay him.'

'I don't want him involved.'

'I'd say that's his choice, isn't it? Or I could just ask him and leave *you* here.'

Tarchon was not happy about any of this, least of all her attitude, but he could hardly blame her given his performance so far. He would just have to prove his worth.

'All right, let me-'

But Kallisto was already on her way. 'What's your name again? Pelopidas?'

'Pelo is fine, miss.'

'All right. You and Tarchon are going to look after me. Ten denarii. Five upfront. How does that sound?'

'Sounds good.'

'Excellent.' Kallisto took the coins from her satchel and handed them to him. She then retrieved some twine from a pocket within the green cloak and began pulling her hair back into a tail. 'You're not alarmed by the prospect of putting those fists to good use again?'

'Not at all.'

Watching her in action, Tarchon doubted that she was used to men refusing her anything.

She turned to him with a "told you so" look and flashed another perfect smile. 'Well then, gentlemen. Follow me.'

*

It swiftly became evident that Kallisto knew the streets of Odessos extremely well. They headed north but followed an indirect path that avoided well-lit and busy areas. Twice they spied watchmen and both times she led Tarchon and Pelopidas into hiding places, waiting for the locals to pass. They also successfully bypassed a legionary patrol, Kallisto commenting that Centurion Panares was concerned about the proximity of the Goths. She hardly made a sound and moved with a speed and confidence that Tarchon knew could only be born from experience.

Even in the dark, he could make out the high arches of the city's aqueduct which they passed to the west. Ten minutes later, they reached a section of the wall that made up the northern perimeter of the city. Here, Kallisto turned towards the coast: the wall to their left, buildings to their right. She eventually stopped by a pig pen. Though the animals were gathered on the far side, the smell was intense enough to make Tarchon's nostrils burn.

'Gods, my nose,' said Pelopidas.

'We'll be out in the fine country air soon enough,' replied Kallisto. 'Now listen. Panares will have stationed men at the gates and weaker sections so we'll get through here. There's a hole, formed where a stream has cut down into the ground and under the wall. It's tight but once we're through we just have to climb out of a gully, then we're clear. Watch your footing.'

'Can't watch anything,' said Pelopidas. 'It's dark.'

'Three- quarter moon,' countered Kallisto. 'That's not dark.'

Just past the pig pen, behind some half-collapsed building, they halted. The wall here was about ten feet high: a collage of stone blocks and sections of brick. Kallisto swiftly found the hole and crawled through. Tarchon dropped down onto gravel-covered ground and a couple of inches of water. It was a struggle to get his shoulders through the gap but he hauled himself under the wall, which turned out to be at least six feet wide.

Once Pelopidas was also through, they followed Kallisto along the bottom of the narrow, steep-sided gully. She paused a couple of times to warn them of rocky obstacles and they covered about a quarter-mile before she started up the right side. The sandy ground was treacherous but there were a few rabbit burrows and hardy bushes to help them scramble to the top.

On open ground, they could at least see a bit more, which turned out to be useful as Kallisto cut across uneven terrain. They soon reached a wide, sandy track that ran out towards the coast through terraced fields and groves.

'Not bad, you two,' said Kallisto as they walked three abreast up a slight slope. 'Men are usually highly adept at tripping over and walking into things.'

Tarchon bit his tongue, certain he'd spent more nights than her negotiating darkened streets without giving himself away. Before they left the Octopus, he'd gone to fetch his sword, dropping it to Pelopidas from their window to avoid undue attention. He had been proud to acquire the blade and was now relieved to have the weapon over his shoulder.

'We just followed *you*, Cassandra,' said Pelopidas keenly. 'You seem to know every step.'

'I scouted the route three days ago. Could have been a cloudy night.'

'None of my business, of course,' said Pelopidas. 'But this all seems very…adventurous. Something tells me I haven't heard the whole truth.'

'You're right,' replied Kallisto.

'That I haven't heard the whole truth?'

'No,' she said, quickening her pace. 'That it's none of your business.'

They saw the fire from some distance away. Tarchon climbed up onto a wall and swiftly concluded that those gathered around it were legionaries. As he dropped to the ground, Kallisto cursed.

'Probably guarding the crossroads. I know another route but we'll have to move fast.'

They rounded two sides of a walled field, followed a dry ditch north, then continued toward the coast along a stony path.

'Should have brought a lantern,' said Pelopidas.

'Oh yes,' Kallisto said drily. 'Announce our presence to the army patrols, Goth scouts and every other Marcus, Titus and Lucius. Lanterns are noisy, lamps are unwieldy and they both slow you down. I have a candle and a fire-starting kit if we need it.'

'Goths?' said Pelopidas. 'You don't really think they could be that close?'

'Why do you think that patrol is there?' Kallisto replied. 'They're not out here stargazing.'

She turned off the path, carefully negotiated a collapsed wall and entered another field. Halfway across, they disturbed some birds which flapped noisily away to the south, startling them all.

'Who is this man anyway?' asked Tarchon, now walking alongside Kallisto.

'You want details, tell your friend to drop back a bit so he can't hear.'

Tarchon did so; and Pelopidas grumpily agreed.

'Name's Aristomachos. A former procurator. When he retired, he used his numerous connections across Moesia and Dacia to broker business deals. Knows a lot about the Goths – and their spies.'

'How did you make contact with him?'

'He's been on Gargonius' list for a while. I got word he was in Marcianopolis a few months' back. I made sure he noticed me and, sure enough, he turned up in Odessos.'

Though she clearly possessed other talents, Tarchon could imagine how easily Kallisto would find it to target, attract and then exploit men. No wonder Gargonius considered her so valuable.

'How did you get the information about the spy?'

'Slowly and carefully. I didn't want to scare him off. He's not a young man. He knows that dealing with Goths *and* Romans is becoming increasingly risky. I suspected that one big pay-out would suit him nicely.'

'And the emerald – how did you get that?'

'That's another story. And a long one.'

Pelopidas jogged up behind them. 'Not far from the sea now – I can smell it.'

'Only another mile or so to the lighthouse,' said Kallisto.

'Lighthouse?' said Pelopidas. 'What lighthouse?'

It was situated on a narrow promontory, the structure stark against the night sky. Here at the coast the wind was stronger, ruffling their hair and clothes as the trio approached through high grass. They had just descended from a low ridge which blocked their view of Odessos and could see nothing of the settlements on the coast to the north. To the east, only a few fleeting wave-tips caught the eye.

'Glad we're here first and no one else is,' said Kallisto. 'Some folk still come here for the view, though the lighthouse hasn't been used for years. Someone at Thalia's once told me that it was built by the Persians.'

'The Persians got to Moesia?'

'Centuries ago,' said Tarchon, whose knowledge of history had come largely from his uncle Hostus. Aunt Cassia often remarked that her husband was more interested in the past than the present.

'Never heard of Cyrus the Great?' said Kallisto.

As they started along the promontory, Tarchon heard the booming surf beneath, and was once more transported to the headland in Bithnyia. He was beginning to wonder if he would ever be free of Green Cove.

After thirty paces or so, the foreland widened out to about forty feet and they were soon standing below the tower. Here, on open ground and with the moonlight reflecting off the sea, visibility was better. Tarchon could make out the lighthouse's arched entrance but also the many gaps in the circular wall and the many stones on the ground.

'Good timing.'

Turning round, he saw that Kallisto had spied a light approaching from the north-east. The three of them stood in a line, silently watching.

'He's not alone,' said Tarchon, when the lantern's glow caught at least one other figure.

'That's why you're here,' replied Kallisto. 'I suggest you go behind the lighthouse. But be careful, the ground has fallen away there.'

'Who will that be with him?' asked Pelopidas, sounding rather less confident than he had in Odessos.

'Not sure. He did have a local bodyguard but I believe that man was called up to the auxiliaries. It may all go smoothly. But if it doesn't, your presence should be enough to dissuade him from forcing the issue. If I want you to show yourselves, I'll cough twice.'

'Shall I look after the emerald?' asked Tarchon. 'That way he can't take it off you.'

'He won't be taking anything off me. Get out of sight and have that sword at the ready. But do *not* show yourselves unless I give the signal.'

Tarchon and Pelopidas walked carefully round the left side of the lighthouse.

'Gods,' said the boxer, no doubt looking down at the water far, far below. There was barely five feet between the ancient tower and the end of the promontory and both men felt their way around with their hands pressed against the stone.

'This will do,' said Tarchon after only a few steps. He then slid back past Pelopidas so that he'd be able to hear what was going on.

'Don't like heights,' said Pelopidas.

'Just be glad it's not daylight.'

'Quite a woman, eh? Certainly knows her own mind.'

'Mmm.'

The wind was not that strong but Tarchon could hear little and so took another few steps. He unsheathed the sword and rested the tip on the ground, estimating that he could get to Kallisto in a couple of seconds. Despite his annoyance at her arrogance, she did seem very capable. He was determined to not make another mistake.

Soon he could see the interlopers as they negotiated the narrow neck of the promontory. Risking a peek around the tower's edge, he saw a man of about sixty, lantern in hand. Behind him were two large figures. When they halted, Tarchon took another step, confident that the light wouldn't reach him.

'Good evening, Cassandra,' came a smooth voice. 'Did I not tell you two that she was lovely?'

He received no answer from his companions, whom Tarchon could still see little of.

'Evening, Aristomachos,' she said. 'You're on time – for once. Who are these two? Judging by appearances, I'll hazard a guess they're not bookkeepers.'

'Astute as always. Two new friends. Wrestlers looking for employment after the cancellation of the games.'

Tarchon grimaced, unsure of how a boxer might fare against wrestlers. Frustratingly, the glow of Aristomachos' lantern was still preventing him seeing anything more than two silhouettes. As for Aristomachos himself, he was well dressed in a pale tunic and cloak, a sly-looking man with a neat white beard. He didn't appear to be armed.

'I did ask you to come alone,' said Kallisto. 'If I can brave the night, why can't you?'

'My dear, while every moment spent with you is a pleasant one, let's get to business. Do you have it?'

'I have it. But I'll need that name first. And I'll tell you now that I know every senior man in the governor's staff in Heraclea.'

'I didn't say he was on the governor's staff.'

'He better be – or he's of no use to us.'

'Ha. Quite right. Let me see the gem.'

Tarchon glimpsed Kallisto's right shoulder as she stepped forward and showed him. There was a pause, then Aristomachus smiled. 'You did not exaggerate.'

'I hope you didn't either. The name.'

Aristomachus paused and bobbed his head from side to side. 'The thing is, Cassandra, the Goths seem to be doing quite well. Better than you expected, quite possibly better than Rome expected. Do I really want to endanger myself by passing on such sensitive information?'

'If you don't, I will counter by ensuring that the Goths *think* you did. You will face the same risk, but without the compensation of the emerald.'

Aristomachus sighed and scratched at his chin. 'I don't want to be...confrontational but, with my associates here, I could just *take* the stone, without giving you the name.'

Kallisto raised a hand, the lantern-light sparking briefly off the green gem. 'Or I could throw it into the sea.'

'But then I would be angry.'

'I thought you didn't want to be confrontational. The name, Aristomachus. *Now.*'

'Ready,' whispered Pelopidas, who had come up right behind Tarchon. Realising his fingers were aching, Tarchon loosened his tight grip on the sword's hilt.

'Very well,' said Aristomachus. 'His name is Mamercus Alfius.'

'Deputy Magistrate.'

'The one and same. He was previously an envoy in north Dacia. That's where they turned him. He has a cousin in the iron trade who keeps him in touch with the Goths. The only other thing I know is the name of his handler: Tulga.'

'I hope for your sake that you're right. Here.'

Kallisto entered Tarchon's field of vision as she threw the emerald to Aristomachus, who caught it with his spare hand. Holding it up to the lantern, he smiled at the light dancing off the well-cut gem.

'Quite beautiful.' He slipped it into a pocket and looked back at Kallisto. 'Almost as beautiful as you. For what it's worth, I am sorry. But I can hardly cut up the emerald, so I had to offer these two another form of payment. *You.*'

Aristomachus gave a theatrical shrug.

'Son of a bitch,' said Kallisto.

'Now, now. There's no need to be unpleasant.'

Aristomachus turned away and handed one of his bodyguards the lantern. 'Here, take this. I'll make my own way back and I'd rather not draw attention to myself.'

Now Tarchon could see the two bodyguards. The wrestlers were very similar in appearance: dark-skinned Easterners – Cilician or Armenian perhaps – with hair cut short and thick moustaches down to their jaws. Their red and orange sleeveless tunics were decorated with all manner of exotic patterns. Neither were particularly tall but they were barrel-chested with arms that looked capable of crushing a man.

'Farewell, Cassandra, I do hope they're not too rough with-'

The wrestler without the lantern grabbed the former procurator around the neck, fingers digging into his skin.

'Jewel,' said the bodyguard in a thick accent. 'Now.'

'What? Your payment is the girl. She's worth-'

'We take jewel *and* girl.'

Tarchon could feel Pelopidas ready to move beside him. He was trying to see if the wrestlers had any weapons; it appeared they didn't.

'Now!' growled the Easterner, squeezing tighter.

'All right,' yelped Aristomachus, swiftly handing over the emerald. The second man handed it to his compatriot with the lantern and turned back to their former employer. He tried to run but the wrestler grabbed his arm. His second hand shot downward and encircled Aristomachus' spindly thigh. Lifting him easily, the Easterner walked to the left, towards the edge.

Tarchon moved around the lighthouse.

'No!' shrieked Aristomachus, flailing at his tormentor.

'No, don't!' yelled Kallisto, her voice suddenly shrill. 'Please.'

The man with the lantern looked at her, amused, then watched his friend. The second wrestler shook off his victim's grip, turned to his side and flung Aristomachus into the darkness. There was no scream, no sound of impact. He simply disappeared.

Clapping his hands together as if he'd just disposed of some rubbish, the wrestler grunted something to his friend.

Though she'd not given the signal, Tarchon knew the pair might easily do the same to Kallisto: they had to act now.

'Let's go,' he whispered.

He and Pelopidas sprang around the tower and rushed in front of her. Tarchon aimed the sword at the wrestlers. They seemed surprised but not particularly concerned.

'Leave here,' ordered Tarchon. 'Now.'

The Easterners appraised him, his blade and Pelopidas, then turned to each other.

'Get the emerald,' said Kallisto.

'What?'

'You have a blade. They don't.' She moved up, between Tarchon and Pelopidas and addressed the Easterners. 'Give us the emerald.'

'We go,' said the man with the lantern. 'You don't want fight us.'

Tarchon agreed with that but he also didn't want to appear a fool in front of Kallisto once again. He stepped forward, aimed the sword at the man who'd spoken. 'Give us the emerald – or you're going to get a much closer look at this.'

The man lowered the lantern. It was then that Tarchon noticed several dots of light just below the ridge to the west. There was someone there; on the same path Aristomachus and these two had used. His attention was drawn for only a second or two but it was enough.

The wrestler swung the lantern into the sword. The light fell to the ground but Tarchon somehow kept hold of the blade. The wrestler followed up swiftly, one great paw clamping his sword hand at the wrist. As the second man closed in, Pelopidas darted forward to intercept him. The agile boxer shrugged off a grab from his foe, went in low and landed a crashing upper cut on the big man's jaw. Teeth rattling, the Easterner staggered away.

As his wrist was now in danger of being crushed, Tarchon had no choice but to drop the blade. The instant he did so, the wrestler chopped his other hand into Tarchon's neck. His entire body seemed to freeze and he dropped to his knees, pain leaping from his neck down his spine. Some instinct told him another attack was coming. He threw himself to his left and lashed out with his trailing leg. Whatever he hit, it was effective. With a grunt, the Easterner fell onto his back, body thumping into the rocky ground.

Seconds later, metal flashed downward, the contact reminding Tarchon of a butcher at work on a block. Getting to his feet, he saw Kallisto holding the blade with both hands. The wrestler was rolling around on his back, choking noisily on his own blood.

'Help!'

Pelopidas had somehow been caught by the remaining man, who was dragging him to the right, towards the edge of the promontory.

Tarchon got there quickly, soon realising that the wrestler had the boxer in a headlock. Almost tripping over Pelopidas' legs, he reached out for the Easterner, located his shoulder and slammed a clenched fist into his ear. He knew from experience how much this hurt and wasn't surprised that the man let go of Pelopidas and turned. As he did so, Tarchon aimed a second punch. He caught him square on the jaw but it seemed to do more damage to his hand than to the Easterner's face.

'Move!' ordered Kallisto. But by then a panting Pelopidas was back on his feet and back in the fray. Coming in from Tarchon's right, he easily evaded the wrestler's flailing arms. A moment after his first punch caught the man on the nose, a second smashed into his chin, sending him tottering backwards. A desperate swipe from the Easterner hit Pelopidas' head but the boxer stayed upright.

Despite the ache in his right hand, the momentary respite had allowed Tarchon to see just how close they were to the edge.

He was about to charge the wrestler when Kallisto came up on his left. She swung two-handed again and could only have missed by inches. Even so, the attack was the wrestler's undoing.

As he retreated, one foot slipped on the grass, then the other. He fell, hands clawing at the ground before his bulk dragged him over the edge and to his death. Again, there was no shout or cry; only a shocked gasp that sounded almost like it came from a child.

'Gods' blood,' said Pelopidas between breaths. 'I thought I'd had it then. What about the other one?'

'Dead,' said Kallisto. 'No thanks to you two. Not much point having a blade unless you know how to use it.'

Tarchon might have said something to that but he was more interested in the lights approaching the foreland. He now counted six, moving swiftly towards them.

'Oh shit,' said Pelopidas.

The noise of their horses was clear as they closed on the landward end of the promontory. For once, Kallisto said nothing, but the situation was clear. They were trapped.

XXIV

She was still holding the sword. 'You two throw the body off. With luck, they won't see the blood.'

'What are *you* going to do?' asked Tarchon.

'Find the emerald,' she replied, as if it was obvious. 'I think he dropped it. Hurry! We have a minute at the most.'

There was no time to argue. Tarchon grabbed the dead wrestler under the arms and instantly felt warm blood on his fingers. Pelopidas took the big man's feet and they carried him to the edge, near to where Aristomachus had met his fate. They got as close as they dared before dropping him but the bulky body stopped short. Tarchon knelt down, gripped the Easterner's belt and rolled him the last few inches. Wiping his wet fingers on the grass, he stood to see Pelopidas already on the move.

Barely fifty feet away, the first of the riders had halted and dismounted. Sprinting after the others, Tarchon found them at the lighthouse door. Kallisto handed him the sword, hilt first.

'Is this thing safe?' asked Pelopidas.

'Probably not,' said Kallisto, 'but it's safer than taking our chances with *them*.'

'Might be legionaries.'

'And if they're not? Come on. And keep your voices down.'

Once inside the lighthouse, they lost the moon and the starlight. Now that a little time had passed since the fight, Tarchon felt pain in his hand and neck – and his wounded arm.

'Can't see a bloody thing,' said Pelopidas.

'Let me go first,' said Tarchon, who reckoned he was better suited to this task than the others. With the sword in his right hand, he bent forward until his left touched the floor: a dusty stone step, to be precise. Feeling ahead, he touched the next step, then the third.

'Seems intact. Go on all fours.'

'They're coming,' said Pelopidas. 'They're coming this way.'

'Go,' instructed Kallisto. 'And try not to poke me with that sword.'

He started up, keeping the sword over to the right. Though the exterior of the tower was round, the stairway was square. The steps themselves were relatively solid, but whenever he touched a wall, a chunk of brick or cement fell off.

'Stay in the middle. We're at the first corner now. Left turn.'

His fingers were already thick with dust and cobwebs but he kept moving, now hearing voices directly outside the tower. The others stayed close behind, Kallisto occasionally bumping into his heels and calves. He counted eight steps on every level and soon they had negotiated six turns. He felt sure they weren't far from the top. Spotting a gaping hole in the exterior wall that showed him a rectangle of sky, Tarchon took it as a warning and slowed down. That caution prevented a fatal error.

The next step didn't exist. His searching hand touched nothing but thin air. Reaching higher, his fingers felt a structure of horizontal timbers bound with rope.

'What is it?' asked Kallisto, her voice harsh in the tower of stone.

'There's a gap here. And some kind of repair.'

'Can we keep going?'

'Not sure we should.'

'We *have* to,' she said. 'They're coming up.'

'They're coming *up* the tower?'

'Yes. Go!'

'All right. Feel for the gap – timbers just above.'

Tarchon couldn't believe the speed at which the situation had worsened. The night had already taken several terrible turns and now here was another.

Despite the dangerous gap, the timber structure felt relatively solid. It was more of a broad ladder than a series of steps, the timbers apparently tied and staked to the stone. The third timber shifted and squeaked, causing him to stop.

'Be careful,' he said over his shoulder, glimpsing Pelopidas' eyes and the suggestion of light below him.

Tarchon continued upward, relieved that the planks were at least well-fixed. Now *he* could hear the men below and they were talking loudly, which might at least cover the noise from above. From the last timber, he emerged through a hatch onto the top of the lighthouse. Here, more planks had been put down, and they also felt solid enough. In the centre was a stone construction, much like an altar, with built up edges. Tarchon guessed this was where fires had been lit when the lighthouse was still in use. The surrounding walls of the top were at a similar height.

'Quiet,' hissed Kallisto to Pelopidas as they joined him. Tarchon looked down the hatch, watching the moving light getting brighter.

'We should never have come in here!' whispered Pelopidas. 'We've had it. We're finished.'

'Kill the first one or two, the others might think twice.' Kallisto moved to the surround, which was four feet high and two wide. 'Some loose stones here. We can use them.'

Though he couldn't help admire her courage and resourcefulness, Tarchon didn't share her optimism. They were outnumbered, with no route of escape.

'Goths,' she said.

'You're sure?' asked Pelopidas.

'Of course I'm bloody sure. I can hear them. They find us, they'll kill us.'

Tarchon heard this but he had another matter on his mind. Running his hands around the surround, he found that the whole exterior had been circled with many lengths of inch-thick rope, presumably to strengthen the aged structure. Some of the stones were indeed loose, as were some of the ropes, but the arrangement had evidently held for quite a time.

'Over the edge,' he told the others. 'There's rope for hand and foot holds. This area feels solid enough.'

It was at the rear of the tower, above the spot where he and Pelopidas had earlier hidden.

'Gods, spare me,' whispered the boxer. 'There has to be another way.'

Kallisto was already beside Tarchon, stretching over the surround, touching the outside. 'He's right. Come on. We've no choice.' She lifted her tunic above her knees and climbed up onto the stone.

'I can't-' spluttered Pelopidas as Tarchon grabbed him.

'You *can* and you *will*.'

The torchlight below was bright now. The Goths were close.

Kallisto was on her front, having twisted nimbly around and dropped her legs over the edge. Placing both hands on the ropes, she lowered herself further, disappearing completely from view.

'Pelo, just do what I do and you'll be fine.' Tarchon had already sheathed the sword. He now put it over his shoulder and leaped up on to the wall. Once on his knees, he turned around and backed towards the edge. Glad to see Pelopidas copying him, he lowered his right boot and found a rope for his first hold. Reaching down with his left hand, he grabbed another rope then descended over the edge. Seeing torch-light glinting off a Goth helmet, he found another rope with his right hand and dropped another two feet.

Perched there, Kallisto to his right, Pelopidas to his left, he told himself not to think about the height – or the ancient, crumbling tower. He – they – just had to hang on. Realising that one of the others was using the same rope, he shifted his left hand. His left foot was still hanging but he found a hold on a protruding stone.

There were several Goths up at the top now, pacing around and talking loudly. Nothing about their low, earthy language was familiar. Kallisto had turned to her right, so he couldn't see her face, but something about the angle of her head suggested that she was listening. The Goths were busy now; one man issuing instructions as they shifted something around.

Tarchon turned to see Pelopidas hanging only from his hands, legs dangling, silently struggling. Grateful for the noise above and meticulous with every move, Tarchon crabbed two feet to his left and two down. He gently held Pelopidas' trembling right calf and placed his toes against the nearest rope. The boxer put his other boot there and seemed to settle. Checking that Kallisto was also secure, Tarchon now listened. He heard the thud of something heavy landing on something metallic and then the glug of liquid.

With a sudden whoosh, a great flame was set alight. Recovering swiftly from the moment of panic it caused, Tarchon realised just how afraid he was. This was a lighthouse: of course they were lighting a fire, presumably a signal of some sort. He just hoped the Goths wouldn't stay too long; the three of them couldn't hang there indefinitely. He reckoned he had a slim chance of making it to the ground but he doubted the others would.

The thought caused him to look down and he instantly wished he hadn't. He could just about make out the rounded end of the promontory and the wave-tops glinting far below. Despite his experience of heights and daring climbs, Tarchon felt his stomach turn over.

Seconds later, he felt a boot softly tap his right arm. With the roar and crackle of the fire, there was no danger of the Goths hearing him, so he climbed up next to Kallisto. She felt secure enough to free her right hand and point out to sea. He saw it clearly: an answering signal fire a mile or two out.

The Goths had obviously seen it too; there were triumphant cries from above.

You've done what you came to do.
Now go. Go!

Suddenly, light flashed above him. He saw the top of a man's head, illuminated by the flaming torch in his hand. The Goth was talking to another, apparently in good spirits. A drop of burning oil fell past Tarchon's right ear, a second landed on his upper right arm. After a few seconds, the tunic began to smoke. Tarchon twisted his shoulder and brushed it against the tower wall, extinguishing the tiny flame. More drops fell as the man moved to the left, and Tarchon bowed his head.

Oil struck the back of his neck. Somehow stifling a shout, he threw his head back. Pressing the oil into his tunic collar, he felt the heat sink into his skin. But as he exposed his face, a third drop struck his cheek. He instantly wiped it against his arm, so quickly that he almost lost his grip. The pain was still there but it was leavened by the sight of the accursed Goth and his torch moving away.

Pelopidas had clearly seen what had happened. He shifted to the left, abruptly dropped a few feet. The ropes moved under Tarchon's hands and feet. Pelopidas was panicking.

The Goth said something to a compatriot, oblivious to the falling oil. More drops fell. Tarchon was already moving, ready to grab the boxer.

Too late.

Pelo's dark form merged with the night as he fell silently from the tower.

Paralysed, Tarchon looked down at the waves, then back at where his friend had been, as if he might now see him there. Was he seeing things? Hallucinating? Somehow mistaken?

No. He was gone.

The Goth continued his circle of the tower, torch still shedding sparks. Tarchon squeezed his eyes shut and pushed his face against the cold stone.

He just hung there, cursing himself, Kallisto, the gods. Once, he looked at the ground at the base of the lighthouse and thought he saw something moving, then decided it was his mind playing tricks. He eventually became aware that the noise from above had lessened, that the lights were all below, that the Goths were leaving. Then he felt Kallisto move in beside him.

'We can...where's Pelo? Did he already climb up?'

Tarchon said nothing. He hauled himself up and over the surround. Upon the stone altar, low flames still burned within an iron cauldron. He walked around it and looked down to see the torches moving away. The Goths crossed the promontory, mounted up and rode off, utterly unaware of what they had done. By now, Kallisto had also climbed over the surround.

'Tarchon? What happened? Talk to me.'

He did not reply and the near-certainty that Pelopidas was dead did not stop him getting down to the ground as swiftly as he could. Despite the dark, he hopped from one timber to the next, dropping the sword when he reached the steps, then sprinting the rest of the way. Once outside, he ran around to the eastern side. He could see no sign of Pelopidas so he got down on his knees and crawled around, feeling the grass. He wasn't there. There was nothing there.

'Pelopidas?'

His only answer was the surging crash of waves. Like Aristomachus, Pelo had simply disappeared. Tarchon imagined his broken body in the water below, being thrown against the rocks. He leaned back against the tower and looked out to sea. The light had disappeared. Feeling as if he was about to throw up, he drew in deep draughts of the chilly air.

Kallisto came around the other side and stood there, only her eyes visible until the moonlight sparked off the sword in her hand.

'I'm sorry. I didn't see-'

'He didn't make a sound. Didn't want to give us up.'

'These ...these things happen.'

'They don't just *happen*. It's *our* fault. Mine and yours. We should never have brought him.'

She stood there, wind blowing her hair up, tapping the sword tip against the ground. 'All right. It's *our* fault. But right now, we have to go and warn the city. We both know what that signal meant. They're here.'

He followed her swift silhouette back the way they had come, the sword on his back. Glad of the dark, he wiped away tears as he thought of Pelopidas' face, which had always seemed to be smiling. The poor bastard had come to Odessos seeking glory and fortune, only to meet such an odd, terrible death. That moment when he'd slipped silently from view would not leave Tarchon's mind.

He thought about stopping, letting Kallisto carry on, dropping the sword, walking away. He could forget it all: his orders, Gargonius and Korax, the Service. Forget Byzantium for a while, go somewhere new. It was one thing to kill; another to get someone else killed. He did not know if he could live with it.

'Tarchon!' Turning, emerging suddenly from the darkness, Kallisto grabbed him by the arm. 'You're not listening to a word I say! All right, *come* here!'

She led him to a slope where a tiny stream gurgled its way down towards Odessos. She kneeled.

'I'm cleaning my hands. You do the same.'

He didn't have the energy to argue. He put his hands in the water and rubbed off the grime, blood and sweat accumulated over the last few hours.

'Now your face.'

The water was wonderfully cool and he took his time, rubbing at his skin and then rinsing it off.

'Better?' she asked when they stood.

'A little.'

'Listen to me. What's done is done. I don't know if you want to beg the gods for forgiveness or slit your wrists. And I don't care much what you do when we're out of here. But I need you sharp. Gargonius sent you to help me get out. And if we make it to Byzantium with the name of that spy, he's going to be a very happy man. And once we've told the men in charge what we've seen, we *are* leaving. Can you get through this night, Tarchon? Because if you can't, we may as well go our separate ways now.'

'I can.'

'Good. And be ready with that sword. I've done my bit.'

Marching between two lines of olive trees, they could easily make out the walls of Odessos because lanterns and braziers were alight upon them.

'You really think the Goths could attack tonight?' asked Tarchon.

'Possibly. But if they were here in force we'd have heard or seen something by now. More likely they're scouting out the approaches, ready for a push tomorrow or sometime soon. But they'll need a lot of troops to take the city.'

'And the ship?'

'Hard to be sure but it doesn't bode well. Most likely a coordinated attack in daylight – might be here to blockade the harbour or land troops. We need to find Centurion Panares.'

'He knows you? Who you are?'

'He knows me – as Cassandra. Looks like I'm not going to be back in Odessos for a while. If I have to blow my cover with a few individuals, so be it.'

'Wait.' Tarchon halted as they neared the end of the olive grove, close to the road they'd used earlier.

'What is it?'

'I saw a light. This side of the walls. Close to where we're headed.'

'All right. Let's take it slow.'

Reaching the road, they both saw a flash of light that weakened, then disappeared.

'Lantern,' said Tarchon. 'Shuttered.'

'You're right. Close to the gully. Looks like I'm not the only one who knows about it.'

'Is there another way?'

'Let's get closer; see if we can work out who we're dealing with.'

Once off the road, they cut across the broken ground and stopped only a few hundred yards from the wall. Now still, Tarchon let his eyes and ears adjust. It didn't take long for him to see the moving shapes barely forty feet away.

'See them?' he whispered. 'Horses. Tethered.'

'I see. How many, you think?'

'More than five, less than ten.'

'Agreed,' said Kallisto.

'Couldn't be soldiers?'

'Skulking around here with no lights – unlikely. Could be the group from the lighthouse. Scouts.'

'I can scatter the horses. That'll put a dent in their plans.'

'They'll have left a sentry or two.'

These were the bastards that had killed Pelopidas. Tarchon welcomed the chance to strike back at them.

'Not a problem.'

'All right but don't get carried away. I'll circle round, wait at the point where we climbed out. Can you find it?'

'Of course.'

'If anything goes wrong, make for the main gate. Half a mile east.'

'Got it.'

'Good luck.' With a tap on his shoulder, Kallisto slipped away into the darkness.

Tarchon gently drew his sword and advanced, hunched over, careful with each step on the uneven ground. As he closed to twenty feet, the horses began to shuffle around, no doubt catching wind of him. He could see individual animals now and it looked like there were eight. He was beginning to think the Goths had left them untended when a man walked around the mounts to Tarchon's right. To stay hidden, he crouched down, placed the shiny sword behind him and bowed his head. After a minute or so, the sentry turned back the way he'd come and spoke some calming words to the horses. Tarchon stood and followed him.

He knew his closeness would panic the horses but he was on the sentry in seconds. As the man spun and reached for his blade, Tarchon grabbed a fistful of his tunic with his left hand and brought the wooden hilt of his sword down with the right, landing a heavy blow on his brow. Stunned, the man fell into undergrowth, moaning.

The horses were now neighing and straining against their ropes. Tarchon found the lines that tied them to a nearby tree and cut them. Slapping a couple across the rump, he soon had them fleeing away to the north, making all kinds of noise.

Retracing his steps, he somehow tripped over a stone and almost landed on his own blade. But he was soon up and circling around to the gully. As he approached, he saw a line of figures emerge: dark heads, shoulders and arms. Whispering to each other, they gathered, then ran to the north.

He was about to continue towards the meeting point, when he heard movement to his left.

'Tarchon?'

'Yes.'

Kallisto extricated herself from a sprawling bush. 'I moved away when they starting coming out. Good work. Let's keep going.'

After a brief pause to check that the Goths were all out of the gully, the pair slid and scrambled down to the bottom. Feeling water come through his boots, Tarchon followed Kallisto to the wall. Once she was heading through, he checked behind him, then crawled after her. This was again such a struggle that he barely noticed the light ahead of him until he pulled himself out and looked up.

Kallisto was standing against the wall, surrounded by four legionaries, one of whom was holding a torch. Despite the circumstances, Tarchon was struck once again by guilt as a flaming drop of oil fell past him. As they looked down at him, Kallisto spoke.

'It's not us you need to worry about, gentlemen. We came across a Goth scouting party just the other side of the wall.'

'Horseshit,' said one of the men. 'You're the ones sneaking around.'

'Let's see what Centurion Paneres thinks,' said another of the solders.

Kallisto answered with a sharp look at the suspicious legionary. 'Fine by me.'

XXV

Odessos possessed a broad, imposing forum, with grand porticoes on two sides and a tall basilica at the southern end. Still surrounded by the four soldiers, Tarchon and Kallisto climbed the high steps to the basilica's entrance. Here a dozen more legionaries stood guard, armed with spears. The group of six passed between two broad, green doors and were met by a grey-haired officer. He told the soldiers that Centurion Panares was currently in one of the basilica's offices. They made their way down a pristine corridor lit by high, three-legged braziers and only now did Tarchon realise how dirty and wet they both were. Kallisto walked with a protective hand over her satchel, which contained the emerald she'd recovered from the promontory. Tarchon's sword had been confiscated.

At the office, another soldier stood guard. He held up a hand, indicating that they should wait. Inside, a centurion wearing a white tunic with red stripes at the sleeves stood over a table, pointing at something. Opposite him was an older man in a toga flanked by two younger officials. Kallisto coughed, causing those inside to look up, surprised to hear a woman amongst them. The older man was a paunchy fellow with wavy, white hair and red cheeks. He peered curiously at Kallisto.

'What's going on?' asked Centurion Panares. He was slight for a soldier; brown-haired with a light beard.

The eldest of the legionaries spoke up. 'Sir, we caught these two sneaking back in under the wall, close to the granary.'

'What do they have to say for themselves?'

'This one claims-'

'I have some important intelligence regarding the Goths.'

Tarchon was not surprised by Kallisto's interjection.

The man in the toga stepped forward. 'Cassandra, is that you?'

'Good evening, Governor Strabonius. Please excuse my appearance.'

'What in Hades is going on?'

'This may make things clearer,' she said, reaching into her satchel and taking out her miniature spearhead.

'Excuse me, sir.' Centurion Panares walked past the governor and out of the office. He took the spearhead from Kallisto and examined it. He then walked back to Strabonius and showed it to him.

The governor smiled at Kallisto. 'Clearly a woman of many talents.'

'Come in,' said Panares, gesturing to them.

Governor Strabonius issued orders to one of his lackeys. 'Fetch some towels for her. Some hot wine for us all. Are you cold, Cassandra – a cloak perhaps?'

'I'm fine, governor, thank you.'

As the man hurried away, Kallisto and Tarchon halted by the table. Upon it were two large sheets of papyrus, one showing the city, one showing the province of Moesia.

Strabonius gazed at Kallisto. 'I was told a while back that the Service had a man here. What a disguise.'

She shrugged and smiled.

Panares dismissed the four soldiers, one of them swiftly returning Tarchon's sword. The centurion looked him and up and down. 'Who's this then?'

'Another agent, sir,' Kallisto explained. 'He...misplaced his spearhead. He was sent to recall me but there was some business I had to conclude. A meeting at the old lighthouse. We were about to leave when a party of Goths arrived. They climbed up and lit a fire. We saw an answering signal from a ship offshore. On the way back into town we came across them or another party – they seemed to be scouting the defences.'

The governor smacked a clenched fist into a palm. 'I bloody well knew it. Why didn't your patrols know anything of this, Panares?'

'They can't be everywhere, sir.'

'Will you at least call out the militia?'

'Possibly at dawn. Do not fear, the walls are secure.'

'*Do not fear*, he says.' Strabonius leaned on the table and stared at the map. 'If they cut us from off Marcianopolis…'

'Do you know any more?' asked Panares.

Kallisto shook her head. 'This ship – could it be one of the two that attacked the *Hercules*?'

'Possibly.' The centurion turned to Strabonius. 'We should bring Captain Brygos in. He should know immediately.'

The governor nodded. 'And I want to know *his* intentions.' He caught the eye of his second assistant and pointed at the door. 'Hurry now. And don't accept any nonsense – tell him I have *personally* requested his presence at the basilica.'

As the second assistant left the office, Strabonius glanced at the centurion. 'You know how these navy types can be.'

Panares was focusing once more on the map. After a few moments, he suddenly called out to the officer stationed by the door. 'Karras – have someone ride down to the beaches on the city side of the wall and consult with the harbour sentries. And have a boat readied – at dawn I want a party to cross the estuary, to see if any landings have been made.'

'By Jupiter,' said Strabonius, gulping anxiously. 'The danger could come from anywhere.'

'We have seven hundred swords and plenty more who'll help us,' countered Panaraes evenly. 'Odessos is *not* falling to the Goths.'

'Quite right,' said the governor. 'Ah – at last.' A maid entered with a tray which she placed on another table. Upon the tray was a steaming silver jug and she poured wine from it into four silver goblets. Tarchon gratefully took his, thanking the maid as he downed the rich, warm wine. If not for the earlier events of this seemingly endless night, he supposed a meeting with the most influential men in the city might have impressed him.

A tribune arrived shortly after with a written message from the governor of Marcianopolis. While Panares and Strabonius discussed it, Kallisto took the towels brought for her and she and Tarchon went to sit on one of the many benches in the basilica. She looked down at her grimy, wet tunic and cleaned off the worst of the dirt. She then dried her hair and wiped her face, missing a muddy mark on her forehead.

'You have a…er…'

She handed him one of the towels. 'Clean it off. Don't miss any.'

He moved up the bench and did so, feeling nervous at being so close to her.

'I need to look at least half decent. I'm going to have to persuade this Captain Brygos to give us passage on the *Hercules*.'

'Is that a good idea? What about the Goth ships?'

Having cleaned off the mud, he moved back. Kallisto turned her attention to her hands.

'The governor may not even know it but Brygos has orders to withdraw south if under threat. That's why they didn't stay and fight during the last engagement. The Black Sea fleet has only eight operational warships and they're not going to risk losing one of them for Odessos. They need them to secure the Straits, among other things.'

This raised numerous questions in Tarchon's mind but something else was concerning him. 'How do you know all this?'

'Some I find out, some Gargonius tells me. You know, it might be better if I handle this captain on my own. Go get your gear, maybe rest a bit.'

Tarchon didn't want to even think about returning to the room he'd shared with Pelopidas. What would he do with the boxer's bag? What would he tell Chremes?

'Listen,' added Kallisto. 'I know this type of thing is all new to you so I'm going to help you out this time. Pelopidas. If it's going to help snap you out of this daze, there is one thing I'd suggest.'

'What's that?'

'You know enough to find his family in Byzantium?'

'I think so.'

'You go there. Give them some money if you want. Tell them it was his. You can even tell them what happened, or a version of it. At least then they'll know and you'll have done all you can.'

Kallisto opened her purse and gave him a handful of denarii. 'To settle your bill.'

'Thank you,' said Tarchon as he stood.

'And if it helps you,' she added, 'blame me.'

Having asked the guards outside the basilica, Tarchon learned that it was the seventh hour of night. He also asked them for some directions back to the Octopus. When they'd finished, one of the legionaries who'd apprehended him and Kallisto left his compatriots on the steps and hurried over.

'Sorry about earlier, mate. Couldn't be sure you were with us.'

'No worries.'

'Here, take this or you'll get stopped by every watchman in the city at this hour.' The legionary handed him a circular wooden token with some kind of insignia engraved on it.

'Gives you permission to be out on the streets at night.'

'Ah. Thanks.'

'What's going on in there?' asked the legionary.

Now Tarchon understood. This wasn't just a friendly gesture; the soldier wanted something in return. Given the situation, he couldn't blame him.

'Busy.'

The legionary pushed a finger below the cheek guard of his helmet and scratched his skin. 'How worried should we be?'

'The centurion seems confident. I'm sure you'll be all right here inside the walls.'

'What about the Goths? How many you think?'

'Just scouts for now, I reckon. Thanks again for this.'

As it turned out, he needed the token. Having the sword over his shoulder probably didn't help and he was approached four times by watchmen and soldiers. There were many of them close to the forum but the city became quieter as he headed south towards the estuary. He did notice that there seemed to be more doormen stationed outside some of the larger residences. His addled mind forgot the instructions but he followed his nose and, after a couple of wrong turns, reached the inn.

Other than a legionary patrol, the quay was quiet. The *Erythrai* had left and Tarchon couldn't help wishing he was on it. The *Hercules* was not difficult to make out: there were dozens of lights and a lot of movement aboard.

It took some time for Chremes to come to the door. After looking out through a spy-hole and questioning Tarchon, he warily opened up. He was holding a stave and his hand was shaking.

'You do know the city is under siege?'

'I do.'

Chremes invited him in and bolted the door. He walked over to the counter and rested his stave against the wall.

'Where's Pelopidas?'

'Busy. I'm going to meet him after I collect our gear. How much do we owe you?'

Though he'd practised the lie during the journey, it was still difficult to get the words out.

'Eight denarii.'

Tarchon counted out the coins and put them on the counter.

'Can I wrap up that chicken for you? Pelopidas really-'

'No.'

Tarchon was in and out of the room as swiftly as possible. He placed all his clothes in his pack and did the same with Pelopidas' gear, though he could barely bring himself to touch it. Hurrying back downstairs, he said farewell to Chremes, who immediately bolted the door behind him.

With the two packs over his shoulders, Tarchon walked to the mole. He almost threw Pelopidas' pack away, then cursed at himself for even thinking of it. He looked out at the silent estuary. There was not a single light upon the water; it seemed impossible to him that a Goth attack was imminent.

It was not a cold night but there was a chill breeze coming in off the sea. With the sword over his hip and a pack on each arm, Tarchon walked out along the mole. The deteriorating structure offered a few spots down out of the wind. Sitting in one of them, he pulled his blanket over himself and leaned back against his pack. Despite the shelter, it was not comfortable or warm and that suited him well enough. He hadn't been there long when it began to rain and he didn't mind that either. It only seemed right that he should suffer.

Tarchon awoke to sunrise, a brilliant burst of yellow that coloured sea, cloud and sky. He felt himself confronted by the eye of the gods, questioning him. He shook off the wet blanket and knelt before the sun. He spoke to Jupiter and to Minerva; asked them to watch over Pelopidas on his passage to the underworld. He told them that he was a kind, just and courageous man. As the yellow light bore into him, he also asked for forgiveness.

By the time he finished, the sun was so bright that he had to turn away. He waited, looked around for some sign of reply but then realised that the sunrise itself was the sign. That was why he'd gone there – been guided there? – and endured the wet night on the mole, in a perfect position to see the dawn. This was a new day.

He didn't want to forget the previous day (in fact, he was determined to follow Kallisto's advice regarding Pelopidas' family) but he knew from the Nicomedia job that he just had to keep going. He had to put all these thoughts aside and concentrate on the here and now. Gargonius, Korax and Kallisto had all told him the same thing. And now this sign.

The bandage on his arm was filthy and torn. He cut if off and threw it away, glad to see that the wound was healing well. He stood, gathered his gear and made his way back along the mole. Turning left at the Octopus, he was overtaken by a party of ten or more: two men laden with bags, wives and children in their wake. The pair cursed when they saw that – beyond the *Hercules* – only two other vessels remained. One of the wives admonished the man for his language but her attention was soon occupied by her sobbing daughter. When the girl was picked up by her mother, she dropped a straw doll, too distraught to notice. Tarchon put down the packs and chased after her to return it. Up ahead, the other man was questioning an officer from a freighter similar to the departed *Erythrai*. The sailor was gravely shaking his head.

Tarchon walked back to the packs and picked them up.

'Get you anything?'

He had stopped beside a tiny tavern where the owner was pulling back the iron grate that covered his doors. Below each of the small, diamond-shaped windows was a table and chairs.

'Hot wine?' added the man, a middle-aged fellow with a curious island of hair that had been abandoned by the receding remainder. 'Milk?'

'Wine, thank you.'

'Anything to eat? I've got a pot of porridge on.'

Though he still wasn't hungry, Tarchon knew he should eat. 'That'll do.'

Before heading inside, the man nodded towards the ships.

'Leaving today?'

'Yes.'

'Lucky you.'

In the short time it took for his wine and porridge to be served, Tarchon watched at least fifty more people arrive at the quay and immediately question the crew of the two remaining ships. The sense of panic and fear was not helped by the fact that both crews were clearly preparing the freighters for departure. There were a couple of coasters and numerous smaller boats further down the quay and these too were now attracting attention.

'I swear there'll be no one left here by nightfall,' said the tavern-owner, standing beside him with hands on hips. 'Lot of folk heading west to Marcianopolis too.'

'Will that be any safer?'

'A lot won't be stopping there but that's where the closest bridge is. Those with family or friends to the south will be heading that way.'

'You staying?'

'I'll stay. Got my mother upstairs. Can't leave her bed. I used to be in the militia. Don't know if they'll want me. Still got my blade. Ah, look here – talking of swords.'

The closest of the *Hercules*' two gangplanks was currently being crossed by a number of marines, easily distinguished by the green tunics that Tarchon had often seen in Byzantium. They were also clad in the typical trousers, socks and light sandals. First off the gangplank was their senior officer. He also wore a dark blue, fringed cloak and carried a vine stick much like a centurion. Ordering a few loitering lads out of the way, he swiftly organised his marines into two lines. All carried oval shields decorated with Neptune's trident and the wings of an eagle. These Tarchon had seen before, but not the remarkable variety of weapons on show. There were hand-axes, swords, spears and a quarter of the men were armed solely with bows or slings. The officer had them stand to attention, facing their ship. He then walked along the first row, inspecting uniform and equipment. He was evidently a hard taskmaster: the third man he inspected was told off loudly and despatched on a punishment run along the quay, spear in one hand, shield in the other.

This continued for some time, with two more marines sent away. At the other gangplank, supplies were being ferried aboard by the sailors, who all wore varying shades of blue. The repairs seemed to have been completed but four men hung from harnesses, either washing or polishing the timbers. Another man sat astride the six-foot bronze ram situated at the bow, which reminded Tarchon of a farmer's plough. Wearing only a loincloth, the burly sailor was oiling and polishing the metal. A large orange eye was painted just behind the base of the ram, which was reinforced by a network of wooden supports.

By the time the inspection had finished, five of the marines were off running. After ordering the rest back aboard, the officer waited for the miscreants. He took off his blue-crested helmet and paced up and down, tapping the vine stick against his thigh. Without his helmet, Tarchon realised how short he was: not much more than five feet. Compact and muscular, his grizzled features and grey, cropped hair suggested that he was at least fifty.

Even this disciplined military man was distracted by the arrival of Kallisto. She wore a pale blue dress, a dark blue cape and laced boots. Recalling what she'd said about winning favour with the captain, Tarchon suspected the colour choice was entirely intentional. Her long, sleek black hair had been tied back in a simple ponytail. She marched along the quay towards the *Hercules,* followed by two men hauling a hand-cart. Directing them to stop by a gangplank, she then walked straight up to the marine commander with a smile. Within moments, the marine had called out to a younger officer, who answered with a wave and headed for the gangplank.

Tarchon paid for his meal, wished the tavern-owner the best of luck and warily approached the ship. By the time he got there, the marine commander had gone to intercept two of his returning men. The young officer was casting an eye over Kallisto's four wooden chests.

'The small one contains my lyre and flute,' she said. 'We must be *very* careful with those.'

'Ah. Right.' The officer seemed a tad taken aback by the prospect of this passenger. He was quite pale, especially for a sailor, and possessed wavy, auburn hair. Upon his tunic sleeves were a single stripe.

'Captain Brygos did tell you that I'd be aboard?'

'He did, miss. Wasn't there a second passenger too?'

'That would be me,' said Tarchon, feeling rather embarrassed.

'I see. Well, at least *you* don't have much luggage. Let's get you two aboard and find somewhere where you won't be in the way.'

'Much appreciated,' said Kallisto. 'And your name?'

'Neratius, miss. First officer.'

Tarchon put the packs over his shoulders and grabbed the chest containing the instruments.

'Careful!' said Kallisto, before leading the way aboard. It was the first time Tarchon had seen her in daylight and in truth it only enhanced her beauty. Her skin practically glowed and her dark brown eyes were as enticing as her full, pink lips. Tarchon was starting to wish she was ugly: it would have been less distracting.

He had seen many warships at the naval dock in Byzantium but he'd never been aboard one. He was surprised at how featureless the deck was, though it was currently being scrubbed by dozens of sailors with pails and brushes. Other than the single mast, there was just the captain's deckhouse at the stern, one firing turret ahead of that, and another at the bow. These small turrets could accommodate only a few (he assumed the archers and slingers) and resembled the top of a guard tower. Tarchon was also surprised by the narrow beam of the vessel. He knew it was built for speed but reckoned it was little more than twenty feet from one side to the other.

As they followed Neratius to the rear hatch, dozens of heads turned towards Kallisto. Tarchon noted that while some enjoyed the view, others glowered and cursed. Like the superstitious crew of the *Erythrai*, they doubtless feared that the presence of a woman would bring bad luck.

The stairs were steep, so Tarchon waited for one of Kallisto's men to help out with the chest. As ever, she had other ideas.

'I've got this end,' she said, grabbing one of the iron handles. 'Go.'

Tarchon took the other end, turned and descended the steps. They went all the way down to the base of the hold, past two levels of oars and benches constructed in a wooden frame. Here, dozens of men in sleeveless tunics sat in small groups, some oiling or cleaning their oars (which were currently not deployed). Like those on deck, they seemed very interested in – but not entirely happy with – the new arrivals.

'This way,' said Neratius, hurrying along the central walkway towards the stern. Tarchon took charge of the chest once more and followed him. On either side of the walkway were the ribbed compartments of the *Hercules*' hold. Some held rocks used for ballast, others contained provisions, timber, sailcloth and weaponry.

'Good morning,' said a slight man of around sixty, who was sitting on a barrel, studying a page of writing.

'Morning,' said Kallisto as they passed him.

'Romillus,' said Neratius over his shoulder. 'Ship's surgeon.'

They came to some spacious wooden lockers built on the side of two small cabins, one either side of the walkway. Many were filled with clothing but a few were empty.

'Your luggage can go here,' said Neratius, gesturing to the lockers. As he placed the chest in one of them, Tarchon noted how immaculately tidy and clean the ship was. It seemed incredible that so many men could live – and fight – in such a cramped space.

'Port oarsmen, breakfast on deck in a quarter-hour,' announced a loud voice from behind them. 'If I see so much as a rag or pin out of place, there'll be trouble. And don't forget the latrine – you can use the two on the dock. I'd like to keep the stink to a minimum. Especially as we have guests!'

Neratius pointed back down the walkway. 'Demades. Master of oarsmen.'

Demades was a predictably brawny fellow with a round face and a blunt nose. Despite his threatening tone, he was soon assisting one of his oarsmen with a troublesome mounting.

Kallisto dismissed her two men with a coin each. Tarchon and Neratius then lifted her remaining chests into the lockers. He also put the two packs in one, hiding Pelopidas' behind his own so he wouldn't have to look at it.

'We've a bed for you here, miss.' Neratius gestured to the cabin on the right. 'Officers will be in and out, depending on their shifts but we've put a curtain up. I don't expect any problems but if there is any…unwelcome attention, let me or the captain know.'

At that point, the captain himself appeared in the doorway of the cabin opposite. Brygos was a tall man with curly black hair and a thick beard, both tinged with grey. He looked weary; dark bags had formed under his eyes. He was dressed very much like the other officers, except for the white rings on the sleeves of his blue tunic.

He was currently looking at Tarchon's sword. 'Good that you have a blade at least. If there's close action, you report to Iraklidis, understood?'

'Yes, sir,' said Tarchon, though unsure who that was.

Brygos turned to Kallisto. 'Miss, as we discussed last night, you *must* keep out of the way. I suggest this cabin or my deckhouse if conditions allow.'

'Very well, captain. May I ask about the latest intelligence?'

Brygos retreated into his cabin, followed by Kallisto, Tarchon and Neratius, who pulled the door to. Within the tiny room was a bed, a stool and a desk. Upon the desk was a silver muscle cuirass and a bronze helmet. Instead of the usual crest, the helmet was topped by distinctive feathers coloured red and blue. Beside it was a navigational chart composed of many pieces of paper glued together.

'The Gothic ship has been sighted off the southern headland,' said the captain. 'From the description it sounds like the *Prince Catalda*. She's an eighty-footer. Hundred and twenty men.'

'She can't keep up with us though?' said Kallisto.

'No. And I doubt she'd take us on alone.'

'Is she one of the ships that attacked you before?'

Captain Brygos exchanged a glance with his first officer. Tarchon guessed that he had not encountered many women like Kallisto, who often acted much like a man, and a confident one at that.

'No. That was the *King Varin* and the *King Filimer*. *Filimer* is identical to the *Hercules* – one of ours that they captured a few years back. *Varin* is slightly smaller – a hundred feet, hundred and sixty men. No sightings since our skirmish but there's fog to the north. I requested reinforcement by the imperial post seven days ago. The *Victory* was in Heraclea but I've no idea if they've even received the message yet.'

Everyone knew the *Victory*: flagship of the Black Sea Fleet. She was like the great warships of old: two hundred feet long, with four banks of oars. Other than a few of the giant grain ships, she was the largest vessel Tarchon had ever seen. He was keen to observe the giant on the open sea.

Kallisto spoke up again: 'I noticed you've no bolt-thrower up on deck.'

Brygos sighed.

'Mounting came loose during bad weather last month,' explained Neratius. 'We can only have a new one installed at a yard.'

'We leave within the hour,' said Brygos.

At that, Tarchon and Kallisto withdrew to the passageway and then the cabin to allow the officers through. Kallisto sat down on one of the two lower bunks. She let out a long breath and gazed at the aged timbers beneath her feet.

'Get any sleep?' asked Tarchon.

'Not a bit. I had to make a few farewells – be Cassandra again for a few hours.'

'Thalia's?'

She nodded. 'Been there almost six months. I think they'd grown quite attached to me.'

'I meant to ask: your singing and playing – I've not seen many better. How do you keep it up?'

'Not many better?' she repeated with a provocative smile. '*None* better, more like.'

Tarchon was fascinated to know more about her. Assuming she had a family, what did she tell them? She was well past marrying age and surely no father would allow his daughter to live like this?

'It's an excellent cover,' she added. 'No one bats an eyelid at a woman travelling alone if she's a musician, or if she acts oddly – in fact they almost expect it. And when people know you're good at one thing, they assume you don't do anything else.' She looked up at him. 'You'll need to work on that – cover stories, deception. You're an open book.'

Tarchon took the sword from his shoulder and sat down opposite her.

'Well, we all have to start somewhere,' she continued. 'You did well last night.'

If compliments from Korax and Gargonius had raised his spirits, this had double the effect. While Kallisto brushed something off her knee, Tarchon found his eyes wandering to her shapely calves, her thighs, her breasts. He imagined holding her in his arms, kissing her-'

'What's up with you?' she said, frowning.

'What? Nothing.'

'Listen, we have a job to do. Don't go falling in love with me.'

Tarchon blushed so badly that he wanted to cover his face with his hands. 'What are you talking about?'

'Don't worry. It happens all the time – just try not to. It's no good for anyone.'

'I won't *have* to try. You're a pain in the arse and you seem to think you're a man. You're not.'

Kallisto giggled. 'Why would I want to be a man? If you're not thinking with your pricks, you're acting like pricks.' She stood up, shaking her head in disbelief. 'I'm going to get some air, you coming?'

XXVI

Many gathered at the quay to see the *Hercules* off. Tarchon and Kallisto stood at the starboard rail, close to the deckhouse, looking out at the crowd. Among them were Chremes and the tavern-keeper; Tarchon waved to them both. A group from Thalia's were also there, shaking their heads and exchanging regretful looks. Several grown men wiped away tears.

'I suppose they all fell in love with you,' said Tarchon, still embarrassed by their earlier exchange.

'Probably,' she replied, 'though I'll give Hippon a bit more credit. A true lover of music. I could make him cry just with my playing. He knows he won't find anyone better on the lyre this side of Rome.'

She gave a final wave to her adoring followers as the *Hercules* was pushed off by the harbour master and several others. Not far behind Tarchon was one of the two helmsmen. He and a compatriot held the two almost vertical tillers that controlled the warship. Captain Brygos was at the bow, leaving Neratius to take the vessel out.

'Oars in,' said the first officer. 'Slow.'

'Slow it is,' answered Demades from below the hatch.

As he passed on the order, a drum beat rang out. The rowers dipped their oars and were soon following the drum in perfect time, propelling the ship forward as Neratius ordered the helmsmen to turn towards the estuary.

Tarchon looked back at the Octopus and remembered arriving; thinking that all they had to worry about was the boxing competition and finding Kallisto. His eyes drifted to the coast. He could not shake the thought of poor Pelopidas lying on the rocks, bloodied and broken.

'Gods, look there,' said Kallisto, when they were several hundred yards off the shore. A large building in the north of Odessos was on fire and they could see defenders manning the wall. Beyond the wall, up on the ridge they had crossed the previous night, a line of mounted warriors looked down on city.

Kallisto sighed. 'It's started.'

As the *Hercules* powered out of the estuary, all eyes turned to the southern headland, where the *Prince Catalda* had been sighted. The captain had ordered cruising speed, which Tarchon reckoned to be about four knots. It felt quicker up on deck because they were heading into an easterly wind. Brygos and his officers were clearly not happy about this because it limited their ability to use the sail and the wind was pressing them into shore, restricting their alternatives.

Tarchon had also learned that Iraklidis was the name of the diminutive marine commander. His green-clad men now sat in two lines in the middle of the deck, either side of the mast. Lying behind the mast was the yard, while ahead of it was the rolled-up mainsail. Iraklidis prowled up and down, vine stick in his hand, occasionally exchanging a word with Brygos. Tarchon had left his sword below and hoped he wouldn't be noticed.

Kallisto was gazing anxiously at the headland. She retrieved a tiny bottle from her ever-present satchel, tipped out some unguent and rubbed it on her lips.

'What are they like?' asked Tarchon. 'The Goths.'

'Ambitious. Especially Cniva. He's expanded his domain, captured wealthy cities and mines and ports. Used the money to recruit more men. He knows the Emperor has difficulties with the Senate, uprisings, possible mutinies in the legions. A good time to strike.'

'Intelligent then.'

'For a *barbarian*, yes.'

'Someone once told me that there is no such thing as a barbarian. Just Romans and non-Romans.'

She waved a dismissive hand at him. 'Goths are basically Germans. Backward pagans with no respect for the true gods or the civilised world. They try to be like Romans – by taking our ships, using our coins – but they'll never best the Empire.'

Tarchon was surprised by all this; she sounded like a legionary.

'They should go back to their forests and their wooden huts where they belong. They have the odd success now and again but they're nothing compared to us. The red and gold flies across most of the known world.'

'You love Rome.'

Kallisto replaced the vial in her satchel and rearranged her hair, dropping her ponytail over her shoulder. 'In a manner of speaking. And you?'

'Love? No. There are some things about it I like, some I don't. My best friend is Persian.' Tarchon wasn't entirely sure why he said it; probably just to shock her.

'I was born outside the Empire,' replied Kallisto. 'A *long* way outside. A land of clans and chaos, feuds and bloodshed, endless cycles of war and revenge. When I was taken from it, I thought my life was over because it was all I knew. When I saw the Empire and learned of Rome, I was glad because I'd discovered a better world; a brighter world.'

Tarchon was again taken aback by the passion in her voice. She didn't seem the type to care about much but herself yet now she sounded like some magistrate or governor. He looked at the red and gold standard flying from the *Hercules*' stern and all the uniformed men. He guessed most of them loved the Empire too.

Captain Brygos had returned to the deckhouse. He came out holding a bound book, studying a certain page. As he stood there, a young sailor approached.

'Sir, lookout reports no sightings but the fog is bad. Estimates visibility at one mile.'

'If that,' replied Brygos, now looking forward. They were approaching the end of the estuary and the fog sat in a great bank ahead of them.

Tarchon glanced upward. He had earlier watched the lookout climb the mast and position himself in the crow's nest. Having once scaled such a mast, he knew how small even the *Hercules* would appear from above.

Neratius spoke up. 'Not much cloud though, sir. The fog will burn away. An offering to Jupiter and Neptune, perhaps?'

'Our time is better spent in *useful* preparations,' snapped Brygos. 'You take the bow.'

'At once, captain.'

Brygos ordered the helmsman to head slightly to the south, then went forward and spoke to Iraklidis. Below, the timing drum continued its relentless beat. Despite the enormous effort being expended, Tarchon heard nothing of the men, only the dip of the oars and the groans from the leather straps that held them against their pivots. *The Hercules* now drew level with the southern headland, which rose some two hundred feet from the waves, turf at the top, rock at its base.

'There it is,' said Kallisto.

Tarchon had only looked away for a moment but now he too saw the prow – then the whole – of the Gothic warship. It was already clear of the headland, moving quicker than the *Hercules*. From distance, the main difference was the great black standard hanging over the stern. Several shouts had already gone up and Brygos went to join Neratius and another officer at the bow. Within a minute, the captain marched back past the marines and issued orders to Demades. The master of oarsmen was sitting on the edge of the hatch, scratching the thick hair visible above his tunic.

'Fast.'

'Fast it is, captain.'

Demades disappeared and was soon bellowing orders. The drumbeat accelerated, the oars matching it with practised ease.

'Helm to port,' ordered Brygos.

'Port it is, captain,' came the simultaneous answer from the helmsmen, who were two of the older sailors. Brygos stood with one hand on the side of the empty rearward turret, watching the bow of his vessel veer left.

'Hold there and steady,'

'There and steady, sir,' came the reply. The *Hercules* was again heading directly out to sea, almost parallel with the Gothic ship. With the acceleration in pace, the vessels now seemed to be moving across the waves at the same speed, which Tarchon estimated at six knots.

Just then, the aged surgeon climbed out of the hatch. Though the sea was calm and the deck steady, Romillus struggled to his feet, then lurched past his oblivious captain to the side-rail. He also had a satchel over his shoulder and from it he selected a small flask.

'Just to settle the stomach,' he told Kallisto after he'd drunk a little of the contents. 'One would think I'd be immune to seasickness after so long.'

'How long have you served?' she asked, eyes still fixed on the Gothic vessel.

'Eight years, is it? No, nine. Before that I was with the legions. I prefer the navy – I like waking up in new places.'

'How was it up north?' she asked.

'A few run-ins with Cniva's ships.' Romillus turned to the enemy vessel, screwing up his eyes. 'I hope we don't engage. We're better at distance. Up close I'm not sure there's much in it. They don't have our discipline, of course, but they're as tough as I've seen.'

Tarchon didn't much like the sound of that, especially as the captain expected him to fight. He wondered if anything else on this accursed mission could take a turn for the worse.

Neratius returned to the deckhouse. 'Looks like the fog's lifting, sir.'

'Not sure if that's a good or a bad thing,' said Brygos before addressing his helmsmen once more, ordering them to turn 'two points to starboard'.

'I'm not going to let him bar our way,' added the captain.

'Understood, sir. I'll notify Iraklidis.'

As Neratius headed for the marines, Brygos waved a hand at the surgeon. 'Best settle in and ready your implements, Romillus.'

'Of course, captain. May Jupiter and the great gods guide your hand.'

'You two can go with him,' said Brygos.

With an artful flick of her hair and another glorious smile, Kallisto approached him. 'Captain, I'd really prefer to remain on deck.'

'Do as you're ordered the first time, girl,' replied Brygos gruffly. 'Or I'll have you thrown over the side.'

Incredibly, she seemed ready to protest, so Tarchon ushered towards the hatch. 'Just do as you're bloody told for once.'

Once there, they had to wait for the slow Romillus to negotiate the steps. Despite the ventilation all around, the air below was now thick with the odour of sweat, which shone on the faces and arms of the oarsmen. Two to each oar, they were pulling hard now: feet braced, jaws set, knuckles white. The drummer sat in the walkway, legs either side of his drum, bald head gleaming.

'Eyes to yourselves!' bellowed Demades as Kallisto and Tarchon stepped down on to the walkway.

'Come,' said Romillus. 'I'd welcome some assistance. My orderly was killed up near Kreminiskoi and he's not been replaced.'

They followed him past the last ranks of oarsmen to a compartment close to the cabins. The depth of the compartments varied but here they were about two feet lower than the walkway, the bases a lattice of timber.

Romillus pointed to a pile of wide planks on one side. 'Spread them out for me, would you, young man? It gives me a flat area to work on.'

As Tarchon did so, Kallisto found a perch with a good view through the closest oar-holes. 'Looks like they've turned north a bit. Not sure we'll get ahead of them.'

Tarchon laid out the third and fourth planks, which had evidently been cut for this space. Romillus returned from the lockers carrying a bronze medical case which he placed in the corner of the compartment. Under his arm was a bundle of bandages, some of them faintly stained with blood. As the way was clear for a moment, Tarchon entered the nearby cabin and fetched his sword. If he did have to fight, he wanted it close by. He then realised his hands were shaking.

How in Hades did I end up here?

He made fists and took some long, deep breaths.

Outside, Kallisto was still reporting on events outside. 'We might be a little ahead now, I think.'

If she can deal with this, so can you.

He could not be sure that there would be another opportunity for prayer so he took it now.

Great and honoured Minerva, I promise to give an offering of great value when next I have the chance. I promise to remain faithful to you for as long as I live. Please watch over me this day. Please allow me to return home.

Once back in the hold, he stood beside Kallisto and looked out at the Gothic ship. It was much closer now, perhaps only two hundred yards away. He could make out individual oars, sailors on deck, and a row of shields mounted on the side. The standard was a simple design: two crossed axes, white on black.

'Cniva's flag,' said Kallisto.

'We're not ahead of it,' said Tarchon.

'No,' she agreed.

'But it's smaller, yes? Should be slower.'

'Should be,' said Romillus after another swig from his flask. 'But she might be lightly loaded. We've got a full complement of marines, plus the turrets.'

Tarchon saw that there were indeed no turrets on the Gothic ship. The two vessels were well out to sea now, perhaps three miles off the coast. Tarchon looked out to the port side and saw that the fog was thinning by the moment.

'Captain won't keep this up much longer,' said the surgeon, now picking through the many implements within his medical box.

'Why not?' asked Tarchon.

'The men will tire quickly at this speed and we've a whole day ahead of us.'

Though no order was given, they began to hear a lot of movement from above: boots on deck and the scrape of metal on wood.

'What is that – a hundred yards?' said Kallisto.

'No more,' replied Tarchon.

They could see a dozen archers lined up on the port side of the Gothic ship. There was no deckhouse but towards the stern was a cluster of men in helmets.

'Slightly ahead now,' said Tarchon.

Just then, Captain Brygos came down a couple of steps and spoke to Demades. In turn, the rowing officer went to speak to the drummer. When Demades turned back towards them, the rowing officer was for once quiet but his mouth was moving.

'What's going on?' asked Tarchon.

'He's counting down,' answered Kallisto.

'To what?'

Romillus sat down beside his box, put an arm across it and wedged himself into a safe position. 'Never a dull moment in the navy. One starts to value them at my age.'

Half a minute later, the drum suddenly increased in tempo and the oarsmen moved swiftly up to ramming speed. Demades roared encouragement, adding to each drum with a shout of his own. Now the effort began to show on the faces of the oarsmen as they heaved the ship onward. Tarchon heard the squeak and groan of gear behind them as the rudders turned. The *Hercules* swung sharply to the right, now aiming straight at the enemy vessel.

He almost fell off the beam he was standing on. Once steady, he gripped another with both hands, watching as the ship came closer with every passing second. There was a flurry of movement towards the stern of the *Prince Catalda*, then the

Gothic vessel also turned. Their manoeuvre was just as neat and soon the ships were on a collision course, only a hundred feet apart.

'This should be interesting,' said Kallisto, leaping away from the side and onto the walkway, close to Tarchon.

The rowers strained at their oars, breathing hard, dripping sweat onto creaking benches. The drummer watched Demades, who stood at the base of the steps, looking up.

'Ship your oars!'

This instruction was carried out with remarkable speed and precision. Completing a final stroke, the rowers pushed down until their oars were horizontal. They then yanked them in, the ends almost meeting each other above the walkway.

'Impact!' yelled someone.

Tarchon and Kallisto dropped low on the walkway.

When it came, it was surprisingly quiet. One low snap followed by several more. Shouts, scrapes, cracks. To the left, the hull of the *Prince Catalda* flashed past: staring eyes, an iron rib on the rudder, a fluttering corner of the black standard.

'He's taken their oars,' stated Romillus without looking. 'Half at least.'

Then came more impacts, but these were against the side of the *Hercules*. Shouts filled the air on deck and it sounded as if every man up there was moving.

But nothing was as loud as the great thump from the stern; a blow that shuddered through the whole ship. Seconds later, the *Hercules* seemed to be hauled backwards. Several rowers fell from their benches with shouts and curses. Fortunate to be already down, Tarchon and Kallisto steadied old Romillus as some of his implements rolled away.

With the sound of splintering wood, the ship abruptly lurched forward again.

'Oars in! Slow!'

As Demades and his drummer spurred the rowers back into action, half a dozen sailors came flying down the steps. They pounded along the walkway to the stern, closely followed by Neratius. The officer's face was flushed, his eyes wide with panic. What was said next alarmed Tarchon more than what had already occurred.

'At least they missed the rudder.'

'Look at the size of the bloody hole though!'

'Sir, we've got water coming in!'

To his credit, Neratius took charge quickly. 'You four, get cloth pegged in across there. You others – timbers and the rest of the repair gear. Er...you! Tell the captain we've a three-foot hole just above the waterline.'

'Me?' said Tarchon.

'Go!' thundered Neratius.

'I'll come with you,' said Kallisto, already moving along the walkway.

'Don't be long,' said Romillus. 'I'll need that help.'

Demades was towards the bow, helping a man repair an oar mounting. The rest of his rowers were heaving with slow but powerful strokes.

Following Kallisto up the steps and on deck, Tarchon saw that the *Hercules* was again heading south-east, away from the shore. The marines were now divided between the two turrets and the port side. Half a dozen sailors were clustered at the rail close to the stern, looking down. The Gothic ship was some way behind them, drifting. The damage was obvious: several shattered oars floated nearby.

'Report from Neratius,' said Kallisto. 'Three-foot hole just above the waterline.'

The captain shook his head. 'Crafty bastards.'

'How did they-'

Ignoring the pair of them, Brygos called one of the older sailors over and began questioning him about the wind and their chances of laying a course south. Close by was a marine hastily restringing his bow.

'What happened?' Kallisto asked him.

'Don't think they wanted a head-on scrap with us,' said the man, speaking as he worked. 'But they had a bolt-thrower hidden under sail-cloth. Fired as we passed and hit the stern. We took out plenty of oars and a few men but I reckon they've done what they intended.'

Tarchon was just absorbing the implications of this when a shout came from the crow's nest.

'Say again!' bellowed Brygos.

'Mast sighted to the north!' replied the lookout. 'Four miles.'

'Any sign of the other one? Sure it's not two?'

'Just the one, sir.'

Tarchon could not yet see the enemy ship.

Brygos grabbed another sailor by the arm and nodded back towards the stationary Gothic ship. 'You watch him. Tell me if he moves.'

'Yes, sir.'

Brygos took off his helmet and stowed it in a basket just inside the deckhouse. He met the older sailor close to Tarchon and Kallisto.

'Well?'

'Pretty much a dead easterly, captain. If we head north, we'll end up in that bloody bay past Odessos. South the coast is more favourable. We could make for Mesembria but with a holed stern they'll likely run us down before we get there.'

Brygos did not reply, instead turning north. The sea fog seemed to be receding by the minute.

The old sailor continued, a grimace on his weathered face. 'Wind will take us back into the Devna, sir, but then we're-'

'Trapped.'

Brygos walked to the port side, the marines making way. He placed his hands on the side-rail and gazed at the fog.

'Cease rowing!'

'Cease rowing, sir!' came the reply from below.

As the oars were lifted, Brygos kept his eyes trained to the east. 'Our old friends, hunting together again.' He shouted up to the crow's nest. 'Lookout – amidships – you see it?'

'I see it, sir.'

'Nicely done,' said Brygos thoughtfully, running his fingers through his dark beard. 'Nicely done indeed, though they were fortunate with the fog.' He approached Iraklidis, who was tapping his vine-stick against his other hand.

'Centurion, we can't outrun them. We're going to have to fight them. I'll try to take them one at a time but the likelihood is we'll face them both.'

'No matter, sir. We'll see off these barbarians for you.'

Captain Brygos met this with an odd look, as if he appreciated the sentiment but didn't quite believe it.

XXVII

The Gothic ships must have been going at close to full speed because they took only a half-hour to reach the *Hercules*. Tarchon was again impressed by the crew, who stuck to their tasks and seemed to accept their inescapable fate with grim determination. Brygos allowed the oarsmen time to rest and take on water while the sailors worked on the damaged stern. From what Tarchon could gather, they had stopped water coming in but hadn't the time to make a full repair. The port rear quarter was vulnerable. As for the marines, they unsheathed their swords and replenished their stocks of ammunition.

The crew had at least faced both ships before and knew of their armament: both were equipped with a heavy bolt-thrower. Captain Brygos seemed particularly keen to establish which vessel was which. Using a page of his own notes, and the contributions of his officers, he'd decided that the *Varin* was the ship to the north, the *Filimer* to the east. The Gothic ships now closed in on bow and port side, no more than a half-mile away. The *Prince Catalda* was a similar distance behind them and still hadn't moved. Neither had the *Hercules*.

Brygos stood alone, just in front of the hatch, arms crossed, eyes flicking between the two ships. He had stood there while a sailor put on his silver cuirass; his helmet he still held in his hand. Neratius and the other officers watched the captain, clearly anxious that they take action.

At Kallisto's suggestion, she and Tarchon had retreated into the shadowy deckhouse and the captain seemed to have forgotten about them. Tarchon didn't imagine that she was any keener on assisting with Romillus' bloody work than he was. He also wanted to see what was going on.

Brygos walked over to Iraklidis and spoke to him briefly. Moments later, the marine commander sent three of his slingers to each turret. Five of his ten archers – all staying low – moved back to the stern. They laid out their quivers and crouched there. Brygos then marched over to the hatch and spoke to the attentive Demades.

Moments later, the master of rowers disappeared and the drum beat began again. Brygos took his oarsmen up to cruising speed and ordered the helmsmen to turn north. Two sailors then came up from below, both carrying two shields. Each man stationed himself beside a helmsman and also crouched down. The captain put on his helmet and walked into the deckhouse. There, he took up his own oval shield, which was green bordered by red, adorned with a pattern of silver snakes. He must have seen Tarchon and Kallisto sitting there but said nothing.

'Fast, Demades.'

'Fast it is, sir.'

The sea was rougher now and the *Hercules* began to rise and dip, the strokes less uniform and effective. They could see the prow of the *Varin* too, cutting through the water towards them. The sea fog and remaining cloud had disappeared. The polished timbers of the Gothic ship shone, every piece of metal sparkling like the rippled sea beneath.

Tarchon moved up to the front of the deckhouse and looked to his right. The *Filimer* looked to be at maximum speed and, if the *Hercules* met the *Varin*, would be on the scene only two or three minutes later.

'What's he up to with those archers and the shields?' said Kallisto.

'Not sure. This is why I'd never join the army or the navy – you can't control a damn thing.'

'I'm with you there,' she replied. 'You're just a little piece on a very big board.'

Shield still in hand, Brygos dropped back to be close to the helmsmen. The warships closed to two hundred yards, bounding across the waves. The captain issued a series of course corrections, clearly determined to keep the vessels prow to prow. At a hundred yards, Demades' head appeared in the hatch, eyes locked on his captain. At fifty yards, the archers at the bow nocked their arrows and prepared to draw.

Then the noise changed. Tarchon belatedly realised that – apparently without instruction – the rowers had lifted and shipped their oars. Though without power, the *Hercules* was still doing three or four knots as it neared the *Varin*, where oars still thrashed away. Tarchon looked at the bow turret: the helmets of the slingers were just visible. Iraklidis was with the remainder of his marines behind the mast, every man holding a shield.

Sure that the ships were going to smash into each other, Tarchon spread his feet and held the left side of the deckhouse, Kallisto the right. At an order from Iraklidis, the slingers now began to swing their weapons. With the *Varin* no more than fifty feet away, the captain ordered the helmsmen to veer right. The Gothic captain saw it and matched it but his ship had barely moved when Brygos countered the order. As the bow swung back to the left, Demades shouted 'Starboard, single stroke.' As every oar on that side dug deep, the movement left accelerated. The Gothic captain was unable to compensate and the vessels passed twenty feet apart.

Even so, the enemy archers were ready, gathered by the side-rail, bows drawn. As they let fly, arrows peppered the *Hercules*' deck, most turned by shields or thudding into the timbers. Then a much larger shape flew through the air, a thick rope snaking out behind it. The great bolt smashed into the forward turret, embedding itself in the wood. Before the harpoon could pull tight, Iraklidis and three others fell on the great rope with hand axes, chopping at the thick fibres. As the ships slid past each other, the rope straightened. On the Gothic ship, the crew of the bolt-thrower watched along with many others as the marines hacked away. At last, they were through and the severed rope was pulled harmlessly away with the *Varin*.

Though his eyes were fixed on this, Tarchon heard movement behind him. Looking around the edge of the deckhouse, he watched the archers spring up as the sterns of the warships drew level. Showing great agility and balance, the bowmen unleashed a volley of arrows straight at the Gothic helmsmen. Even so, the movements of ship and sea were considerable and only two found their targets. One was already screaming and reaching for the bolt lodged in his throat, the other gazing dumbly at the projectile stuck in his shoulder. The men staggered away, the ship momentarily without steering.

The rest of Brygos' plan then became clear. Demades' men had already prepared their oars. At the captain's order, the *Hercules* performed a tight right turn, the helmsmen pushing the tillers hard over. The archers had already nocked a second set of arrows, which they duly launched at the men who'd replaced the fallen helmsmen. One was struck in the chest and all in that area were forced to take cover.

Once her turn was done, Brygos ordered the *Hercules* straight up to ramming speed. A third and fourth volley from the archers stationed at the bow caused chaos at the rear of the *Varin*. Though the enemy oarsmen were still working hard, the lack of control was evident.

'Where's the *Filimer*?' yelled Brygos.

'Port side, sir,' answered someone. 'Two hundred yards and closing.'

Roared on by Demades and his drummer, the Roman oarsmen propelled the *Hercules* towards the *Varin*, which was now veering across their bow. It was evident to Tarchon that the Gothic crew lacked the experience and skill of the Romans.

'To port! We strike his stern!' bellowed Brygos, perhaps realising that he had only once chance to take out the *Varin* before joining battle with the *Filimer*. As he braced himself, everyone else did the same.

The bow of the *Hercules* was not far from the rearward starboard oar of the enemy vessel and the change of course brought it straight into the stern. The bronze ram sliced noisily through timber and spun the Gothic vessel around. Had it hit straight on, the two ships would have come together, but the angled attack allowed the Roman warship to plough onward, ripping more wood from the *Varin*'s stern. Tarchon winced as he heard oars cracking but they pulled clear of the *Varin* with the archers smiling, apparently sure that they'd crippled a second vessel.

Then came their turn.

The prow of the *Filimer* smashed into the *Hercules*' port side, nearer stern than bow. Four unsecured sailors went flying, rolling across the deck. The Roman warship was pushed away but then stopped, impaled on the deadly ram. Suddenly, the Goths were there, clustered at the *Filimer*'s bow. Most wore bronze helmets but some went without. And though he saw dark-haired, dark-skinned warriors like his own people, Tarchon saw others with blonde and auburn hair. Some had shaved it at the sides, others boasted luxuriant beards and moustaches. Their spears jabbed the air as two gangplanks were pushed out on either side of the bow.

Captain Brygos, two other officers and the sailors got clear to avoid the rush of the marines. Iraklidis' men spread out in a double line, covering the port side. Tarchon saw a grappling hook fly through the air, closely followed by another. The first hook landed amidst the marines and was skilfully knocked back over the side before it could be pulled tight. The second was instantly tugged in and locked against the rail: until it was knocked off by a Roman spearhead.

But there would be no chance of escape. From the middle of the *Filimer*'s deck, a harpoon shot across the waves, trailing a line. It impaled the *Hercules* close to the bow, the well-judged shot too low for the marines to reach.

'Don't let them swing into us!' yelled Brygos, now sheltering behind his shield and protected by several armed sailors. Iraklidis nodded his acknowledgement without turning round. Brygos now looked over the starboard quarter at the *Varin*, prompting Tarchon and Kallisto to do the same. Several

Goths were at the stern, looking down at the damage. Many broken timbers could be seen but the forward rowing positions still looked usable.

'She's not out of this,' stated Brygos.

The first of the *Filimer*'s gangplanks dropped towards the port side. Attached to the top were two lines used by the attackers to hold the plank and control it; at the base was a spike. On this occasion, the Goths showed great skill and, at the first attempt, landed the end neatly on the side-rail. It was in fact, more than a plank: a reinforced miniature bridge complete with ropes along each side.

This time, Iraklidis and his marines did not interfere. The first attackers climbed onto the gangplank, shuffling forward, each holding a circular shield. The shields were painted bright white, with a black wolf's head around the central spiked boss. Two more came up behind the first man but, when they were halfway across, the marines in the turrets opened up. Two slingstones pinged harmlessly off the first shield, damaging nothing but paintwork. The lead man was only feet from the *Hercules* when an arrow embedded itself in his left foot. He faltered and fell to his knees, fatally revealing his head for a second. A slingshot caught him on the cheek and he fell back, bouncing off the plank then hitting the water. A cheer went up from the marines but the Goths did not stop. The remaining two continued, crouching even lower, now having to negotiate a thicket of arrows at their feet.

Leaving his marines, Iraklidis ran towards the bow, shield expertly guarding his left side. The Goths were now hauling the harpoon – and the bow of the *Hercules* – towards them using a winch. This had the effect of slowly levering the prow out of the Roman ship, causing yet more damage. After a few instructions from the marine commander, two of his men sprang up and put their shields over the side. Handed a spear by Iraklidis, a third man stood and leaned over the rail, clearly trying to dislodge the harpoon. The commander himself held onto his belt and arranged his own shield to protect him.

Tarchon noticed that Kallisto was no longer beside him but now sitting inside the shadowy deckhouse. Despite the noise of the battle around them, she was gazing calmly into space, hands clasped in her lap.

'Kallisto?'

'Looks like you were right. We shouldn't have risked this. Worse, I didn't send a message over land. If we don't make it, Gargonius won't get the name.'

It actually took Tarchon a while to realise what she meant.

'The name? The spy? There's plenty else to worry about right here and now!'

'I was in Odessos a long time. It's the one really valuable piece of intelligence I uncovered. Now we're going to die in a bloody sea battle.' She shrugged. 'At least there's a bit of glory in it.'

A cry went up from the bow. Iraklidis dragged his man back over the side-rail, a bolt lodged between his shoulders. He laid the shuddering marine on his side, then left him, obviously concluding that he was beyond help. Shield still up, he seemed to curse. His team had, however, again succeeded in cutting the harpoon line: the severed rope was in the water.

Though he knew nothing of the Gothic language, Tarchon could see the name of the vessel etched in white close to the stern. The oars had been shipped and the entire deck was crowded with warriors, most clutching wolf's head shields. It seemed to Tarchon that the Romans were badly outnumbered and he wondered why Brygos was yet to summon his many oarsmen to the deck.

Moments later, the captain approached. 'You two – get below while you still can. Help Romillus.'

Tarchon reckoned that this was a better – and safer – duty than joining the marines. 'Yes, captain.'

Protected by officers bearing shields, Brygos hurried away towards the stern.

'We don't have shields,' said Kallisto, eyeing the hatch.

'Then we better be quick.'

They got below unscathed and found the place considerably less orderly than when they'd left. Due to the effects of the harpoon and the winch, the *Filimer*'s ram had been pulled clear, but it had left a five-foot gash just above the waterline. Sailors were already closing in with timbers, nails, cloth and pegs.

Of even more concern was the damage to the stern. Neratius stood watching anxiously as his crewmen laboured. There were so many of them packed in there, that Tarchon couldn't see what was going on. What he could see was two separate teams working pumps to clear the bilges. Others were using pails, scooping water out of the rearward compartments and chucking it out through the oar holes.

Tarchon and Kallisto moved under the steps and out of the way as Brygos ordered Demades to deploy his oarsmen. While some were already assisting the sailors and a few had been injured, there were still at least a hundred men available. Demades organised them into a double line while his senior men assembled weapons and equipment below the steps. All were given a spear but there were only a few spare shields and these all seemed to go to older men. Tarchon saw many fearful looks; unlike the marines, the oarsmen would have to fight without helmets and armour. The steps shook above his head as the men filed upwards.

'You there!' It was Romillus. The surgeon was kneeling on the boards, with four patients laid out in front of him.

'Coming,' answered Tarchon. He and Kallisto waited for more oarsmen to join the line, then hurried down the walkway.

'I must move to the right side and forward,' stated the surgeon.

It wasn't difficult to see why. The men now working on the damaged hull were very close and the bilges were overflowing under at least two of the planks that Tarchon had earlier put down.

'Take this man, then the timbers,' said Romillus, nodding to the sailor closest to the walkway. This man was on his side, groaning. A ragged wound above his left hip was bleeding heavily and his eyes were rolling.

'On to the walkway first,' said Tarchon. 'You take the legs.'

For once, Kallisto actually did as she was told. Though they tried to be gentle, the wounded man cried out. Having deposited him close to a compartment on the other side, Tarchon leaped over him and cleared a space, rolling kegs and wicker baskets aside, stumbling several times. Returning to fetch the planks, he tried not to look at what Romillus was doing with his patient: cutting away flesh around an arrow to pull it free. Kallisto was gripping a vertical timber, also trying not to look.

'Grab a timber.'

She helped him move the planks – one of them dripping blood – and place them in the new compartment. As he continued to shift baskets to make space, Tarchon realised how the volume of the battle had changed. It sounded as if every man was now engaged in the fight; an impression reinforced when the few oarsmen left below grabbed spears and shoved them out through the holes. Some seemed to be trying to push the *Filimer* off, others were targeting the enemy.

When Tarchon and Kallisto moved the patient onto the boards, he moved from groans to curses.

'Help here!' demanded Romillus.

Joining the surgeon, Tarchon and Kallisto saw that he was no longer working on the sailor with the wounded side. This man's face was motionless and a long line of drool hung from his mouth.

'Is he-'

'Forget him, girl. You help that man. A glancing wound but bleeding badly. You'll need to bandage him.'

This young marine was able to sit up and had bravely tried to bandage his wounded shin. But he was pouring with sweat and breathing as if he'd just run a marathon. As Kallisto grabbed more bandages and went to his aid, Tarchon knelt beside Romillus, who swiftly washed his blood-soaked hands in a nearby pail of pink water. His numerous instruments were laid out on a similarly blood-stained length of cloth.

Fortunately, the man they were dealing with was unconscious. He was on his side, head as limp as his arms. He was a lean fellow, his blue tunic pushed up over his belt to reveal thighs several shades paler than his lower legs. One of those thighs had been struck by an arrow, midway between knee and hip. The bolt had gone clean through but was leaking a surprisingly small amount of blood.

'Evenios,' said Romillus, wiping his brow before holding the thigh on either side of the wound. 'I know his father. I must do what I can. You see the arrow has gone through. We cannot leave it there – not so close to the artery. We must push it *all* the way through and out. Grabbing a set of heavy iron pliers, Romillus cut off the head and feathered tail of the bolt.

'Oil it,' he told Tarchon. 'Vial in the medical case there.'

Tarchon took a length of cloth, dipped it in the oil and applied it to the rear of the bolt. Meanwhile, Romillus repositioned the patient's leg so that the extraction would be easier. Tarchon was feeling sick – partly because at least one of the men had soiled themselves – but he knew he could deal with this. Growing up on the streets, he had seen most things, including numerous gruesome injuries from fighting – or more commonly – accidents. Looking down at the arrow poking out the back of this poor bastard's leg, he saw not only blood on the tip but pieces of skin and cloth from his tunic.

'He'll likely wake,' said Romillus. 'With him on his side, it will be difficult for you to keep him still but you must.'

'Understood.'

Sitting astride Evenios' legs at the knee, facing him, Romillus placed one hand on each end of the bolt. He made a few initial movements, causing Evenios to move and stir.

'The start will be the worst,' explained the surgeon. 'I can't be too rough – not this close to the big vein – so it won't be quick. Ready?'

'Yes.'

Tarchon leant over Evenios and placed a hand on his shoulder. As the surgeon began to push the rear of the arrow and pull the tip, Tarchon locked eyes with Kallisto. Still bandaging her patient's shin, she gave a tight-lipped smile of encouragement.

At Romillus' first real application of force, Evenios awoke. He initially seemed dazed but another jolt from the surgeon brought his arms up to Tarchon, as if to fight him off.

'What are you doing?'

'You're injured. We're-'

Evenios began to struggle. Romillus pressed down on his knees, still holding the arrow at both ends. Tarchon leant his right arm onto Evenios', pressing it against the board, but the wounded man's left arm was free and he flailed at Tarchon, catching him across the nose.

'Still, Evenios!' yelled the surgeon. 'I am Romillus, ship's surgeon. You *must* let us help you!'

With that, he gave another yank on the head of the arrow, pulling the severed end into the wound.

Gripped by a paroxysm of pain that arched his back and made his teeth grind, Evenios then let out a scream the like of which Tarchon had never heard. Showing enormous strength, he continued to thrash around.

'Keep him still, lad!' shouted Romillus.

'Easier said than done. Can I knock him out?'

Kallisto was there in an instant, stuffing a thick strip of leather into Evenios' mouth.

'Bite down on this,' she said into his ear. Her tone seemed to calm him, even when Romillus pulled again.

Face dripping with sweat, red eyes bulging, Evenios' lips trembled as the surgeon did his terrible work.

'Slight blockage,' said Romillus. 'Ah, we're through, I think. One more, Evenios. You've done well, son.'

Another pull and it was over. Evenios immediately slumped back and lost consciousness once more. After he'd let go and moved back, Tarchon was stunned at the amount of blood. Romillus dipped his hands in the pail again and calmly watched the blood issuing freely from both sides of the wound.

'Quite a bit but we've not nicked the big veins.'

He grabbed a bandage and wrapped it tight around the thigh, tying it off an inch above the wound. He handed a second bandage to Tarchon.

'The whole length of it. Tight – but not as tight as the one above. Oh gods. More.'

Sailors were carrying injured marines down the steps. The poor sod with the wounded side was still blocking the walkway. Only yards from him, the repair crew had given up trying to stem the flow from the second attack but had at least prevented the water reaching other compartments.

'I'll do this,' said Kallisto, 'you get him on to the planks.'

Leaving her with the bandage and Romillus gathering his implements, Tarchon went to the man and dragged him on to the boards. There was only space for four so he moved him to the edge, close to the hull. He had barely set him down, when something thumped into that side of the *Hercules*.

Knocked off balance and toppling forward, Tarchon only avoided the casualty by stretching for a beam and arresting his fall. Rolling on to his side, he looked out through the oar-holes. He glimpsed dark timbers, the stump of an oar, a white dragon on a blue shield.

'The *Varin*'s alongside,' uttered one of the newly-arrived sailors, hardly seeming to care about the injured marine he was holding up by the straps of his armour.

'We've had it,' said the man holding the soldier's legs.

'Cease your mutterings!' yelled Neratius, emerging from the crowd of men at the stern. Behind him, Tarchon saw water now spilling over the edge of the compartment.

'Put those men down and clear space for them,' Neratius told the sailors, helping Kallisto move her patient to the other side.

Tarchon had to drag his gaze from the enemy ship, which now seemed a blur of activity, the Goths shouting with what sounded like excitement and confidence. Soon the thumps and crashes on the starboard side were as loud as those on the port. Like the others, he soon found himself staring upward, fearful that they'd already been overrun.

'Look at your bloody work!' yelled Neratius, cuffing a sailor around the head but also snapping Tarchon back into action. He and Kallisto helped the sailors lay out two more marines as Romillus began to check the new arrivals. The first of them had an awful wound to his face that had caved in his cheek and rearranged his eyes and nose. He was not moving and Romillus' assessment was a mere shake of his head. The next man was a marine encased in armour. A blade had found its way between mail and helmet and torn flesh from his neck. He was holding the wound with his hand.

'Somebody get that bandaged.'

Yet more wounded were appearing on the walkway.

'You!' snapped Romillus. 'Make more space for us.'

Tarchon moved into the next compartment, which was mostly taken up by two large sails, wrapped in yards of twine. He hauled one out and Kallisto helped him with the other.

Once the new arrivals had been laid down, Neratius ordered the sailors to the stern. 'Back there – we need more hands baling.'

'Hold that order!' Brygos came flying down the steps. 'All of you up! Every spare man. Now!' The captain dropped his shield and began bodily pushing sailors up the steps. None of them had armour and only a couple possessed helmets. Those who'd lost their spears took new ones from the pile below the steps.

Vaguely aware that Kallisto was helping one of the wounded, Tarchon tried not to catch the captain's eye.

Brygos first looked at those still dealing with the hole in the port side. 'How's it looking there?'

'Bad, sir, but just above the water at least.'

'Keep at it.'

Neratius looked desperately to the stern. 'Sir, the repair's not holding. We've got more and more-'

'Then you better keep baling, first officer! We're barely holding them off up there. You – didn't you have a sword?'

Tarchon found himself face to face with the bearded captain.

'Yes, sir.'

'He's an agent, captain,' said Kallisto, 'and new to the job.'

'I need *every* man up there. You, girl, will help the surgeon.'

'Am I to have no other assistance?' demanded Romillus, his voice wavering.

'When I can spare men, I'll send them down,' said the captain. 'Find your sword, grain man, and report to Iraklidis.'

Trying not to think about the scene on deck, Tarchon went to get his sword, only to find it had got stuck beneath a heavy coil of rope. Once armed and back on the walkway, he realised that Kallisto hadn't been treating a marine; she'd been removing his mail shirt and the quilted undershirt.

'Here.'

Tarchon took the undershirt and put it on, tying the straps around his waist that would hold it in place. The mail-shirt was far heavier than he'd expected but he was grateful nonetheless.

'Find a helmet too,' said Kallisto. 'But stay out of trouble. This isn't our fight.'

'I think it's everyone's now.'

XXVIII

Tarchon was sure of one thing: he wasn't going up on that deck without a helmet *and* a shield. Fortunately, the continuing flow of injured men had created a new pile of equipment close to the bottom of the stairs. He grabbed a helmet and strapped it on, fingers trembling as he buckled it. The captain's shield was still there and he picked that up too, surprised by the weight. Once a sailor with a visibly twisted ankle had hopped down the steps, his path was clear. Bizarrely, all he could see beyond the hatch was a blue, peaceful sky. But what he could hear was a battle now louder and more violent than at any point; the sounds of men moving and fighting; killing and dying. He supposed he could have hidden somewhere, perhaps helped the sailors out of Brygos' sight. But he was an agent of the Empire now and he'd been given a direct order. And what would Kallisto think if he avoided the fight? He reckoned there were worse reasons to die than trying to impress a woman.

He didn't stop until he reached the deck, sword still sheathed over his left hip, shield at the ready in his right hand. Seeing Iraklidis crouching down with Captain Brygos outside the deckhouse, he ran towards them without a single glance at the wider battle. When he halted beside the marine commander, Iraklidis grabbed the edge of the shield and turned it to the right, towards the *Varin*. Even though he was close, there so much noise that Tarchon couldn't hear what the two leaders were saying. Instead, he looked to the left.

Here, the *Filimer* stood just off the *Hercules*, gangplanks hanging limply on either side of the bow. Archers and slingers were still massed at the front of the ship, taking regular shots.

Tarchon had seen their victims below and now saw many more. At least a dozen lay on the deck behind the thinly spread defenders, arrows stuck in their stomachs and chests and throats. Most were the unarmoured oarsmen, spears abandoned on the deck beside them. The green tunics of the marines were evenly spread amongst the remaining sailors and oarsmen. They could do little but hide behind their shields, be ready in case another attempt was made with the gangplanks. Many of the timbers below their feet were sticky with blood and, as the *Hercules* shifted, lead shot rolled past the deckhouse. Tarchon also spied numerous arrows sticking out of shields and several embedded in the mast. Iraklidis' turret archers must have been low on arrows; they were out on their hands and knees, scouring the deck for usable bolts.

Moving back a couple of steps to give himself more protection from the deckhouse, Tarchon moved his shield so that he could see through a gap between it and the one held by Iraklidis. The situation on the starboard side was very different. The defenders could not even attempt to push the adjacent *Varin* off; they were too busy repelling the charges and thrusts of the attackers. A thicket of spears traded blows, clanging off helmets and shields, sometimes finding a human target. It was mostly green tunics at the front, with the oarsmen to the rear, their spears deployed over the marines' shoulders.

Suddenly, no more than twenty feet from the deckhouse, round shields were thrust forward, carving out a space. Three Goths wearing studded leather armour and wielding axes leaped on to the *Hercules*. One was instantly halted by a sword thrust into his groin, underneath his armour. Face torn by a silent scream, he fell back. The second attacker pulled a marine's shield down and hacked into his face, sending the defender spinning away. Blinking blood out of his eyes, the unfortunate defender was pulled clear by two sailors. The third Goth was a fearsome fellow with mad eyes and a grey beard. Barging a pair of defenders aside, he raised two hand-axes high, then cleaved one man's helmet in two. The second axe was turned by a shield and a big oarsmen stuck the attacker with his spear. As the mad-eyed Goth collapsed, the defenders fell upon him with a quiet brutality that forced Tarchon to look away. All the horrors he'd seen since entering this violent new world were nothing compared to this deadly battle.

From the port side came the sound of oars in the water. Turning that way along with Brygos and Iraklidis, he saw the rowers of the *Filimer* heaving their vessel backwards. Though the full complement of oars could not be deployed due to the collision, the water was churning. However, the *Filimer*'s rowers took only another two strokes before lifting their oars and twisting them. As they dipped them again and drove their ship forward, the men redeployed, lining up along the port side. The Goths were clearly intent on laying alongside the Romans, trapping the *Hercules*.

'Can we stop them?' asked Brygos, sweat dripping from his nose on to the gleaming surface of his cuirass.

Iraklidis shook his head. 'They'll board us on both sides. I'll tell my men to port to let them approach.'

To Tarchon, it sounded like the marine was giving up.

'Fatigue?' said the captain.

The marine commander nodded. 'If we allow them to harry us over the next hours, we've had it. They have more men and two operable ships. If they want to force it, we must let them.'

Up close, Tarchon realised how lined the face of the veteran marine was. He was at least ten years older than the captain.

'And when they board?'

'We defend what we can in numbers – just the stern. Three-sided square including the hatch. I don't hear many orders at the lines. They have no marine contingent. They'll attack quickly but without control. They come on to us, we kill more of them. Is there anyone left below?'

'I'll fetch any I can spare. What about the wounded?'

'They stay where they lie for now. Be careful, captain. We need you alive.'

With a clap onto Iraklidis' shoulder, Brygos ran to the hatch and descended.

Iraklidis hailed the nearest marine and gave a couple of hand signals. The soldier passed the message along the line as the *Filimer* pulled alongside. The side of the Goth ship was filled with shields of various sizes and at least five grappling hooks could be seen.

'Name?'

Though he heard this, Tarchon's eyes were fixed on the approaching ship. Then something hard hit his chest. It turned out to be Iraklidis' fist.

'Name?'

'Tarchon.'

'You stay behind me, cover us with your shield. And I mean *right* behind me. If I get an arrow in my back, I'll make sure I stay alive long enough to cut your throat.'

'Yes, sir.'

To Tarchon's surprise, Iraklidis first went to the starboard side. The marine commander moved at a swift, crouching walk, shield top just below his eyeline. He began close to the stern, forcing his way through or dragging his marines back to bark instructions. He didn't speak to every man but those he did looked like his veterans. Tarchon stayed close, switching his shield to his left hand, trying to emulate the marine's technique. One Goth arrow thudded into the shield's leather-covered timbers and another pinged off the bronze boss. He was surprised there weren't more targeted at the diminutive officer wearing the blue-crested helmet but glimpses to port showed the warriors on board the *Filimer* were more concerned about securing themselves to the *Hercules*.

The worst of it all was the wounded. Dragged out of the line and mostly abandoned, there were many on both sides. Where he could, Tarchon used his spare hand to pull them away from the boots and weapons that could hurt them further. Most appeared beyond help and had been struck several times. Some of the blows inflicted in the melee had gone through their armour but many were to the vulnerable spots – faces, necks, forearms. Twice Tarchon slipped in their blood and twice men grabbed him, pleading for help. And that was just on one side.

The front of the *Hercules* was curiously empty, the deck clean and unoccupied between the forward turret and the bow. Stopping at the turret, Iraklidis ordered the four men stationed there back to the rearward structure.

The defensive line was thinnest at this end on the port side, which now faced the *Filimer*'s stern. The enemy clearly sensed this because – just as Tarchon and Iraklidis arrived – three grappling hooks came flying over. The ships were already side by side but these lighter hooks were thrown for a different purpose. Pulled in with impressive power and expertise, they dragged three shields – and the men holding them – on to the adjacent side-rails. One defender, a blue-clad sailor, neatly slipped his hand from his shield handle and reeled away. But two others were killed in seconds, axes hacked into their backs and necks by roaring Goths.

More of the attackers charged past their cohorts, straight into the fray. A marine was first to them, knocking one Goth back with a shield edge to the chin before being clubbed across the head by an axe shaft. But the momentum was entirely with the fresh attackers and three more leaped aboard; shoving, driving, slashing. Two oarsmen fell back, one of their spears rapping Tarchon across the knees. A fleeing sailor tripped over the same spear, landing between two casualties. It seemed the first real breakthrough would come here.

Iraklidis had other ideas. The closest of the Goths was equipped with a small hand-shield. Exploiting his lack of height, the marine commander dropped his own shield and went in under it, swinging his sword upward and catching the Goth on his elbow. Though not a mortal blow, it opened his defences. Raising his sword up above his head, Iraklidis heaved down at the youthful warrior. His sword cut a line from the man's right shoulder down his chest, carving through leather armour and skin. He didn't go down immediately; only when another marine smashed him across the head with the blunt end of his spear.

Iraklidis wasn't done. After a quick glance along the line, he closed on the second Goth, who had both hands on a defender's shield. The clashing warriors were so close that there was no room to swing. Picking his spot, the compact commander instead drove the blade into the attacker's unarmoured flank. Screeching with pain, the man twisted away from the blade, blood leaking down his side.

The last of the three Goths had seen this. Batting Irakilidis' blade aside with his shield, he pushed him out of the melee and raised his axe, ready to hit his vulnerable trailing arm.

For some reason, Tarchon had still not drawn his sword: but he knew he could help. Situated behind the commander, he thrust his shield out over Iraklidis' shoulder. The impact reverberated through his arm but he had blocked the axe and given Iraklidis the time he needed. With a neat spin and dart, the marine drove his short sword into the Goth's armpit. The blade crunched deep and the warrior spasmed, dropping his axe. His eyes had an odd, yellow tinge and seemed to register an outraged surprise at his defeat. A short slice of Iraklidis' sword across his throat sent him to the deck, where he was promptly stamped upon by the defenders. The commander shook blood off the tip of his sword and recovered his shield.

Tarchon again tore his eyes away, feeling sick rising up his throat. Without so much as a word for him, Iraklidis hurried along the line, briefing three more men with a word in their ear. It was obvious to Tarchon that a wider breakthrough was imminent. The men on this side had been fighting for at least half an hour and their weariness showed in their grim expressions and sluggish movements. Many had two hands on their shields while others just leaned against their compatriots, hoping to simply keep the Goths at bay.

Six archers were crammed in the rear turret, each holding a quiver full of arrows. Brygos came up through the hatch, followed by four more men, each holding numerous shields and spears. Iraklidis collared two of the men instantly. Not sure if he should follow, Tarchon did so anyway, watching the marine commander place one men just left and forward of the hatch, the other man to the right. Each of the sailors had a shield and sword and now formed the corners of the defensive square Iraklidis had mentioned. They looked terrified but stayed where they were as he withdrew, once more squatting beside Brygos. Tarchon returned to his protective duties.

'How's the damage, captain?'

'Bad. I think we'll lose her. But not yet.'

'Now then?'

'Do it,' replied Brygos.

Tarchon followed Iraklidis forward, as did a third man, who was carrying a horn just like legionaries used. At Iraklidis' instruction, he raised it to his lips and sounded two short notes. The first men to leave the side-rails were sailors and oarsmen. In their rush, some stumbled or collided with each other. As they ran to Iraklidis' position, he shouted at them: 'Find a shield or a spear. Line up, facing forward, then kneel. Shield or spear! Line up! Kneel!'

Within a minute, he had them arranged in neat rows. By now, the outnumbered marines had been forced to retreat too, leaving a second signal redundant. If anything, they were even quicker, swiftly forming three lines of green, shields facing outward, most with short sword in hand. Tarchon found himself a few feet ahead of the rear turret, now in the middle of around seventy crewmen, with eight marines on three sides of the square.

'If you're right behind my marines, spears at the ready,' ordered Iraklidis. 'You others – stay low, shields above your heads.'

The Goths poured onto the *Hercules*, more coming from the *Varin* to the right, many unleashing war-cries and jabbing their weapons in the air. The marines barely had time to interlock their shields before the closest warriors attacked.

Some of the Goths never made it. The archers in the rear turret were firing at very short range and hit four of the enemy instantly. They had time to release another volley and strike three more before the archers on the *Filimer* took their turn. A deflected bolt clattered onto Tarchon's helmet as he crouched there, surrounded by defenders.

Someone on the *Filimer* was clearly in charge because men were sent to stand on the rails and angle their shots down into the mass of sailors and oarsmen. But by then Iraklidis had them squatting with their shields over their heads, much like the classic Roman tortoise formation. Tarchon had seen it used during military manoeuvres at the arena. The weary sailors and oarsmen were far from precise but the effect was the same: not many of the arrows found their targets.

His own shield was covering both he and Iraklidis but he saw enough to tell that the well-drilled marines exacted a heavy toll from the first Goths. Expert at keeping their shields up, then dropping or shifting them for a timely strike, they initially held their positions. But as the liquid press of troops surrounded them, filling the *Hercules*' deck, the lines began to falter. A scowling Iraklidis watched as his marines retreated two or three steps but – without a single order from him – the line of spearmen jabbed at their foes, driving them back.

Tarchon had no doubt that it was a temporary victory. The Goths were roaring each other on, all sailors and all warriors, apparently confident that victory was near.

Iraklidis pulled a few men out of the square's centre and sent them back, to cover any attackers who tried to get around the sides to the stern. Tarchon glimpsed two older men at the rear of the *Varin*, both clad in dark red cloaks and bronze helmets. Their confident expressions reminded Tarchon of some he'd seen at the arena; certain that their preferred gladiator was going to prevail.

And yet the lines still held. Leaving Tarchon, Iraklidis raised his own shield and waded into the fray, directing any spear that could be effective towards the enemy. When he returned, he was dragging a dead marine, whose face was masked by blood. Tarchon took him past the turret and into the deckhouse, then did the same with another dead man. He resisted the urge to crawl in there himself, cover his ears and just wait for the battle to end.

'What more can we do?' yelled Brygos.

'Nothing,' replied Iraklidis, picking up a flask from the deck and swigging back some water. 'We hold our shape.'

Tarchon found himself wondering if he should go down into the hold; he wasn't doing a lot of good and knew Romillus and Kallisto would need help.

Then the left side gave way. It was a simple matter of weight and pressure, with four marines falling back into their counterparts, removing the line of shields. The Goths were ready to take advantage. While two jabbed their long swords into fallen men, more drove their spears into the defenders. One of them was shouting in their language, guiding more attackers into the breach.

Still crouching, Tarchon was knocked into Iraklidis, then on to his backside. As boots and knees thumped into him, he feared he might be crushed. Abandoning his shield, he pulled himself past knees, elbows and sword-hilts to his feet. Iraklidis squeezed past him to the left, still bellowing:

'Hold the left flank! Hold the left!'

A panting Captain Brygos stumbled past Tarchon, into the ragged gap now left in the middle of the previously neat formation. The press of bodies was so tight that Tarchon willingly followed. He was relieved to see that the front part of the wall was still intact, the right side too. To the left was utter chaos: a morass of steaming, sweating bodies; red blades and battered flesh. Some men fought with a never-ending shout, others remained tight-lipped and silent, drawing on every sinew just to free themselves, help a compatriot, strike a blow.

Sword still in hand, Tarchon just stood there beside Brygos. Muscle cuirass now smeared with blood, the captain just turned and blinked, as if trying to make sense of what he saw. But he did nothing. And said nothing. Around them were many men; some wounded, some not. And they did nothing either. They looked beaten.

Tarchon was looking at the hatch, wishing he could go down below, when Kallisto came up.

At first, he half-believed himself to be dead and dreaming.

Hair slick with water, her soaking, blood-stained dress clinging to her form, Kallisto bounded up the steps, sword in hand. Both her forearms were red and, as she looked about, her hair flicked through the air. It was as if some legendary huntress had been conjured from a legend or the stories of old.

Tarchon was expecting some well-chosen words of encouragement, a rousing speech for the exhausted, wounded men. But then he realised that no inspirational words could match the sight of her. She ran up to the closest line, simply shouting 'Fight! Fight on!'

Her high, clear voice cut through the cacophony, momentarily halting Roman and Goth alike. Tarchon wasn't sure if it was her beauty, her courage or simply the sword in her hand but it spurred the defenders to renew their efforts.

'Come on!' yelled a newly-galvanised Brygos. He grabbed the nearest wounded man and pulled him into empty space behind the hatch. He picked up a spear and handed it to a man sitting, transfixed by Kallisto. 'You – fight! Fight on!'

Within moments, others were up, doing what they could.

'You can do it!' cried Kallisto, dark eyes set in an unblinking glare. 'Fight for your mates! For the *Hercules*! Fight on!'

She reached down and helped up a big oarsman. Though he'd been sliced across the brow, he stood and took the sword she offered him.

'Keep going! You can do it!'

'Yes, miss,' he said, in bizarrely formal fashion.

Another wounded man staggered out of the fray, his right arm butchered. He fell in front of them and Tarchon went to help Kallisto drag him clear. For the moment, that was all they could do but it seemed that the defenders were somehow still hanging on.

Trying to assess what the enemy was doing, Tarchon glimpsed an archer on the *Varin* take aim at Kallisto. He grabbed her and dragged her down, the pair of them landing in a heap. Moments after an arrow clanged off his helmet, he found one for her. Once she'd put it on, they stayed low but kept at their work; pulling injured men out of the melee, helping others to the hatch.

After what felt like a few minutes, Tarchon turned his attention to the left. There was only a single line of defenders, a ragtag of marines, sailors and oarsmen but they had held firm. Iraklidis had lost his helmet but the few men with him were still fighting hard, shields solid, spears punching out at the enemy.

Suddenly there was a great crack from the direction of the *Varin*. Tarchon stood and looked right in time to see the ship's sternpost explode, sending timbers flying and the two cloaked officers ducking for cover. From the rear turret came a shout:

'It's the *Victory*! *Victory* coming up from the south! Quarter-mile!'

Tarchon found himself next to Brygos once more. Another great smash went up, followed by agonised cries from the *Varin*. One of the sailors grasped his captain by the arm. 'The catapults, captain. They're dropping stones on her!'

It took that comment for Tarchon to realise what they were talking about: the Black Sea Fleet's flagship. Brygos' plea for reinforcements must have reached the ears of his superiors and the ship had been sent north. The *Victory* was twice the size of the *Hercules*, more than a match for the Goth vessels. Tarchon could not yet see it but the effects were immediate.

Shouts went up from their enemies, many on the *Varin* immediately heading below. Within a minute, the ship was moving off, the two cloaked officers yelling orders. One was sent sprawling again as another stone thudded into the deck. Lethal splinters flew up, one warrior staring down at the wooden daggers stuck in his stomach and thighs.

As quickly as they had stormed the Roman ship, the Goth warriors melted away; running from the battle, vaulting over the rails. A few didn't reach the starboard side in time and had to flee back across the *Hercules*' deck. On the *Filimer*, sailors were cutting the lines holding the grappling hooks. As the last men returned to their own vessel, others with boathooks and spears pushed it off. On what had been the left side of the square, many of the exhausted defenders fell to their knees. Iraklidis, however, took up a spear, barged his way between two sailors and threw the weapon. It struck a retreating warrior just above his backside. Body arcing in pain, he fell forward over the rail and tumbled into the sea.

Tarchon saw a tall, grey-haired Goth at the stern of the *Filimer* take charge of the tiller. The ship's oars entered the water in random fashion but were quickly propelling her northward. The warriors on the deck seemed as weary as their Roman counterparts, many with heads bowed. The grey-haired man gave a last look at the *Hercules* then turned to the north.

Iraklidis wiped his brow on his green tunic sleeve and marched over to Brygos. Other than a cut on his hand and a bruise on his cheek, the marine commander appeared uninjured. Seeing him seemed to bring the captain to his senses. Iraklidis pointed to the right and the pair watched the *Victory*, which seemed to be pursuing the *Varin*.

Tarchon almost smiled when he saw the huge vessel cutting across the sea, vast banks of oars pushing the water aside. The flagship dwarfed the *Hercules*, the upper half of the hull painted blood red. Tarchon knew that it possessed two bolt-throwers and two catapults. He could see one crew hastily reloading a catapult; it took four men just to shift one of the stones.

'What fortune,' breathed Brygos. 'Half an hour more and they'd have finished us off.'

'They should have finished us off half an hour *ago*,' remarked Iraklidis, as if commenting on a sporting contest. He spat on to the deck. 'Barbarian rabble.'

Poor old Romillus had fainted. Tarchon and Kallisto went downstairs to help the surgeon, only to find him laid out on two sacks of grain with Neratius trying to rouse him. As if this wasn't bad enough, it was also clear that the *Hercules* could not be saved. The water was up to their knees, with many oars and several bodies floating around. Tarchon and Kallisto stayed with Romillus as Neratius went to the stern with Captain Brygos. The ship had listed to the left, meaning that both holes were now submerged and that water continued to pour in. There were only sailors below; the vast majority were on deck, assisting the wounded.

'Come on,' said Kallisto, sprinkling water on the old physician's face. When he did not respond, she gave him a light slap. This did the trick and, when he awoke, Romillus sprang up with remarkable energy. He gazed wide-eyed at the rising water, Tarchon keeping a hand under his arm just in case.

'You passed out,' said Kallisto. 'But you're needed on deck.'

'Yes, of course,' he replied. 'My things?'

Someone had at least thrown his instruments into his case and placed it on the sacks with him. Kallisto took charge of it, while Tarchon held on to Romillus. Before leaving, they had to wait for some oarsmen, who were carrying wounded up the stairs. Some of them were so pale and had lost so much blood that Tarchon thought it impossible they would survive.

'She'll be gone in minutes,' said Brygos as he waded back to the submerged walkway, Neratius and five sailors with him.

Neratius said nothing. The first officer looked as spent as the warriors above.

'Save what you can,' said Brygos, already on his way into his own cabin.

'You should get our gear,' Kallisto told Tarchon.

As she escorted Romillus up the steps, Tarchon headed in the opposite direction. Fortunately, the lockers were quite high up and he quickly salvaged Kallisto's chests and his pack. Of Pelopidas' pack there was no sign, which he thought was perhaps a gesture from the gods.

He was about to collect Romillus' chest when Brygos waded out of his cabin. The captain was carrying his own chest but it looked very heavy and, struggling through the water, he dropped it. Instead of trying to recover it, Brygos just watched it float back to the surface and drift towards the stern. Upon his helmet, several of the feathers had been broken and hung down at odd angles.

'Captain? Captain Brygos.'

The mariner just stood there, eyes glazed, breathing rapidly.

'I'll send someone down to help you, sir.'

It took Tarchon two more trips to bring up the luggage and this felt somehow selfish considering the scene on deck. Dragging the last two chests to the deckhouse, he saw that the shape of the defensive square could be discerned purely by bloodstains. Romillus had not yet treated a patient; he was still examining a line of fallen men. Iraklidis and all his surviving marines were there too, trying to staunch bleeding and bandage minor wounds. Many of the sailors and oarsmen were also helping but some now gathered at the starboard side. Having seen off both Goth vessels, the *Victory* was approaching. Another of the officers had gone down to help Brygos and the captain seemed to have recovered himself. He stood at the rail with Neratius, watching the *Victory*.

Kallisto had found a pail of water and was now cleaning her arms. Tarchon thought of the moment outside Odessos when she had told him to wash himself. There were undoubtedly people to help but neither of them was doing so, nor did Tarchon want to. He'd had enough of mutilated bodies and screaming and crying and suffering. Though she'd not removed all the pink stains from her skin, Kallisto stopped for a moment. Kneeling over the pail, she gripped the sides of it, apparently about to vomit. Drawing in a deep breath, she regained her composure.

'Talk to me,' she said. 'Say something.'

The dying *Hercules* shifted again, timbers groaning under the strain. Tarchon had to adjust his feet and Kallisto had to hold on to the pail. Injured men wailed and abandoned blades slid across the deck.

'Iraklidis,' said Tarchon. 'He...he did it. Organised the marines, everyone.'

'Experienced man.'

'Yes.'

From the injured came a shriek. Romillus had some instrument in his hand and was digging into a sailor's shoulder.

The man was being propped up by two others and now crying like a child. The deck moved again and even Kallisto's heavy chests began to slide. Tarchon held them steady.

'Thank you.' She opened one of the chests and grabbed a fresh tunic and a cloak. 'Can you stand in front of the deckhouse please? I simply *have* to get out of this dress.'

Taking the wounded off the *Hercules* was not easy. Tarchon wondered if Brygos had sustained some kind of unseen injury because the captain climbed off at the earliest opportunity, leaving Neratius and the others to tackle the problem.

The *Victory* was much taller than the *Hercules*, the rail ten feet higher. Those capable, however, could scale the rope ladders dropped at bow and stern. Kallisto had no trouble finding two sailors to take her chests and was one of the first off behind Brygos. Tarchon reckoned she had earned that right; especially after the remarkable impact of her appearance from below.

He kept his pack on his back and assisted the sailors. While some of the injured could be helped up the ladders, the seriously wounded had to be tied to ropes and hauled up, a slow and agonising process. But the enormous *Victory* had a crew of over four hundred, so there were plenty of hands to help. And it was just as well; the *Hercules* was visibly sinking by the moment, the water now halfway up the steps.

Tarchon counted thirty dead and Neratius' last order was that they be dropped through the hatch to go down with the ship. By then, Romillus had finished off four men who were beyond help by slicing their throats with a hand over their eyes. Iraklidis had offered to do it but the veteran surgeon insisted.

"I've done it to hundreds,' he told the marine. 'Their faces come to me in the night. A few more won't make any difference.'

Even though he could barely form a thought, Tarchon reckoned he'd been lucky to see two such experienced men fight the battle in their own ways.

He was one of the last off the ship; climbing up the forward ladder and hauled on to the spacious deck of the *Victory*. He watched as sailors hurried efficiently down four hatches, ready to man their oars once more. Boathooks pushed the *Hercules* away and the foundering ship was soon all but submerged, waves sloshing across the deck, filling the deckhouse. Soon only the top half of the mast was visible.

'Here you go, lads, you've earned this.'

A big sailor with a ready grin was walking along with a bucket full of mugs in one hand, a great jug of dark wine in the other. Tarchon waited for his turn and took a mug. The sailor filled it with wine.

'Not a drop of water in there. That's the festival day stuff.' He stopped for a moment and looked the new arrival over. 'You a sailor?'

Tarchon shook his head.

'Passenger?'

'Yes.'

'Gods. Drink up then, lad. I reckon you need that.'

XXIX

Tarchon spent the night on the deck of the *Victory* with the men of the *Hercules*. He saw nothing of Brygos, Iraklidis, Romillus or Kallisto but a marine named Chabrias took him under his wing. He had seen Tarchon defending Iraklidis and also happened to be a native of Byzantium. Tarchon was deeply glad of his company. The sailors and soldiers sat in a circle until nightfall, at first discussing who had been hurt and lost, then recounting the battle through their own personal stories. The general feeling was that Brygos had done pretty well given the situation but that they would have lost without Iraklidis. Though grateful, the marines were clearly not surprised. Tarchon learned that Iraklidis was an islander from Samos, who had spent twenty years with the Green Sea fleets, fighting Persians and pirates.

When they weren't talking about him, they were talking about Kallisto. Those who had seen her rallying cry described it to others with admiration and awe. One man said she was, "as true a Roman as any man", another that she was a "goddess in human form". A third stated that he would never again believe a woman's presence aboard ship to be unlucky.

Tarchon sat there and listened, discovering that reliving the battle seemed to help him deal with it. When they were given a second helping of wine, the marines offered thanks to the great gods and honoured their fallen fellows. There was praying and joking and laughing and crying. As the sun set, Tarchon opened his pack and pulled his blanket over him, laying out amongst the crew.

At night, he did hear shouts and the noise of flapping sails and groaning blocks but his weariness always dragged him back into sleep. He was awoken by a song. With the great dark sail full above him, the *Victory* sped south, the wind over her port quarter. Many of the oarsmen had been allowed up and there were at least three hundred men crowded onto the deck. Their first song was familiar to Tarchon: a rousing tune that referred back to the Roman navy's greatest victories. It was followed by another that was more like a rhyming poem. This song mocked the Goths, berating their ugly women, unpleasant personal habits and small cocks.

As they sang, the noise almost deafening him, Tarchon thought about what Kallisto had said; her pride at being Roman. These men clearly felt it too, though fighting for the Empire had cost them friends and injured many. Amongst the sailors, there was a fellow who'd lost two fingers and another with a mutilated ear. Others were being treated below.

Korax thought the same; presumably Gargonius too. In that place, at that time, Tarchon felt some of that pride and unity. But he had come close to death several times; was Rome worth dying for?

Not to him. Not now, anyway, and he didn't reckon ever. If it meant so much to these people, good for them. For him, it was about the money and being a man who had earned – and deserved – respect.

With the wind favourable, the *Victory*'s sail remained full and pushed the great ship south at what Chabrias believed to be a good seven knots. Around midday, they were given some navy rations: hard biscuit and dried sausage. The sausage was more fat than meat – and the biscuit hard as stone – but Tarchon was ravenous and ate everything he was given. Later, he noticed the first of what turned out to be dozens of bruises upon his legs and sides. He eventually concluded that they'd been sustained during that awful press in Iraklidis' defensive square.

In mid-afternoon, the marine commander came up on deck, swearing viciously at his men when they dared to greet him with a cheer. He gave them a report on the casualties and informed them that they'd reach Byzantium by nightfall (the sailors had worked this out already). Just as he was about to leave, Chabrias warily reminded the commander of Tarchon's intervention. The marine commander said nothing, though he did knock a fist against Tarchon's arm before he left. According to Chabrias, this was a rare gesture of respect.

Later, as they neared Byzantium, Tarchon saw Romillus up on deck. The aged surgeon leaned against the rail, gazing out at the sea. It was as Tarchon had seen it many times: calm but ominously black, like some great pool of oil. In the sky were a few patches of thin cloud, below them a strip of yellow, then orange, then red just above the horizon.

Tarchon considered approaching the surgeon but he had no idea what he would say to the man. He suspected that, like him – perhaps like all the survivors from the *Hercules* – he just wanted to reach dry land.

Though the sun had set by the time the *Victory* docked, there were many present to observe the flagship arrive. Three gangplanks were laid and the *Hercules'* survivors were sent to the one closest to the bow. From here, they filed steadily ashore, some carrying bags, others with only their clothes and weapons. The deck was so high that the planks met wooden towers with steps down to the quay. Here, the officers were directing the men to a line outside a large building. Looking on, gathered between two braziers, was a collection of high-ranking army and navy officers, and three men in togas.

Once on solid ground, it took a while for Tarchon to feel steady. He said his farewells to Chabrias and the others, the sailor telling him where he could find his family's home at Fourth Hill. Like Tarchon, he was a White and insisted that they go together to the chariot races some time. As Chabrias jogged after his compatriots, they were already being barked at by their officers. Brygos didn't seem to be among them.

Tarchon suddenly felt a hand gripping his forearm. Passing by, a great pack on his back, was Neratius.

'Sorry we couldn't have given you a more pleasant trip,' said the first officer.

'Sorry you lost your ship. Have you seen Kallisto?'

'I think she already got off,' said Neratius, continuing on his way. 'May fortune favour you.'

'You too.'

'That depends which ship they put me on.' With that, Neratius disappeared into the crowd. Tarchon looked around but on the dark, busy quay, it was hard to see much of anything. Though he'd not seen Kallisto while on the *Victory*, he'd expected to leave with her; perhaps even go straight to Gargonius with the information about the Gothic spy. Tarchon told himself that he wanted to get some credit for bringing her home safely, but in truth he also just wanted to see her.

It was a chilly evening but he couldn't be bothered to fetch his cloak from his pack. He set off along the quay, trying to remember the quickest way back to his apartment. Though it was nice to have a home to go to, what he really wanted was some company. He was thinking about going to Mehruz's place when he felt someone walking along beside him.

'There you are.' Kallisto smiled. She had only her satchel over her shoulder.

'Ah...oh.'

'Ever considered a career as an orator?'

'What? Er...where's your gear?'

'It'll be sent to my inn later. I have all my valuables in here.' She tapped the satchel.

'Are you going to see Gargonius?' asked Tarchon.

'That can wait until morning. What are you doing?'

'Going home.'

'Really? My inn is close. Fancy some wine, Tarchon?'

He was a little confused. It was unlike her to be so friendly. But he liked it.

*

The creature possessed a man's body and was holding a green spear in one hand, a yellow dagger in the other. Upon the head were thick strands of black, beaded hair. But the face was not human: it was a long, green snout filled with jagged teeth.

'Petesouchos', said Kallisto, returning after a few minutes away. She seemed to have something in her hand but Tarchon couldn't see what.

'Sorry?' he said turning back to the tall, colourful fresco behind their table. The nearby lamps seemed to have been arranged to make the image all the more frightening.

'The crocodile god,' she added. 'From Egypt. Why do you think it's called the Palace of Phragonis? The owner's family has been here for five generations.'

'Nice place.' Tarchon had actually been to the inn once before; to the back door, to be precise – delivering milk. It was indeed very close to the harbour, on a prestigious street amongst many other expensive establishments.

Kallisto sipped from her bronze goblet and made a face. 'I asked for true Falernian – that's not it.'

'I like it. Strong.'

'Falernian is *always* strong. But the colour's not right.' She held the goblet closer to one of the lamps. 'Too dark. You know, they harvest it very late, even when there's frost. That's what makes the flavour distinct.'

'I didn't know that.'

She returned her attention to Tarchon. 'We shall have to get you some clothes.'

His new tunic was so damaged and blood-stained that he'd had to throw it away and was now wearing his old one. Though there weren't many people in the dining room, those present were very well-attired. The pair had given their bags to a male attendant, who'd cast a disapproving look at Tarchon. As for Kallisto, she seemed to fit in everywhere.

'You're not saying much,' she said, leaning onto the table, towards him.

'Sorry. It's...it feels like we were at sea for an age. I've not stopped in one place for a while.'

'Listen, I know I've been harsh on you a couple of times but, considering it's all new, you've acquitted yourself well. I'll tell Gargonius as much.'

'Thank you.'

'You have family here in the city?'

'Not really. Some good friends.'

'That's something.'

'Must be difficult for you – always on the move.'

Kallisto forced a half-smile that disappeared as swiftly as it arrived. She picked up her goblet and downed the remainder of her wine, wiping her lips. 'You can have the rest of it.' She pushed the glass bottle towards him.

'Right,' said Tarchon, disappointed that he'd not been able to make more of the occasion. 'I expect you're tired.'

Kallisto opened her hand and put one of two keys on the table. 'Number nine. I'm in eleven. I've asked for hot water for both – you want to come and see me, make sure you use it. And don't leave it too late.'

An hour later, Tarchon was in room nine, standing on a towel, scrubbing every inch of his naked body with a flannel. He kept running over exactly what Kallisto had said but she hadn't really left much room for doubt. He'd been so excited in the moments after she'd left that he'd been forced to rest his arm over his lap when an attendant approached. Downing the wine had helped him calm down a little but now he wished he had more.

With the excitement came a lot of nerves. He hadn't been in bed with a woman for more than a year and, though pleasant enough, she'd been no Kallisto. Tarchon just hoped he wouldn't embarrass himself.

Bearing in mind her advice to not leave it too late, he swiftly dried off and arranged his hair as best he could. The room was the nicest he'd ever stayed in by some distance. It contained not only a bed but a chest of drawers, a wardrobe and a desk. One entire wall was taken up by a fresco featuring a mighty river, complete with palm trees and waterfalls. Once dry, he went to investigate the tray of complimentary toiletries on a table beside the bed. One vial was clearly scented hair oil and that he left alone. The second he wasn't sure of. He took out the stopper and detected a faint flowery smell. He put his finger in and licked it. Whatever it was, it wasn't intended for the mouth. Cursing, he spat it out into the nearby water bowl. The third vial smelled of cinnamon and honey, which he knew was used for the teeth. Sticking his finger in, he rubbed the sweet mixture all around his mouth.

Then he got dressed. It was a shame he didn't have a fresh tunic but at least he was clean. All was quiet in the corridor. He locked his door and walked barefoot to room eleven. He knocked softly and waited.

Kallisto opened it with a smile. She was wearing an almost translucent gown. He could see the shape of her breasts and hips. Like him, she had a few bruises and cuts on her brown skin.

'Almost missed your chance,' she said. 'I was starting to doze off.'

He laughed nervously, embarrassed by how loudly it came out.

She locked the door. The room was similar to his, with only two candles alight, close to the bed. She came up behind him.

'Let's get this off.' She pulled his tunic up over his thighs but couldn't reach high enough so he hauled it over his shoulders.

'Sorry. Nothing clean.'

'Don't worry. You smell nice now, at least.' She walked around in front of him and glanced downward. 'Not bad, and improving by the moment. You do have a pretty nice face but the body…really quite excellent. You better be careful around Gargonius.'

With a giggle, she walked over to a table and took two goblets of wine.

'I met him at the baths once,' said Tarchon.

'His suggestion, I'm sure.'

'I only dipped my toes in the water.'

'Literally or metaphorically?'

Unsure what she meant, Tarchon took his drink and was glad of it, for he was the only one naked. Kallisto sipped some more and stood close, looking up at him, her nipples hard against his bare chest.

She ran a hand over his right arm and shoulder. 'Nervous?'

There didn't seem much point in lying about it. 'A little.'

'Don't worry. I know you're young. Leave it to me. Drink up.'

When they'd both finished their wine, she put the goblets back on the table. Stopping in front of him once more, she slipped the gown from her shoulders, ran it down over her hips and stepped out of it. Tarchon just looked at her. Kallisto was even more exquisite than he had imagined; and he *had* imagined.

'You can touch me, you know.'

He reached out and held her shoulders; her skin was warm and soft. She stepped forward, gripping his back then feeling lower and squeezing his backside. She tilted her head and pursed her lips. He kissed her, felt her tongue sliding over his. They kissed for a long time and then she turned and walked towards the bed.

'Remember what I said – don't fall in love with me.'

'I'm not making any promises.'

He awoke to the sight of Kallisto, standing at the window, looking out. She was again clad in the gown, her sleek black hair on the sleek pale material. As Tarchon sat up, he felt himself flushing at the memories of the night before. He had learned a good deal during the first bout (which had ended quite quickly) and a great deal during the second, which had taken place on the bed and on a chair.

'Why are you so tired? I did most of the work.' She walked over and sat on the edge of the bed.

'Er...'

'Just joking. Stop saying "er". Better not to say anything.'

'Right. Sleep well?'

'I did. I like nights like that,' she added thoughtfully. 'They help you forget.'

'You do it a lot, I suppose?'

Her immaculately maintained eyebrows dipped towards each other. 'What do you mean?'

Tarchon lifted his hands in surrender. 'Nothing. Can we get some breakfast?'

'We can. And then you can go and get ready. Message arrived while you were sleeping. From Gargonius. We're to meet him at the fourth hour. The Gardens of the Temple of Bacchus.'

'Ah. How did he know we were here?'

'I sent a message to him last night. As far as he's concerned, we stayed in our own rooms, understood? And you don't tell Korax – or anyone else.'

'Very well.'

'Before we leave, you *must* go and buy a new tunic. I can't be seen around the city with you in that old rag.'

'Right.'

'Are you getting up then?' she demanded.

'Do you have to be like this?'

'Like what?' she said with a shrug. 'This is me.' She picked up his tunic and threw it at him.

Tarchon crossed his arms and sighed, depressed that the wonderful glow of the previous night had disappeared so abruptly.

I know why she's like this. She doesn't want me to fall in love with her. But I already have.

Kallisto wasn't happy with his choice of tunic – ill fitting, apparently – but said there wasn't time to get another. She advised him to go shopping with a woman, preferably one who dressed well herself. She had also lent him the money, which meant that he was now eleven denarii in debt to her: he hoped Gargonius would help him pay her back.

Tarchon did not particularly enjoy the walk to the Temple of Bacchus, which was situated west of First Hill. Kallisto asked him a few questions about the city but he sensed that she was just trying to ease the tension and found he didn't have much to say himself. He had already realised that what had seemed like the start of something might in fact be a one-off occasion. That didn't stop him wishing that – instead of going to see Gargonius – they could take walk, spend some time together, actually get to know one another.

Even though she claimed to have never lived in Byzantium, Kallisto clearly knew her way around. He had wondered how a striking woman like her would negotiate a busy city without attracting attention. Her solution was simple; she raised her hood and moved swiftly and surely at all times. A couple of hawkers and one very opportunistic young drunkard tried to intercept her but she dodged them all with ease. While in her room, Tarchon had seen the slender dagger she kept in a neat compartment on the outside of her trusty satchel.

At the temple, a password from Kallisto to a middle-aged priest was sufficient to see them escorted to the rear. The priest unlocked a gate and gestured for them to walk through to the small, square garden. There was no sign of Gargonius yet, so they sat on the single bench. If not for the air of tension and the upcoming meeting, Tarchon would have enjoyed the garden. It was immaculately ordered: divided into neat flower beds and box hedges. At each of the four corners was a small, potted cypress tree, foliage cut into the shape of a long, rounded tear. The scent of rosemary hung heavily in the air.

Hearing footsteps, Tarchon was gripped suddenly by a question that had been on his mind. 'Kallisto, after this, will–'

But the fast-moving Gargonius was already there, sweeping in to the garden. Today his slender frame was clad in a pale green tunic. Through the vegetation, Tarchon spied the bearded

Solon lurking near the gate. There was not room for three of them on the bench so he stood. Gargonius touched his back briefly before taking, and kissing, the hand offered to him by Kallisto.

'Daughter.'

'Father.'

'How wonderful to see you safe and sound. You do not look like the survivor of a sea battle.'

'One must retain appearances.'

'Indeed one must.' The agent sat down and crossed his legs. 'And thank you, Tarchon – for bringing this one back to me.'

'When he frowns like that, it's best to give him an explanation quickly,' said Kallisto. 'Master Gargonius was kind enough to adopt me into his family several years ago.'

This at least made more sense than her being his real daughter. It was a common enough practice, something a few young men and women actually aimed for.

'The pleasure was entirely mine,' said the agent. 'Having established that you're both fit and well – to business.'

Kallisto nodded, brushing her hair out of her eyes. 'Aristomachus named Mamercus Alfius as the spy. His handler is named Tulga.'

'Alfius, a name I know. Tulga, a name I don't – even better. Well done. *Very* well done. We will act on this immediately. How was it up there?'

'Not good. We ran into a Goth scout party. I daresay they'll have attacked Odessos by now. Any news?'

Gargonius shook his head. 'I have no source as far north as you were. The army reports will be in soon, though no one is expecting good news. By all accounts, spirits at naval headquarters are little better. A warship lost.'

'Three of theirs damaged,' countered Kallisto.

'The sailors fought bravely,' added Tarchon. 'The marines too.'

Gargonius gave a sly smile and gestured towards Kallisto. 'And apparently a warrior woman was sighted amid the battle. It is said that she inspired the crew of the *Hercules* to fight on.

The story is spreading throughout the city. We shall have to find you a new assignment, and swiftly.'

Kallisto actually blushed. It was odd to see her so respectful for once. But she did then look up.

'Don't forget Tarchon. He didn't take a backwards step. The sailors adopted him on as one as their own on the return journey. He was also a help to me in Odessos.'

'Very good,' said Gargonius, which pleased Tarchon. 'We shall have to find something for you too, young man. But you certainly deserve a rest. I'll send for you in a day or two. For now, I need some more time with Kallisto.'

'Of course.' Tarchon was determined not to say "er" and speak clearly as these too. 'Sir, I owe Kallisto some money. Could-'

'Not an issue, young man.'

'Unfortunately, I also lost my spearhead.'

'Ah, well, that will have to come out of your pay but ...anyway, we shall call on you before long. Korax is away but don't leave the city without notifying us, understood?'

'Yes, sir.' Tarchon forced himself to stay composed, despite the unavoidable feeling that he would not see her again: for some time, at least.'

'Good day, then. Kallisto, good fortune to you.'

'Good bye, Tarchon.'

He turned and left the garden.

Mehruz's place was busy. Arriving there, he saw that every one of the eatery's ten tables was occupied. The customers looked like some kind of religious group; all were male, with shaved heads and identical circular medallions hanging round their necks. Mehruz was busy behind the counter and Anahita was delivering and collecting plates at an impressive pace. It was obvious to Tarchon from her expression that the lunchtime rush had been fraught. Though Mehruz was hard at work preparing dishes, he still found the time to smile and wave at departing customers. Not wishing to disturb the pair, Tarchon sat outside the clothier's opposite, which was closed.

Only when most of the customers had departed, did he join them. Mehruz was standing over a huge pile of dirty plates, running a hand anxiously through his curly hair. Anahita stood beside him, shoulders slumped, drinking from a mug.

'Table for twenty, please.'

She looked up with a frown; he looked up with a curious glance that turned swiftly to a smile.

'Tarch! You're back.' Mehruz extended his hand across the counter and Tarchon shook it.

'Yes.'

'Welcome,' said Anahita evenly. 'Want to give us a hand?'

Mehruz grimaced. 'Ana-'

'Of course,' said Tarchon. He was more than happy to keep busy; especially as he still hadn't decided how much he was going to tell his friend.

When their last two customers left, the couple decided to close for an hour or two while they cleaned up and got some more food cooking. Tarchon first brought the tables and chairs in, then put up the wooden screen that covered the counter.

Later, he stood next to Mehruz, drying the crockery the Persian was washing. He gave vague answers to a couple of questions but tried to avoid an interrogation by asking his friend about the eatery, the children and everything else he could think of. They had both moved on to chopping vegetables when Anahita nipped upstairs to check on the children, who were being watched by a friend.

'Come on then, Tarch,' said Mehruz. 'You're being very secretive about all this. Don't worry about Ana, she'll take the chance for a lie-down. We won't see her for a bit.'

The next thing he knew, Tarchon felt his friend's hand gripping his arm. 'Hey, what's wrong? Tarch?'

He belatedly realised that he had not responded; had hardly moved. Mehruz took the knife from his hand. Tarchon let out a long breath, turned, and leaned back against the counter.

'I knew you were holding back on me.'

There were at least one, possibly two incidents, that he could not disclose to anyone, even Mehruz. But he feared for his sanity if he didn't tell someone about what had occurred in these remarkable last few months.

'If I tell you, you have to promise to tell no one else. Not even Ana. Swear it!'

'By all the gods.'

'Forget *all* the gods; swear by *your* god. I mean it, Ruz.'

'By Ahura Mazda, I swear it.'

'All right. It's...some of it ...it's not good. I can't give you names but I just...I have to tell someone.'

'Take a breath and start at the beginning.'

'All right. This job. Basically, I got it because I tried to rob an army pay cart.'

'What?' Mehruz frowned. 'You did what?'

'Oh, that's nothing,' replied Tarchon. 'That's just the start.'

Historical Note

This story is set some twenty-two years before the events of 'The Siege' but the issues faced by Roman emperors in the third century remained lethally consistent. As well as the many enemies beyond their borders (including the Goths, the Carpi and the Persians), there was the ever-present threat of being assassinated, betrayed or usurped – occasionally all three at once!

Philippus (known as Philip the Arab due to his origins in what is now Syria) was elevated to the purple following the death of his predecessor, Gordian III, in AD 244. As is often the case, the circumstances of Gordian's death remain opaque and some sources claim that Philippus conspired in his murder. In any case, his first act was to secure a peace treaty with the Persian emperor, Shapur. He then travelled to Rome to secure his position by maintaining good relations with the senate. In 248 – the year this story is set – he threw a huge amount of money and effort at the celebrations of Rome's one thousandth year. Among the many events in the capital were games held at the Colosseum. We're told that over a thousand gladiators were killed along with many exotic animals including hippos, giraffes and a rhinoceros. It is to be hoped that Philippus enjoyed the celebrations: his reign and life would last only one more year.

King Cniva was indeed the leader of the Goths at this time and his armies penetrated deep into Roman territory, threatening multiple provinces. The Goths probably originated in Scandinavia before migrating into modern Germany and eventually as far as the Black Sea. A later iteration, the Visigoths, carried out the infamous sack of Rome under their leader, Alaric, in AD 410.

Galla's experiences reflect the times in which she lives. In Roman society, it was considered entirely acceptable for seriously disabled babies to be killed at birth via 'exposure'. Scapegoating, isolation and suspicion were also common and there is much mockery of the disabled within Roman poetry, theatre and comedy. Having said that, we do know that some Roman parents chose to raise their disabled children.

Historical texts suggest that, though they were very much like legionaries, Roman marines may have worn blue like the sailors. However, green was also worn and – with a bit of dramatic license – I have assigned that colour to the marines here as a method of differentiation. What is undisputed is that they wore sandals and socks! In this period, the smaller, more manoeuvrable 'liburnian' type of ship was preferred to heavier vessels such as the *Victory*, which had dominated in earlier centuries. This was partly because the navy's role had become less about great naval battles than patrol duties and interception. Smaller vessels could be more easily deployed around coasts and within rivers.

Could there have been female agents? I've been unable to find any direct evidence. The evidence we do have suggests that men dominated all fields within the ancient world and the areas of the military, politics and espionage were no different. However, there are examples of female rulers, advisors, priestesses and warriors who were hugely influential. I find it inconceivable that, over the many centuries, the emperor and the empire never made use of female agents in some capacity. Common sense suggests that an asset such as Kallisto could have been hugely useful. Indeed, the marginalisation of women might have made it easy for them to gather intelligence unnoticed.

Acknowledgments

This novel was written between November 2020 and December 2022. Thanks to my editors: Milena Brown, Neil Brown and Sarah Brown. Once again, Leila Summers did a great job formatting the document. Diogo Lando of Red Raven Design produced another excellent cover. The brilliant Nigel Peever will again be narrating the audiobook.

I must also thank what I think of as the 'faithful few'. *Agent of Rome* has never been a huge seller but my enthusiastic band of loyal readers has always motivated me to keep going. Financially, it's probably not an efficient use of my time but I have enjoyed returning to this world with a new protagonist. I have grand plans for Tarchon but the sequels will only happen if I sell enough copies. With that in mind, anything readers can do to spread the word is greatly appreciated. Obviously, recommendations are very beneficial but, if you have the time, please do share links via social media or write a review. I do hope this isn't the last *Agent of Rome* novel but, if it is, sincere thanks for your support!

Also by Nick Brown

Agent of Rome Series
The Siege
The Imperial Banner
The Far Shore
The Black Stone
The Emperor's Silver
The Earthly Gods
The Last Battle

Marik's Way

Printed in Great Britain
by Amazon